SAVAGERY

BOOK ONE
THE CROWN

ERIK PETRAVICIUS
MANISELA PRESCOTT

SAVAGERY: THE CROWN

Copyright © 2024 by Erik Petravicius and Manisela Prescott

ISBN: 978-1-966111-00-9

Publisher: E & M Renegade Creative Works, LLC
Edited by Jonas Saul the editor-in-chief at Imagine
Press Cover designed by Istvan Szabo

DEDICATION

We would like to dedicate this book to everyone who inspired this story. Those who are lost and caught up in "the life" trying to find their way. Especially those suffering from mental health problems, drug and alcohol abuse, and poor decision making. Also, to the Special Forces community, most notably the army Rangers and to all the service members who serve and continue to serve, some of whom offered the greatest sacrifice of giving their lives for our freedoms.

ACKNOWLEDGMENTS

A big thank you to Scott Bertinetti, Robert Connell, Marc Novak, Mitch "Casper" Fergason, Ronald Milcoff, my brother Jared and his wife, the rest of my family and friends who helped and supported me while writing this book.

- Erik

First and foremost, always, thank you to the most high, God, for whom without, I undoubtedly would not be alive to tell this story. Thank you to those who believed in my change and fostered my Growth. Thank you to my dearest mother who raised me tough, kisses to the sky Ma.

- Mani

A special tHanks to

Jonas Saul, who is the bestselling author of the Sarah Roberts Series and an active International Thriller Writers Inc. member.

Travis Davis, author of "Flames of Deception."

- Erik and Mani

Author's Preface

We are presenting a crime/fiction book based on actual events from our lives adding in fiction when necessary but keeping it true to a harsh reality. Although our story tells a tragic tale of two individuals going down the wrong paths in life, there is hope, as it is also a redemption story. It is a raw and honest take on the real workings of a Pacific Islander crime syndicate involving street gangs, prison gangs, biker gangs, Native American crime families, the Russian mafia, Mexican cartel, the US military, DHS, and Gypsies and more.

This story is told through the eyes of our two main characters. Tone' a former army Ranger who becomes a CID agent while going down the rabbit hole of a criminal enterprise. Then there is Preschool, a hardened criminal rising to the ranks of a top drug kingpin partnered with the fourth largest Mexican drug cartel distributing from the Pacific Northwest through Utah, California, Nevada, Hawaii, Australia and the pacific islands.

Preschool tells his story after recently released from the feds for being part of a huge drug trafficking pipeline going from Mexico directly to the United States and into the pacific islands (Hawaii, Guam, Palau, Tahiti, Australia, etc...) through him. He partied like the Wolf of Wall Street, having tons of chicks like playboy bunnies, and spent money like a billion-dollar whale.

Writing this book based on his paperwork (arrest records, court documents, etc.) which reads like a novel. His story entails not just drug trafficking and racketeering, but real-life situations in dealing with relationships and betrayal. His family was always known in Hawaii for being mafia-like and the feds were never able to get them until 10 years ago when he was sentenced to 10 years. All this can be substantiated by court documents and legal work containing over 3,500 pages.

These guys are the islander version of the sopranos, telling the tale of corrupt federal agents working with them, to brutal and savage acts of violence. This shows a different side to the islands that it's not just palm trees and hula dancing. On the island of Hawaii his uncle ran the locals for quite some time and when he was alive no one could make a movie in Hawaii without paying the islander tax. For example, Teamster trucks were blown up and burnt for not paying. Only when his uncle died did all these movies of Hawaii start airing.

His demeanor of being a really, nice and gentle man, is genuine. However, there is a dark and sinister side to him. This guy apparently ran a gang that compromised leaders of his community from California, Utah, Washington, Oregon, and Hawaii with far reaching tentacles deep back into the pacific. This guy had the FBI, DEA, Homeland Security, Postal Inspectors, and local law enforcement agencies all involved in his take down, yet you would never think this guy was capable of any of this.

His cartel connection was with the most dangerous group in Mexico, The Knights Templars. The cartel who started the beheading of enemies and introduced that idea to the south.

Tone', who was along for the adventure, tells of his humble beginnings and the trappings of the criminal underworld. Sharing memories of his childhood and military service leading up to his involvement with the USO's.

While serving in the military he transitioned from special operations as an army Ranger to becoming a CID agent. Eventually, he finds himself involved not only with organized crime syndicates, but also with the CIA and other government intelligence agencies.

His personal demons begin to unfold as he travels down the rabbit hole of crime and street life. His PTSD and depression are brought to the forefront as his decision making becomes more and more radical. Fighting his pain and suffering he begins to self-medicate with alcohol and a life of excess, especially indulging in the pleasures and comforts of women.

All while keeping up appearances and trying to juggle his military career with his personal life, coupled with his enthusiastic entrepreneurial spirit of building his own business empire.

Although he is a bit naïve and reluctant at times his demeanor makes him a natural leader for the streets and criminal activity which he is slowly pulled into. Inevitably he finds himself in over his head swimming with the sharks of the underworld.

Preschool and Tone' are kindred spirits forming a lasting bond and quickly find themselves intertwined in each other's lives and futures.

TABLE OF CONTENTS

PROLOGUE

MSG PRESCOTT:

"In an ancient Polynesian tribe, there was a saying that goes, 'In the land of the blind, the man with one eye is a warrior, the man with two eyes is the chief, and the man with a third eye is a god." Master Sergeant (MSG) Prescott seemed to be talking to himself more than to the audience of soldiers huddled around. MSG Prescott, spitting on the ground in disgust at what he was ranting about, continued. "You know, in those days, the Sons of God slept with the daughters of man as foretold in the sacred texts. All kinds of demi-gods spawned from this intimacy. Yeah, they had numerous half-bred humans roaming the Earth freely with superhuman strengths and abilities. Can you imagine that? X-men type shit." He went on, "I've heard English people tell the story saying that the man with one eye is king... Ha. A guy from the British Armed Forces, an ally, told me I had it wrong. That it was 'a man with one eye is king.' Can you believe that shit? That's typical of English colonial thinking and how they believed their kings and queens were greater than the gods."

Laughing, MSG Prescott ranted, "I laugh at them and how they refer to their kings and queens as 'My Lord' or 'My Lady'... 'Your Highness' or 'Your Holiness'. They show divine reverence to these mere mortals like these people were divinely birthed. These English did nothing but bring smallpox and sicknesses to the islands of sacred spiritual secrets. Divine kings? Ha, I spit on all of them."

"You know it's funny that before the infestation and invasion of paradise, the Polynesians fished, hunted, and sailed the seas without worrying about hunger. Having their essential needs met, Polynesians were afforded time to build their hierarchies and villages on the focus of worshiping gods."

"Polynesians were considered pagans in those days with gods like Lono, the god of rain, Tagaroa, the god of the ocean, and Nafanua, the goddess of war, and more. We had a god of fire, a god of fertility, and a god of the forest. They had so much freedom that they were able to form their own little patriarchal society, which taught the value of strength in family and unity before the English screwed everything up. We lived. The English survived. Their mentality was that of takers where they take, take, take. The English had nothing. I mean, history taught us that they would travel for weeks and scavenge for deer to find bone marrow, just to travel miles and miles back to bring meals for their own kind."

Prescott talked and talked of how his culture was overridden by cultural pollution and indoctrination imposed by the invaders to survive and thrive in their new world order. "My own people are struggling to survive now. They live with a survivor mentality, turning them into cutthroats, forgetting life's true value."

MSG Prescott would go on to tell us about the fables from the islands. About how things were made to be used by men who had value. And how men are now made to be used, and things are being valued. He spoke about how Polynesian tribes believed, "The world is blessed with eyes, but only a few men were gifted with seeing." That everything beneath the seeing eyes is sheep, which are vulnerable and weak, requiring protection from slaughter or guidance from a shepherd. He spoke of religion and how, from the U.K. to America, it was used to control the 'sheeple.'

He would tell of how this story dates back to the legendary times when the tatau (tattoo in the Polynesian language) was first introduced to the Polynesians and said to be from the gods over four thousand years

2

ago. How the tattoos of those days had a sacred divine meaning in its pattern. Every triangle was symbolic of the mountains. Dots were the sun. Sharp-pointed triangles were spears used for war.

Going on, he said, "Today, the meaning of the story is fulfilled in all its prophetic glory with officials turning a blind eye, people seeing but not believing, and others lusting after the possessions and lifestyle of someone else. And how, if love is the greatest commandment in the Bible, then why don't these followers of the Bible see that jealousy and hatred are the worst of all its sins?"

I usually let him rant and rave when he's had a lot to drink because there's never anyone here to listen to us. However, this time, a much bigger audience is present. It is sometimes the most bone-chilling thing when he is accurate and on point, like a drunken mind speaks a sober truth. People have been long waiting for a divine seer who is to help them find freedom from slaughter, while the anxiety of the truth that they might be all alone on this one kills them off faster than the grim reaper's blade. One by one, they are being plucked off by the leaders who are supposed to lead them to freedom. Disgusting.

He continued, "I mean, look at us! We're in the middle of the desert, fighting a war where we were duped by the 'All Seeing Eye' in Langley and the White House. I can't even believe we are out here fighting this war and losing our brothers, friends, and men, and for what? Blood oil? Black gold? Bullshit! My family will never see any of the benefits of my blood and tears out here. I wonder if they'd even send my mother a check. Heck, rumors are floating around of guys going back home from tours and turning to the streets to cop dope because their veteran affair benefits are a few years out from taking effect and providing them the medications they need. United. Fucking. States. Of. America. The kings get rich while the jesters turn to junkies after being sent on a wild goose chase in the desert looking for an Iraqi royal family on a stacked deck of cards. (Sings) *Oh, say, can you see, Muthafucka.*"

CHAPTER ONE
FROM DUST BOWL TO PRISON HOLE

REYES:

The wipers moved back and forth like a metronome as I sped down Ruston Way. The rain washed over my windshield, blurring my vision. I gripped the steering wheel, continuing to tear at the vinyl already being pulled away by my inner rage beginning to manifest itself. It became a game of sorts as I played chicken with my own life, moving my pistol to the side of my head, then in my mouth—back and forth. It was the spring of 2005 in Tacoma, Washington, as I was driving down Ruston Way.

That night, I was having one of those episodes. That's the thing about traumatic experiences or PTSD: some triggers set it off. Everyone's trigger is different, and often, there's more than just one trigger. It so happens that that episode was set off by my then-girlfriend Monica. I was distraught and had an emotional and mental breakdown. Swearing and yelling about intangible things, just yelling anything that came to mind. The fits of rage would've been evident to anyone who saw me, as well as the intense pain I was experiencing by the tears rolling down my cheeks.

I was at one of her mom's famous barbecues earlier that day. These were big outdoor events with plenty of food and alcohol to go around. Always a big gathering of people, her mom went full out being a magnificent host. I was relaxing, enjoying drinks and good food; it was a good day. That was until Monica started in with her bullshit. I bet her mom was talking shit about me again, opening the floodgates of Monica's mouth. Whatever internal self-hate she had come pouring out to any undeserving victim within earshot, which happened to be me that night. Every time she drank, she would get so mouthy and belligerent.

Monica was absolutely gorgeous, half Cuban and half Italian, with a fiery attitude. The ass on her was so perfect it had been validated by the necks it's broken. Oh yes, any time I was out with her, whether it was the bar, the mall, the beach, or anywhere, I would catch guys doing triple and quadruple takes, trying to see that ass of hers. I always got a kick out of it, especially since she seemed oblivious.

Anyway, there I was with a pistol to my head, crying like a loser. It had been a couple of hours since she spewed all her venomous poisons into me, but I could still hear her voice in my head saying, "Fucking loser." I swear if she had been some dude saying that shit to my face, I'd have pummeled him and let all that rage out. But instead, there I was with a pistol to my head, driving with my eyes closed, having no regard for the road on which I was driving.

Briefly, I put the pistol down on the passenger seat and closed my eyes. Just letting the car take me where it wanted to go. Maybe a telephone pole or oncoming traffic. I remember thinking at least my family wouldn't have to live with the pain, guilt, and shame of me killing myself. No luck. The car continued on a straight path. I opened my eyes, picked up the pistol again, and repeated this several times.

I was intoxicated and so fucking angry. Actually, I was enraged. The flashbacks of the early part of the evening kept playing repeatedly in my head. Hearing her berating me, calling me a loser, and digging into me over and over. That one word by itself was enough to set me off. I was no fucking loser, fuck her. By the time I was twenty-one, I had done more with my life than most people would do their entire lives. I was a motherfucking Airborne Ranger, a combat veteran, and an aspiring entrepreneur. What did she ever do with her life other than party and enjoy the luxuries of her freedom provided for by men like me? What a little fucking cunt. And if that ass of hers wasn't so damn sexy, I would've been done with her a long time ago, but what can I say? I have issues … haha.

I remember opening my eyes, lifting the pistol to my head, and determined that time to squeeze the trigger, saying, "Fuck it, I'm just going to do it. I'm going to end this mental and emotional pain once and for all."

Just as I was about to squeeze the trigger, my cell phone rang. It continued to ring as I held the pistol to my head, poised and ready. Lowering the pistol, I stared off blankly. The ringing of the cell phone was hypnotic and took my mind to the data bank of memories I had tried forgetting. Ever unsuccessful. I vividly remember the flight on a US marine medevac helicopter while flying over Iraq. I lay there watching as Navy corpsmen were at work desperately trying to stabilize my friend. We were both badly wounded. I was helpless and could only think to myself, *Fuck! Fuck, fuck, FUCK! Brother, don't fucking die. Fight through this shit.*

Then I heard one of the corpsmen say, "He's gone." I could only watch and look into his eyes as he faded away, his soul leaving his body. In my mind, I was saying *no, no, no, I don't want you to die.* That day, Master Sergeant Tavita LemaokaOAli'i Prescott was mortally wounded, saving my life. It has been hard acknowledging my own sufferings from the events of that day, especially when one of my best friends, a brother from another mother, paid the ultimate price. I wasn't only severely wounded physically but mentally and spiritually as well.

The cell phone must've gone to voicemail several times, but whoever was calling me that night was persistent in wanting to get a hold of me. The next thing I remembered was the cell phone ringing again and me with the pistol to my head, yelling at it, "What? What the fuck do you want? "At that point, I just didn't care anymore and wanted to escape my pain. I was shouting, "Is this what you fucking want me to do, God? You want me to kill my fucking self? Fuck that bitch, fuck you. Fuck everyone! I don't give a shit because I should already be dead. Fuck it, I already am.

Just a dead man walking." I laughed when I said the last remark because that was exactly how I felt at the time—like a dead man walking.

Defeated, I continued with my final thoughts. "Why the fuck am I even alive?"

After a long pause of what seemed like an eternity, I confessed, "I'm so fucked up. Fuck me, I don't want to die." And just like that, I made up my mind to live.

I looked down at my phone because it was ringing again and decided to answer it that time. I set my pistol on the seat and picked up the phone. "Hello."

It was Sergeant First-Class Allen Thompson calling to check up on me. "Hey brother, I'm sorry. I know it's late, but I couldn't sleep. I keep thinking about you and the rest of the guys."

"No worries, man. Is everything all right?"

"Yes, I just wanted to check on you. You know, a brother check."

I couldn't help thinking, *he couldn't sleep, huh*? I guess we all have our demons. Maybe he had his own pistol to his head and was reaching out from the great dark abyss. Looking for just one reason not to pull the trigger, and that night, it happened to be me. Maybe not, but either way, someone loved me and was looking out for me. I said, "Man, you don't know how much I appreciate you checking up on me."

"Ya, brother, it's been too long since we last hung out."

"Too long indeed. We should get together and catch up soon. Where you at now?"

"Retired and back in Montana."

"Well, shit, brotha, I need to come out that way for a visit."

"Love to have you come through any time."

"Ya man, that sounds good."

We said our goodbyes and hung up.

Darkness will always creep into a man's soul from time to time, and the dark voices will come whispering dark thoughts of suicide. The trick is learning to deal with them and putting them in their place. One thing was for sure. I had to get away from that crazy chick. Every time with her nonsense, she would trigger my PTSD. Mixed with alcohol, I knew nothing good would ever come of that relationship. Eventually, I did just that. However, it took some time and wasn't easy to do.

CHarLie aka "PresCHOOL":

"IN A WORLD OF CHAOS, THE ONLY CONSTANT IS CHANGE."

I had read that quote every day for the two years I lived in the Segregation Housing Unit (SHU). The SHU, or "the Hole," as it's known to prison inmates, is solitary confinement. A prison inside of prison. A Hell inside of Hell. It is the epicenter of the black hole in a dark, empty universe where inmates are isolated in the middle of nowhere. And yet, this is where I chose and managed to spend most of my years while I was incarcerated. In the SHU, consorting and bonding with other troublesome inmates who were always fighting, gambling, or disobeying the laws of the land when they were out in the general population.

I had been in and out of the SHU for everything from fighting and assaulting an officer while being investigated for ordering a stabbing of another inmate to actually stabbing another inmate. I had been there for two years straight because of a hostile takeover prison riot at Cedar Creek Correctional Facility in Little Rock, Washington. A riot that involved attacking the warden and taking over the prison.

That incident earned me a first-degree prison rioting charge, which added to the lengthy rap sheet of charges I already had. That incident, which solidified my infamy and stupidity in the Washington state penal system, could have been prevented, I believe, had the warden done his job.

The riot, which had been brewing over staff targeting me, had finally kicked off when they plucked my last straw. The staff had asked me to clean up poop that someone had splashed in their duty office. When I argued that I wasn't trained in hazmat, the officers responded that it wouldn't kill me. When I complained that I worked in the kitchen and that they got unit porters to clean the units, they retorted, "You are going to clean this because we're telling you to do so."

After relentlessly trying to plead my case, which they weren't hearing, I politely stated, "I know you guys are trying to mess with me because I have a reputation for being troublesome. So kindly, if you guys would leave me alone, I promise I won't break your jaws if you call me on the P.A. system again to clean this mess. Okay?"

Then I walked off. And as I was walking back to my bunk, they called on the P.A. system, telling me to come clean this poop. NOW!!! This concluded that the only thing these pigs understood was violence. With my history and predilection for violence as a teaching tool, who better than me to show them?

I calmly took two fire extinguishers off the wall after lighting a cigarette (smoking was not allowed) and walked back to the officer duty station. I threw one of the fire extinguishers through the window of the staff duty station while they were all inside laughing. I threw it so hard that it launched like a torpedo through the office window, leaving a huge hole in the center. I then proceeded to take the other fire extinguisher, stuck the hose inside the hole, and sprayed the officers powdery white. It was not so funny then because no one was laughing. They were scrambling to get out through the backdoor while one officer stood there stunned, continuing to get sprayed. I reached in through the hole, grabbed the phone that was linked to the P.A. system, and made an announcement. "This is your new warden speaking. Please evacuate the building, as my new staff is going to be burning down the place." Before I could tell the other islanders to burn the place down, the place was already engulfed in flames.

The quote, etched out from the paint on the door, intrigued me because it was like a brain teaser. You could drive yourself nuts trying to figure it out. It was like some kind of philosophical BS that some random Joe, dying of boredom, would post online. Or some random Joe, literally dying of boredom here, had carved out on the door. It was probably some random guy parroting wisdom he heard, but for whatever strange reason, it was quoted. It was deep enough to spark questions in me. So much so that it piqued my philosophical interest, left me uneasy, and bugged me every day for the two years I was there.

In the SHU, a "yellow" line is painted on the floor near the door. If you want to go to the yard, you must be up and standing on this line by five-thirty a.m. You must be naked with your pumpkin orange jumpsuit and underwear in your hand, ready to be handed out through the tray slot so the staff can search it for contraband while watching you through the window in the door. The search is routine for security measures.

"Stretch your arms straight out while using the spirit fingers. Run your fingers through your hair. Show me the back of your ears. Open your mouth wide, exposing the insides. Lift up your junk. Turn around and show me the bottom of your feet, one at a time. Each time, wiggling your toes. Squat down, spread'em, and give me two good coughs."

When they assess that you do not pose a danger, they will hand you your clothes back, and you can get dressed and cuffed up (let them put handcuffs and shackles on you) so you can be transported to the yard area. Everywhere you go in the SHU, you are handcuffed and shackled.

If you are hungry, you better be on that yellow line come breakfast, lunch, or dinner because otherwise, they will wheeze on by you, leaving you starving and waiting for the next meal. I was usually up way before the meal cart arrived, trying to get my daily five hundred push-up count before bed. It didn't take me long to lose weight on the involuntary diet. Every day, up, down, up, down, reading the etched quote, "IN A WORLD OF CHAOS, THE ONLY CONSTANT IS CHANGE."

In the 18th century, the SHU, or solitary confinement, was first experimented with in the Eastern State Penitentiary in Philadelphia. It was said that the Quaker Group (Benjamin Franklin, Benjamin Rush, and others), some of whom were our nation's founding fathers, believed that prisoners isolated in stone-cold cells with only a Bible would use the time to repent and find spirituality.

Consequently, instead, they found that many of the inmates went crazy and couldn't adapt to society when let out, so the practice was slowly done away with. However, because prisons have become popularly a lucrative business in the United States recently, the profiteers who built the prisons across the U.S. built every one of them with the SHU intact. Hoping they could succeed where the founding fathers failed. The profiteers who built the new solitary confinement built it with the psychology in mind that they could improve on the old method by now incorporating generic mandatory rehabilitation programs to educate inmates on behavior modification benefits.

One of the privileges for learning about "behavior modification" was extended visiting hours. They used extra visiting hours as an incentive to try to attract inmates who had families driving from far away towns. Coincidentally, that is 99.9% of the prison population because prisons are commonly built in some Schitt's Creek backwoods far, far away, and its occupants are mainly inner-city kids from impoverished backgrounds.

The profiteers believed that their method would be similar to putting a child in a corner and then explaining why they were put in time out. To encourage the child to keep from misbehaving, they allowed him to play with friends (visitors), like there's a huge difference between the implementation strategies they used compared to those of the founding fathers.

Well, let me tell you something. Solitary confinement is not a good rehabilitation method for humans. The corners of a home are far different from the dark corners of a cement concrete cell in freezing cold temperatures, with a thin blanket for warmth and a Bible for a pillow.

Studies have shown that long periods in solitary confinement have led to anxiety, severe depression, and suicide. If you have ever spent time in solitary confinement, you can hear kicking doors and screaming from cells where guys are losing their minds.

If the prison systems worked at rehabilitating anyone, then why is the number of incarcerated persons in America drastically rising instead of declining? Why does America have the highest incarceration rate of persons per country around the world? And why did it take so long for anyone to finally come out about the systemic racism targeting certain impoverished areas of the country filled with minorities to occupy these new prisons?

None of the generic programs the profiteers implemented have ever been proven to work. There is no data or statistical study to prove that these programs have ever effectively kept a guy from wanting to come back to the SHU.

They have offered programs like the 'Step-Down' Program, where an inmate would have to denounce his gang affiliation and/or debrief. That inmate, working his way back into the general population, would be targeted and attacked by his former gang the minute he is let out for having joined such a ridiculous program.

Other similar programs, such as the 'Legacy' and 'Integrity' Program, have similar failure rates. In truth, these programs seem like just another avenue in which the state used to request more funding from the federal government. The only programs that boast any success rates are the ones founded by inmates, who are most likely not supported by the state and are strongly discouraged.

cHapter two
war is Hell

Reyes:

The incident that began a very dark period of my life took place near Baghdad, Iraq, in 2003. While serving with the 75th Rangers as part of a special mission's team, my squad was tasked out to pick up a reconnaissance team belonging to the Regimental Reconnaissance Detachment (RRD). My dear friend Master Sergeant Tavita LemaokaOAli'i Prescott was part of that RRD team.

We had just linked up with the RRD team when we came under heavy enemy fire from insurgents. Upon enemy contact, we maneuvered our six Humvees into a defensive position, returning fire. Both my Alpha and Bravo teams, along with the RRD team, dismounted, setting up a secure perimeter, allowing me time to assess the situation with MSG Prescott.

The concentrated fire came from two small two-story structures with a common courtyard surrounded by a six-foot wall. The next closest dwellings were across a field just beyond the compound, with more buildings spread out across the landscape. This was a typical layout in the countryside.

We decided to assault the small compound with the two structures. Four members of the RRD team, including MSG Prescott, would move in with us to secure the compound, and then they would clear the structure on our left. My Bravo team, consisting of four soldiers, Sergeant (SGT) Davis, Private First-Class (PFC) Hernandez, Private (PVT) Jackson, and Specialist (SPC) Malone, plus myself, would take the dwelling to our right.

Alpha team and two RRD guys would stay back with the Humvees and continue laying down suppressive fire and overwatch. The RRD guys could maintain good command and control, monitoring the radios and giving situation reports to higher-ups. Plus, they were more experienced and better able to assess the battlefield and paint the proper picture for higher-ups. More importantly, they were able to call in any indirect fire missions or close air support with great proficiency.

As we moved through the front gate, Bravo and I split right, and the RRD guys split left. As we approached our target house, all four of my soldiers stacked on me: one soldier in front of me and three soldiers behind me. Stacking is the tactical term, which means a gathering of soldiers just outside a door, passageway or entryway in preparation to breach it. Everything must be synchronized and expedited to move each soldier quickly through the entry point known as the fatal funnel. Ultimately, stacking ensures violence of action, speed, and surprise.

We stacked outside our target dwelling. The lead soldier, PFC Hernandez, would be responsible for breaching the door. Quickly following the initial breach of the door, PVT Jackson would toss a flashbang grenade inside. After the flash and the bang, I would be the first through the doorway. Visually clearing the center, then peeling left and punching through to my points of domination. Clearing the first corner, following the wall, and engaging any enemy threat along the way. The next soldier into the dwelling was Jackson, coming through the doorway, peeling to the right, and doing the same on his side of the room.

Our third man through the door, SPC Malone, would come through and peel to his left, clearing his sectors of fire visually or with fire, engaging any enemies in the center of the room, and working ahead of me to the far corner. Our fourth man, SGT Davis, would come through the doorway, peeling to the right and doing the same on his side of the room. Following close behind would be Hernandez coming through the doorway, peeling left along the wall doing the same, and then providing rear security in case any insurgents unexpectedly decided to follow us inside.

This initial entry would all happen within a matter of seconds. Once inside, we would have the task of clearing room by room, engaging any enemy until the whole building was secured. The bigger the building or, the more hostiles in each room would dictate just how long it would take. Usually, we could clear an average-sized building within minutes unless met with a barrage of resistance.

As I moved through the door, initially focusing on the room and covering my sectors of fire. I immediately saw a man in my sector. He looked to be in his thirties and was modestly dressed in a robe and sandals. He seemed surprised to see me there as he was holding a rifle in his hands, lifting it towards my team, at which point I engaged the enemy combatant. I put at least three, maybe five rounds into his body, causing him to slump over.

I remember the burning sensation in my thigh as another enemy combatant caught me in my right leg, the bullet grazing me. Thankfully, Malone was already putting steel on target. Otherwise, instead of grazing my thigh, the man would've been grazing the inside of my skull.

It was such a chaotic moment. I can only clearly recall the first man I killed. I can see his face and each of the expressions he had made before taking his last breath. Everything else is still just a blur. I think I remember him so vividly because I don't want to remember anyone else. I shot and killed that day. But I do. How could I ever forget?

During that brief and chaotic firefight, my whole team received injuries, and numerous insurgents were killed and wounded. A total of eleven individuals in that house had become enemy combatants. Four men, three women, two teenagers, and two young boys. Only one woman and one child survived the exchange of gunfire, but not without being wounded.

For that brief moment in time, we had enemy gunfire coming from what seemed like all directions. Then, just as quick as it began, it was all over. Not before I killed that boy with the AK-47 squeezing off rounds who aimed his rifle at one of my rangers. In a fraction of a second, I did exactly what I was trained to do and neutralized the threat without hesitation. Yes, even an eleven or twelve-year-old with a rifle will kill you just the same as anyone else, and sadly, they are still just children. Just one more reason why "War is Hell."

After all, these were just normal people living ordinary lives on their farms and orchards until the war kicked off, and we went looking for bad guys. Don't get me wrong, some really bad people needed going after, but there must've been a better way. And there was, as we would later learn, that the top CIA officials whose job was to monitor the Middle East had devised one.

The Bush administration ignored those plans and followed the advice of the white-shirted pencil-pushing brigade. None of whom ever saw combat, and most never even served in the military. They were counting dollar signs while the two top military advisors in the room, both of whom had been in combat, were on board with what the CIA had recommended as a plan of action. Oh well, all the unnecessary blood is on their hands, and it's just too bad they don't ever have to sit down with any of the people their greed has impacted. If they actually had to face the consequences of their actions, so many future wars and conflicts would be avoided.

Even with the sounds of the chaos inside and outside, I could distinctly hear a cell phone ringing repeatedly as we worked systematically clearing and securing each room. While most of the wounded insurgents lay incapacitated, dying from their wounds, we secured and searched their bodies, removing any firearms and such. While we finished clearing and securing the building, I kept hearing that cell phone ringing over and over.

As we approached the last room we needed to clear, I saw it lighting up and vibrating on the floor with each ring. As we stacked and entered the room, I saw a woman on the floor holding a child around the age of ten or eleven. On the floor next to the woman was the cell phone, along with two weapons. The woman cradling the child in her arms pleaded with her eyes for someone to help her child. We momentarily locked eyes, and understanding her needs, I felt compassion sweep over my face and through my eyes.

In an instant, that moment was gone as I stepped over to her, knocking her to the floor face down. I then secured her arms behind her back and searched her and the kid for more weapons. So, there I was, standing over this mother and injured kid while she started getting hysterical, and that cell phone was still ringing and ringing. I was about to lose my shit.

I spoke to her, and I doubt she even understood. "Hey lady, I fucking get it, your kid is injured. Maybe you fucks should have thought about that before you tried killing me and my guys. You're yelling and screaming at me? Bitch, I should be yelling at you. Who the fuck shot me in the leg? Was it you? Was it the kid? Just shut your fucking mouth."

The rage was building inside of me, and I was already amped up on adrenaline. Fuck, I felt like just smashing her face in just to get her to shut her fucking mouth. Somehow, the ringing of the cell phone was the only thing keeping me sane at that moment while I was on the verge of snapping. Maybe subconsciously, it was a soothing melody to calm the beast inside of me trying to get out. I felt myself going dark.

Thankfully, Malone had his head in the game and came over to finish securing the woman's arms behind her back with zip ties. As he was doing that, she turned her attention to him, and instead of yelling and screaming at me, she started crying and pleading with him to help her child.

Don't judge my teammates or me. We were professionals. We were just doing our job the same way you do yours. You go to work every day, and you do your job as professionally and as thoroughly as you can. Most of you even pride yourselves on how well you perform at your job. That's all we were doing. We were being as professional and as thorough as we could, priding ourselves on how well we performed at our job. And make no mistake about it. Our job was to find the enemy, fix the enemy, and kill the enemy. It didn't matter if the enemy was the boogeyman, a woman, or an eleven-year-old kid.

When Malone finished securing the woman, he began to render first aid to the boy and patched him up pretty well. So, what if she was zip-tied and restrained? We couldn't leave her unsecure. We weren't just going to let that woman roam around free with all kinds of weapons within arm's reach. After all, she had just tried killing us. What makes you think she had had a change of heart? Especially with her child being wounded. You can't be mad at me or my team. It was what it was. Hate the game, not the player. Besides, those were your tax dollars hard at work. You can thank George W. Bush and his greedy bitch brigade.

While Malone was busy with first aid, Davis was checking on the rest of his team, and I was on the radio giving a situation report (SITREP) to the RRC team outside, who passed it along to a higher-up. I let them know that I and all of Bravo team members sustained non-life-threatening injuries and were good to continue the mission. In addition, I informed them of our two new detainees. I could also hear over the radio that Master Sergeant Prescott and the other RRC guys had secured their building and were coming out and getting ready to move to the Humvees.

Preschool:

Well, with all the trouble the founding fathers went through trying to help man find God, discipline, and change, they are going to be sorely disappointed to find out what we have brewing in the works today. Today, we are going to prove to the profiteers why their generic methods of rehabilitation do not work. We are going to show them how keeping us in the SHU for two years resulted in a maladaptive growth rather than a spiritual one and how dangerous we can be when we want to be. Today, we are going to execute a prison attack on a prison guard, and we are going to do it all from right here in their solitary confinement. This is what happens

when the belly of the beast starts grumbling and becomes upset, and this particular guard knows just how to stir things up.

They say rehabilitation is defined as taking a person out of their environment, fixing them, and returning them to their natural environment better than before. The thing is, some of our natural environments have an influential impact on us far greater than we can withstand. No matter how much prisons change us, a breath of fresh air surrounded by the wrong people in our natural environments can change us right back.

To restore the criminally broken to a state that is far better than they found it requires a tremendous amount of hard work. Work that the profiteers don't want to pay for because mental health expenses are a costly budget. Moral Recognitive Therapy through a textbook is not effective therapy, despite what they believe. The people in the SHU, people like me, usually are the sick-and-crazy, above-the-law, can't-stop-themselves, or unable-to-adapt-to-society types. We are not bad people who need to be good. We are sick people who need to get well. We don't need to be punished. We need to be treated. Everyone in the SHU has addict-like behavior that makes us prone to easily get addicted to something or susceptible to violence if we don't get it. This is a sickness that is treatable through counseling and therapy. Not through some "Do It Yourself" booklet. A broken brain can't fix a broken brain, no matter how many psychotherapy books you throw at it.

Prisons, to me, always seemed like hospitals for the spiritually sick, with the SHU being its insane asylum. The easiest way to describe a prison is to liken it to The Walking Dead television series. There are a bunch of walking dead zombies just wandering about in the general population, aimlessly, where there are only a few survivors left. The survivors band together in groups and try to isolate themselves from these airheads, just roaming about as if they are sleepwalking. The walkers are those who are shunned and looked at degradingly by the survivors. Rapists, pedophiles, and such are categorized as walkers. They are soft targets and are taken advantage of frequently. They are not really hardened criminals. They are hardened weirdos. They go in and out of the system continuously because they can't seem to break free from the cycle once they begin. There is a huge difference in prison between a walker and a survivor. Inmate and convict. Being shunned and being respected. An inmate—or walker—will get into a situation he can't get himself out of. Meanwhile, a convict— or survivor—will walk right by a situation and pay no mind to it. If it doesn't involve his friends or himself, it's not his business.

Sometimes, you can watch a prison crowd move and tell who the walking dead are and who the survivors are because a walker will bump into a survivor absentmindedly and get himself stabbed in the head. I truly believe prisons mold some of the best survivors in life because I have seen a lot of survivors get out and adapt to any situation or change. I know many who are successful in their careers and in their home lives. Regardless of how many people return to prison, statistically, based on the seventy percent of the inmate population that will come back within only a two-year period of being out, the chances of a survivor returning are slim. They do possess social-pathic traits and have no regard for the law and consequences, doing the necessary evil to survive, so there are some that return. But not many.

To prove my point that survivors fare well in situations, I had a cell phone in my prison during the COVID-19 epidemic. I started a food blog of dishes and desserts I created. Dishes that made people's mouths water like I was at a five-star restaurant. Fancy cheesecakes and blueberry pies. I showed the prison morale and how everyone was positive and hopeful. The U.S. was on a two-week isolation, and ordinary people were letting the squirrels in their heads drive them nuts, so much so that the suicide rates spiked upwards nationwide. We inmates had been confined to our units since the start of the epidemic, and prisons are where the outbreaks pretty much started.

I call this place a hospital for the spiritually sick because, growing up, I was taught prison was the opposite of a church. But it's worse than a hospital. It's a dang concrete cemetery with numbered doors like they're marked graves, with souls buried alive inside, awaiting a resurrection. I was always made to believe this was where the wicked atoned for their sins with time. A lot of the walking dead, you would be surprised, are well-educated and very intelligent. These guys are actually educated dummies who can explain psychology, anthropology, sociology, technology, and whatever else-ology but don't know what to do to save their own lives in the midst of an economic collapse, an animal attack, a flat tire, or even worse, a zombie apocalypse breakout. These types aren't entirely hopeless in prison, though, because I've seen some of them get out and use what they've learned to get rich. Legitimate or not.

Every prison across America is usually the same. They're commonly built in some backwoods remote locations where some hillbilly inbred from Schitt's Creek is hired to work. Prisons pretty much operate the same way everywhere. Operations are typically standardized nationwide. In the SHU, however, things are entirely different depending on the staff. You are stripped of all your privileges and are pretty much sitting in a cell for twenty-four hours a day at the mercy of the inbred guards on shift. If you are lucky, you get twenty-three hours in your cell and are let out for one hour of recreation time. This is probably the only privilege you have left to enjoy while down here.

Many men look forward to this single hour out because they can be outside basking in the sun even though they are caged in a tiny yard area. This area is usually as small as a dog kennel or a glass box room, and it is fixed with fences all around you. I don't know why they put the fences on the ceilings, as we would somehow figure out a way to steal the stars and sky had the fences not been there. But hey, some mental genius designed this place with layering fences over fences and razors over razors. I'm just lucky if I can get one hour out when I do. No complaints.

On this particular day, though, the staff we're targeting, a hillbilly Schitt Creek corn-fed High School dropout of a guard, decides he is going to burn us (deprive us) out of our yard. He blames it on being short-staffed. He also condemns us for being bad, stating, "If you didn't come to prison in the first place, you wouldn't be beggin' to see the sun now, wouldya?" He decided that not only was he revoking our yard privileges, but he decided why not push the envelope further. Why not burn us out of our dinners, too, right? There's nothing we can do about it. He walks right by our doors while we are standing there looking famished and silly right on the yellow line. To add insult to injury, from the windows in our cells, we can see him in the officer station eating our meals.

These types of people feel it's their job to punish the inmates, not considering that being sent to prison by the courts was punishment enough. He doesn't consider that we have families who have to endure our every struggle and suffering we go through, worrying when we don't eat or write. Every time he's on shift, it's the same thing with him. The inmates are tired of this and want to teach him a lesson he'll never forget. If they think two years in this hell hole will fix our bad behavior, then they have something else coming because one thing about prisoners you should know is that they know all about their rights but don't know a dang thing about their wrongs.

Eating our dinners and starving us caused a commotion among the inmates, which caused the plan to be hatched. It's the staff's world, they believe, and they can do whatever they want to inmates, and they think no one will do anything about it. But we're not just your average inmates. We live in the basement of this spiritual hospital for a reason. We are the worst kind of sick. The kind that will hurt you and themselves just to know they got revenge. The kind of sickness that there is no cure for. We know every routine minute by minute. We know the exact amount of steps from our rooms to the next, all the way down to the shower and yard. We know the mechanics of the prison and how it operates. Since the SHU usually has no supervision or oversight for this kind of staff behavior, they typically get away with it. But we survivors feel it's our duty to regulate this behavior and stop this from happening to us or anyone again. The sad thing about the SHU is that most of the guards who get in trouble for some bad behavior in the general population get sent to work here. This particular staff member has had his fill of being a problematic jerk. To say crap trickles downhill is an understatement because we also get the butt end of it all.

Before I go on, I have to explain that in the SHU, there are protective custody cases here in the SHU. Inmates who are afraid for their lives are housed here for their own protection. Usually, sex offenders or snitches or, sometimes just scaredy cats. Then there are guys like me. The fighters, the gamblers, the rioters, and so on. Because of this reason, secret communications are necessary and vital to the success of our secret planned covert mission because rapists, snitches, and scaredy cats are never included in our reindeer games. The Green River Killer, Gary Ridgeway, was amongst one of those inmates housed in this SHU. Robert Yates, the Spokane Serial killer, is another among the protective custody cases and lives a few doors down from me. The most troubling thing to me about these guys is that every day, during mail calls, these weirdos get tons of marriage proposals and money orders sent in by both women and men strangers. The staff would have to literally open their cuff ports just to pour their mail in because they would have stacks of it. Most of us are stressed, hoping to get a letter from our girlfriends or loved ones just to feel alive.

I'll never understand the fascination of it all, but down here, they are just another numbered door with a sick spirit inside. The plan is simple, and the inmates have coordinated their plan of attack by communicating through the vents and toilets. Some things that are too sensitive to yell through the wire, we have taken the risk of writing on toilet paper and "fishing" over to each other. Fishing is sliding an issued Bob Parker comb with a string from our clothes tied to one end, with the note attached to it. This can be slid under each other's doors from the next room or from down the hall. We can slide this fishing rod out, and the intended recipient will do the same. When our wires tangle, he can then pull the line into his house and read the note. Since I speak four languages, I am designated as the communications coordinator for this simple plan to work. The same poop bomber from the riot who blew up the staff office and caused the staff to target me for cleaning is with us in the SHU from the riot incident. We've designated him to be the bomber, with one other bomber on standby.

CHapter THree
casualties of war

Reyes:

It was determined that since we had two detainees with us, my team should move to the Humvees first while MSG Prescott and his guys provided rear security for us. I was told to get back to the Humvees ASAP because more hostiles were moving into the area, and enemy fire was increasing. The RRD team outside suggested that we move our asses before more insurgents arrived and started blowing shit up.

Bringing Bravo team together inside, I quickly advise them of the situation. Then, I instructed them to prepare to move. Checking our ammo and equipment, we prepared to move out, ready to leave the building and rejoin the rest of our squad at the Humvees. Slinging my rifle over my shoulder, I picked up the boy in my arms as Malone secured the woman. Bravo team was ready to move. Davis and Hernandez were the first ones to exit, followed by me, then the woman, Malone, and Jackson bringing up the rear.

Almost exactly as we crossed the center of the roadway, we came under heavy fire, with bullets whizzing past us and pieces of dirt bouncing off of us. We were trying to make tactical movements back to our squad at the Humvees. I say, trying because we must've looked like a dance troupe performing some weird dance routine as we each scrambled for any kind of cover we could find in the haze of gunfire.

I remember hearing the .50 caliber machine gun from one of the Humvees open up a heavy stream of return fire into enemy positions all over. The gunner on that Humvee was like a madman, putting rounds everywhere, causing the enemy combatants to duck and cover. I wondered if they were doing a dance similar to ours and looking just as silly.

During that brief lull in enemy gunfire, while our .50 caliber gunner kept the enemy busy, Bravo team and I attempted to continue to move back to the Humvees about fifteen yards away. When we started moving, Bravo team and I came under fire again, along with mortars. Several mortar shells landed within close proximity to me and the rest of Bravo team. I was thrown backward off my feet as a mortar landed about thirty feet away. Hernandez was about ten feet in front of me. I was on the ground, covered in dirt, blood, and human flesh. I couldn't feel my body and was unable to move.

PFC Hernandez was killed instantly. His body, along with the boy's body I was carrying in my arms, absorbed most of the blast and shrapnel, killing them both and saving my life. The boy's mangled body was a few feet from me, and his eyes were staring blankly as he took his last few breaths. The woman and Malone lay on the ground motionless. Everyone, including the enemy, must have thought I was dead, too, which was a good thing for a short time because no one was shooting at me anymore. On the bad side, I was in the middle of the street and unable to move.

I could only watch as the chaos unfolded around me. I could see Jackson struggling to pick up Malone's limp body and Master Sergeant Prescott running over to help. He ran over quickly, scooping up Malone. As they were moving toward the Humvees, Jackson was hit and fell. There was Master Sergeant Prescott carrying SPC Malone and half-carrying and dragging PVT Jackson along with him. I could see in slow motion as all three of them were being shot as rounds penetrated and passed through their bodies while they moved back toward the Humvees. They went out of my field of vision. I could then make out Davis, who was thrown to the ground by the same mortar that had exploded in front of me.

Davis had landed face first and was low crawling to the Humvees. At that point, I couldn't feel anything and was struggling to move. At the time, I was thinking to myself, "Man, I am so fucked." Thinking, *this is it. This is how I'm going to die.* I began to reflect on my life. It didn't last long, however, as my self-reflection was interrupted by a familiar voice. "Uce, you're all right, you're going to be okay. I got you, Uce."

Master Sergeant Prescott was pushing debris off of me and what was left of the bodies of Private First Class Hernandez and the boy. He picked me up and carried me back to the Humvees as rounds were whizzing past us—I think some were whizzing through us. Just as we were back at the Humvees, before he could set me down, we both fell hard to the ground. What happened was he was struck in the back of the neck, the bullet shattering one of his vertebrae, ricocheting up through his jaw, and exiting out through his cheek with fragments of bone and bullet slicing into his carotid artery, causing severe internal bleeding.

Thankfully, a Battalion of Marines was conducting operations within close proximity to where we were, and after what seemed like an eternity, a quick reaction force (QRF) arrived on site (Semper Fi, you glorious "Devil Dogs"). A platoon of Marines in their LAVs accompanied by two M1A1 Abrams tanks and a pair of Cobra gunships made short work of the insurgents. They wreaked havoc on our enemies, dishing out our revenge for us. Good. Fuck all of them. Our medic and a Navy corpsman (the marine medic) were tending to the wounded, myself included. They kept saying to us, "Hang on. The MEDEVAC is on its way. You're going to be okay."

When I began to regain some feeling back to my body, I was relieved and happy at first. Then, I quickly wished I couldn't feel the pain running throughout me. It hurt everywhere. As they were loading us, the wounded, onto the helicopters to be MEDEVAC, I couldn't help noticing the remaining body parts of Hernandez being placed into a body bag.

As I watched my friend, Master Sergeant Prescott, die that day on the helicopter, I remember thinking of this old rap song by Scarface playing over and over in my head. "And realized killin' men meant coming up, but it still hurt, and can't nobody change this? It's nineteen-ninety-four, and we wake up against the same shit. I never understand why. I could never see a man cry 'til I saw that man die." The only difference was Master Sergeant Prescott didn't cry. I did. The tears slowly rolled down my cheeks as both he and I died that day.

PreSCHOOL:

The Four Part Plan.

STEP ONE: We have the bomber brew up what's called a 'poop bomb.' A concoction of poop mixed with water in a cup. When the staff opens the cuff port (a metal slot in the door for sliding trays in to feed the inmates), the shUNI bomber will pretend to reach out for the tray but instead grab the guard's hand and pull him down with his other hand to stick the bomb out and splash the lazy punk in the face with the surprise attack. When this happens, all the other inmates in participation will proceed in unison to flood their cells. By the time the guards shut off the water supply in the realization that there's a Wild Waves theme park in the unit, we will have moved on to step two.

STEP TWO: Cover the cell windows with wet toilet paper. In the SHU, it doesn't matter what prison you are at in the United States of America. If an inmate covers his window, for security purposes, the staff MUST remove it to be able to see the inmate. If not, this is a safety hazard not just for the inmates but for staff alike. If an inmate refuses when the staff asks him to take the covering down, then the staff will have to suit up and request the help of a team of goon squad staffers armed with a riot shield to take the coverings off personally.

Distressingly for the prisons, getting the goon squad requires the prisons to then get other staff members to leave their posts and come join in the fight at the good old SHU. This could halt prison operations, especially if they are already understaffed, which is most likely the case.

Or at least according to the targeted staff, they are. Once they get their goon squad suited up and ready, they come in a single-file formation, with the first staff holding a riot shield in front of him or her. The way things normally work is that they would try to gas the inmate out first. The way the gassing works is that they stick a canister of oleoresin capsicum (OC) aerosol dispenser in the tray slot and spray you full of gas. This would be in the hopes that the inmate surrenders after suffocating from the gas inhalation and disorientation. But if you are determined to give them hell, though, then pepper spray or gas won't hurt you any. It's a small price to pay for the execution of the big plan.

I bet some of you have watched TV shows and seen peaceful negotiations between the guards and inmates. That's what they display on shows like Lock Up. They only show the things that depict their cordial and peaceful tactics. They don't show how cruel and vicious these cops can really be. That's to avoid risking a major lawsuit for cruel and unusual punishment of inmates. I can guarantee you that if you have made it thus far to where they must suit up and get the goon squad, you are going to be punished severely for it. And it's not cordially done like you see on TV at all. TV is all a song-and-dance pony show for the public and is phony as heck.

Once they've sprayed the inmate, they open his cell and then rush in to subdue him with restraints and take the coverings off the window. Afterward, they go about their business like it was just another day at the office. The inmate who was misbehaving is taken to a tiny cell called isolation, where he is stripped naked and left there for three to five days, handcuffed to a single metal stool in the center of the floor (until he gets his act together). Remember that the SHU is freezing cold and is sometimes called the "morgue" because of this. Isolation is pure torturous Hell.

CHAPTER FOUR
IT'S NOT SO BAD REALLY

REYES:

Not long after returning from Iraq while still recovering from my injuries, my window for reenlistment came up. I had to decide on re-enlisting or getting out. I wasn't ready to leave Uncle Sam yet. I felt we still had some things to do together. Due to getting injured, I had to change my military occupation specialty (MOS) because my body was not ready to endure the stresses that would be placed on it if I continued life as an Airborne Ranger.

It took a little convincing, but I decided to change my MOS to 31B, which is the Army's classification for Military Police (MP), and then I could go to the military police investigator (MPI) course to get my victor five (V5) skill identifier. Then after some time as a military police investigator I could put in my packet for the Army's criminal investigation division (CID).

CID is a federal law enforcement agency whose counterparts include other federal law enforcement agencies such as the FBI, ATF, CIA, etc. Each of those agencies has its own specific purview of operations and these overlap from time to time. CID deals with all criminal activity pertaining to the military and overlaps with many other agencies in intelligence gathering. In addition to the global war on terrorism and national security matters. That all seemed like some pretty fucking high-speed and thrilling shit.

For the most part, though, being a military police officer seemed a little lame to me. Although, and I'm not going to lie, the opportunity of becoming a special agent was appealing. It was high-speed enough to satisfy my need for adrenaline rushes, and I would have plenty of thrills from it. Plus, I really wanted to catch child abusers and pedophiles, giving them some rough treatment before bringing them into custody.

If I was going to stay in the Army, then changing my MOS seemed like the best thing to do at the time. Additionally, it would give me more time to deal with my injuries and newfound anxieties. So, I changed my MOS and got the additional skill identifier as an investigator. Oh boy, was I in for a ride.

PreSCHOOL:

STEP FOUR: This is the utmost important of all steps. Stick to the script and see it through. Give them hell when they enter your battlefield, which is the tiny cell you've prepared for a counteroffensive. This is the most critical of all steps, considering you have followed the steps in order. I know ... you must be thinking, well, whatever happened to STEP THREE? Well, that's the thing. Step three almost always fails in prison plans. Let me tell you why. Plans usually go awry when you don't consider everything, especially if you don't follow the plan as instructed. This is how it went awry for us on this cold, wet, and dark day. In life, things don't always go according to plan, and I learned that the hard way on that day, like on many days in my life, because I don't always plan for everything like an educated dummy. But this one was the most memorable experience of all because it left me shell-shocked. Literally. So pay close attention.

On D-Day: The guard hands the tray to the bomber and is met with surprise.. The poop bomb exploded beautifully. Waterfalls started streaming out of the inmates' cells who were participating. The goon squad comes in, and the first house they go to is mine. They figured it out through confidential sources or just plain common sense that I'm the ringleader in this whole mess. They figured if they could get me to succumb to their terms, the others would follow suit. I had my bed rolled and tied with sheets, which is what inmates use as shields. My face is covered by my wet T-shirt like a ninja mask, which is what's supposed to be technically STEP THREE. Shield your face from gas. Use your bed shield sheet as protection against their shield, and no matter what happens, DO NOT abandon your shields. It's all you have.

I'm sticking to the plan and taunting them with all the bad words I could get out. I'm like a demon-possessed raving lunatic. They gas me, but it's a small thing to a giant. I'm screaming for more. Begging for it. I refuse to back down and play their pony in the song and dance show. I'm still jumping for joy all around my flooded/ gassed cell. I can hear the cheers from my fellow inmates and the loud kicking on the doors for moral support. The guards finally open my door, and they rush in like a defensive tackle line, with everyone behind the first guy carrying the shock shield. Where I screwed up was, for the life of me, I made the educated dummy move. I abandoned my shield and improvised step three in the midst of battle, hoping to gain the upper hand advantage by jumping on them first.

The door cracks cracked open. I abandoned my bed shield and rushed forward. The first guy with the shock shield shocked me, and I went down. Timmmmmbbeerrrr!!! I didn't know about the shock shields up until then. Like I said, I was shell-shocked— no, pun intended. I dropped to my back like a quarterback sacked, laid out on the floor in about four inches of water. The first guy falls on me. Then the entire team does a six-man pile-up on him.

All the while, the shock shield is jolting me with 50,000 volts flowing through it mounted on my chest. I was lying in the water, and I could feel myself painfully separating like my spirit was trying to leave my body. Then I all of a sudden was watching myself, standing over my body, trying to tell them to get off him —meaning me. Before I exited my body, all I could remember was the first guy with the shield in between us. I'm looking at his angry face through the Plexiglas shield, and I can't bring myself to scream or utter a single sound. No one told me that the shields were armed with electricity racing back and forth on the front end and that this surge of electricity would shoot right through me like a lightning bolt coursing through my veins, locking up every muscle in my body. This made me a complete statue under this human pyramid of guards. I could smell burning like someone was cooking human flesh. I regretted my decision to get on this wild wave ride, but it was too late, and there was no going back now.

They had me squished to the floor thinner than Sunday prison pancakes, and all I could do to cry was formulate a tear that would not drop but hang out on the corner of my eye. It was like that one tear was just loitering on the street corner of my face. Every muscle was shocked and stiff. I found myself under this human pyramid, feeling like I was getting electrocuted with the worst bladder infection ever, times ten. I'd finally sailed Schitt's Creek's raging rivers with no paddles and had gotten more rage than I bargained for. My muscles and everything were so constricted that even weeks after the incident, my body would twitch with spasms. Still, to this day, I am easily shocked by electrostatics from just taking clothes out of the dryer or just someone touching my hand. I'm telling you if you have never been shocked to where you feel you are suspended in time, and you can watch your life pass before your eyes like you're on your social media feed scrolling in rapid flipping motion—with each passing post being an important life events event flying by—trust me, you don't want to try this. I had been jumped by a rival gang and left for dead. Shot by a rival gang and left for dead. Stabbed in prison during a gang fight, and none of it was as bad as this incident. It just never occurred to me that "In a world of chaos, the only constant is CHANGE" and that if I wasn't willing to change, then chaos would be the price I paid for living.

Oh, and everyone in the SHU that was participating in the fight that day? Hooting and hollering and rooting and kicking? Well, the guards rightly figured out how it played out. After the shock therapy that was administered to me, they scrapped the plan and decided it wasn't so bad to go without a yard and food for a couple of days or so.

CHapter Five
TransiTioNs

Reyes:

With the new mission came a different perspective, not only into the military but also into life. Instead of only having to deal with my own internal fucked up shit, I also had to deal with everyone else's fucked up shit. So, seeing just how fucked people were, especially at their lowest moments, was eye-opening. I learned firsthand why police officers are so jaded toward their fellow human beings. Oh, and the politics of being in the MPs is maddening.

As an MP, you got it from everyone, and that was definitely not good for my new anxieties or my PTSD. It would also feed and manifest the whole contemplating of suicide thing. You see, in the U.S., service members and police officers are high on the list of occupations most at risk for suicide. Which, obviously, was not a great combination for someone already on edge. Combat veterans also suffer from the risk of suicide for many reasons.

Maybe you can see where I'm going with this. I not only suffered a traumatic brain injury from being blown up in Iraq, but I'm also a combat vet with some very dark shit in my closet. Then I picked a job that is extremely stressful and a high risk for suicide brought on by a politically rich environment (the military is almost all about politics), and to top it off, I was an alcoholic, only I didn't yet realize it at that time (it would take me years of denial and understanding before I would come to terms with it).

Add in some fucked up childhood traumas and survivor's remorse, and I was this perfect rage-filled storm waiting to unleash my destructive powers. Oh well, I was in the shit then, and I could only laugh about it. Besides, as I've already told you, I'm better now, I promise. That is something I need you to understand. I promise that I am really better now. That whole killing myself episode was many years ago and hasn't gotten to that level since. I've learned how to handle the darkness much better since then.

The thing was, I came into the Army as an infantryman, and our mission was and still is exactly this: to find the enemy, to fix the enemy, and to destroy the enemy by any means necessary. So, within the infantry and other combat MOSs, they must create killers willing to kill and die on their order. That is our job, killing is our business.

Then they continue the conditioning at your unit and, in my case, the 75th Ranger Regiment. A group of stone-cold killers willing to destroy and die for Uncle Sam at a moment's notice. We were conditioned daily to execute our mission perfectly, physically, mentally, and emotionally. They are perfect killing machines in every way. I'm sure the co-ed hospital soldiers didn't prepare for killing and dying the way we did. I often think about the cadences we would call out on our morning runs and such.

"Hey, hey, Captain Jack, meet me down by the railroad track with that knife in your hand. I'm going to be a stabbin' man, the best I can, for Uncle Sam, re-up you're crazy, re-up you're outta your mind, hey, hey Captain Jack, meet me down by the railroad track with that gun in your hand I'm gonna be a shootin' man, a stabbin' man, the best I can, for Uncle Sam, re-up you're crazy, re-up you're outta your mind ... "

And my personal favorite ... "Left, right, left, right, I begin to kill, left, right, left, right, oh what a thrill, I went to the market where all the people shop, I pulled out my machete and I began to chop, left, right, left, right, I begin to kill, left, right, left, right, oh what a thrill, I went to the playground where all the kiddies play, I pulled out my Uzi and I begin spray, left, right, left, right, I begin to kill, left, right, left, right, oh what a thrill ..."

Not only did we call those kinds of cadences day after day and year after year, but we became them down to our very core. How else would we be able to do what we needed to do for Uncle Sam?

Actually, there has been a great deal of controversy over the years about what cadences are allowed. I imagine all the dental techs and such who had sensitive ears and complained about hearing such sociopathic glee coming from combat arms units as they passed formations. As if all their sensitivity training mandates could fix any of it. What the fuck? Sensitivity training? Oh, I'm so sorry, mister enemy combatant, but I am going to have to shoot you in your fucking head today before you shoot me. I hope you have a nice day, and I don't say anything to offend you. That's Army politics for you, haha.

As I've gotten older, I've come to have a better understanding of how the mind works and how the military machine breaks down the human psyche to build up obedient robots so that the machine can move along with limited snags. They call it conditioning, but it's really brainwashing to varying degrees, depending on what level of conditioning is needed to get you to perform your military occupation and what unit you're assigned to.

They like to say we are all the same and receive the same kind of training, but that isn't true. Good old Uncle Sam always controls the narrative, which is laughable. It's really not like that at all because someone serving in combat arms has a completely different job than someone who is a dental tech, for instance, just like someone in a line unit has an objective that is entirely different from someone working in a hospital. The mindsets are not the same.

Don't get me wrong, they go through it, too, but it's different. There are levels to this shit. Some are operating on level one shit while others are operating on level fifty type of shit, and everything in between. The things they do to us in combat arms are definitely at a much higher degree of "conditioning," as they call it. That is just the way it needs to be to do the job that needs to be done. Thank you, Drill Sergeant, for conditioning my mind and my body.

And I really do understand why they do the whole "sensitivity training" and "we are the same" propaganda stuff. It's because they need us all to get along so we can function as a whole. But why not "de-sensitivity training" and "some of us are killers, and some of us are not?" I mean, I still respect everyone who has the balls to sign on the dotted line and serve their country, potentially being put in harm's way. Regardless, it's the normies who make up the rules, and it's probably better that way.

The truth is we are not all the same. In fact, the psychological match between death row inmates and special forces operators is almost the same. The number one thing that sets us apart, and maybe the only thing, is that we have a twenty percent greater moral calculator in our head. We break the rules, think outside of the box, and tolerate authority. That difference in making better moral decisions and choices, and not by much, is what keeps us out of concrete cages. It also causes us to look for the best legal ways to channel our defiant energies. And believe me, when push comes to shove, we will both fuck up your world, and for us, it's not just words; we mean it wholeheartedly. In fact, we both rather enjoy fucking up shit. Just that one of us has a higher tolerance for your bullshit. So yeah, I was a little fucked up, but I was learning to deal with it. Savagely.

PRESCHOOL:

Transitioning to the streets from prison is hard. Transitioning to the streets with the weight of the USOS wealth on your shoulders is even harder. USO is the Samoan word for "brother." USOS is an organization founded in prison, which stands for Uniting Sons Of Samoa. A prison gang that has spread its tentacles far beyond the walls of its birthplace. The founding and formation of the USOS organization is the result of congested prisons and overcrowding relief efforts by the Department of Corrections nationwide. Private prisons were more than eager to benefit from prison profits that they welcomed any state prisoner to their new prison facilities, which would turn out to be killing fields and racketeering havens. Private prisons provided the thunder dome and cannibalistic atmosphere by taking only the strong. Anyone who had a medical condition would be weeded out and not fit to be housed there because the private prisons didn't want to be liable for the sick, thus rendering the private prisons a gladiator environment where only the strong survived. And what happens when you get a bunch of bulls in a bullpen? Eventually, they lock horns.

Me coming home without a pot to piss in and a window to pour it out from made me desperate and eager to get things off the ground. I was faced with all the typical apprehensions and fears that came with being released.

The anxiety was a motherfucker. It felt like I was sent from another planet and expected to infiltrate Earth without drawing attention to myself. The problem with that was that being on probation and under the scrutiny of the law added to the compounding stress I was already dealing with. I'm a hustler. It doesn't matter where you put me. I'll get money. You can send me out in space to another planet, and I'll come back with some alien hoes and a bag full of alien dough, driving the latest alien model, the UFO.

It was just coming home with the watchful eye of John Law that made things tricky. Being held up by the arm of John Law with a probations shock collar didn't give me a lot of wiggle room. But shit, I did what I knew how to do. I was an operator with one focus in mind. Being an operator on the streets and a smart operator at that, stealth and secrecy were your strongest allies. It was how the mafia lasted for so long operating in this country. Remaining covert and out of sight. It wasn't until the new age group came along with the disease for attention that it brought the greatest secret societies crumbling to their knees.

The first rule to success for anyone coming home was proper planning and preparation. A failure to plan was a plan to fail. I networked from inside the prison through correspondence and female connections. I had a sexy Hungarian female staff member named Ms. Basque who taught me the most valuable lesson I learned from prison. She said, "You know, I sit here and watch guys come in and out of prison. Day in and day out. I hear about them in the streets. The who's who of the towns. And you know, none of them have money saved. They all hustled for ten years or so and gave it all to the feds when they got caught up. Now, they go home after serving ten to twenty years, and they have nothing to go home to. Do me a favor?"

"What's that?" I said.

She said, "If you go back to doing what you do best and accumulate wealth, be smart about it. Save it where these motherfuckers can't ever touch it or reach it. Will you do that for me?"

I smiled. I wanted so much in life at that moment to marry her. To promise her I'd be back for her that I'd do right by her. But we both knew the truth in the situation was only what she had said and nothing else. It always stuck with me, though. The truest shit sometimes comes from the least likely person we think it would. Who'd ever have thought that a prison guard would give me the one piece of gem that I would wear in my crown when being king of the streets?

She said, "And one more thing. Stay out."

I smiled. "Yes, ma'am."

See, behind every strong man is a wise woman. Women are the lifeblood of any organization. Especially prison gangs. They keep members in communication. They help with the leg work that is needed on the streets. They are the sounding board to our prison voices. Anyone who defies them knows that doing so would be defying us indirectly. It's why guys get out to go and get laid up like fuck boys with their girls. They feel they owe them the world. But not me. I knew that there was much more to be had ...... and I wanted it all. The world was not enough. I wanted Mars, Venus, and Neptune too.

My first visit was to the criminal lawyer who worked with us in building our foundation for successful members transitioning. He was a long -time friend of the USOS and helped many members beat their criminal convictions and come home early on appeal. He was one of the most brilliant legal minds who believed in justice for all, and not justice just for the rich.

Having that reputation made him sought out by many gangsters looking at time. His integrity made him a well-respected and loved member of the streets as well as the Washington Bar Association.

When I got there, the first thing he said was that everything was everything. That was all I needed to hear. Heck, the lawyer was such a great lawyer that he offered up his hot-smoking legal secretary and the conference room for a sexual consultation. Well, not exactly in that manner. But he did say, "Hope's been checking you out since you walked in. Be Careful. I know that look. She's got the hots for you." And I asked Hope to help me in the conference room, which was all she wrote. What? I'm human. I had just walked off a seven-year stretch in prison, and there was no way I was going to leave that office without giving her dreamy and hungry eyes the satisfaction they desired.

The next person I went to see was my long-time girlfriend of five years, Mimi. She found me on the internet and started writing to me two years into my sentence, and we developed a long-lasting friendship/relationship. The thing about her was she grew to move away from being jealous or insecure about herself. She knew that entering into a relationship with a man from the lifestyle I was from would require patience and adjustment to her beliefs. Having been part of my life gave her meaning and purpose to hers. It gave her the independence and confidence that most women could only dream of.

I knew there were people out there who were judgmental in the sense they considered her stupid for putting up with a man like me. She would get it all the time from her mom, her friends, and even her co-workers.

They would tell her she was worth more than I had to offer. That didn't seem to be the case when I met her, though. Those people didn't know shit. They didn't know what I had offered her. This girl, like many women I knew, seemed to have their shit together when they really didn't. She was up to her neck in debt she couldn't afford to pay. She was working at a dead-end job she didn't enjoy. She was suffering from anxiety and depression and did not feel loved or lovable. She was in such a bad place that was dark and gloomy that she would question her existence and oftentimes think about un-aliving herself.

I changed all that. I helped Mimi clear all her debts and build her credit from prison. Gave her the funding to start her own business and attend college. Got her working for herself and earning money, which she enjoyed. She had four employees working for her. As for the anxiety and depression, I know you want me to say it went away with conjugal trailer visits in Prison and the erotic stimulating phone calls at night. Nah, it didn't. It went away with her finding and believing in herself to where she was able to know her true worth and priceless value. The trailer visits were a bonus. I would take her to the moon and show her the brighter side of it, too, where she lit up every time she saw me. She became so independent she didn't need me. She wanted me. She loved me for loving her. Not too many women can say they are with the man who gives them financial security and is the best lover they have ever known. Nah, most women are with a man they enjoy financial security from, yet this isn't the man that she dreams of or thinks about in her downtime. It's the man that made her eyes roll back of her head and her toes curl. The man that made her heart skip a couple of beats that she fantasized about. Let that man call her while she's in a new relationship, and watch how quickly she forgets everything and spends hours on the phone clutching it like it's her life support. Bet she still masturbates because her man does not fulfill her like that other man does.

The third person I went to see was Momma. Every gangster in his right mind knows that Momma is a high priority to visit when they come home. Why? Because Momma was always there when times got tough. It is the mommas of the world that won't ever believe what they say in court about their baby. No matter if the evidence is stacked against her child, be it a smoking gun, a video recording, or a bugged telephone call admitting to killing the victim. Momma's will always argue, "There is no way my son did it." On top of that, no one can top Momma's cooking. There ain't no competition. Many women have come close, but never close enough to where a son would not want to visit his Momma.

Armed with the financial backing from the lawyer, the support of one of the strongest prison organizations as my backbone, and a small cache of firepower that I left stashed at Momma's house, I was ready. All that was left was attending neighborhood street meetings set up and organized by the members of the USOS in prison, and I'd soon have the Army I needed to take this town by Storm. I had a reputation of being ruthless preceding me. Now, I had to live up to it.

CHAPTER SIX
ENTERING THE DARKNESS

REYES:

During that helicopter ride back to the field hospital, I lay there for what seemed to be an eternity, thinking in the darkness, alone. I was thinking I almost died and maybe still was going to, and also thinking about everyone who did die. MSG Prescott, SPC Malone, PFC Hernandez, the crazy screaming woman, and her kid. It was in an instant that PFC Hernandez exploded in front of me, and my brain kept playing that scene over and over in my head as I drifted further into the darkness, alone. I was having my life flash before my eyes, each time with flashes of Hernandez exploding. Then I was thinking about what I was going to do with my life if I lived. There were plenty of things I still wanted to do. I still wanted kids and family. I remember thinking who this man in the darkness was and what he was supposed to be doing.

After spending some time in the hospital and recovering, I had to make some choices in what direction my life would go. I could get out and medically retire, or I could stay in the Army. It would break my heart every time I would think how if I stayed in, I wouldn't be able to fulfill my duties as a Ranger and would have to go down to a regular line unit. Then, I would think about how I could do something different for a while until I could get back to the special forces community I loved.

I thought maybe I'd go to the Green Berets and one day have a chance at CAG (Delta). Until then, I needed to let all my wounds heal completely, physically and mentally. Then, I could recondition my body to take on the rigorous and strenuous physical demands that were placed on the body during special forces recruitment, training, and operations. Going into the MPs with a career path in CID would still give me an option of going back into special operations while having something to fall back on that I wouldn't hate if my body didn't heal up right.

After spending eight weeks for my 31B MOS reclassification course at Fort Leonard Wood, Missouri to become a military police officer I made the short trip across base to the Military Police Investigators course for another eight weeks of training. While attending the investigators course, I became interested in two other training opportunities there, SRT and PSD.

The first one I wanted to attend was the Special Reaction Team (SRT) course which was five days long. It's basically the military's version of SWAT training for MPs consisting of building clearing, breaching, vehicle assaults and planning; things I was already familiar with from being through all my Ranger training. It would be more like a refresher course for me and give me a chance to learn some new things as well.

The other one was the military's version of the Secret Service called the Protective Security Details (PSD) course, lasting another twenty days. This course would teach us how to protect dignitaries on military installations as well as in hostile environments and combat theaters of operation.

Using my advantages of being a noncommissioned officer (NCO) with a Ranger tab and having both a 75th Ranger combat patch and combat infantry badge, I was able to easily ask around. It was the combat patch that gave me the most respect from whomever I talked to. Everyone in the Army has an idea of what a Ranger is. They know we are elite warriors, a special breed of men admired and respected. Our motto, "Rangers Lead the Way," is famous Army-wide as Rangers have led the way in over fifty military campaigns for more than sixty years.

What I found out was that upon graduation, I would be assigned orders to the 504th Military Police Battalion in Fort Lewis, Washington.

What this meant for me was that if I could get an officer's approval from the 504th, I could then attend one or possibly both of those courses. I decided to make a call into my new unit, which turned out to be on a redeployment back stateside from an eighteen-month rotation in the sandbox (Iraq). As luck would have it, the major on the rear detachment didn't have a problem with letting me attend those courses. It turned out the major had attended Ranger school, having earned his own Ranger tab, and he loved his Rangers. As far as he was concerned, a sergeant with a combat-patched and fully tabbed Ranger could get as much training as he wished.

Fort Lewis is situated in the Pacific Northwest in beautiful Washington State. There are lush rainforests, the Puget Sound containing a bunch of islands, Mount Rainier, and the Cascade Mountain range. Located right on the I-5 corridor, making trips to Seattle, Portland, and Vancouver, Canada, took one to four hours or so, depending on where you want to go and when you go. Washington State had a lot to offer. There was skiing, hiking, mountain biking in the mountains, floating down a river, and even downtown shopping or clubbing, all of which could be done on the same day. There were plenty of places to go and sights to see.

Out of everything, Tacoma caught my attention most, and I just seemed to fit in there. Tacoma locals were rough around the edges, but once you broke through the roughness, you would find real solid people with warm hearts. It was funny to me that everyone outside of Tacoma would always warn you to stay away from Tacoma, saying how rough and dangerous it was. Then, the Tacoma people would tell you to be careful and stay out of the hoods in Tacoma.

I would ride my mountain bike everywhere as part of my own self-rehab program. It was cool because of their mass transit system. You could catch buses or trains with bike racks and go exploring everywhere from Fort Lewis to Tacoma to Seattle, all in a day. So, I kept an eye out while riding around, looking to avoid those hoods in Tacoma that I kept hearing about. I was doing that for a couple of years, thinking, "Like damn, how big is this Tacoma anyways because I haven't passed through any hoods yet."

One day, Monica, a girl I was dating, started telling me where all the hoods were located. At that point, I thought to myself that all those neighborhoods looked and felt just like where my grandma lived. Of all the years she lived there, only a couple of shootings took place on her street. Of course, one of the parks down the street from her apartment had a part of it that was off-limits to us kids. This was the same park we would all play football in over our holidays and summer vacations.

One Thanksgiving holiday, when my parents and brothers were visiting grandma, I remember us kids having a friendly neighborhood football game. Since my cousins lived there year-round, they had all their friends over to play a game in the park. It was great because there were plenty of bodies to fill out the two teams. I'll never forget as we were coming out of our huddle and lining up on the line of scrimmage, one of our teammates began running away. This kid, Chris, was always into something and pissing someone off. Apparently, he pissed off the wrong ones who were coming to collect on his ass that day. It was kind of like our little half-time show. All of us kids just watched as Chris went sprinting off across the field and down the street while these gangbangers with shotguns and pistols went chasing after him. Damn, he was fast and a good thing, too. After the show, we all went back to playing football, minus one player.

The hoods in the Midwest are just different, I guess. Chicago, Detroit, Milwaukee, Saint Louis, and Gary have hoods, real ghettos. Thankfully, I never lived in any hoods. My parents and relatives, on the other hand, had lived in them. My father grew up on the south side of Chicago during a time when it was at its worst. I actually had an aunt who was born in Cabrini-Green, one of Chicago's most notorious housing projects. It was made famous from many movies, including *Candyman* in 1992 and the TV show *Good Times*, which aired in the 1970s. At one point, Cabrini-Green turned into a national symbol of urban blight and a failed housing policy. Then, from 2000 to 2011, the City of Chicago finally demolished those projects.

The hood and the ghetto are places you are taught from a young age to avoid, and if you find yourself in one of them, you better know how to carry yourself to safely navigate it. One time as a teenager, around when I was seventeen, I had that lesson driven home. One night, I was in the front passenger seat of my cousin's car, and we were heading home from hanging out with some friends. We passed a group of five or six cute girls hanging out on the sidewalk in front of an apartment building. I told my cousin to pull over, and I hopped out. As I approached the girls, ready to spit game, the situation dawned on me.

Behind the girls in the shadows were a bunch of gangbangers chilling against the brick walls of the apartment building. The shadows had concealed them from any passerby on the street. I had, unfortunately, gotten the attention of these gangbangers, and not in a good way either. At this point, I'm already on the sidewalk a few feet away from the cute girl I was starting to spit game to as the gangbangers came off the wall and circled me. You see, my cousin had only slightly pulled over, not realizing what I was going to do, and when I got out of the car, he went to park the car. Thankfully, he didn't have far to go to find a parking spot. The gangbangers circled up around me and started verbally checking me. All I knew to do was to stand my ground, be cool, and never back down like no bitch. They were going to give me a stomping for disrespecting their hood, which I had no business being in. At that point, I knew I was fucked.

My cousin finally made it over to us, and he started shaking hands with a couple of the gangbangers and speaking to the leader of the group. My cousin explained that I was his cousin, just up from Michigan, visiting for the summer, and squashed the situation so that we could leave. Not one of those gangbangers was happy to see me leave. They were really looking forward to whooping my ass just for the fun of it. As it turned out, my cousin grew up with most of that crew and played middle school football with them. The leader of the group and my cousin were good friends at one point, one choosing to go into "the life" and the other choosing not to.

Plus, maybe an even bigger deal was once they knew who I was, they knew who my grandmother was. She probably changed diapers on all of them, and she was always looking out for the kids in Chicago Heights. Out of respect and love for her and my cousin, I got a pass and learned a valuable lesson that night. You really should look before you leap.

My grandmother, whom I am named after, was Antonia, and my name is Antonio, but everyone calls me Tone for short. She was loved and respected by the whole community for the love and kindness she gave to everyone from Cabrini-Green to Chicago Heights, who had lived in the latter for over twenty years by that time. She was active in city hall and worked for a non-profit dealing with the poor and underprivileged adults and kids of the community, which reminds me of another incident involving some hood girls again. It seems to me that women always have a key role in problems that occur to me. At that time, I was at my cousin's apartment with him and his friends. One of the females started talking some crazy shit, making stuff up. I challenged what she was saying, so she got upset and left. Turns out she's a cousin to some gangbanger. She tells him I was harassing her and blah blah blah whatever else she said to make it out that I was some terrible guy that he would have to deal with.

The next day her cousin showed up with some of his gangbanger buddies and started harassing another cousin of mine, asking where I was. Now my cousin wasn't going out like that and didn't care that it was six to one. This one cousin of mine was wild and welcomed the fight because he definitely wasn't about to betray his family for nothing. Fortunately for my cousin, as these gangbangers were making threats and getting ready to do the business on him, his dog got loose from inside the apartment. This mutt named Baby, mixed with Beagle and Pitbull, had quite the reputation around the neighborhood for biting dicks and balls. Apparently, none of these six gangbangers was into involuntary gender reassignment surgery and promptly vacated the front porch.

While all of that was transpiring, I was at school taking some college courses at the local community college. The incident occurred around noon, and when I got home around four in the afternoon, my aunt, the same one born in Cabrini-Green, had filled me in on what had happened. She then told me we were having some guests over for dinner and going to watch a movie after dinner. At dinner, an older Hispanic man and his wife arrived. My aunt and grandmother greeted them, invited them inside, and introduced me as the "nephew" and the "grandson."

We sat down and ate the dinner my grandmother had prepared. My aunt and grandmother talked most of the time with our guests. The man only made small talk with me, but I could tell he was sizing me up the whole time. I can never forget the movie we watched that night, unbeknownst to me at that time it was very fitting for the situation I was now in. The movie was *American Me* starring Edward James Olmos who was made famous from the TV show *Miami Vice*.

The Hispanic man sitting there in the apartment with us was one of the top members of a notorious street gang, both of whom I don't have permission to say by name. But if you put two and two together, there are similarities to the movie we were watching. This man and my aunt were childhood friends, and my grandmother had taken care of him and looked out for him countless times while he was a kid. After the movie, the man and his wife thanked my aunt and grandmother, saying their goodbyes. I honestly don't remember the man saying goodbye to me. He saw what he needed to see, and that was that I was a good kid, not in the life and not a troublemaker, well, not the gangbanging kind of troublemaker.

I learned some lessons that night, too: the art of politics and diplomacy, the importance of knowing the right people for any given situation, and having power. Only a few will ever know the man who visited our apartment that evening wielded power. His words were law in the world to which he belonged, and disobeying him could result in death. Nor did I ever again have trouble with anyone from that crew. If any of the girls or guys from that affiliation saw me, they looked the other way, and at the same time, they also made sure no one else had any issues with me or my cousins. Just like that, I had instant protection in and around the hood.

Don't get me wrong, Tacoma has its hoods and rough areas for sure. It was built differently than the Midwest, with its own unique looks and set of rules. From what I've learned since my mountain biking exploration of Tacoma days, I was there during a time of relative peace and order. What happened in the 1980s was what everyone talked about and how they still viewed Tacoma. It stemmed from a combination of law enforcement cracking down on all the gangs in Los Angeles and California coupled with those same gangs trying to spread out to new untapped areas to increase their profits. Especially in the drug trade, due to the crack epidemic, many California gangs migrated north to Washington and east to Utah, New Mexico, and Arizona.

For some reason, Tacoma became the hub of the Pacific Northwest, and it wasn't ready for the mass influx of LA gang members. These gangs ran the streets unchecked by insufficiently funded and under-trained police departments. Adding to the complication, they didn't have enough manpower for the surge in crime and violence. What happened next was Tacoma became a city under siege from the 1980s to the mid-1990s, in effect making it Washington State's ground zero for gang activity. It would take law enforcement agencies and local governments almost two decades working together to bring it under control. Eventually, by the end of the 1990s, law enforcement statewide began to have sufficient funding, manpower, and training. They got a handle on the gang violence and criminal enterprises that had invaded their state over a decade ago.

I guess most would say it is one of, if not the most notable, incidents that occurred in Tacoma, solidifying the severity of the gang problem that happened in 1989. On Saturday, September 23, on Ash Street in the Hilltop neighborhood, a staff sergeant in the Army Rangers who had recently purchased a home in that neighborhood was having a BBQ with fifteen of his Ranger buddies (one of whom was another staff sergeant who worked in military intelligence, who we will just call CW5). The staff sergeant who bought the house had recently become a target of one of Washington State's most notorious street gangs, the Hilltop Crips. He and his fellow Rangers were more than ready for whatever the Hilltop Crips would throw at them. The BBQ was more of an antagonistic way of inviting the violence that would soon ensue later that day. Reports indicated that the Hilltop Crips took to intimidation antics and even verbally threatened the staff sergeant that they were going to kill him and burn his house down that night.

The Rangers, bringing their personally owned weapons and ammunition, formulated a tactical plan, setting up defensive positions around the house. Later that night, the Hilltop Crips began an assault on the house. The Rangers were ready. After all, this was exactly the type of shit they trained for. The firefight lasted about ten minutes, and over three hundred rounds were fired. After that incident, there was no longer any denying or hiding the gang problems of the Pacific Northwest. There were even talks from the then-governor about having the National Guard brought into Tacoma to deal with the gang problem. I'm sure Uncle Sam had a lot to say regarding this, as I'm sure he wasn't happy having his soldiers assaulted, particularly his Rangers.

I can only imagine the phone calls from the president's office to the governor of Washington and the mayor of Tacoma. George H. W. Bush was a hard-core Republican, tough-on-crime, no-nonsense type of politician with strong ties to the CIA. He was just finishing up his first year in office, and that was the kind of thing that made a president look bad and inadequate. Americans like to feel safe and believe they are protected. If your own soldiers aren't safe in public, then how could anyone else be? Needless to say, Tacoma and Washington State found the funding and resources to deal with their gang problems after all.

Preschool would be incarcerated with most of the older generation from that era, and the Hilltops loved him ...

PreSCHOOL:

My first big break came when I settled a long-time neighborhood rivalry. I had gotten the blessings and the controlling power from the O.G.s in the prison system to educate their young ones and put them to work. Or eradicate the bad ones from the brood. The word hit the streets before I did, and everyone was eager to have someone to look up to. The streets had been left so long without organization and structure that they had been in complete and utter chaos for decades. The feds, having removed the heads of the gangs in the streets, had caused civil wars and chaos to erupt all over the city. I don't know when they would realize that taking the older heads off the streets makes things worse. Every time you remove a leader from power, you create a power vacuum, which results in a territorial dispute that always ends bloody. Power without a leader is nothing but chaos. Look at Operation Iraqi Freedom. Good job, Georgy Boy. You're the only one who came up out of that war richer than a Turkish sultan without a bruise. And you didn't even break a sweat. Ironically, in the streets, the heads of organizations are always strung up on RICO charges for crimes that members of organizations do. Yet, when removed, the voice of reasoning goes to jail, and the balance of power and control on the streets are left to the shooters and muscle who ain't really great at thinking on their own. How is that supposed to make sense?

Settling the dispute earned me a few street cred points and brownie points to add to my character. I knew that I had to be everything that my reputation said about me since it preceded me into the free world. All I had to do was show guys that I meant business, and there's nothing that displays that you mean business more than violence. A cutting away of the cancer in the group with one swift finger motion. Establishing yourself with crazy people takes a lot more craziness. This lets them know that you might be crazy, but there is someone out there who is crazier and willing to go beyond your extent of the meaning. The word spread quickly to the streets, and to the jails, and the prisons. Before you knew it, the message came via kite. Good job. We are a culture that celebrates violence. Like I said, it's a reason we love extreme contact sports and action films. We're warriors. Having the approval come from the top levels of the prisons means they were expecting someone to come out preaching their bylaws with an iron fist and not with a bunch of flowery words. With hot lead and not hot air. I was on the right path. The boys approved. For the first time in a long time, there was someone doing the thinking and shooting at the same time. They couldn't have been happier.

It's a dog-eat-dog world in the streets, and the following is all based on the messenger. I knew that words would not soothe the years and years of rivalry that deepened into the hearts and minds of these guys who carried with them anger and resentment that turned into bitter animosity and poison. The only way to cure this cancer had to be with a cut at the root entirely so that it wouldn't form again. Making sure that the surgical procedure was made public was the idea of preventing the wound from spreading again. See, a lion does not always act violently, but when it does, it makes sure that others know it's something they do not want to witness or experience again. They prefer him just roaming the jungles in peace and sleepy quiet.

CHAPTER SEVEN
NEW BEGINNINGS

REYES:

Military police have a complicated role within the military. They are what are called security and mobility support assets having both combat zone responsibilities (field MPs) as well as law enforcement duties (garrison MPs). In the field, MPs conduct mounted and dismounted patrols, route reconnaissance, intelligence gathering, anti-terrorism, convoy and personnel escorts, critical site security, area damage control, and cordon and search operations. MPs are also responsible for detainee operations from the battlefield to detention centers.

Additionally, MPs conduct criminal investigations on and off the battlefield. In garrison, they operate much like any other police department, providing police and emergency services to the military communities, often consisting of soldiers and civilians on military installations. At Fort Lewis, this included active duty and reserve soldiers, the National Guard, ROTC cadets, veterans, civilian family members and friends, civilians employed by the government, private contractors, and visitors.

Also located on Fort Lewis is Madigan Army Medical Center, the U.S. Army's second-largest medical treatment facility and a state-of-the-art and technologically advanced medical center. It's been deemed a level two trauma center, making it one of four in the state of Washington and one of three in the Army.

At any given time, there were two hundred thousand plus people on Fort Lewis, resulting in an interesting mix of activities concerning law enforcement. It has it all, theft, assaults, drugs, burglary, rape, murder, arson, domestic violence, etc. As required, upon being assigned to law enforcement duties, e.g., working the road or garrison duties, MPs, along with their civilian counterparts, the Department of the Army Police Officers would go through an additional two weeks of training and briefings. It was in one of these briefings that I learned about the meth problem of the northwest, making it one of the meth capitals of America during that time.

Those labs were being set up in the training areas, which consisted of thirty-two training areas covering approximately sixty-four thousand acres of densely wooded and hilly terrain. Those meth labs would often be guarded and booby-trapped with explosives and other nasty traps. This posed just one more problem for MPs, who then had to receive additional special training to deal with those meth labs.

During that two-week training, I had to undergo OC training. OC stands for oleoresin capsicum, which is commonly referred to as pepper spray. Basically, they take the hottest peppers in the world and extract their oils into a concentrated aerosol spray easily deployed up to ten feet. Let me tell you, that shit really sucks, and having gone through the gas chamber, I'd choose the gas chamber over OC spray every time. CS gas, which is commonly called tear gas, sucks while you are exposed to it, but soon the gas dissipates. Within ten or fifteen minutes after you remove yourself from the gas, you begin to feel normal again. It is not the same with OC. The effects of OC last for hours and sometimes days. This was worse during hotter temperatures, too, because that's when your pores open up wide versus in cold weather when your pores are more closed up.

There I was in June on a sunny afternoon in eighty-degree weather, pushing into the nineties, getting sprayed with that OC shit. No, not fun at all. You stand there with the instructor about ten feet away, telling you to look at him. He won't spray you until you are looking at him with both eyes open. That motherfucking bastard actually got off on that shit, too.

After you get sprayed, you go through an obstacle course of sorts, having different tasks to perform at each station.

When I got sprayed, my eyes shut immediately because they burned instantly. When I was a kid, I used to be on a swim team, and sometimes the chlorine levels would be so potent that if you tried opening your eyes underwater, reflexes would kick in, and your eyes would shut involuntarily, and you'd have to force them open through sheer will power. That OC shit was way worse, and if there weren't so many bystanders watching, I might have curled up into a ball on the ground and cried.

The cadre yelled at me to open my eyes and directed me through the course. Stations one through four were something along the lines of me having to throw a bunch of knees and elbows against attackers holding pads. Then, in the next few stations, I had to draw my dummy firearm, engage targets, and apprehend a suspect. The last stations were calling out on the radio my location and requesting backup. Trying to read the street signs and building numbers with that shit in my eyes was no easy task. The whole time, I kept thinking how I wanted to hurry up and get that shit out of my eyes. That motivated me to complete each station and move through the course as quickly as possible. The idea of relief from the pain at the end was very compelling.

What those assholes didn't tell us in the safety briefing was that once we completed the course and began our decontamination, there was no instant relief and that the shit was going to linger. In my case, I was messed up for a couple of days while enduring the effects. I don't know; I might just prefer to be shot instead, but I haven't decided which is worse yet. At least I know OC spray works on most people, so there's that.

I would later witness confrontations between Samoans and the police. Those Samoans were fearless and ready to do battle. They didn't care about the police having guns, batons, Tasers, or even working dogs, but as soon as a cop would pull out the OC spray, well, those Samoans would suddenly want to comply. Those giant warriors would rather be shot, beaten, tased, or mauled by a dog than get sprayed with that fiery venom, and I couldn't blame them one bit because I almost felt the same way about it.

Getting settled on Fort Lewis and into my unit was a fairly smooth process. However, I wanted to get out and explore the area but didn't have a car, which put me on the market for one. I heard about this guy, Jimmy, who helped service members acquire automobiles at a very reasonable price. As a licensed car dealer, he could go to both the public and commercial auctions reserved only for dealers. Jimmy would go to those car auctions on behalf of the service members and secure a vehicle that met the specifications of the buyers. He didn't charge as much for his service in comparison to the other car dealers. He only charged a commission on the purchase of the vehicle and some small administrative fees. He didn't really have a car lot or anything, just a small office in South Hill. That kept his overhead and cost of business at almost zero, which was what allowed him to make those great deals for the customer.

This saved the customer anywhere from thirty to fifty percent on the purchase of a car and sometimes even more depending on what kind of vehicle and year they wanted. The only thing about this way of doing business was that it kept him on a constant grind. Since he didn't advertise or have a car lot, his business was exclusively done by word of mouth. Good thing for him that he tapped into the military market because one thing for sure is that service members and veterans love to talk about getting a great deal on a car. Jimmy always delivered on these deals if you were lucky enough to hear of him and this unique service he offered.

When I met Jimmy at his small office, I was impressed by his high energy level. The guy was in his fifties, a combat veteran of the Vietnam War and was on a constant go status. He was a likable person and had great stories to share. He honestly liked helping service members, especially veterans. They were his favorite customers.

When he asked me what kind of vehicle I was looking for, I told him it was a sports sedan like a Lexus or a Camry that was slightly used. He asked me my budget, and I told him it was around twelve grand. He just smiled and said that it wouldn't be a problem; he could definitely find me something really nice in that price range, and I would be happy with it. I gave him my contact information, and he said to give him about a week or two and that he should have something for me by then.

Just as promised I heard from Jimmy just under a week later. He had some good options for me. He asked me if I could meet him at the auction so I could come take a look and test drive them if I wanted to. I was excited to hear this telling him yes and asking where and when I needed to meet up with him. He told me to go to the auctions in Auburn and gave me the directions and time to meet him.

Auburn was only about a forty-five-minute drive from Fort Lewis. Once I arrived, Jimmy was happy to show me the options he had found. I honestly think he was more excited about the cars than I was. I don't think he could help himself because he was such a naturally enthusiastic person. I test-drove all of them on the little track that they had set up just for that purpose. There was a black Nissan Altima, a maroon Nissan Maxima, a black Toyota Camry, and a gold Lexus to choose from. Honestly, I was a fan of the gold Lexus from the jump and probably didn't give the other cars a thorough look over. Although, the Maxima was a pretty sharp car and fun to drive.

When Jimmy told me I could probably get the Lexus for under ten grand, I was sold on the idea of him getting it for me. I told Jimmy that if he could do that, I'd be extremely grateful and impressed. He told me he would know in a few days after the auction, but he would be able to secure one of those cars for me at a very reasonable price. After giving Jimmy my approval to proceed, I headed back to the car.

While walking back to my car a strange thing happened. I heard this whining childish, impish soft tone voice call out to me. "Are you looking to buy a car?"

When I turned around to look at who was talking to me it was a rather heavy-set man, short and round like a beach ball. He was well dressed in designer clothing and wearing expensive jewelry puffing on a cigar. He says to me, "Ya, I can help you get what you are looking for."

"How's that?" I asked.

"Oh, I come to these things all the time and know most of the people here. They like me, and it's easy for me to make a deal with them. I buy cars all the time for different dealers in the area and for myself. Would you like me to find one for you?"

That dude was just too slick, and it felt like he was trying to run some kind of hustle on me. My life experiences told me this much, but I've always tried to remain cool and diplomatic with people, to be friendly and at least hear them out because in my playbook you could always use a hustler or scam artist to your benefit. As long as you understood what they were and didn't give them any real in roads.

So, I asked him, "What's your name? Do you have a business card or anything?"

"My name is Milo."

"Okay, Milo, I'm Tone."

"Hey, nice to meet you and I'm really sorry but I don't have any business cards to give you."

"That's okay. How about I just get your number, and if I need anything, I can call you."

"Sure, I can do that."

After Milo gave me his number, I was on my way back to base. Two days later, Jimmy called to inform me that he was able to get the gold Lexus for me for eight-thousand six-hundred and eighty-four dollars. I remember thinking eighty-four dollars was a very specific number, and I think that's why I remember it. After I paid him his commission, title, and taxes, it came to around eleven thousand five hundred dollars. Jimmy was really excited and told me if I bought that same car at a dealership, it would cost me about twenty-eight thousand dollars. He also told me that if I wanted to sell it to a private party right now, I could sell it for around eighteen thousand dollars. I remember thinking I could make seven grand just like that. Of course, my mind went to work on how I could do it. I needed more information. I began asking Jimmy some questions, and he explained the process to me in detail.

What it came down to was him finding the deals and me providing the cash. However, as a private seller, I could only sell five cars a year. Any more than that, and I would have to become a licensed dealer, which was pretty fucking expensive to do, and I wasn't interested in running a dealership. Overall, it didn't sound too bad to me; selling five cars at seven grand each would give me an extra thirty-five grand in a year. That was wonderful news to me, and this made me get excited about the prospect. Maybe that was why Jimmy was always so excited.

Jimmy also explained to me that if I wanted, I could become a quasi-investor. I'd front Jimmy the cash to buy the cars for other potential buyers who didn't have cash on hand. Typically, they had to take out a bank loan. Banks didn't lend private parties money to purchase automobiles at auctions, and the auction required a cash deposit on cars that were bid on and then cash on delivery upon winning the bid. Car loans are written against the car being purchased because the car is the collateral that the bank owns until paid off by the borrower. The bank doesn't write "what if" loans on bids. So, the only option for a private party to secure a loan from a bank other than a car loan was to get a personal loan. For most people, especially ones with bad credit, that would be significantly less money than they would need to purchase the car they wanted.

That was the other side of Jimmy's business, helping people with bad credit purchase as nice a car as they could without getting gouged on a loan or by a dealership. If a person had terrible credit, they could purchase a car through Jimmy three to ten thousand dollars below the Kelly blue book valuation. Therefore, the bank was much more inclined to approve a car loan with more favorable interest rates for buyers with bad credit.

Instead of fourteen to twenty percent interest, they could secure a loan for maybe eight to twelve percent interest. Plus, they paid lower taxes, which gave them more money for a down payment required by the bank.

I would front the necessary capital to make the deal happen and get paid at the back end. It was a win for everyone: Jimmy, the banks, the buyer, the auction, and me, the investor. Besides, who doesn't like helping out those who are less fortunate or who have fallen on bad times? Sure, I wouldn't make as much as I would as a private party seller, but I could make anywhere from five hundred to a thousand per car without the five-car limitations set by the state. In my estimation, I could do that ten, maybe twenty times a year, giving me another twenty thousand dollars or more. Just like that, I increased my yearly income by almost sixty thousand dollars without lifting a finger. This is when I began reading books on business and finance, satisfying my newfound addiction. Did I mention I have an addictive personality?

PreSCHOOL:

Raising a gang or running a mob is not a simple task. It requires a lot of time and attention. It's like extreme babysitting. It's even more extreme when it comes to a prison criminally run organization because a small issue could send the prisons across the states into a violent frenzy, and the backlash could end up spilling all the way out to the streets. In prison, they have guys that are known as "reps," short for representatives for each group. These reps are guys who try to diplomatically iron out situations between their group and the opposing groups should a problem arise. Reps all know that bloodshed and battle in all-out race riots in the past has been nothing but painful and costly, and so they'll try to reach a peaceful resolution that is satisfactory to both sides as the better alternative than war. The reps are usually smarter than average Joe's. They are good at defusing and de-escalating a problem civilly knowing that freedoms of the hire-ups are hanging in the balance, and that SHU programs being ten years at a time, are to be considered and factored gravely and wisely.

A lot has changed from the old days. See, back then, no one hesitated to kick off a riot for a simple disrespect, and everyone was willing to risk their lives trying to save face or puff their egos. These days, after the old timers have been put in the SHU for ten years at a time, prison politics has softened with how delicately prison gangs approach the topic of war. Everyone is looking for a more amicable way to resolve issues now, other than bloodshed. It's no longer knives first, questions later. The reps report to the leader of the pack, the old timer who calls the shots. Our old man is Paulie, the brother of "Vikaly" Tavita LemaokaOAli'i Prescott, the sergeant who died in the war in Iraq while serving with Tone.

Before the old man's brother died, they were working on a project supposedly with the government to allow felons to enlist in the armed forces. The old man believed that it would've made more sense to send guys from the joint out to the battlefield, considering they were experts at urban warfare, and most of them were already suffering from PTSD or some mental health of sorts. The USOS are brown and don't look American at all. This would've made their transition easier, considering that the Asian/Islander group had strong ties to Muslim radical organizations, the cartel, and every other criminal network from the American prison systems. Guys were excited with the prospect of going to war in real life. They summed it up as being "just like playing *Call of Duty* in real life." When the old man's brother died, they scrapped the plans to move troops to Iraq, and the old man-made new plans for extending his reach to the community. The old man came up with an idea to economically enrich his community and empower his people by investing the USOS money into building businesses and opportunities for the future. The plan got approved by the USOS committee, and so everything I'm sitting on is the product of that plan coming to fruition. Yes, I was entrusted with the role of organizing and babysitting one hundred soldiers. I was the guinea pig for the old man's pilot program. But I had a lot of practice and experience from watching the old man when I was inside. He took a liking to me after having seen me perform like a man who had nothing to lose, so he had his henchmen summon me to his cell one day.

"You confuse me," he said. "You have visitors and letters daily from the outside world. A family that loves you. Yet you go to war like you're serving a life sentence, and you could care less if you go home. You are very educated and highly intelligent, which is a rarity for our kind. You spend countless hours in the library studying stocks, economics, government politics, and the mob. You don't play basketball when we are all out there in the yard because you're reading. You earned a degree while here that would be a waste of time if you catch a murder rap and never get to apply it to the streets. Tell me, what makes you so smart but so dumb at the same time? You're like an educated dummy."

"I know it doesn't make sense to you," I said. "I study not just books but people. I've watched and studied the way the pigs operate, and I'm mindful not to get caught when I do something."

He laughed. "If you keep taking chances, eventually you will lose against the odds. You need to learn the cost-benefit analysis and the risk versus the rewards mindset. Quit playing the odds. It's always stacked against you. Remember that."

Paulie ran the biggest gambling tickets in prison, so he knew the odds like no one else. He has a little brother on the outside involved in Casinos so he's getting the numbers first thing in the morning and the inside scoop on the sports players and games. Paulie probably wins ninety percent of the time so I know he knows what he's talking about.

Since that day, he has always kept me close to his side. He wanted me to learn to mentor and lead. To mellow out. I did a lot and it's because I started to take the 'lifers' lives into consideration. I'm just visiting. They have to live here. If they are thrown into the SHU the jobs they have in laundry, the kitchen, or the units go to someone else. These jobs are how they are able to run and maintain their gambling and other operations. The list of names of our people showing up to the facility gets handed down to the laundry workers and they can have a care package for brothers that are new. Or have a return to sender package awaiting someone who testified against a member or committed a sexual felony charge. Sex offenders and snitches are not welcomed at all.

chapter eight
Promotions

Reyes:

A lot had happened since arriving at Fort Lewis, and I quickly made many new acquaintances in and out of the military. I began to live a dual lifestyle. In one instance, I was a decorated soldier in the military with great career progression and opportunities, while in the other instance, I aspired to be my own boss as an entrepreneur. I can honestly say things were good and moving in the right direction for me in both cases. For the first year, while assigned to the 504th MP Battalion, I worked the road conducting law enforcement duties. Working four twelve-hour shifts during the week, sometimes more and hardly ever less. Actually, it was a lot of sometimes, especially when adding in all the additional training requirements and mandatory formations.

A typical workday included getting in an hour early before a shift started to draw weapons and equipment, inspect the assigned police vehicle, and attend the pre-shift briefings. At the end of the shift, completing all necessary paperwork from calls during the shift was a must, then turning in weapons and equipment needed to take place. All of this usually meant a fourteen-hour shift at a minimum. Time off was a commodity. During my time off, I chose to pursue business opportunities and party, which included drinking and fucking.

Looking back on it all, I had made an erroneous decision to mix business with pleasure. At the time, it all made good sense and actually seemed like a practical idea. Even now, it still makes sense on paper, but in all actuality, the practical application was much harder to control. It was difficult to cultivate a net positive outcome versus a negative one under those circumstances. Honestly, I probably should've just stuck with the car enterprise and made moves into real estate or something less fun and exciting.

I was making money with cars, and it was relatively easy with no real work on my part, but still, it was boring, and I needed adrenaline rushes. Quite frankly, my ego needed to be satisfied in ways normal and boring could not. I wasn't trying to do anything illegal or hurt anyone, but adrenaline rushes and ego-boosting activities tend to break the rules, which lean more toward illegal activities and people getting hurt—go figure. This is how I started down a questionable path in my life.

There was this club, The Loft, in downtown Tacoma, on 21st Street and between Pacific Avenue and Commerce Street, which was the spot to be. Since it was on a hill, the backside and upstairs were on Commerce Avenue, while the downstairs and main entrance were on the Pacific Avenue side. The top side was split between a separate martini lounge called 21 Commerce and the VIP area and upstairs of The Loft. It was the hottest club in the area, with about a thousand-person capacity just in the downstairs area and probably another two or three hundred upstairs. Thursday and Saturday nights were the busiest nights, and it became one of my weekly establishments where I could drink and party.

There were four colleges and several junior colleges located within the Tacoma area, plus all the military members from McChord Air Base and Fort Lewis, in addition to all the locals, so you can imagine all the young party goers a place like this would attract. This club was pulling in at least forty thousand dollars a week on the books, plus who knows how much off the books. This is how I learned about cash sales versus credit card sales and the value of a perishable, unmeasurable product like fun and alcohol.

One night, while I was there, the bar manager made the suggestion that I should help promote the club. I had absolutely no idea what he was talking about, but I was interested nonetheless in what he had to say. Basically, all I had to do was pass out these business card-sized flyers that gave free admittance into the club. There was a blank white space on each of the cards where I could write my name, and for every card that came back to the club, they would pay me a dollar, plus I wouldn't have to pay or stand in any lines to get into the club anymore.

I liked the idea, not for the money but for the clout and status it would give me. Besides, I really hated standing in lines. I agreed to do it, and he then introduced me to one of the owners, who was responsible for marketing and managing the clubs daily. Oh yes, clubs with an "s" because it turned out they owned several of the clubs in the area. That mega club, the martini lounge, a comedy club, and a sports bar. I began promoting for all four spots. I was a foot soldier for the clubs, something that also resonated with me. Those little business cards easily earned me forty to a hundred dollars a week, which basically amounted to drinking money. I was being paid to party instead of paying to party. I really loved that part. While at these clubs, I was treated like an insider by all the staff, security, and owners. Those little cards were also a great way to meet and talk to the females, instantly breaking the ice.

Although I never directly hit on any of the women while I passed out the cards, it was a different story once they were at the club. They were easier to talk to and flirt with, giving me easy access to their pleasure spots. That would later become a problem and complicate my life in more ways than I could've imagined. Needless to say, I was a very motivated foot soldier passing out my little fuck cards. Ha-ha.

I must've been doing pretty good on my weekly numbers because, after a few months of this, the owner suggested I meet with a fella named Danny Duke. He said by teaming up with him, we could do our own events and promotions. There were a lot more opportunities to make significantly more money. Instead of forty to a hundred dollars a week, we could be making a few hundred to a thousand dollars a week. This idea appealed to me, and I agreed to meet with Danny Duke, who was a DJ, they used from time to time as a fill-in. I got his phone number, called him, and set up a face-to-face meeting at Tully's downtown on the corner of Broadway and 9th.

Danny Duke was all smiles and a genuinely good person with warm, friendly energy. He was full of life, and I instantly liked that guy. We talked about a lot at that first meeting, mostly about his background and where he was from. He was from the Midwest, a little farther east from where I had grown up. There's always something about meeting someone who brings familiarity to you when you're in a strange land. I could tell from how he described back home that he came out west to get away from something and start a fresh new life.

Danny never told me exactly what it was that he was running from, but it didn't matter because he had put that part of his life behind him, and that was good for him. Leaving the past behind is hard for a lot of people to do. God knows I was always on the run from my own past, and that would be the case for the foreseeable future. Outside of the military, I never really discussed what I did for the military and rarely spoke about my time as a Ranger. My usual response to civilians was that I was a supply sergeant for a medical unit, living a very boring existence within the Army.

We drew up a quick business plan and came up with a name for our enterprise: Duke Entertainment. This actually took some persuasion on my part, as Danny was a bit modest and apprehensive about using his name. I told him using my last name, Reyes, wouldn't sound as good. Reyes Entertainment just didn't flow off the tongue the same, even if Reyes in Spanish meant kings. Maybe King Entertainment might have been just as catchy. We also discussed the way the nightlife attracted certain elements and that he would never have to worry about any of it, as I was more than willing and capable of dealing with any of the darker elements within "the life."

Often, what happens in the nightlife is that it's a breeding ground for drugs and illicit activities. There is a lot of money to be made both legally and illegally, so there is always the temptation for people to make power moves to establish dominance and gain access to the money. A lot of club owners and promoters were often victims of shakedowns from different criminal elements, either well-organized enterprises or just loose cannons. At the very least, I felt I had a basic understanding of the language spoken by those characters. I was also more than willing and capable of going the distance to back up my word. Danny Duke was safe with me, and no one was going to fuck with us or our money.

Things for Danny and me worked out well, and we were doing pretty good with our promotions, bringing in about three hundred dollars each, every Wednesday night. Not that it was great, but after all, we were new to the game of promotions and starting at the bottom of the ladder that's why we were given a Wednesday instead of a weekend night. The best three nights of the week were Thursday, Friday, and Saturday, all of which were already spoken for by other promoters who had been in the game longer.

Danny and I were given the opportunity at the smaller comedy club on 9th Street called Cans, which was a nice little club, and for a Wednesday night, we had it going. We decided on a Latin night theme, and we did this promotion for a few months. It was a good start, but it wasn't enough. I needed more. During that time, I learned about the industry and met most of the players around the Tacoma area. Those of whom I didn't meet personally, I knew of them, and they knew of me. I was certain of one thing, and that was I needed muscle and lots of it to solidify myself in "the life."

PreSCHOOL:

There was a time when the USOS became infamous for our ability to move in on any nightclub we wanted within the Seattle-Tacoma area. My culture is already infamous throughout prisons and the streets as muscle and great at it. If you look at shows like *The Mayans*, the spin-off from

Sons of Anarchy, you see they have Samoans robbing the cartel in the first episode. They have the Samoans in *Den of Thieves* as hijackers. Robbers. They even had Samoans showing up in the Show, *Animal Kingdom*, where a family's business is to commit robberies, for no apparent reason but to show that Samoans are stigmatized as criminals of violent force.

Anyways, it was quite simple to take over any club to control. Months later, when I had informed the lawyer that we were in the "contracting" business with local nightclubs, he was thrilled at the prospect that we might be doing something legit. Except when he found out what it entailed, he spat out his calamari at lunch and said, "That's not a legitimate business. That's a fucking racket. It's called extortion. What the fuck. We never shared anything with him that could incriminate him or us. But he was smart he could read between the lines?"

Our approach was simplistic, sending out our enforcers to each of these establishments, seeking out their heads of security. The designated USOS would go up to the security staff and ask who was in charge of security. After finding out who it was, they would then propose that they hire the uces to work security. If the answer was not a yes, then the USO would beat the shit out of the lead security and anyone else who decided to get involved. We would smash the bars and smash the patrons who were unaware of how painful being a hero would be. Heck, one time, there was a huge wedding after-party where the bride and groom were seated in a VIP section as guests of honor. The uces confiscated all the cameras in the room, breaking them on the ground and stomping on them. The groom, who was related to a well-respected motorcycle club, decided to play hero and started a fight with an uce. He had three guns pointed at his face before he could get close enough. Trigger hit this guy so hard that he spent six months of his honeymoon recovering in the heroes hotel (St. Joseph's Hospital), rewiring his jaw and his dislocated body parts.

The USOS approach was very effective, but it did create a degree of violent retaliation from the individuals affected by our hostile takeovers, resulting in some unfortunate deaths. This also tended to put us on the radar of the local police, who didn't like us already. Overall, this cut into our bottom line and profit margin, which was not good. After all, this wasn't the prison yard, no matter how many times they tell you prison is a microcosm of the real world. It is a much more chaotic environment with so many more players and variables to consider. Even though we had the strength and the numbers, the cost soon became too much to sustain.

Honestly, I came to the realization that we needed a more diplomatic approach to the clubs and bars. We needed business reps. There was a lot of money to be made at each of these venues, and the one problem with violence is, as it's been said before, violence begets violence. The Godfather couldn't have said it any better, "blood is a very costly expense." Taking over these establishments by force wasn't the problem. Maintaining control of them once taken through violence was. The economics of that situation couldn't sustain a long-term war over territory and control of the club scene. Besides that, The USOS needed the ability to expand into establishments that had an upscale profile and higher undetected return. It was hard to make money while fighting a street war. We needed a more peaceful solution. While trying to figure things out, a serious issue led to our encounter with the Russians, which could not have come at a worse time or ended badly.

CHAPTER NINE
PROMOTION PROBLEMS

REYES:

Both my grandfathers were summa cum laude graduates of the party life. I grew up partying. It was in my blood. I had my first drink at six years old. It was a warm can of Old Style beer that my older brother had stolen from my grandfather's secret stash. The first time I got drunk, I was going into the seventh grade. The first time I got shit-faced was at the beginning of my ninth-grade year. By the time I was going into the eleventh grade, I was a full-blown alcoholic.

At fourteen, I went to my first teen club, a place called Pebblewood, and it was the place to be. Of course, they didn't serve alcohol to a bunch of teenagers, but that didn't stop us from getting our drink on before the club or sneaking it in. By the time I was seventeen, I had acquired a college ID card that allowed me into clubs that hosted college nights. I also orchestrated two of the biggest house parties in the town I grew up in, bringing people from as far as three hours away. These parties were legendary. All of that was in a time before social media.

My best friends growing up were of a different breed and caliber. Most people never get to have friends like them. We are more like brothers than friends. We're a family, loyal to one another to a fault. Throughout life and even in the military, I've only ever met a few individuals of the same caliber, loyalty, and true friendship. The last summer before I left for the military, we had formed the PHOG clique (Penthouse Original Gangsters), and we partied in around a two-hundred-mile radius from Grand Rapids, MI, to Detroit, MI, to Evanston, IL, to Bloomington, IN. It was our pond, and we had a blast meeting all the females we could possibly meet during our travels.

On my last night out with my clique, we got into a huge brawl at a club, going from the dance floor to the parking lot. That was the first time I literally split someone's wig open. I had caught this dude with an overhand right at just the right angle, and I remember seeing his forehead split open, skin flapping, and blood oozing out. We fucked them niggas up. Then we all jumped in the car, and I remember being worried that we were going to get pulled over and arrested, causing me to lose out on going into the Army. I was afraid of missing my opportunity to escape my own path of destruction, most likely ending up in jail or going to prison, disgraced and dying prematurely. I didn't even want to go out that night because I was leaving for basic training the next day and was trying to stay out of trouble, but the calling of my family was stronger than my commitment to my own future. Thankfully, we were never pulled over, and the next day, the Army recruiter picked me up in the afternoon and took me to Kalamazoo to begin my journey into the military and my future.

My concerns regarding promotions came to fruition on a hot sunny day in August as I was out with Monica, Danny, and a few others. We were at Flaming Geyser State Park on the Green River. It was a popular summertime activity to float the river. People would grab inner tubes and flotation devices to float down the river, stopping along the way to party at certain bends. Aside from that, you just lazily floated and drank, enjoying the day and conversation with the people you were with.

My inner tube was attached by a rope to another inner tube carrying a cooler of beer. Everyone was drinking and having a good time. At certain points in the river, you could stop to enjoy the deeper water, diving in and swimming. As we neared the end of our journey downriver, we stopped to smoke a joint—everyone except me. Standing on the riverbank while they were smoking, Danny started to discuss business with me. He was telling me things were all set and looking good for our new promotion. It had been about eight months since we had started working together, and we were both excited about our new opportunity. We agreed it was going to be a whole lot of fun for us.

While we were talking about the new promotion, I was unaware that Monica had walked up behind me and was listening in on our conversation. Things between her and I weren't going well, and our relationship was coming to a head. She was so resistant to me doing those promotions and always using them against me. She would constantly tell me what a loser I was doing those promotions and how the club owners would laugh and make fun of me behind closed doors. The only reason those comments held some merit was because Monica's little friend, supposedly her best friend, was friends with a girl who had close ties to the owners. It turned out that her best friend at the time was supplying Monica with pills like Percocet and oxycodone, which I didn't know about at the time. What a great friend to have.

So, whether the owners actually made those comments about me or not, it didn't matter because Monica only wanted to hit me where it hurt—my pride and ego. Deep down, I knew I couldn't be with someone like her. She was all wrong for what I wanted to do in my life. It didn't matter that I was more than willing to make her my wife and have kids with her. Maybe if she had appreciated that fact, things could've been different.

At any rate, my desire to accomplish things and be a self-made man, starting from the bottom and working my way up, was more important to me. So, I said to myself, *fuck those motherfuckers if they're really talking shit behind my back.* They didn't know me, and if they were too chicken shit to say it to my face, then they were nothing but little bitches, and I'd use them to get what I wanted.

Danny was telling me that the promotional fliers would be in on Friday and how he had been grinding away on Myspace promoting the hell out of our new night. As I was in the middle of telling him that I'd get the military crowd, I caught a glimpse of Monica looking extremely agitated and ready to explode.

She did her best to speak calmly. "What the fuck! Why are you getting involved with that shit? You said you were done with the nightlife shit. You know how I feel about all that! You just need to worry about doing your military stuff."

I could see Danny looking at me nervously, a bit confused because I was grinning, and Monica was clearly in a state of high agitation. So, with a cheesy grin and wink to Danny, I turned to Monica and began using my charm to calm her down.

"It's nothing," I said. "You don't have to worry about anything. I'm not really all that involved anyway, and I'm just helping my dude out so he can make some money." I just wanted her to relax, hoping I could charm her into going along with what I was getting involved with. Monica wasn't buying into my charm that day.

"Fuck this," Monica exclaimed and stormed off.

"Monica," I called out to her, but to no avail. She got onto her inner tube and floated down the river alone. I turned my attention back to Danny.

"What's wrong?" Danny asked.

"Man, I don't know. She just gets jealous because she knows that we are going to be dealing with a lot of females, and she thinks I'm going to fuck all of them. She doesn't get it. The girls bring the dudes, and the dudes bring the money."

"Sorry, dude, if I said anything wrong."

I could see the concerned look on his face and tried to reassure him and with a big smile. "Nah, man, it's all good. I probably should've told her already. I just didn't feel like dealing with her, though."

He nodded and smiled. We got back onto our inner tubes and tried to enjoy the rest of our afternoon. I was just going to have to deal with

Monica later when we were alone. She didn't even know that ownership of The Loft and 21 Commerce had changed, and the new owners and general manager wanted us to bring our Wednesday Latin night promotions to 21 Commerce. Doubtful, her little friend even knew. So much for their intel on the previous owners. The venue was a much better setting for the Latin night. Not only was it a classier place, but the floors were also made of wood instead of concrete.

The wooden floors at 21 Commerce provided a better surface for Latin-style dances such as salsa, bachata, merengue, etc., which our Latin crowd appreciated. Our idea was to set up a DJ on the 21 Commerce side playing Latin music, and on the upstairs side of The Loft, we would have another DJ playing hip hop and top 40 music. The general manager really liked that idea. In fact, he liked the idea so much that he brought in another promotion team called the Doll Squad to promote the hip-hop and top 40 side of the venue.

That didn't sit well with Danny or me, but we understood why the general manager was over-excited about having two promotion teams promoting the night. The club was looking at some financial problems, and they needed every event to bring in as much business as possible. Still, I didn't like having to share the night.

During the rest of the day, Monica and I barely spoke to each other. During the car ride back to her place, we spent it in silence, only listening to music. It was later that same day that Monica and I would have it out, saying our final goodbyes. When we were back at her place, we both took turns taking our showers. She took her shower first. Before taking mine, we still hadn't spoken to each other. When I finished my shower, Monica was in the kitchen wearing a little sundress.

Damn, she looked so good from behind, as always. She was putting away dishes and looked sad. I went up behind her and wrapped my arms around her, hugging her from behind. She just kind of melted into my arms as I began kissing her on her neck. Then, her cheek and lips before kissing her full-on mouth. I pulled her away from the sink, pushing her up against the kitchen table, all while kissing her passionately. I maneuvered her onto the table and overwhelmed with passion, I found myself with my head between her thighs, enjoying her clean shaved honey box. She went crazy with desires and pleasures being fulfilled by my skilled mouth and tongue. This time, my charms were more persuasive than at the river earlier that day. I was hypnotized by the level of ecstasy I was giving to her. I stood and grabbed her by the back of her neck, and staring deep into her eyes, I penetrated her with a level of excitement I believe neither one of us had experienced before. This session of make-up sex took us upstairs to her bedroom. It was good, too, maybe the best sex we ever enjoyed together.

We fell asleep in her bed, and sometime after midnight, I could feel Monica becoming restless, waking us both up. I rolled over and tried going back to sleep, and I felt her give me a gentle kiss as she got up out of bed. She walked over to her desk, picked up a book, and climbed back into bed. As she was reading, she was having trouble concentrating and was clearly distracted by something. Frustrated, she set the book down and climbed out of bed again. She walked over to her dresser, dug through a drawer, and pulled out her marijuana and rolling papers. I was still lying there half asleep as I watched her walk to her desk, sit down, and begin to roll a joint. She lit it and began to smoke. Exhaling deeply, Monica sank back into her chair and relaxed. She continued to smoke her joint as the room filled with smoke. Suddenly, realizing just how filled the room had become with smoke, she frantically opened the windows and turned on the fan.

Still half asleep and overwhelmed by all the smoke and smell of marijuana, I found myself shouting, "Monica! What are you doing?"

Nervously, she sat down at the window and tried to act like nothing was wrong, answering nonchalantly, "Nothing."

Her could-care-less attitude set me off. "What the hell? The room is filled with smoke."

With a shrug, she sarcastically remarked, "Is it? I hadn't noticed."

"Are you fucking high already?"

"No." She chuckled.

By then, I was sitting up in bed and glaring at her as she ignored me. There she was, passively sitting at the window, still smoking her joint as if nothing was wrong, not caring that I was bothered. Trying to get her to see why I was so bothered by her inconsideration, I said to her, "I can't believe this shit. You know I'm on active duty and working in law enforcement. And you know how they fucking do random urinalysis. It doesn't matter if it's secondhand smoke or not. There is zero tolerance for that shit in the military. What the fuck, man?"

Monica looked at me and then looked back out the window, not even acknowledging what I was saying. Her indifference really pissed me off at that point, and I felt the rage building inside of me. Why couldn't she just acknowledge what I was saying and apologize? She probably couldn't because she was still caught up in her emotions from earlier that day. What a shit show.

Agitated at the situation and her behavior, I got out of bed and walked toward her and, as calmly as I could, asked, "Are you trying to fuck me? Do you want me to get in trouble again?"

Playing dumb and dismissing what I just said was a legitimate concern, she said, "Why are you so worried? You're not the one smoking it, are you?"

"That's not the point. I can't have anything at all in my system." I began getting dressed and gathering my things, hoping she would stop being so hardheaded about the situation.

Monica was still sitting by the window, smoking her joint and laughing. "You can't get a contact high."

I snapped back, trying to prove a point. "Are you serious? You *can* get a contact high. If you shot gunned that joint to me, I'd get high. You can get cancer from secondhand smoke; you can get a contact fucking high!"

"I'm not smoking a cigarette."

"Okay, you wanna be an ass? Then be an ass." We looked at each other, locking eyes. I was waiting for an apology, anything that would've kept me from leaving. She was almost lifeless and uncaring. After a long time of silence and blank stares, I shook my head in disgust, grabbed my keys, and went to leave. Before I walked out of the room, I was hoping to snap her out of her defiant attitude. I exclaimed, "I can't do this shit. I'm out. Peace."

As she watched me leave the room, I looked back from the hallway, at which point she swallowed hard and turned back to the window. I knew she could hear me going down the stairs and could hear the front door close behind me. Just like I knew she was watching me as I walked down the walkway toward my car. As I got to my car, I made it a point to look up at her in the window. She was just blankly staring out of it and then looked at her joint in dissatisfaction, flicking it out the window. She wiped away what must've been a tear and continued staring out the window at me. Vaguely, I could hear her begin to cry. Sadly, I got into my car and looked back at her house in the rearview mirror, thinking it was the last time I would see her.

CHAPTER TEN
BLOOD LUST

REYES:

After my first year working as a patrol, I eventually moved up to the MPI office. It was shortly after, while coming back from leave, that I caught a horrendous case. It was just bad timing all around for me and was another log to add to the fire leading up to my suicidal tendencies. The human psyche can only take so much before it snaps. In those time periods, we needed emotional support and understanding, not more chaos and torment. Unfortunately, Monica provided neither the support nor understanding that I needed and craved at that time in my life.

For me, none of it made any sense since Monica and I had just returned from what I thought was a fantastic summer vacation. We had taken a cross-country trip back to my hometown in Michigan. Although we had only recently met and started dating, within a month or so, I invited Monica to come with me. The plan was to drive one of my cars and drop it off for my younger brother so he had reliable transportation. Then we would fly back. It was a fantastic trip.

I got the call the next day after getting back from the cross-country trip with Monica. Coincidentally, it was also the week prior to her mom's barbecue and my suicidal meltdown. The perpetrator was about ten years younger than me; shit, he was still just a kid. He had recently returned from Iraq receiving a purple heart, suffering injuries from an explosion. The call out over the radio said he told his therapist that he had killed his eighteen-year-old wife. The couple lived in on-base housing and had been having marital problems, even receiving couples therapy provided through the Army. It was the same therapist he and his wife had been receiving family counseling from who had made the call to 911. I guess the kid felt comfortable telling them about his deeds.

Finding her on the kitchen floor was a real gut check, and I wasn't fully prepared for what I walked into. I don't think anyone working on that case was prepared. Entering the front door, I could see a blood trail going from the front door through the living room and into the kitchen. When going into the kitchen, we saw her tiny body lying on the floor with a meat cleaver still in her neck. She had a pentagram carved into her stomach, and her body was mutilated with stab wounds—seventy-one stabs, according to the official report. Blood covered everything. I remember my heart sinking into my chest, feeling cold and numb, thinking, man, they were so young. Nothing could be done for her. She was dead, dead, and had been for some time.

A few years later, while working as the duty investigator, I would catch another terrible case first thing in the morning, just after coming on shift. It was about a female soldier who thought she might have killed someone. It turned out that she killed two someones. She was living in the barracks and decided to kill two soldiers with whom she had been having romantic relationships. A husband and wife decided to break it off with her because the wife was just giving birth, and the married couple wanted to focus on their family.

That didn't sit well with the female soldier, so she shot them both in their home off base. Then, she tried to chemically dispose of the bodies in their bathtub. She took the newborn baby back to her barracks. It was while she was sitting on the steps at the barracks that another soldier in her unit saw her. He asked her why she was back from the field already. She proceeded to tell him she thought she had done something terrible and that she thought she might have killed someone. The soldier, feeling uneasy about her demeanor and what she told him, decided to call 911 to report the suspicious behavior and odd remarks.

Getting her back to the MP station and interviewing her was quite an ordeal, even though she was cooperative. She acted helpless and confused. After interviewing her and hearing the details of the crimes she recently committed, I had to notify CID and Pierce County Sheriff's Department because it was a multi-jurisdictional occurrence. The couple lived off-post but were members of the military, as was the perpetrator, so both agencies had to work together.

Seeing the bodies of the victims partially dissolved in acid was an unforgettable sight to see. It was enough to make anyone lose everything in their stomach and then some. As for me, all I could do was make a joke in order to cope. "Shit, it looks like she missed a spot."

An older detective from the sheriff's department who was just as jaded as me let out a chuckle. I noticed as we both locked eyes that he had suppressed tears. His eyes glossed over, making them look darker than they were. We were human, after all, and in touch with our emotions even if we sucked them way down deep. If people suppress themselves from the cruel realities of this world long enough, they enter into a void of darkness, obtaining an empty, emotionless state of being.

Preschool:

With my help while in prison, Mimi started two business ventures, a hair salon and a nail salon. Both were in the same building next to each other on Meridian Avenue in Puyallup. It was a great location for her, with all the Army wives and their dependents as established clientele; having the monthly government paychecks to pay for her services kept her businesses busy.

One day, I got a phone call from her. "Hey, baby. I'm just leaving the lawyer's office," I answered.

I could hear Mimi crying hysterically. "I just got extorted by these two biker dudes. They threatened to come back."

"WHAT?" I shouted. "Okay, what bike gang was it? Do you know them? And what do they want with you and the salon?" I was trying to understand her through heaps of sobbing, and it was frustrating me and making me yell at her.

"Yeah, it's Natasha's boyfriend. He's a prospect for the Deadhead Riders. She was ..."

"Hello? Slow down. Okay. Okay, I'll handle it. Don't worry. I'll call you later."

Infuriated but not wanting to do anything too drastic until I obtained more intel, I called an old friend. He was a patch member of another bike gang that was really close with the shot caller for the Deadhead Riders. Uncle Vic was in one of the biggest motorcycle clubs in the world, and that's exactly who I placed a call to. "Aye, unc. It's me."

"Hey Charlie Boy, you out? When did you get out?" He was surprised and excited to hear from me. I explained the situation, to which he immediately switched over to his mediator role instead of his uncle role. "Look, DO NOT do anything stupid neff. I will call them and talk to their guy, then call you back."

"Okay, uncs," I said.

Vittorio Gigante was an uncle. I started calling him uncs because he had treated me like family since we met in prison. In the Polynesian culture, everyone who is older is an uncle or aunty out of respect. He was a relative of a mob boss in New York and well respected amongst bikers. He was part of that Canada mobster/bikers connection and only moved out west to spread the connection's reach.

He called me right back and said, "Okay. So, I talked to them, and they want a sit-down. Are you willing to talk to them?"

"Sit down? Shit, I'm ready to send them to the moon. Set it up."

"Well, I invited everyone here to my house. I figure you can see your aunt and say hello. Plus, everyone knows it's a neutral zone."

"Okay. Perfect. But Uncs, I'm looking to make them Deadhead for real today," I said.

"Relax, nephew, I want you to hear them out. Their shot caller, Tricky, is a longtime friend of mine. He'll fix it, believe me".

I'd only been out of prison a few months, and this is the type of issue I would run into daily while trying to maintain a peaceful resolution outlook on issues. A day in the life for me. I called four of my most trusted Uces (Uce is short for Uso or brother). We got to Uncle Vic's house first. I made sure that we were set up right so as not to get ambushed. I had "Pistol P" at the door with an M4 modified scope and an extended drum magazine. "Whiskers" and "Juney" against the walls. And me sitting, with "Boxer" standing behind me. All of us with the most exclusive weapons out of our arms cache. They showed up with about ten guys riding in on their motorcycles.

All of them carried handguns, and one was armed with a shotgun. The main guy was not even armed. Being a stand-up guy, he approached me straight away. "Hey, my name's Tricky. I want you to know that, first off, I asked about you inside. A lot of the "Old White Boys" upstate love you. You know a free bird? Goose? Billy 'Never Never,' right?"

"Yeah. Good people. Love those guys," I said.

He went on, "I want you to know that no patched or prospect member of my club ever laid hands on your old lady. Mimi, right? Yeah, well, she might not be telling you the entire truth about the situation. See, she was offered a high-paying position to teach cutting/coloring hair in Seattle. She left the shop with her best friend "Natty" (Natasha). We even bought a piece of the place from her for twenty K, yet it was not worth that much. But we figured we could move our money through it undetected, so it worked out. There's a lot they don't pay taxes on. Tips and things. Shampoos and color. We paid for the water pump that blew. The roof that caved in. For almost two years, we've been running this place without Mimi in sight. We have a lot of money invested in that salon. So, we're here to claim our vested stake in it."

I was baffled and caught by surprise. "Fucking Mimi. Hold on. Let me make a call to this bitch and get this straightened out."

The phone rang several times on speakerphone before Mimi answered. "Hello?"

"Hey. So, I'm here with the biker dudes. I want you to be truthful because it can be all bad here. Do you understand me? I mean real bad. I have Juney and the boys with the bikers. You understand, understand?"

"Yes."

"Okay, Mimi, did you not tell me that two patched members, one of them Natasha's boyfriend, extorted you? Pushed you off the property or some shit?"

"NO. I NEVER SAID THAT!" she exclaimed, hanging up on me.

I tried calling her back and vocalized my frustration, "FUCK!"

Tricky turned to me and said, "Well, looks like you guys got some personal issues to sort out. Communication issues that don't involve us. So, you didn't disrespect us, and we didn't disrespect your cause. I say we've concluded our business. Half the salon stays ours as paid for."

"No, bro." Their eyes all perked up at my response. I continued, "What's fair is fair. What's right is right. What's wrong is wrong." The tension went from zero to a hundred and everyone then clutched their weapons in anticipation. "You guys own it outright. This bitch lied to me and could've caused a wreck. The selfish bitch doesn't deserve to own any parts of that spot. Thank you for your time, brother."

"Look," he said. "I appreciate that. If you ever have an issue with my guys or something you want to relay to my club, please feel free to hit me up. I'll be more than happy to work with you, seeing that you didn't overreact to misinformation that could've put us all in a wreck, as you call it."

In prison, every group is called a "car," and the last thing you want to be responsible for is a car wreck. Especially if it takes the car years to fix. In a case like that, it takes years because many members of opposing sides get snatched up and taken to the SHU for years at a time. It's the correctional department's way of trying to broker peace. By taking the shot callers off the yard. I know why the bikers were so keen on keeping the hair salon. They had shampoo bottles filled with dope and were moving it through the salon without suspicion. I already knew this and had the boys clear out the saloon, taking all their shampoos and inventory while the meeting was in progress. I figured they would be too preoccupied to notice. What? I need a good hair wash.

CHAPTER ELEVEN
THE WOLF, THE SHEEP AND THE SHEEPDOG

REYES:

The soldiers who venture off into the darkness, unable to overcome it, usually end up committing horrible acts of violence; some choose suicide, not wanting to harm others. Once the beast is out, it's hard to put it back in the cage.

Soldiers have been tasked with performing the ugliest and most horrific acts of violence based on the needs of society even before the dawn of the rise of civilization. Roman soldiers were known for their callousness in carrying out their orders, even cutting down defenseless women and children. The Samurai, known for their brutality, cut off heads and performed seppuku on a regular basis. Vikings believing in Valhalla encouraged soldiers to shed blood because dying in combat was a sure way to get there.

The primal instinct of human nature is extremely dark, although I'm not sure the darkness is within each one of us. For some, it seems just as natural as breathing, and they are rare specimens. Then, others can obtain and develop it through training or hardships. In ancient times, these gritty individuals ensured the survival of the tribe. The brutes allowed the thinkers to have time to think in relative safety, only if the brute was there to protect them. These savages were the champions of ancient times, treated with high regard, and even worshipped. Heroes, warlords, kings, and champions. They were the inspirations of mythology and legends. It also seems that the vast majority of humans have no kind of fight in them at all and are as docile as sheep.

In modern times, these harsh warrior behaviors are frowned upon and are only allowed in certain instances, such as if someone is a soldier, police officer, or athlete. If they carry themselves honorably without reproach, then they'll be able to exercise these natural aggressions for as long as they like without any condemnation. For so many, the warriors, savages, go down a path of self-destruction, turning to the streets and a life filled with bar brawls and criminal behavior. In actuality, they are all one and the same, just having chosen different paths in life. It's been said the difference between warriors and soldiers is that soldiers follow orders, and warriors follow a code. I was a good soldier and an even better warrior.

I read somewhere that if individuals with sociopathic and psychopathic traits and characteristics were to become involved in organized sports at an early age, it would help them to channel their aggression into a positive outlet. That same rage exhibited by violent offenders is the same rage that makes the Lawrence Taylors of the NFL, as well as making soldiers into highly functioning killing machines. The difference between the right and wrong paths is that controlled rage has strict protocols as to when to turn on and off the rage. The socially acceptable behavior of individuals rules over their own rage, allowing them to channel it to accomplish a successful life in modern times. The others fall victim to their own undisciplined, chaotic rage that rules them, laying waste to their modern life.

There is an astronomical difference between a man who can just kill at will versus a man who must be trained to kill. Yet, there is a certain kinship between them, such as a wolf and a sheepdog. There is really no comparison between the wolf and the sheep. Law enforcement officers like to refer to themselves as being sheepdogs protecting the flock. Regardless, a wolf is still a beautiful animal and a natural, perfect killing machine whether in a pack or alone. Most sheepdogs are just a presence to let the wolf know there will be trouble if the wolf decides to attack one of the sheep. Like most predators, a wolf will weigh the risks, often choosing easy prey over hard-fought ones that could potentially cause injury or death. If the sheepdog gets a lucky bite in, causing a severe enough injury, the wolf could end up starving in the wild. The big difference between these sheepdogs and wolves is that dogs can be trained, and wolves will always be wild at heart. It is because they are wild that they will always run free, living their best life, whereas dogs will always need their masters in order to live their best life. Not all police officers are sheepdogs. Some of them are wolves. I never really feel like a sheepdog.

Among the military, I see special forces units more like well-organized wolf packs when compared to the rest of the military, which is composed mostly of sheepdogs. The tier one units, such as Delta Force and Seal Team Six, are the most wolf-like and have the most freedom in which to live their best life suited to their true nature and instinct. I knew, ultimately, that was where I belonged, and I couldn't wait to make it back to my pack. I wanted to hunt down the real bad guys and end them. Facing down death as a willing participant. My soul cried out from within me, sharing kinship with all those who have gone to their glorious deaths before me. I'm a warrior. It was my design, my nature, my program till Valhalla.

PreSCHOOL:

When we started the security business after I came home, half of our employees were from the penitentiary and the other half from Uncle Sam's scandalous war in Iraq. Both sides suffered from some kind of trauma, whether it be PTSD, TBI, BDSM, STD, CNN, or anything else. Picking reps and leaders for an islander car is slim pickings. Not too many of them have the mindset to broker peace. USOS are mostly laid-back, chill people. But don't poke the bear. They will put the hurting on their rivals no matter how outnumbered they are. During the famous riots between the islanders and the whiteboys, the blacks asked if the islanders needed help. The islanders laughed. Nah. This is going to be fun. Indeed, it was. Islanders are known for their physical strength, which makes up for their lack of numbers. Their brain muscle, though? I plead the fifth.

There's a joke that goes, "A guy went to the brain doctor looking for a new brain. He wanted an upgrade. When he gets to the doctor, the doctor says, 'So here, we have an Asian brain. Good for computation, business, and other things. This brain is fifty thousand.' The man says, 'Fifty thousand dollars! What else do you have?' The doctor shows him another one and says, 'This here is special. It's a white brain. This one is a little more expensive. It's good at colonizing, building corporations and industries, and other things like traveling to the moon.' The man says, 'Okay, how much?' The doctor says, 'One hundred thousand.' The man, stunned at the price, says, "Wow … what else do you have?' So, the doctor takes him and shows him the last brain they have on their display. He says, 'You can't afford this brain. This brain is a million dollars. It's an Islander brain.' The baffled man scoffed. 'A million dollars? An Islander brain?" Looking puzzled and confused, he asked the doctor, "What's so special about this Islander brain?' The doctor looks up and says, 'It's never been used before." Haha.

I know the other USOS won't really like me for this, but ah. It's a joke. They think I am arrogant and cocky. But aren't we all? People who love being comfortable in complacency hate being brought out of their comfort zones. They don't want to be challenged to do things that give them a better advantage if they think what they have already is all they're worth. Or if it takes too much effort. If you have to dumb down to communicate with others, then you're going to dull yourself out by picking up their slang and speech, mannerisms, and characteristics. And before you know it, you'll sound more like them and less like you. It's like chess. You don't get better by playing someone who's worse than you. You get better by beating the best. That's all I want. For us to be the best.

Every day breathing is a second chance at getting this thing right. I just hope I can pull it off before my everyday life runs out. With all the bullshit I have been faced with daily, I felt like I was pressed for time. Trying to groom my men to be ready for the mental warfare of things was going to be challenging. It's why none of them were given the opportunity to put things together.

CHapTer TweLve
VaMPireS

Reyes:

It had been a few years since my best friend and brother, Master Sergeant Tavita LemaokaOAli'i Prescott, died in Iraq. I was sitting here with my business partner, just a couple of years since I almost killed myself. He's a giant Samoan man. On the streets, he's called Preschool. It's the funniest shit ever. Someone as big as him with that nickname, but whatever. We were running a security and promotions company, plus a classy little strip club called Muy Bella.

Typically, I liked keeping a low profile, wearing average clothing, and driving a car one step above a beater. If you asked anyone, I was always broke but lived in a nice house and always had money to go out. Go figure. That particular night was kind of a celebration, so I got dressed up for the occasion. Preschool and I had just made our first million after expenses, five hundred K for him and five hundred K for me. We split our partnership equally. After all, we were in it together. Deciding to treat ourselves, we suited up, putting on our expensive suits, thousand-dollar pairs of shoes, some expensive jewelry, and our accessories. This wasn't a regular occurrence, but when we suited up, we went all out.

From the expression on my face, you would have thought I was the happiest kid in the world. You could not have been more wrong. I was still dead on the inside. I couldn't help but notice how dead everyone else looked to me. They say crazy recognizes crazy, so maybe death recognizes death. Sure, they all acted the part, like they were living it up and having such a wonderful time. The thing was, I could see deeper than the surface. All those glazed-over eyes from alcohol or some other intoxicant almost never fooled me. Those souls were mostly empty and searching for something that just wasn't there in the nightlife.

I was a people watcher, and I watched all the different people at our club and all the other clubs we frequent, mostly on the account of business. It occurred to me the longer someone would spend in the nightlife, night after night, weeks, months, years and even decades, the less alive they really were and often the more miserable they'd become.

It starts out all fun and exciting, with everything being new and surrounded by other new people experiencing the same new, fun, and exciting things. It was nothing more than a hook, just like any other addiction. The scene in and of itself is intoxicating, having multiple levels of a high that would play on almost every human desire and emotion.

For instance, the thrill of meeting a new, young, beautiful woman. A bonus if she was brand new to the scene because she would inevitably have more life in her. If you were the first one to take her home, you could be the one turning her out, making you her first for just about everything the scene had to offer: sex, drugs, excitement, etc.

The energy in everyone is different. Some have low energy, some have high energy, and some have either more positive or negative energy. There is hateful energy or loving energy. Regardless of the energy, all of our hearts and souls crave energy. When we are healthy, we crave only healthy exchanges of energy, recharging each other positively.

Occasionally, a healthy person will exchange positive energy for negative energy with an unhealthy person. This is usually because they are trying to help the sickly soul, but this exchange of positive energy for negative must be brief and a rare occurrence. If frequent or long exchanges take place, the positive, healthy person will eventually drain below healthy rechargeable limits by taking on too much negative energy. It's then when we are drained and starving, we ourselves turn into energy vampires and will be drawn to any kind of energy to feed ourselves.

Everyone is different with varying appetites and interests. Although the majority of us have very similar tastes and desires there are those who have their kinks, fetishes, or addictions outside the main group. A lot of people find themselves while in this darkness and move forward in life with a newfound purpose and drive. While the rest lay in the darkness being drained until they are completely dead inside.

The problem for most is that they don't even realize what is happening until it's too late. It just drains them night after night, like spiritual leeches sucking up tiny parts of their heart and soul until they're completely empty. They never even feel those first pieces of their heart and soul go missing, getting sucked out of them unnoticed because they were too busy embracing the new excitement and thrills they were experiencing. Almost in the same way in olden times, men would deflower virgins by biting them on their necks or elsewhere at the moment of penetration of the hymen so they wouldn't feel the pain of their innocence being taken from her.

Vampires. They all become vampires sucking on the positive energies of the new heart and souls of the innocent. There are two things that determine how fast they will turn into vampires themselves. How much positive or negative energy do they have entering the scene, and how long do they stay in the life? Most turn into energy-sucking vampires in only a few months. That's exactly what happened to me. Already depleted of positive energy from my life force by combat and such, I entered the nightlife scene, and into the darkness, I quickly went. Thankfully, my early life and the military prepared me better than I thought for handling the darkness.

Anyway, I was sitting there with my friend and business partner. Probably watching him think. He was always thinking about something and lost in his thoughts. A lot of people don't think. Sure, they may have random thoughts running through their heads, but nothing that constitutes actual thinking, though. Working on a plan, formulating an idea, solving a problem, learning something new, creating art, exploring the inner workings of our own emotions and opinions, etc. That is real thinking.

This was something I admired about him and drew me to him because when he speaks, it's with understanding, not only of the topic of discussion but with insight into who the audience is he's speaking with and an inner understanding of himself and how the self fits into the equation. In other words, he knew himself better than most people know themselves. That was something we both had in common; our minds worked constantly. Most live life in a happy-go-lucky auto-pilot mode, but not us. We were thinking men.

He would often say to me, "Everything is everything." It would take me many years to really come to understand what Preschool meant by that saying, but he was right. Everything is everything. Just think about that for a while. Opening your mind to the universe is no easy task, and if it was, then everyone would do it. I only wish I had done so sooner.

Preschool:

As my luck would have it, that time came. I'm sitting here with my uce Tone, with $100k cash on the table, throwing it at strippers like an old man sitting in the park throwing breadcrumbs to pigeons. Yeah, $100k is considered breadcrumbs because this was chump change compared to what we took in last week. The strippers being compared to pigeons? Well, it was true. It was only a matter of time before one of them tried to cozy up to you and then shits on your sleeves like only a pigeon would.

Every day, the business grew larger and larger, and every day, the nets of the feds got tighter and tighter. I was very aware and mindful of this. Keeping in mind that they worked just as hard as I did, and I couldn't ever look at the feds the way the others did. I wouldn't underestimate them. Others in my circle gave those hoes with pigeon toes more respect than they did the feds. But I learned a long time ago to give them their fair share of respect, to an extent. I respected that they were doing what they thought was best while all along getting a shitty return for their life's investment. While I did what I did, I got a huge return so that I could feed those stripping pigeons. I was making twice what the feds made in one year, in one sitting.

Some of the greatest destruction in the world was caused by people doing what they thought was best to change the world for the better. That's what the feds were doing. I knew people who believed in the government's no-fault image and probably thought I was the crazy one. Naively, they have either never experienced the corruption in the system or found a reason to believe that it exists. It's why the world is blessed with eyes, but only a few men are gifted with seeing. It's why they have the woke mob and the sleeping beauties in the country.

There are illegal black ops that the feds run that some people may never believe to this day. Ops such as the "Invasion of the Bay of Pigs" on April 17, 1961, in which the feds employed the mob to try and overthrow the communist regime of Cuba. It was one of the more embarrassing moments in American history because America got its ass handed to them by the communist rebel regime led by Fidel Castro. This era was known as the Cuban Missile Crisis.

Another ops run by the feds that employed the American Italian mob was the invasion of Sicily. There are way too many to list. One that still baffles me is the Jeffrey Epstein case. How could they let this serial child molester continue to operate and hurt children while supposedly under the watchful eye of the law? There were so many things in that case that should show how the United States attorneys handling the cases were corrupt. Hell, they had secret meetings in the Marriot to discuss his plea deals instead of in a government building. They had politicians and princes all involved in that scandal, and the victims were made out to look like prostitutes and drug addicts when they were mostly underage children.

I said that I respected the feds to an extent. That extent is to those who fight crime by the book, which is rare these days. With the recent scandals involving the former FBI Director Comey, I still can't believe people think that the feds operate without trickery or fuckery. Every day, there is some bullshit tactic employed by them to try and turn people in organizations against each other. It's a high-stakes intelligence game when it comes to them, and I feared the weakness of many people in my circle was that they underestimated them.

In *The Godfather*, Don says, "Keep your friends close, but keep your enemies closer." What he didn't say, which was apparent in the movie, was that your friends today can be your enemies tomorrow. So many organizations get taken down, not because of good detective work done by the feds but because of the testimony the feds gather from informants. Information was gathered and extracted a lot of times through illegal means and tactics. A lot of which is also bullshit that those paid informants were told to say. Every day, playing in the streets was like a mental chess game, with them trying to gain my pieces and gain an advantage in our business. Little did they know, I already had one of their key pieces sitting right in my pocket, and that trumped everything.

Chapter Thirteen
What a Mess

Reyes:

There I was, sitting here and enjoying my night with my business partner. At that point, I was drinking like a fish, watching Tiffany dance around on stage, showing off that sexy body of hers. After she finished shaking her ass, she came over and sat on my lap. She kissed me on the cheek and tossed back a few shots of tequila. There's something to be said about hot girls and tequila. Tiffany was starting to show signs of being inebriated, something that always annoyed me as I knew all too well that soon she would begin to trip out and ruin any fun we were having. She was oblivious to the situation and looked off into the crowd and giggled. She never even noticed the glare and scowl coming from me. I caught Preschool looking over at me from across the table and did a quick nod and a wink before he burst out laughing. I was glad someone besides me saw the situation for what it was and found the humor in it.

Preschool's burst of laughter was abruptly cut short by screams and a wave of people rushing from the front entrance and pouring into the club. We both looked at each other with a what-the-fuck expression. Something really bad must have been happening because people couldn't get into the club fast enough, tripping and falling over each other. It was doubtful that Tiffany was even aware of what was going on. Lost in her own little world, heavily intoxicated, she probably thought some celebrity was outside, and to this day, I'm sure she still thinks that.

As we got up from the table and began moving toward the front entrance to see what all the commotion was about, we could hear people saying someone had been shot. As natural of an instinct as breathing is, upon hearing those remarks, I was already drawing out my Glock 22 (a full-sized .40 caliber pistol). In those days, the Glock was used by many law enforcement and government agencies because it was the happy medium between the 9mm and the .45 caliber. With the .45, typically, there are only seven rounds per magazine. The 9mm had a high-capacity magazine capability, allowing for fifteen rounds. The .40 cal had both stopping power and a high-capacity magazine.

When we got outside, we could see people hiding behind cars and anything they could to protect themselves from being shot. After observing that chaotic scene, it was evident that the threat was gone. We were then in the aftermath of whatever had occurred. In the parking lot, lying on the ground in a pool of blood, was one of our security staff.

When the police arrived on the scene, a crowd was already gathered outside of the club. After securing the scene, they began their investigation as to who was responsible for the shooting. They asked if they could retrieve the surveillance footage. When we went inside to the back office to show the video footage in hopes of identifying the shooter's car, they saw more than they bargained for. Apparently, my partner, Preschool, was a little busy that night. If only I had known, I could've run interference on that video footage, delaying giving the police access until we reviewed it and had time to figure out what to do with it, like talking to our lawyers. After seeing the footage with the police, the best I could do was make them go and get an emergency warrant to take the footage with them. That gave us a window of time for Preschool to leave the area and contact his lawyers, and it gave me time to call CW5. It really didn't matter much as they weren't going to make an arrest that evening because they would want to launch a full-scale investigation before making one.

We had access to some of the best legal professionals in the state of Washington, and they were popular lawyers in Tacoma who were famous for suing the Tacoma Police Department for over eleven million dollars awarded in a settlement. Preschool's personal lawyer would later be responsible for taking down the biggest online child trafficking ring, Backpage.com. He would also successfully sue the internet giant Craigslist. That relationship with the lawyer would also lead Preschool to use the USOS manpower to rescue a lawmaker's daughter. None of that would matter much for the current situation, though, because that video footage was pretty damning. The police would inevitably launch a major interagency investigation, bringing in the feds as the heavy hitters for team police. That random act of street violence was really going to throw a monkey wrench into everything we were doing. The questions that needed to be answered were just how random that act of violence was and who was responsible and why.

Being dragged in by the feds weeks after the shooting and interrogated was not on my bucket list, but there I was, an unwilling participant being questioned by federal agents. While I was sitting there in the interview room, I found the irony in how many times I had placed a suspect or witness into one of those rooms and made them wait alone with their thoughts, allowing for anxiety or guilt to settle in on them. It was a great tactic, and most people caved in those moments of waiting for the inevitable to happen. They opened up at the first chance they got to speak to someone.

Since I had been trained in interview and interrogation techniques, studied psychology, and trained as a Ranger, none of it was going to work on me. However, it was going to be painful for the poor sap who had to try and break me into spilling the beans. That shit just wasn't going to happen, which was why it was going to be painful for both of us, in that I would have to witness them failing so much. I would be stuck in there longer than I cared, listening to them ask their questions and making their accusations. I would only answer their questions vaguely and uninformatively. A dance of wasted time that could have been avoided if only those jokers actually did their homework and understood what they were dealing with.

Sitting there alone with my thoughts, I began thinking about why and how I always seemed to find myself mixed up with criminals of varying degrees. I couldn't help thinking about the time I almost became a drug dealer myself. I was seventeen, living with my grandmother. There was this club in Harvey off Halstead Street called Jubilations that we frequented to meet girls. I had been going to that club for years prior to moving to Illinois to live with my grandmother. We would pile into a car or two and take the hour-long drive from Michigan just to meet new girls each week. There was one time when I couldn't go. A bunch of my friends went to Jubilations and got into a huge brawl. Unfortunately, my friends were severely outnumbered, being run down and jumped by forty-plus gang members. My friends ended up having to run for their lives as they fought off their attackers until they could escape to safety. Later, back in Michigan, when they were telling us what had happened to them, one of our good friends who wasn't there exclaimed that he had already heard about what had happened. Those were his people who had put down the ass-whooping that nearly beat our friends to death. See, he grew up in the Harvey area, and lots of his family and friends were among those who comprised the gang from that evening.

On another occasion, one of my friends met this girl at Jubilations. She was living with her aunt, and we would go over to her apartment to hang out and party with them. Well, as it turned out, her aunt's live-in boyfriend was one of the heads of a street gang mostly composed of Latinos. He had taken a liking to me and my group of friends, frequently playing spades and dominoes with us. He would share stories with us, and one in particular he told us I can remember even to this day.

He was out on the street corner hustling, selling cocaine. A car had pulled up, and when he went to the window, he gave them their product, and they paid with hundred-dollar bills. As he was breaking down the hundreds, counting out their change, he had to bend down because it was so windy, and he didn't want his money blowing away or exposing his wad of cash. As he was bent over counting, he felt the hard metal of the barrel of a handgun being pressed against his temple. They told him to give over the money and the rest of the product he was holding. At that moment, he made the split-second decision that he wasn't going out like no punk. He grabbed the gun, pushed it off his head, and began trying to wrestle it away. Hanging onto the dude's arm, he was trying to break it. All the while, he clung to the arm and car as it began pulling away, dragging him down the street. He finally bit the dude's wrist as hard as he could, forcing the would-be thief to let go of his grip on the gun. By then, the car was picking up speed, and he went flying onto the pavement as his crew shot at the car, but it got away.

At that young age, his story inspired me and a friend to talk it up with him about us getting cocaine from him and then selling it in Michigan, but we never pulled the trigger on it because my friend moved to California. So, a little while later, when I moved in with my grandmother, I got it in my head to sell drugs to make some money. I went over to his apartment to line everything up, and he agreed to be my supplier. In between talking with him and getting the product, I had some time to think about what I was getting myself into. Ultimately, it was the thought of breaking my grandmother's heart that kept me from going through with that plan, and when I told him the reason why I was going to pass, he understood, but that also meant I had to break ties with him as well.

I only ever saw him one more time when I snuck into a club using a fake ID. The rapper Yo-Yo was performing when a huge brawl broke out, and someone grabbed me from behind, pulling me away from danger. When I turned around to see who was pulling on me, it was him. He smiled and said, "You need to go. Shit is about to get really bad." He probably saved my life that night because as I was leaving, a whole lot of gunshots rang out from inside the club. I never saw him again after that, but I have always been thankful he was looking out for me that night. Not all guardian angels are saints.

Well, there I was, wondering why I was being treated like a criminal. It wasn't like I shot up my own club. I was a witness and a victim, so why all the cop drama? What were they fishing for? I knew all my guys weren't exactly exemplary citizens, but I wasn't the type to go around telling on people. Being in that room alone and not knowing why wasn't actually bothering me. I could do it all day. Shit, I could do it all year. Those bozos had nothing on Ranger school. Now that shit was miserable and will break any man. In Ranger school, we all break, eventually. This alone time was kind of therapeutic and gave me a chance to re-evaluate my relationship with Tiffany. What was I going to do with that girl?

Just as I was beginning to settle into my thoughts concerning Tiffany the door opened and in walked this guy saying, "You know why we pulled you in?" The guy was Joe Matagi who was a Homeland Security agent.

"I don't know. Let me guess, you guys are trying to meet quota, and the feds are broke, so you guys are pulling over innocent civilians in hopes of making them pay fines?"

Joe Matagi laughed. "Nice try, smart ass. You think we'd go out of our way to drag you down for a traffic violation?"

"I don't know. You guys do weird things these days. I kinda lost faith in the system." I shrugged.

"Oh yeah. Is that why you are involved with this lowlife USO Preschool?"

I shrugged again. "If you say so." Any time you shrug, it really pisses them off, especially when they believe you know what they are asking.

Joe was getting agitated at my could-care-less attitude and tried to level the severity of the situation on me. "Oh yeah, we have you on all our surveillance footage, and I'm going to tell you now, you can save yourself and save us the trouble if you tell us what he's up to. We already know. We just want to give you this opportunity to save yourself. Yeah, your boy is in a lot of trouble. We got him for racketeering, murder, and armed robberies ... robberies as in plural. Yeah, your boy's been really busy since he's been home from the can. And we intend to send him back for good, this time welding the metal doors shut. Yup, and we're going to add extra bolts and bars on the door this time."

As Joe was saying this, I leaned my head back on the chair and rolled my eyes. He then said in desperation, "Look, my braddah. I am trying to help you. From one law enforcement officer to another. I don't think you truly understand the gravity of the situation you are in. It's not good."

I laughed. "I'm not your 'Braddah,' sir. No matter if we are both in law enforcement. Guys like you are nothing more than bureaucratic puppets who go after their own kind. Now, I've come down here and cooperatively answered all your questions to the best of my knowledge. Can I go now?"

PreSCHOOL:

"FUCK." After the shooting, I left immediately. I knew the place would be crawling with cops, and the last thing I wanted was to be on their radar when they arrived. Especially being on paper (probation). I called the boys to meet up at the gas station across the street. I needed to do a full assessment of what just happened. My first thought was, who had the balls to do this to us? Was this retaliation by the Russians for roughing up their messenger? Was this one of the clubs that we shook down sending us a message? I NEEDED TO KNOW.

"You mean to tell me you guys are all on the streets day and night, and none of you know anything about this?" I look at the boys suspiciously because I don't trust anyone in this business. For all I know, this could be an attempt on Tone and me by one of the boys who is unsatisfied with our command position. Haters are a real thing. People will hate you for no reason other than they can't be you. I'm not arrogantly saying this like I'm the guy to be. However, jealousy and envy come from people counting other people's blessings and not counting their own. In this life, no one is ever satisfied with their position. Not even if they are second in command—hell, we can have the world, and it wouldn't be enough. Greed has everyone by the balls, no matter how much money they have in their pockets. It's why we still do what we do even when we no longer have to. Many of us amassed enough of a fortune to settle down and live a good life in the country. Run a legitimate business. But none of us would be able to maintain abstinence from this life. We would end up blowing our brains out at the boredom of a regular life. What's a regular life? Well, whatever it is, fuck it. I want mine fast. Fast money. Fast cars. Fast women. And Fast food. Haha

I can promise you this is why men are restless and irritable when they sober up and go straight. We are meant to be active creatures. We are meant to be warriors. It's why we love football and mixed martial arts and boxing and everything that displays blood and guts. Action movies. That's what this is.

Chapter Fourteen
The Video

Reyes:

In 2006, I took an advanced military police course called The Crime and Criminal Intelligence Analyst Course. This two-week course covered a lot of interesting subjects revolving around crime and criminal organizations dealing on a global scale. This was an important military course because the military is a global organization and a branch of the United States government with bases and interests all over the world, making law enforcement within the military a particularly unique endeavor.

Per their website and course overview, "The Crime and Criminal Intelligence Analyst Course (CCIAC) develops basic Police Intelligence and Investigative Analysts who conduct Law Enforcement Intelligence Analysis within the Department of Defense (DOD). It covers police intelligence operation (PIO) and strategy, critical thinking and crime indicators, legal and ethical requirements for PIO, crime pattern analysis, law enforcement, and investigative resources, file and data evaluation and management, collection plan development, structured data maintenance and management, analyze collected data, analyze work products, social network analysis, and briefings and reporting intelligence findings.

"This course provides the student with an introduction to the methods and techniques of criminal intelligence analysis and strategic organized crime. The rapid increase in multinational analysis and transnational organized crime, corporate drug trafficking organizations, and the impact of crime on national and international policy has created a critical need for law enforcement intelligence experts in the relatively new field of criminal intelligence. The course shows how to use criminal intelligence analysis to predict trends, weaknesses, capabilities, intentions, changes, and warnings needed to dismantle criminal organizations. This course provides knowledge needed by law enforcement professionals at the federal, state, and local levels, by criminal intelligence analysts working in private industry, and by military intelligence personnel making a transition from military to a law enforcement career. The course provides a background on the use of intelligence to dismantle criminal organizations and businesses. This course emphasizes criminal/law enforcement intelligence, as opposed to criminal investigations."

One day, I was pulled aside by one of my course instructors who told me to report to a briefing at the auditorium. Inside, there was a stage and theater-style seating. The lights were dimmed, and only the podium located on stage right was illuminated. A large movie screen was used for the PowerPoint presentation as the speaker behind the podium gave the presentation.

When I arrived, the briefing was already in progress, and I quietly took a seat in the back.

In attendance were both military personnel and civilians from a bunch of three-letter agencies and their respective representatives. The more well-known ones, of course, included the DOJ, ATF, DEA, BOP, DOD, CID, CIA, and NSA. Also in attendance was the U.S. Deputy Attorney, along with some U.S. senators and congressmen. Additionally, there were some top brass from all five military branches (Army, Navy, Air Force, Marines and Coast Guard).

Most of the briefing was delivered through a PowerPoint presentation by a two-star general and some suits. It went into detail about certain organized criminal organizations and gangs operating around the globe within proximity to military installations. It was discussed how certain terrorist cells and foreign governments were utilizing these criminal organizations to infiltrate critical areas and personnel that were vital to national security. A brief synopsis was given of each of the agencies involved, their ability to collect intelligence, and how they could work in tandem concerning national security and the global war on terrorism.

I found the briefing extremely informative and interesting. However, it all seemed way above my pay grade. After all, I was just a glorified grunt buying my time until I could go back into special operations. Although, what was being discussed was intriguing and reminiscent of a James Bond movie about bringing down some sinister plot. I definitely felt out of place and was wondering why I was even told to attend that briefing in the first place. When the formal presentations concluded, we were all invited to enjoy refreshments in one of the adjacent banquet rooms.

Feeling out of place as I made my way toward the exit, a familiar voice from behind called my name. When I turned around, sure enough, it was exactly who I thought it was. My first company commander at the Ranger battalion, Captain Connelly. It had been about ten years since I had last seen him, although we kept in contact periodically over the years. Rumors had speculated as to what he did after leaving his command of Bravo Company. I heard he went onto CAG and later the CIA. It turned out he spent six years in CAG and was then in his fifth year with the Agency.

We shook hands and had a short conversation talking about old times. He told me he was currently working closely with the NSA as a civilian consultant before mentioning he wanted me to meet some people. He explained that it was he who had arranged for me to be at the briefing after he came across my name on a list of potential candidates for a special intelligence gathering assignment at Fort Lewis. There were some security breach concerns regarding force protection, along with national security suspicions of potential terrorist cells aided by foreign agencies. Holy shit, the threat was bona fide and already happening in real time.

For that assignment, they didn't need some straight arrow square do-gooder boy scout. They needed someone who could fit in with the streets and party scene. He explained to me he had been working with Master Sergeant Prescott and the Department of Defense, along with others, to bring a special program to life. The program would allow for certain felons of Pacific Islander descent an enlistment packet into the military. They then would've been used as intelligence assets to infiltrate different hostile countries using their ties to organized crime and the underworld. Unfortunately, the program died with Master Sergeant Prescott. He told me that my name was also on the list for that program, which was submitted by none other than Prescott himself. Connelly shared how he remembered hearing about why I wanted to be a Ranger, and that was what stuck out in his mind while looking over the potential candidates for that assignment. Of all the candidates, he believed I was the only one who could legitimately blend in among partygoers, drug addicts, drug dealers, and thugs without suspicion while still performing my military duties as an MP assigned to the Fort Lewis Provost Marshal's Office. No easy feat.

Connelly told me that if I was interested in the assignment, then I should walk with him over to another building. I told him I was, and we should get to stepping. We left the auditorium and headed to a building just a short walk away. Once inside, he introduced me to the same two-star general who had given the briefing, a chief warrant officer five (CW5), and a representative of the NSA. I assumed Connelly was working for the CIA, but he never confirmed or denied it. He always stated he was a private consultant for various government agencies. I could tell from the patch on his uniform that the general was part of the Intelligence Support Activity (ISA) group. They are a tier-one special forces unit specializing in human intelligence. They were a lot like the CIA. The CW5 also wore the same patch and would act as my handler.

The suit from the NSA did most of the talking and explained to me what I was supposed to do. He said that since I was already doing promotions and private security, it would serve as a perfect vehicle for me to find and recruit my assets. They didn't care about anyone breaking the law or having to build any kind of criminal case. As far as they were concerned, the bigger the criminals and their ties to organized crime, the better because it would lead them to the big fish. As far as they were concerned, this was an intelligence-gathering assignment designed to support national security and aid in the global war on terror. The focus was on finding terrorist cells (foreign and domestic), enemy foreign agents, and threats against military installations and key personnel within the Pacific regions. This gave them a very broad and general scope for them to basically do whatever they deemed fit to accomplish their mission.

After he finished giving me the rundown, he asked if I had any questions. I explained that I was only doing the military police thing while I waited to see if my injuries would subside enough so that I would be cleared for jump status, which would allow me to attend the selection for either CAG or RRC (Regimental Reconnaissance Company as it was then called). It really wasn't my prerogative to ruin people's lives over petty nonsense. Shit, most of the people I know are into something because of one vice or another but are generally harmless. I wanted to make it a point that what I cared about was going after genuine threats to national security. Only terrorist or criminal activity that violated children and truly innocent people. I told them that I didn't mind if a case came across my desk as an MP or something happened while I was working, but I wasn't interested in being a narc.

The general spoke up, saying, "Listen, son, I understand your position, and hell, I can respect it. I assure you this is only about national security and thwarting terrorists and any hostels against our great nation. This assignment is all about exposing and eliminating security threats, not about prosecuting knuckleheads. We aren't the police, and we aren't asking you to betray anyone. We are only asking you to serve your country in the highest capacity."

Connelly interjected, saying, "In a way, you'd be picking up where Prescott left off, continuing with his program. Well, a modified version of it anyway."

Man, Connelly sure knew how to play me. I mean, how could I say no to that? How could I turn down this badass, super-secret James Bond general? Almost everything I did for them would be off-book, just the way they liked it. They were saying none of my assets or anything illegal they were involved in would be disclosed to any law enforcement agency as a direct result of my involvement. This was a way to protect me and keep both me and my assets out of the criminal system as much as possible. They didn't want the judicial process to complicate or impede any of their intelligence gathering, which meant anything I was directly involved in or connected to would be swept under the rug. If any of my assets ended up taking a full ride through the legal system, then they really had to work hard at getting caught and in trouble on their own accord. On the flip side, we would have access to almost all law enforcement agencies and assets that we needed. Well, shit, I guess that's how I kind of became a spy, serving my country.

So, when the police showed up at the club to retrieve the video footage from the door cameras, I just chuckled to myself. I already knew what they were going to find. I knew they were going to get a real hard-on thinking they were going to fry some big fish. They were doing good police work and wanted the footage in hopes of identifying the shooter's car. To their delight, they saw more than they could've bargained for. The video footage showed Preschool coming and going from the bar with large duffel bags. It showed the bags being emptied of the cash they carried onto the back table. The footage revealed Preschool pistol whipping someone outside the club. Then, another incident of him shooting into a parked car. What the video footage didn't have was the club shooter's car and occupants. This made the detectives more interested in Preschool and everyone around him. For the local police authorities, Preschool became their public enemy number one. Unfortunately for them, I happened to be present in almost all the video footage while these things were occurring. Even though I wasn't directly involved with what was happening, I was still there. I thought to myself, you fellas are out of your league. I mean, the only reason there was any of that additional footage in the first place was because CW5 had previously told me not to get rid of any footage.

PreSCHOOL:

[Automated phone service] *"Hello, you have a prepaid call from an inmate at a Federal Bureau of Prisons in California. To accept the charges, press seven now …*

I pressed seven. "Hey, Uce. Wassup?"

"I hear the party was a no-go. What did the cake fall through or what?" the caller asked.

"Nah," I said. "The party had to get rescheduled, but the cake was saved, and I had it taken to the fridge until we rescheduled the party. All is well. But I have to say. Seriously. The caterers you guys sent me suck. I mean, how do you guys expect me to promote parties if the caterers are shit? I need guys that know what they fuck they are doing. Guys that take this business seriously. Sorry, you have to hear that your brother's party is getting rescheduled. But in all fairness, I'm working the catering and parties single-handedly, it seems like."

The caller said, "Okay, bro. My dad was just concerned, is all. He just wants a celebration for my brother. He's kind of pissed at how things are sounding."

"Look, tell him I got it under control. I got party vans and buses, and venues are now better scheduled. He doesn't need to worry about me. Last I checked, everyone was eating well at my parties and enjoying themselves." Click.

Calls from prison cannot be a good thing. It never is. They only called because they were concerned that the club was getting shut down. The club is the bread and butter we all eat from. The rescheduling means that it will be reopened soon enough. A cancellation would mean that it's shut down for good. The cake is the money that flows through it. Hearing that the "cake" fell through means they have heard that the money was seized. But nah. All was well. It was just going to be trickier than ever to get things back up and running. The dad is the old man Paul. I knew he was questioning my ability to make things happen when the calls started coming in more frequently. Ughhh. It's a bad thing that guys send kites to the prisons complaining. It makes the old man worry. The thing is, the USOS have a code that you cannot talk bad about the organization or how it operates. They consider it treason. Even if you are within earshot of another member talking badly. You both are in violation and might as well off the other guy talking. That's how they kept things strengthened and solidified. I just wish they had a fucking rule for guys talking about each other. Gossip always weakens an organization.

First things first, though, I had to find out what the heck happened and why. The video footage from door cams the police confiscated in hopes of identifying the shooter's car led them to see more than we wanted them to see. The videos show a much more sinister and darker side of the club owner, Reyes, than he is letting on to be. It shows me coming and going from the bar with large duffel bags of cash, emptying them on the tables. It shows me pistol-whipping my nephew outside the club and another incident of me shooting at a car. The video shows incriminating events that could put me back inside for violating my parole and some more shit.

Hell, violating my parole is the least of my concerns. This video will definitely raise eyebrows at the precinct, and I'm aware of just how crazy things are going to get. Trickier just got trickier by tenfold. I know I need to get the lawyer on the horn to do damage control. Ughh. I can never have a good night, I swear. Something's always got to go wrong when it feels too damn good. It's like everything's too good to be true at times. I'll put out a fire, and then another fire will break out. I'd rather die in the burning building with them than live to be the only one who made it out to talk about it.

The phone rang at their office. "Hello, Law offices?" the voice on the other end stated.

"Hey, Hope, put the lawyer on the phone. Tell him it's urgent."

"Okay, Charlie. Give me one second."

This is the type of phone call I dread making because I know what's waiting for me on the other side. The phone calls about the boys tearing up stuff and shootings. This, oh man. It's all bad.

"Hey, Charlie. How goes it?"

"Hey, Counselor. The cops picked up the video footage from the club hoping to see if they could identify the car in the shooting."

"Shooting?"

"Yeah, the club got shot up. We don't know who by yet, but we're working on that right now."

"Okay? I'm listening." The lawyer sounds like he's expecting the worst.

"In the video, I come and go with large duffel bags of money. I'm pistol-whipping my nephew. And everything else under the sun."

"Why the FUCK did you guys let them take the video?"

"It was Tone. He didn't know. Or at least I don't think he knew. Shit, we didn't even know there was a fricking video attached to the damn camera. We thought it was for show."

"Well, now you know. Fuck. This is not good. I'm going to call our guy and see what I can dig up about this. Whether there's an investigation or not, I can also try to get something ready to file to suppress the evidence if so. They were there for the shooters. Not you. That would make it legally inadmissible without a warrant. That doesn't make it go away, however. They can still launch an investigation and then gather evidence where the video can be used. In the meantime, drop out of sight. Take a trip to somewhere far away."

"Okay, Counselor. I'm gone."

"Charlie, I thought you had this shit under control? I'm going to visit the old man this week, and he's not going to like this at all".

"I know."

Whoever thought that our own damn cameras would cause everything to come unglued? I didn't expect that to be the way it all ended. It was crazy because when you are thinking of everything that can go wrong, you don't expect it to be the littlest bit of detail. Trying to cover all your bases can be exhausting. It's like Buddhist monks. I wonder if they ever get tired of meditating. I mean, they can float in the air and jump from tree to tree, but what was that skill even necessary for? I was not planning on evading capture by jumping from tree to tree in the forest. This was the concrete jungle. I needed to be able to leap buildings in a single bound to avoid capture. Fricking cameras. And fricking Tone. Why the fuck did he give the cops the damn tapes? This is not good. Not good at all.

CHaPteR FiFteeN
RecruitMeNt

Reyes:

When I started a security company, I didn't expect it to be met with so much opposition and stress. My first security contract was for this crazy Mexican bar on the Eastside of Tacoma. It was not the best place to start out, but I didn't know any better. I had worked on various contracts in the past with this Korean lady who had introduced me to the owner of the bar. She was older and took a liking to me like a nephew or something. She was like my own little Korean, Mrs. Miagi, but for business instead of karate. In her broken English, she was always explaining business to me and how it all worked. Like the real way, it worked with government bidding behind closed doors. She was hip to that racket and all the bureaucratic games. Originally, she was going in with me on my security business and even put together a board of directors for me. That all abruptly ended when one of the gentlemen who worked for the city in the contracting/finance department was investigated by the city and law enforcement. Just before that occurred, Mrs. Miagi had secured this one contract, the bar, for me through her Korean business sources.

The Koreans are all about business and understanding the value of family, community, and the dollar. Within the Asian community, a dollar will remain within that community one hundred and sixty times as compared to the black community, where it only circulates once before leaving the community along with its wealth and prosperity. All because of others' selfishness and greed within the black community, especially the ones who are in a position to help their own families and communities.

The Koreans also have this unsaid board of elders who decide who gets funded with private money to start new businesses. The money is pooled from Korean-owned businesses and other sources and then used to finance new business ventures. They are quite strict and secretive but very prosperous, like their very own Korean-only venture capitals. She knew all the right people to put on the board and had all the funding. She was even remodeling an old bar to open as a club in support of our business venture. It was only a couple of months after starting the bar contract that Mrs. Miagi had bad news. The city worker had decided to get out of town in a hurry, and no one knew where he was going. She said she couldn't work with me anymore because she had to deal with some things she didn't want to drag me and my business into.

I was appreciative and excited upon getting that first contract. I even tried to promote it before the first day of the contract. When I saw the first group of hot females, I began talking about the bar and telling them how I worked there. As I'm telling them my name and who I was, and for them to come through, they're laughing and giggling, but this time, they're laughing and giggling in a different way. They're actually sneering at me, not laughing, but uttering words of disgust while they're giggling. At least, that's what my eyes were telling me as I read their faces and the body gestures they were making. You know, like rolling their eyes or smacking their gum in the only way that the most bitchy of bitches could whenever she said something out of disgust.

Were all these bitches on their periods today, or what? I've been promoting some of the best and hottest spots in town. Usually, when I tell them what club I'm working with, they get all happy, and almost without fail, they want to know if I could get them on the "VIP" list. That was code for "Hot-ass-bitch-who-doesn't-have-to-pay list because she was going to end up fucking one of the men from one of three groups: the staff (bartenders/security), promoters/DJs or "G's" (men with money). If a female came with my invitation, then I usually stood a good chance it would be me they chose. The owners always landed somewhere between promoter/DJ status, but it was typically dependent on how much money they had. I could write a book about the mating rituals of the urban princes. Those were the only guys getting the hot bitches on a regular basis. While they were banging eights, nines, and tens, everyone else was banging sixes and below.

Then it dawned on me what kind of shithole this little Mexican bar really was. These bitches weren't on their periods after all. I was all smiles and shit with them, too. I really thought I was talking about something spectacular. I was temporarily blinded by my own giddiness and excitement of getting my first security contract. In my mind, I had been picturing the kinds of atmosphere and crowds I had grown accustomed to. Then, just like that, the fantasy was lifted, and the reality of that bar sank in. Thinking, what the fuck did I get myself into now? It's in the hood, the most ghetto part of Tacoma. It doesn't mean there aren't eights, nines, and tens. It just means now there are bullets, knives, and a whole lot of ass-whoopings involved. The hood's hood. I was like, *fuck, I'm gonna get shot*. On the bright side, the odds of me getting laid remained the same regardless. Besides, CW5 liked the prospects of that bar. Very promising, he said in his estimates.

At first, I started by myself. That first night, I walked in wearing a windbreaker and introduced myself to the owner. She was Korean and barely spoke English. Her Spanish-speaking clientele barely spoke English. She barely spoke Spanish, if she even did. Now, I may be half Puerto Rican, but unfortunately, I never learned to speak Spanish. There was definitely a three-way communication barrier. Anyway, she was sizing me up and was evidently not very impressed by my size. I'm barely five foot eight. She had this look of disappointment and concern on her face, worried for me and my safety. She wondered if I could even handle that kind of crowd. However, I instantly saw her gleefulness and approval upon me, removing my windbreaker and revealing my muscular build and large biceps.

After that first night there alone, I recruited anyone who could work security for me. I needed six more, at least. My cousin, C'zar, and some soldiers from Ft. Lewis were the first ones I brought on. So now, the next night, I'm there with my cousin, three Puerto Rican cats, and one Mexican dude. I had C'zar, Diggs, Padro, Tito, and Chavez doing security for me, and they all spoke Spanish. Everything was cool and going well for almost half a year. Then I had to go away on a training exercise for a couple of weeks. While I was gone, all hell broke out because Diggs, Padro, and Chavez all had other military obligations to attend to. Which left only my cousin and Tito working for the bar by themselves, and that night, the two of them were caught up in a huge brawl. When I got back, they told me what had happened, and Tito told me to find some more people before he had to go.

I was able to recruit this big white guy named Norm and this boxer kid Malik. For a while, it was only me, my cousin, Norm, and Malik. Surprisingly, we kept the peace for quite some time without incident. Even Chavez came back for a while.

Then, one night, when it was me, C'zar, Chavez, and Norm working, Chavez signaled me over to the dance floor and, pointing, told me one of the patrons needed to go. I went over to the patron to explain to him he needed to come outside with us so we could talk. That guy, seeing over my shoulders that Chavez was already walking away, unknown to me, decided I was outnumbered, and he and his buddy could take me. He threw a punch, and I did some combative shit I learned, throwing him to the ground and then parrying strikes from his buddy, putting him on the ground also. I then grabbed the leg of the first guy and dragged him about twenty-five feet to the front entrance.

Dragging him by his leg was a bad idea. First, it really pissed off his friends, who probably wouldn't have cared as much if I had simply walked their buddy out—dragging him was just plain disrespectful. Secondly, do you know how much effort it takes to drag another human adult male twenty-five feet while they are resisting you? I was gassed and out of breath by the time we reached the door. That's when the group of angry friends bum-rushed the door, pushing me up against the cashier's counter. When Norm saw it, he bear-hugged three of them and proceeded to push them, along with me, outside along with a few others.

Once outside, Norm continued to bear-hug three of them, and I tried to talk calmly to another one of them. As we were talking, one of their friends decided to run up to Norm and start punching him, hoping he would release his friends. Norm just squeezed harder, grinning, growling, and saying, "Come on fucker. Hit me again." That Mexican obliged two or three times before I could get to him. Each time, Norm gave that same grin and response while continuing to squeeze. Norm looked a bit psycho with that grin and blood oozing down his face. Warrior!

I grabbed the dude who was punching Norm, and we began to tussle. Then, I was pushed between a car and a minivan, fighting. That first dude in front of me was the one who had been punching Norm. After dodging a flurry of punches, I took him down hard, slamming him into the side of the minivan. I slammed him so hard it put a large ass dent in it. For a brief moment, I fought off three more attackers coming at me from both sides between the two vehicles. Me, Norm, C'zar, and Chavez were all outside fighting against nine of them. Just as quick as the melee began, it was over, with the four of us ending up back inside and the rest of them outside.

That one incident made me think about Master Sergeant Prescott's advice about always being able to reach out to his family in time of need. No matter what, the Uces always come through for you. I had his mom's number, and there were a bunch of Samoan and Pacific Islanders around here. I always saw them doing most of the security around Tacoma. I called Prescott's mom in Samoa, and she was happy to talk with me about her son. Then I told her of my problem, and she said, "Well, cousin so and so's cousin of so and so's is their nephew. He's down there. Do you want his number?"

I didn't know much more than needing guys to stand at the door. Hell, I have guys who kick them in, too. Guys, that shoot up shit. And guys that fucking get shot at. Who would ever think? It took me so long to figure out that I needed the blend of both military and street guys to run a good crew. It went even deeper than that; there was also street politics involved, involving who did security in what place in what part of town, all based on different races and affiliations. Since that bar was such a shithole in the worst part of the hood and filled with a bunch of drunken Mexican cowboys, no one saw any real value in it. Therefore, they didn't want anything to do with it, leaving me free and clear from being under any obligation to anyone. I was a neutral party to the Koreans, the Mexicans, and anyone else around who was involved in one way or another. Involved means having anything to do with any of the prostitution, drugs, or security attached to the nightlife scene.

I met the giant Samoan one night down at the bar when he came to see what I needed help with. He introduced himself as Preschool and was the nephew of so and so. I felt a good vibe and an immediate connection with him upon our first meeting. Just like me, he was one of those "My word is my bond kind of man." He would later explain to me why guys like him and I have problems with many others, and it was because "We were loyal to a fault." He would say, "For a lot of people out here, they are selfish and only in it for what they can get out of it. They never think about anyone else. I'm always trying to feed my people. To us, it's more than just about the money."

After I explained my situation to him, he said he could help me out with it. I made it clear to him from the jump that the security was a legitimate business venture. However, I knew things had to go on, and that would already be going on if I was there or not. I told him I only did law enforcement on Fort Lewis. As far as anything in the gray, I need to know about it so I can appropriately deal with it. The other stuff I didn't need to know or be involved in and was not part of the business. That's how Preschool and I began our partnership over a handshake like men. As I said before, I needed the muscle to start making my moves. With the help of the Uces, we cleaned house. The Uces were our security's security and regulated the outside stuff, too. Word spread around, and the exposure from this little rinky dink bar was the first brick laid on the yellow brick road to riches. By yellow bricks, I'm talking gold bullions yellow. Preschool was talking about gold bricks and kilos of crack yellow. Haha. Showing that we were capable of handling ourselves and had the manpower to control the crowds landed us more and more gigs. Now, that didn't happen overnight, and it was quite a learning experience.

Over time, as our business grew, Preschool and I became good friends, having a lot of the same perspective on life and sharing similar values. While doing all this stuff with the security at that one shithole bar, I was still working as an MP on Fort Lewis and also doing promotions. I don't remember when I ever slept, but I do remember beginning to drink heavily again. It was through the promotions that I was able to take Preschool to all these different clubs, getting us in free and to all the parties. He was having fun, for sure, and I'm quite certain he was seeing all the dollar signs as well. For Halloween that year, the hottest party on the Latin scene would be at the "Yuppy 21" club, not to be confused with the 21 Commerce Martini Lounge. This club would also later end up being the source of another fire we would have to put out.

It turned out later that CW5 liked that "Yuppy 21" club and would congratulate me on a job well done. At the time, I was clueless as to why I was being congratulated. Preschool was happy with it, too.

Preschool:

Entering into business with Sgt. Prescott's boy wasn't the last option, but still it was a desperate one. A security business under Tone was a good cover for us to start taking the street businesses without any real attention from the law, but we didn't know if Tone was street enough for this business. I mean, he is a law enforcement officer of some sort. But MSG Prescott was smart in that he sent us someone he knew would have the credentials to help and not hurt us. Desperate moves of taking on someone in a business endeavor would have cost us a huge setback if he didn't turn out to be solid like the MSG told his brother Paulie he'd be. It's too bad the MSG wasn't around anymore. He was far smarter than his twin brother Paulie. MSG Prescott helped coach the USOS member in beating a murder trial. The case came back to haunt the USOS for perjury, but doing time for perjury beats doing time for murder any day.

Most of the club owners in the town are weaneys, but they weren't rats. I give them that. They almost always have someone already to whom they answer. Some gang or group that they are paying protection to. Telling wasn't safe for their business and their persons. They knew this to be the silent code of the streets and honored it.

Since I had so many soldiers to feed and not enough capital to feed them, I figured the best thing going would be to start getting contractual agreements from other clubs that needed security. Having security already at clubs didn't mean anything. We were going to offer them something better. Promotion and financial loans with high interest. What people don't realize is that running a club is a tough business. A lot of the clubs in the town are in debt or are suffering from some kind of legal issues. Gangs and organizations that were extorting them weren't concerned about them going belly up. These groups of extortionists were nothing more than pump fakers with a gun. Shit, we all have guns. In fact, since we started operating, I ordered all my street dealers to buy every gun. Every vet that came back looking to get high and wanted to trade their assault rifles was our go-to. They would always try to add a flat-screen TV or a laptop, but we only wanted the guns. We wanted any and all guns from vets, boosters, dealers, crackheads, and all that the streets had to offer. The pump fakers were a breeze to scare off. I'd show up, and they would kick gravel and travel. They knew that I had the bigger guns and the reputation for using them, so they almost always left without a single shot. In one week, I pulled fifteen fully modified AR15s off the street and four M4s. That should tell you how dangerous the town is.

The reason for me wanting all the guns? Simple. Art of war. If I don't buy it, then these addicts would go down the street and trade it with the other races. Blacks. Mexicans. Whites. If I ever had a race issue on my hands, I'd be outgunned. And one thing I learned from reading General Patton's autobiographies was, "I'd rather have a handful of guns than a mouthful of arguments." So yeah, knocking over clubs for contracts was easy. Getting rid of their extortionists was easy. Promoting clubs and having women come there frequently with their marks was easy. But consequently, though, there's always that one, and we just happen to flip it over. Yup. The "Yuppy 21" club, which none of my guys knew about, belonged to the Russians. A club that catered to young, rich Mediterranean people with Lamborghinis and Ferraris parked out front. Hell, there were more people in the parking lots than in the clubs at times. Showing off their car engines and stupid shit. Parking lot pimpin'. But yeah, that club. It belonged to the Russians.

chapter sixteen
war chest

preschool:

In the short time I was out, I managed to take the three million in cash entrusted to me by my USOS and get things in full swing. I helped Tone acquire twenty-one contracts from other nightclubs, worked on a Native American land and development deal with two mockingbird construction companies, and pulled in two hundred grand a month. Not bad for what the feds call a low life. Haha. Suckers.

[Phone rings] [Automated service] "Hello, you have a prepaid call from an inmate at a Federal Bureau of Prisons in California. To accept the charges, press seven now … and then this.

These guys send me flunkies and junkies from the joint, and they think I can make miracles. I don't have guys who spend all their time in law libraries and educational programs. I got guys who were getting high and spending all their time in the yard looking cool. One of the new guys that just came home already got us in some shit. He hadn't had ass in eighteen years. He showed up for work drunk and high out of his mind, making sexual advances on girls in one of the clubs. It's not good for business. In prison, it was easier to discipline guys because we had the pack to do it. Out here, these guys ain't worth the bullet, so it's easier to send them off to work construction.

The American mob's greatest downfall was that they adopted a cannibal-like mentality. They were whacking their own guys for dumb shit. Most of these guys that get sent out are already patched but don't act like it. They are more concerned about catching up in partying and bitches they missed out on all those years. Sexual acts, though, are highly forbidden. Everyone in prison knows that shit. We beat sex offenders to a pulp in prison. I've watched one run by me with his hand trying to hold blood from spewing out his neck because someone gave him a prison necktie with a razor. Now I have to deal with this situation, and most likely, the old man will call for a bullet, which is coded in conversation, to give him his tattoo.

My lawyers deemed three million in cash legal. That's how all this got started. The lawyers used the insurance claim on Sgt. Prescott to draw up documents that really weren't worth the papers on which it was signed. Legitimizing the money through the lawyers made the money legit enough to invest and get things going. But sometimes I wish I never signed up for this shit. All the fancy cars and clothes and pussy in the world don't pay out well to the stress I deal with on a daily basis. That's what guys in the inside and out here don't fucking realize. They all think they can handle my role. Guys out here complain to the joint that I'm living lavish and plush while they work the doors for fifteen dollars an hour. Ungrateful fucks.

I remember the Native brother who worked with me on the land project. He was one of those ill-prepared people. I mean, he could never get all his ducks in a row. Shoot, some of his ducks might've been pigeons, and he'd not even know it. The first day he got the contract in motion, we were expected to pave the new county jail parking lot for the tribe in southern Washington. He calls me panicking on the first day.

"Hey, brother?"

"What's up, Chief?"

"We got a problem ... "

"You gotta be kidding me. This is a million-dollar deal. What's the problem?"

He says, "The fucking guy that was supposed to bring us the steamroller didn't show. When I called the company, they gave me some bullshit answer saying they won't have one available until next week."

"Next week? So why don't we wait?"

"Because I got all these tribal leaders down here with important people, and I can't tell them to leave and come back next week."

"Can we rent one?"

"No."

"Okay. Let me call you back."

I called the white boys. If there is anyone who can get the steamroller or whatever it is you need, it's these guys. The crankster gangsters of Tacoma. Heck, everything in my home is from shopping on the whiteboy booster network. They can steal airplanes and yachts for the cartel. They can steal you anything.

"Howdy?"

"Hey Lep, it's me, Preschool. I *need* you, bro."

"Preschool. What's up motherfucker? I'd ask you how you've been, but I know your ass is all about business. So, let's hear it. What can I do for the golden child?"

"Look, I need you to get me a steamroller."

"A wha ... a steamroller? What the fuck are you building? A landing strip?"

"Nah uce. This is serious. I need one delivered to the address I'm going to send you at the reservation. Can you help me or what?" Irritation crept into my voice.

"This is going to cost you twenty big ones."

"Okay. Twenty grand. I got you."

"No." He paused. "Not twenty grand. Twenty keys."

"I'll shoot you fifteen, but you have to get this thing going asap."

"Done. I'll have it to the place. Send me the address."

And just like that. I didn't even think about it until later that night when I got home. I thought about it and called the chief. "Hey brother, did these guys ever bring you the steamroller?"

"Yeah. An hour after we talked. These white guys are whack jobs. The guy, what's his name, Leprechaun? I think that's his name. He says to tell

128

you it's twenty. They had to steal the semi-truck to steal the steamroller."
All I could do was laugh hysterically. What the fuck? Fucking Leprechaun.
A solid white boy I met in prison who ran the younger generation of his
group. He came home and hit the ground running like me. In a short time
he was out, he managed to organize his little crew of white boys and
became well known for being the face of the whiteboy boosting shopper's
network. He'd steal your ring if you shook his hand.

I always warned guys to check their pockets after they leave his
presence. To which he'd feign injury from the insult and say in his mock
red dot Indian accent, "Thank you, come again."

Reyes:

During this time and while Preschool was handling his other obligations
outside of security, I also had obligations outside of security consisting of
Army and club promotion stuff I had to do. Well, to be honest, the other
obligations I was enjoying consisted mostly of ladies. I was dating six or
more at a time and smashing new ones on a weekly basis. At one point,
my dating roster included a Panamanian, Ecuadorian, El Salvadorian,
Guatemalan, Native American, Filipina, a black chick, and two white
chicks. Don't judge me. The ladies have always loved me. As far back as I
can remember, I have always had female attention. Outside of a few rough
patches and a learning curve in my adolescent and teenage years, dating
came easy. Now, as an adult, with the club promotions and all the nightlife
activities, it was as easy as clubbing baby seals. For the life of me, I couldn't
figure out why Monica wasn't impressed with the fact that I was willing to
give up most of my activities in order to settle down and start a family.
Anyway, I had moved on from her onto greener pastures.

Not too long after my breakup with Monica, I met the Panamanian
at The Loft, the club I'd been promoting for the longest. I saw her at the
club on a regular basis and noticed she was always on her phone texting
and stuff. One night, I approached her in the stairway as we passed each

other. I was going up, and she was going down. I stopped her and introduced myself. We chatted for a minute before I invited her to join me for a drink upstairs. When I walked her to a private booth, I sat down and started making out with her. We were already into each other, and the drinks weren't necessary. She worked for the state and would prove to be one of my most loyal female confidants over the years.

The Ecuadorian was one of the gate guards at Fort Lewis, who was contracted through a private security firm. Anytime I was working on Lewis, I'd stop by and talk with her during my shift; by talk, I mean flirt. I really liked her, and she seemed to have a good head on her shoulders. She had ambitions of going into federal law enforcement and was using her current job as a stepping stool while she was in college. After stopping by and flirting with her for a while, I got her number and eventually went out with her. Then, there was this beautiful El Salvadorian soldier working as an MP. Since she lived in the barracks and had her own room, we would hook up during one of our shifts and sometimes while we were both working. She was great and a lot of fun.

I had known the Native American chick for a minute. While doing promotions, I met her younger sister, who then introduced us. It was a few years later that we eventually hooked up. She was more than ten years older than me and treated me like a king every time I went over to her place. My affair with her lasted probably five years or so. I could always go see her anytime. Through the years, I would often get calls in the middle of the night from her, asking me to come spend some time with her. If I didn't answer, she wouldn't leave a voicemail but would instead just let it record with the background music she was listening to at the time and play out the recording.

I had a weakness for the Guatemalan. She was only four foot nine inches tall, but she was well proportioned for her height with a thick ass and nice breasts; she had a beautiful body. The chemistry between us was absolutely great. Some of the best sex I ever had was with her. She would do pretty much anything I wanted. One time, she was all dolled up, looking as beautiful as ever, and I had her dance on top of the bar at one of the clubs we promoted. Me, the general manager, and staff were the only ones in there at the time, getting ready for the night ahead. The staff were busy doing other things, and the DJ was still setting up and doing a sound check with his equipment. I told her to get up on the bar and show off that sexy body of hers, and she did. Being so tiny, the bar was like a stage for her, and she gave the two of us a wonderful performance. Man, she really turned me on.

As usual, not only was I always the one to start a conversation with the females, but I was the one to always bring the females around. On more than one occasion, the comment was made that I had my own harem. Meeting the Filipina was no different. It was outside one of the clubs we provided security for, and I saw her with two of her friends. They were new to the area and looking for good entertainment venues and places to party. I brought them back to my house, and at the time, I had four roommates, so something was always going on at the house. It was a designated party place, especially for after-parties. While her two friends hooked up with two of my roommates, I put her in my friend zone. As they continued to come over and party, the tension between the two of us grew to a boiling point.

She always dressed up really nicely, wearing classy outfits. One night, she was wearing this black dress, heels, and the sexiest stockings I think I've ever seen. The pattern on the stockings, combined with her long, sexy legs and beautifully curved body, had really caught my attention that night. So, while we were alone in the kitchen and everyone was downstairs partying, I made a move. On the main floor, all the lights were either off or dimmed, and we had just been talking in the faint light. She was leaning up against one of the countertops. I walked over to her and stood in front of her without saying a word. Then I put my hand on the back of her neck. Gently pulling her into me, I kissed her. For more privacy, just in case anyone came upstairs, we moved from the kitchen into the dining room, kissing and touching each other as we moved. In the dining room, she was up against the wall facing me. My hands slid up her thigh to her pleasure spot, ripping open her leggings. I first entered her while we were both standing, then bending her over the dining table, I took her from behind. We eventually went to my room to finish out the passion-filled night.

I had pulled the black chick from that hole-in-the-wall shitty-ass bar where I got my first security contract from. She was easygoing and a lot of fun, but she loved the hood shit. I kept her around for a few years, establishing more of a friends-with-benefits relationship with her. I'd help her out from time to time and, at one point, even let her live in one of the vacant rooms at my house. She was going through some issues and just needed a safe place to lay her head while she figured out what to do with herself. She didn't have any money and offered sex as payment. You can't offer me something I already have access to, so I told her not to worry about it and to just fix whatever she needed to fix in order to get back on her feet. Ironically, we didn't even fuck the whole time she was staying at my place.

The one white chick was a nine-one-on-one dispatcher on base, and we started flirting with one another every time I would stop by the FLECC (Fort Lewis Emergency Call Center). She was a cute red head with beautiful blue eyes and the cutest freckles on her nose. Every time she would have to call out to me while working, we would flirt. As investigators, we would be dispatched by either radio or cell phone. We probably flirted with each other for about a month or so when I invited her out to my birthday party at one of the clubs I promoted. That night at my party she told me she was my birthday present and was going home with me. She was a lovely birthday present indeed.

I had met this other white chick while working on Fort Lewis. She and her friend were witnesses to an incident. I had responded to the base hotel for a call involving a rowdy guest breaking up some stuff. I often refer to them as the Italian and the Blonde. They were both getting ready to transition out of the Army and were temporarily staying at the hotel until they got their apartment. They were both gorgeous, solid eights. Since I couldn't decide which one I was most interested in, I decided to let them decide which one I should pursue. I gave them both my number and told them to hit me up sometime when they got themselves situated in their new place.

One day, out of the blue, the Italian called me to see if I wanted to hang out that night. She wanted to know if I had a friend I could invite along for the Blonde. Thinking to myself, *I don't want to share. I want them both*. I decided I would send out a text message to all my friends, simply asking who wanted to hang out. I didn't include anything about the Blonde or any party. I just asked who wanted to hang out with me. Sadly, no one responded, which I pretty much expected since I was always taking everyone else out to the club, some party, or arranging female companionships. I would've actually been surprised if someone had responded. I texted the Italian back, explaining that it was such short notice, and everyone already had other obligations. I also told her it was no big deal if just the three of us were hanging out. She responded, letting me know that we could do that. They picked me up a couple of hours later. It turned out that the three of us had a fun time that night, shooting pool and having a few drinks. It was so good that they invited me back to their place to have some more drinks and continue to hang out.

I took the backseat of the Blonde's car while the Italian was seated in the front passenger seat. Every time we stopped at a red light, the Blonde and Italian began making out and turning to me to ask if it was okay with me that they were doing so. The first two times they did it, I just played it cool and said to them that it was really cool that they did that. At the third stoplight, I leaned in and joined them in the short make-out session, kissing both of them. We arrived at their place, a two-bedroom apartment.

The Blonde showed me her wine collection and poured me some wine to taste. After only a few sips, the three of us went to the Blonde's bedroom. That was my first threesome, and what a fantastic experience, especially with those two beautiful women. I ended up dating the blond until she moved away.

The Army stuff and working twenty-four-hour shifts wasn't easy. It was supposed to be twenty-four on and twenty-four off, at least on paper. The problem was that it never worked out that way. For example, the schedule would say zero nine hundred (nine am) to zero nine hundred (nine am) the following day, technically twenty-four hours. The thing was, you had to report an hour early for your shift to draw your weapon, inspect and sign for your duty vehicle, and get briefed by the outgoing duty investigator. Then, as the duty investigator, you had to sit in on the morning briefing, going over the blotter report (everything that happened during the twenty-four-hour shift) with the other department representatives and supervisors along with the provost marshal. This briefing generally began at zero nine hundred hours (nine a.m.) and lasted thirty to forty-five minutes, depending on how much activity had taken place during the twenty-four-hour shift. So, no matter what, you were pulling twenty-six hours every day with less than twenty-two hours of downtime. It could take a drastic turn if you caught a case close enough to the time you were scheduled to be off. That case was a priority, and you had to stay until the preliminary investigation was completed. It could take you into the late afternoon to finish all the initial investigation and paperwork involved. I really hated those long days.

How I even had time for everything was beyond me. All I knew was that I was in constant motion and always on my phone, dealing with one thing or another. It was during this time that my alcohol use began becoming excessive. It wasn't like I was drinking while on duty or any of the times working security. However, I would drink in the morning after my scheduled MPI shifts to unwind, relax, and fall asleep. Then, I was drinking while we were partying at one of the venues that we promoted. Then, I would drink at my own parties first to stay awake, and then so I could fall asleep and be ready for work the next day. I kept up this pace for almost two years.

CHapter Seventeen
PTSD

PresCHOOL:

"I know it's the fucking Russians. They sent that kid here yesterday."

"School, you don't know that for sure," Tone said. "Stop, or you are going to get these guys riled up for nothing."

"Nah, I know it was them. That frickin' Yuppy 21 club. That's what this is all about. Don't you get it?" I said in a self-righteous voice.

"What Russian kid are you talking about anyway? Came here yesterday?" Tone asked.

"Oh, bro," chuckling, "this guy showed up. Scrawny ass dude weighs about a buck ten, talking like he is 290 and eight feet. He wasn't a buck twenty, even if he was wet. We slapped him up a little."

"What the fuck, Uce? Really? You want to start shit with these motherfuckers? We don't even know if it was them. Are you nuts?"

"Yeah, fuck them."

"No, bro. What the fuck is wrong with you? That's the last thing we need right now. Some bullshit with the Russians. You just got into it with the Mexicans last week."

"Yeah, and how did that turn out? In our favor, I'd say," I mocked. "Mexicans are supplying us now, which is what I've been needing all along. A new plug."

"Yeah, but it could've been all bad. And while you're needing a plug, shit I'm hoping to just stay off the fucking radar and run a legitimate business. Is that too much to ask?"

The incident with the Mexicans could've been all bad. Tone was right. But it wasn't like I was thinking. I've been having so much shit on my plate that it's hard to think anymore. Something I'm known for inside the walls. Flashbacks have been kicking my ass and sending me on a mental spiral. Bad.

This Mexican guy always comes to the club from which we operate. He is always with his entourage of about ten guys. He thinks he's some kind of Tony Montana. Some big shot. They've been selling dope out of the club and acting like they own the place. Well, that's got to end. See, in Mexico, you can do all that shit and get away with it. But this is America. I run these streets. I've been shot and stabbed on these streets all my life trying to make it out alive for these guys to come here and think they can just shit on people. This guy, in particular, is a fucking peasant. A farmer back home. Throws his weight around like that cartel shit flies out here when it doesn't.

I approached him to discuss his selling dope out of our bar, and he bucks up on me. I tell him that he should kick us down something. Not a lot. But something. We're the reason the cops don't come around. We see what he's doing in our club, and we let it slide. As I'm telling him this, he pushes my face back, and I push him. The others from his entourage jump in, and now it's a Mexican standoff. Literally, I'm at the club alone. So, I said okay, chill. I walk outside and call all the boys to meet me at the club and to come heavy. Everyone showed up armed to the teeth.

I sent a hot blond girl into the bar to get this guy's attention. He starts dancing and moving off rhythm like a white guy trying to two-step. She lured him to the door. Meanwhile, his entourage pushes him to her. They cheer him on. He probably never gets pussy or something because he came floating on air like a puppy in love on cloud nine. As soon as he got to the door, though, I yanked his ass out. We shut the door and locked it. I just started wailing on this guy's face. Knocked him out to where he was snoring and in a frozen position. I was going to cancel his Christmas if it weren't for Dog grabbing the pistol from me. Dog pushes me in the car and has the boys drive me away to our hangout at a house up the road.

Dog goes inside alone and tells the Mexican entourage that things can go one of two ways. If they want to see their friend again, pack it up and leave. We will drop him off at an address they provide. If not, there's a parking lot full of USOS outside, heavily armed, that is going to send everyone, including the girls they were with, up to the Creator.

I called Tone, and he was livid as usual. I start to wonder if he's like the Mexican in that they both aren't getting laid. What the fuck.

He tells me, "Look, there's only three things that can happen, but we have to wait it out and see. One, They can retaliate, which I doubt. That spot is a gold mine for them. It's also a gold mine for us, don't you forget. They know and value that. Two, they can regroup and try some shit, but I'll talk to them. Let them know they are outgunned and outnumbered. Or three, they can reason with the devil and come to the table to talk. Let's see what they decide. I'll reach out to them tomorrow. In the meantime, fuck, can you please do this for me, bro?"

"What's that, Tone?"

"Can you lay low? I mean, really lay low. I'll pay for you to take a vacation to the islands to chill."

People are always telling me to fucking lay low. There is so much work to put in, and I question if these guys have the drive and motivation to do it. I mean, I'm not even supposed to be doing half the shit I'm doing. I'm on probation. These guys should voluntarily jump at the opportunity to do shit. Instead, they're volun*told* to do shit. That's the thing with prison guys. Guys should have toilet handles instead of ears. They are so full of shit. They all talk a good talk about what they are like on the streets. Everyone's a gangster until it's time to do gangster shit. Then it's sex operation. They act like chicks. Fuck. I wonder if these motherfuckers would even send me a note when I'm down or bail when I'm in jail. I know Tone would. He's solid like that. These guys complain about Tone not being of blood relation or from our thing but fuck. This guy's been more loyal than any of them. Blood makes us relatives, and loyalty makes us family.

"Tone?"

"Wassup Uce?"

"Did I wake you?"

"Nah. What's up, brother?"

"Call the Russians. Talk to Laddy. Tell him we want to do a Saufa'i with them."

"Okay, brother. I'll get on that first thing in the morning."

"Oh, and Tone? I'll take you up on that vacation. Maybe I need to get away and clear my head on the beach somewhere."

Reyes:

Even though our attentions were focused elsewhere, including our own personal problems, Preschool and I both took care of our obligations to each other and our business. No matter what needed to be taken care of as far as security concerns went, we both put in the necessary work to ensure its success. As we expanded to more clubs, we also needed to continually recruit more security. While Preschool kept a steady flow of Uces, street cats, and those recently released from incarceration, I brought in military and law enforcement types along with some party boys and athlete types. It was essential that we related and appealed to a variety of people. Believe it or not, there are a lot of politics involved within the club industry, especially from a security perspective. You not only have to keep the club owners happy (your clients), but you must also keep the staff and patrons happy, as well as the streets. Not understanding those politics was where most security teams messed up because they only saw the need to please the clients.

At the end of the day, taking care of the owner came down to two things: protecting their liquor license and their bottom line. It was a business, not a party, despite what it looked like from the outside. By protecting their image, we ensured both were covered from our end. That meant not letting in any problems to begin with and, if needed, removing those problems and finally keeping problems away. This included inside and outside of the establishment. So many bars and clubs got shut down because of too many incidents involving their establishment.

The local municipalities kept records of every call to service at the bars and clubs. A call to service refers to when any emergency service is dispatched, whether it is police, fire, or ambulance. This included the area around the business establishments as well. For instance, any time the police or an ambulance was called in because of a fight, noise complaints, litter in the streets from patrons, or a drunk driving incident miles away from the venue, it was tallied as a strike. If the establishment was part of or mentioned in any complaint, it then became a strike against them, plus elicited a closer look by those in power. When there are too many strikes, they are forced to shut down.

It was a fine line with keeping the staff happy because they were there to make money and have fun. Most of the workers at any bar or club tend to be alcoholics and usually partake in party drugs as well. That included most of the security team. The staff enjoyed a certain level of clout that came from working at a certain venue. They loved to show off by trying to let anyone in and over-pouring drinks. On top of that, the staff and their friends they allowed in often believed the rules of the establishment didn't really apply to them. If not handled properly, it could cause major problems with other patrons. As security, we couldn't just come in acting like Johnny Law, condemning and ostracizing staff and their friends, because we needed to blend in and fit in.

That was because good staff helped bring in paying customers. They had their following of friends and regulars ranging from the hundreds into the thousands. The best bartenders and staff always worked at multiple venues throughout their work week. I always had my favorite bartenders, probably knowing their work schedules just as well as they did themselves, where and when they would be working. So, security needed to make sure the staff were safe and could retain their clout while having fun with limited interference from security. Keeping them safe was easy for us, but their clout and fun were always a delicate dance.

The patrons were divided into two categories, men and women. Then there were sub-categories and a person in our industry better know what those were and who belonged to which sub-category. The reason for breaking it down into men and women was because they must be dealt with differently, and it was also important to understand that the women brought out the men, and the men spent the money.

Women tended to look for safer and cleaner environments to patronize and frequent. Their bathroom better be spotless and fully stocked. In contrast, in the men's bathroom, the urinals could be running over and shit running down the walls, and they wouldn't even care as long as there were plenty of hot women in the club. Not only did we need to provide security for the women, but we also needed to provide a sexy look, which was one of the things that always made our teams stand out. There's nothing more appealing to an average female partygoer than a good-looking, athletically built man wearing an undersized security T-shirt who can spit game and kick ass. When dealing with the men, it always came down to respecting them and allowing them to save face whenever possible.

The sub-categories were the rich and powerful, the popular, the thugs and gangsters, business professionals, the college crowd, the military crowd, the squares, and the randoms. Each group had to be dealt with differently, however, fairly and equally enough so as not to upset any one group in particular.

So many businesses were tied to the streets one way or another, and the nightlife industry was no different. In fact, there was probably more involvement from the streets than in most other industries because it was so cash-heavy. Clubs and bars were also ripe for drugs, prostitution, controlling territory, and flexing nuts. All of that took place whether the owners, staff, and patrons were aware of it or not, and sometimes they were even in on it. I kind of always knew that instinctively, and from growing up in the scene as a teenager, that first hole-in-the-wall bar solidified what I already had known. It was important for security to be a neutral party and be as unbiased as possible. Motherfucking Switzerland or the UN.

We were allowing everyone to do what they were going to do anyway, but they had to follow the house rules and respect everyone's hustle. Not everyone working at the bar or security was trying to be a part of any kind of illegal activity and didn't want their jobs compromised just because someone else was. A lot of our people were on the up and up or trying to be so they didn't end up back in trouble with the law. As security, it wasn't our job to upset the natural order of the jungle. We simply had to moderate it and keep the peace.

It was important to understand and acknowledge that every race, culture, affiliation, and such spoke their own language and had customs only familiar to their group. However, cool speaks cool, money speaks money, Army speaks Army, street speaks street, Russians speak Russian, etc. Balancing out security teams was the key to addressing that. I had a good mix of security, representing various groups of people with different backgrounds. That way, the teams were able to accommodate the many venues we served and had common ground with the patrons who would frequent our spots.

If there were too many street cats, then there would be problems, too many military guys, then there would be problems. Too many Uces, then there were problems. For instance, if it was all Army dudes working security together and a situation with some street dudes occurred, then there might be a breakdown in communication. The Army guys might overreact to the street cats just being the way street cats were. If it was just the Uces and a group of soldiers who were out for a night on the town and began doing the kind of dumb shit soldiers do, then the Uces might take it as a sign of disrespect or something. Soldiers spoke soldier, street cats spoke street, and Uces usually got along with mostly everyone and could speak to the Samoan patrons. This was very important because it only took one unruly Samoan patron to wreak havoc at a spot.

It was especially important to be in good standing with the local municipalities, police, first responders, and the community. Being in the military and working in law enforcement was a big help with that. It allowed me to meet other law enforcement officers either during a call, training or on an agency assist. That gave me some leniency with the responding officers anytime a call came out for them to respond to an incident at any one of our spots. We even utilized the local police to work security for our venues, either in uniform or out. They loved the extra money going into their pockets as well. Everyone wanted to eat, legally or illegally. CW5 helped out, too. He was quite well connected through various means and could sway officials to see things from a certain perspective, if need be, negatively or positively.

Preschool was a master of the streets and community relations, and everybody loved him. I loved him. He was an extremely likable guy with charisma and a way of speaking to others that was relatable regardless of who they were. Being half Samoan and half Tongan, he got along with both sides of warring factions. Samoans and Tongans were always at odds with one another for some cultural reason, but not Preschool. Since he grew up in Hawaii, the islanders have loved him. He represented both flags, red and blue, so he got along with both sides on the streets. He was probably one of a few people who could wear a blue flag in an all-red neighborhood and not get shot over it.

In most instances, red, blue, Samoan, Tongan, Hawaiian, black, white, whatever—they answered up to him anyway. He was in charge and had earned every one of his stripes. Needless to say, he was a crucial component in handling all the street stuff. I needed him to walk a more diplomatic line, though, which was going to be easier said than done. He had his way of doing things that had been working for him for his entire life, for the most part, anyway. Since he was still on probation, he could've been sent back to prison at any time if he had been caught in violation. I needed him out and free, and so did our business. Plus, he was my friend, and I didn't want to see him go away.

Trying to get him to see that was like trying to get a blind man to see the safest way to walk across the freeway. In that case, maybe it was more like trying to get the blind man to see that the bridge he often traveled had been washed away. I was pretty sure he was suffering from post-traumatic syndrome (PTSD) from all those years incarcerated. It wasn't like I was judging him for it or anything. Shit, I had my own PTSD issues to deal with. I just wish he would've chilled more instead of trying to start World War Three with the Mexicans and then the Russians. Man, I wondered if he was even getting laid.

CHAPTER EIGHTEEN
FEDS

REYES:

It landed on my lap to deal with the Russians in order to help with the Preschool cleanup. Yet another mess he had created. All because he was dead set on doing things his own way and not dictating those under him to do the necessary things. See, I'm not really saying he was right or wrong about how he handled it. All I'm saying was he shouldn't have been the guy out front taking the heat. He had graduated from foot soldier to leader but didn't realize it. So, it was up to me to work my diplomatic approach to get everything on good terms with them.

I had been friends with some of the Ukrainian community for a few years, as they were some of the first people who took me in when I got out to Washington. One family, in particular, treated me like one of their own because I helped their son get out of street life. Setting him down a better path for his future and affording him the opportunity to have a family of his own. I was even the best man at his wedding and there for the birth of his firstborn. He was like a brother to me, even to this day. Whenever I go over to the house, it's Uncle Tone to the kids.

He was always busting my balls about all the "meetings" I would have to run off to. He'd say, "Ya, sure, another meeting. This guy is always running off to some meeting," and then we'd both look at each other and laugh. He was streetwise and had an idea of what I was getting involved with but never said anything about it. He knew I respected him and loved him too much to involve him in anything that would cause him any problems. Although he wasn't directly connected to any of the Russians I now had to deal with, by default of the close-knit Ukrainian community, I was at least aware of them, and they were aware of me. Plus, having spent time with him and his family, I gained valuable insight into how Ukrainians and Russians thought.

As far as I was concerned, everything had been going smoothly since the time Preschool and I started working together. He helped clean up that shit-hole bar, got guys to work, and gained new business. Everything was moving like clockwork with all the spots we had, and the problems that came with the business were manageable. It was so much that Preschool and I had enough time to go to a bunch of parties I was privy to. Even a Halloween party hosted at none other than that "Yuppy 21" club. It was a nice club in south Seattle owned by the Russians, and everyone knew it. The Latins loved to party at that spot, and those were my people by birth, so I was always familiar with their events. We had a great time, and Preschool even got into the festivities wearing a costume. Which kind of threw me off guard because he was this giant Samoan fresh out of prison. I wasn't expecting it at all, but there he came with his girl, dressed up as Julius Caesar and Cleopatra with his henchmen dressed up as Roman soldiers. The shit was dope, and I think they even won the costume contest. I remember walking from the parking lot to the club, and all these different Uces working security knew him and gave much respect to him. Preschool didn't waste any time telling them about our security business either.

Yep, things that first year going into the following summer had been nothing but forward progress for us. This afforded me the opportunity to constantly host after-parties at my house. This eventually led to throwing the biggest Latin indoor venue at the time, and I don't think anyone has done one bigger since. I had the hottest Latin DJ around, a Puerto Rican rapper with a big following who had just got out of the joint. There were also these Puerto Ricans from the Army on active duty who performed and were a big deal with the local crowd. We hit the streets old school doing a gorilla marketing campaign passing out fliers. I had everyone passing out fliers—shit, I had thirty thousand of them printed up and was dead set on having them all passed out. Over twelve hundred people came out that night, making it a hit. Even the Uces loved it.

In fact, Preschool enjoyed it a little too much. He was so hammered and feeling the vibe that he and Juney had attached themselves to the general manager (GM) and started taking over the place. It got to the point that when the GM slipped away from the pair of Samoans, he came over to me. He asked me to do something because he couldn't have these guys running his club. He was terrified of them. I just laughed and told him I would talk to them. I told Preschool, and we laughed even more about it. I loved seeing my Uce having so much fun and getting his fill of things to come.

It was briefly after this concert that things began to get bumpy. For starters, the GM informed me that the owner had to close the club and that the Latin concert was the last night the club would be open. We had that place overcapacity and would have every weekend after that. Damn, if I had only known it was a one-time shot, we would've done things differently. See, we gave away about half of the door. This means we didn't charge at least four hundred people the twenty-dollar cover charge. That's eight grand if you do the math. Plus, we didn't even ask for any kickback from the bar money that night. Eighteen percent of the bar sales of twelve hundred people that night would've been about another ten grand for us. A total of eighteen thousand dollars was lost because they didn't tell me what was up. Even if we only charged fifteen dollars, the people still would've paid it. We sold ourselves short just to get the night up and going so that we would, in turn, have the money coming in on a weekly basis. I would've been happy making ten grand a weekend from that spot. Fifty-two weekends a year, and that would've been five hundred thousand dollars of legitimate money for the business. To their credit, both the GM and owner tried making it up to us by giving us some other spots they owned and managed, but they were just not as profitable.

Anyways there I was with my dick in my hand, thinking about all the legitimate money we could've made, and Preschool was thinking about all the other money he could've made. Instead of focusing on how we were going to bounce back, Preschool got agitated. He never took anything out on me, but he got short with the guys. I think that was what put him over the top, causing him to handle the Russian messenger the way he did. Losing that club was costly for him in more ways than one. None of it was in his control anyway, which was probably an even harder pill for him to swallow. The problem was he couldn't just sit back and enjoy the ride because he wanted to be in the driver's seat. He needed to be in control.

Sometimes you have to be the passenger, and sometimes you have to be the driver. This is hard to do, especially if you are used to only being in the driver's seat and making things happen. In the Army, it's not uncommon for officers to fight among themselves or with NCOs or NCOs fighting among themselves for this very same reason. So much so that it is a popular saying in the Army for someone to say, "Stay in your lane." Which simply meant mind your own damn business and focus on what you need to do because I'm in charge of this and have it under control.

Preschool was driving in everyone's lane. I wasn't even mad at him. I loved that dude and appreciated him. I decided to just be cool about it and let him do his thing. I figured later, he would cool his jets, come to his senses, and trust that I had my end of things under control. Eventually, we would come to an understanding between the two of us, but not before some turbulent times.

Now, before I tell you about this thing with the Russians, I have to take you back about a year. Remember that CW5 and the intelligence gathering mission they presented to me? Turns out that not only was the nightlife stuff a good inroad, but I also needed to become comfortable with the world of illicit drugs. CW5's simplistic logic was that the drug market leads to people doing illegal things, and people doing illegal things lead to those who would want to undermine the government and national security, and those who would want to undermine the government and national security lead to terrorists.

It was CW5's opinion that getting in with the Native Americans would provide the exact access to the drug market that he wanted. It was also his opinion that the Native Americans were less organized and sloppier than the rest of the other organized crime syndicates and street gangs. It was because the Native Americans were too comfortable for their own good.

Native Americans have their own governments and land, so they get to operate a lot differently than everyone else. They are a country within a country regulated by the Bureau of Indian Affairs, which falls under the Department of the Interior. Within that bureaucratic nightmare, all the federally recognized tribes get to self-govern as they should. Keep in mind that there are five hundred and seventy-four federally recognized tribes in the United States. As far as tribal governments go, some are well structured, operate quite efficiently, and thrive, while others are not. Anyone on tribal land is subject to tribal law enforcement and technically federal jurisdiction. Some tribes have better relations with state, county, and local law enforcement, but some do not. Outside of state and local jurisdiction, there is only tribal and federal jurisdiction on the reservations. The feds usually aren't too involved with tribal law enforcement issues because they're not invited in, and most of the federal law enforcement agencies don't even care about or are aware of things surrounding the reservations. This makes most reservations a no man's land with a small police force and a large area of land to cover.

The Puyallup tribe is unique in that, however, because they are the most urbanized reservation in the United States. Their reservation flows seamlessly with the cities of Tacoma, Federal Way, Puyallup, Milton, and Fife. To put this into perspective, the populations of each city at that time were Tacoma two hundred thousand, Federal Way ninety-thousand,

Puyallup forty-thousand, Milton six thousand, Fife five thousand, and the Tribe thirty-five hundred. Half the time, you didn't even know you were on tribal land because you would think you were in one of those cities. The law enforcement jurisdiction issues are a delicate balance between the tribal government and the state, counties, and other city governments. The reservation also extends into two counties: Pierce and King counties. During that time, many tribal members hemmed up by the local law enforcement agencies could request tribal law enforcement if they were on reservation land. In addition, they could have their charges and case moved to tribal court as well as being housed in tribal jail if arrested. The tribal jail at that time was a converted mobile home. Things are a little different now, but still the same in many ways. All of that is why the Native American syndicates were the easiest ones to infiltrate because they were too sloppy. They didn't have much to worry about other than a slap on the hand and funny stories to tell about how dumb someone was and then right back to their criminal mischief.

CW5's plan was for me to use my party lifestyle to find someone who would bring me into the Native American fold. From there, we would see where it took us and move accordingly with the intel gained. This actually came to be through one of my roommates who hooked up with this white girl who had kids with one of the tribal members. She was in her early twenties, a fun party girl, and easy enough to get along with, too. Plus, it turned out that she was loyal as fuck and would put it all on the line for any of her friends. This was his operation, and that was what he believed and wanted me to pursue. My job was just to follow his orders and pursue any lead he thought viable.

One day, we were hanging out at the Red Robbins. I told her she needed to hook me up with some of her friends—the crazier, the better. This she did, and plenty of them, too. This part of the assignment I didn't mind at all. Young hot, twenty-something-year-old party girls down to fuck. This is how I met Tiffany, who was a Puyallup Tribal member so deep in over her head in the street and a loosely organized Native American crime family. Through them, CW5 and I would be led to the Nigerian doctor supplying the local area with pills. We didn't care about the pills or any of the criminal activity, but we wanted this doctor and his Nigerian contacts. Why Nigeria, you might ask? That country produces, supports, and funds terrorism across the globe. It was precisely what CW5 was looking for.

Okay, back to this situation with the Russians. Having a war with them was not good for anyone or any of the things we had going on. From CW5's perspective, going to war with them would cause them to be even more cautious and make it harder for us to collect intel on them. They were already a sophisticated group to begin with. It wasn't good for Preschool because it messed with his money and street business. A war with the Russians would've most certainly brought in the feds in full force, as this type of thing is what they sit around and wait for to happen. They can't wait to get their hands on someone committing a murder or violent enough crime so they can flip them using the full weight of the law. It wasn't good for our promotion and security business either.

As far as I was concerned, I needed to quash it as fast as possible. It wasn't good from CW5's perspective either because it would make it even harder to collect intel on them as they were already a sophisticated group to begin with, as I said. He told me the feds were already interested in Preschool's activity in the streets, and this war would make it so even he couldn't help. He assured me that if I could get Preschool and the Russians to make peace before war started, then he could get the feds to become interested in someone else, hoping they would lose interest in Preschool altogether, leaving him to the local authorities to deal with.

Chapter Nineteen
The Russians

Reyes:

I knew a guy who knew a guy I could talk to about straightening out the situation with the kid Preschool had roughed up. My first two security contracts were for the hole-in-the-wall bar and for this gypsy securing his private residence. As it turned out, the gypsy, Milo, the car guy, was involved in a criminal enterprise working with the Russians. Milo was a gypsy from Romania who had gotten into a little hot water with some of them and needed private security. One day, shortly after starting the security company, I was checking out some cars at the auction when I bumped into him again. He asked me what I had been up to, and when I mentioned that I just started my own security company, he smiled. Then he asked me if I did any private security contracts for people's houses and stuff like that. I told him it was something I could do. He then told me he needed someone to do security for his house and watch over his wife and kid when he wasn't home. I told him I could do it, and that's how I learned about dealing with gypsies. Big mistake.

One of their biggest hustles is to drive around in their new SUVs and approach people in a parking lot, offering to sell them some jewelry because they ran out of money while vacationing and needed to get gas in order to get back home. Sometimes, they would stake out a gas station, pulling the same scam over and over. The jewelry was fake, but because they were riding around in a new SUV and dressed nicely, they created the illusion of having the kind of money to afford fancy jewelry. Most people are kind-hearted enough and figured these guys were just down on their luck during the worst possible time while on vacation with their family. Oh, ya, there was no shame in their game. That scam was a family affair; husband, wife, kids, and even grandma were all in on it and riding around together. They probably cleared a few thousand a day from that scam.

They were also big on the stolen car game. They ran that scam in conjunction with the Russians who chopped the stolen cars. The Russians and the gypsies also had numerous used car lots all over the Pacific Northwest. On a few occasions, I even helped move some of Milo's vehicles. I would drive a car from one of the lots in Tacoma all the way down to Portland. I'd drop that car off and pick up another car for my return trip back to Tacoma. I did that a few times; the money was good, but I did have an idea of what was taking place, and that never sat well with me. Honestly, I had no business messing around with the stolen car game. It wasn't about the money because even though it was quick, easy cash, it wasn't the kind of money a guy like me should've been risking jail time for. It came down to an adrenaline rush for me walking on the edge. So, all in all, I only did it a few times before deciding no longer to get involved with that hustle.

As it turned out, one time, when Milo had me meet him at one of the dealerships, I knew the owner, Alexus, who greeted me warmly upon my arrival. That caught Milo off guard, and he even seemed concerned that I knew some of the people he was dealing with, causing him to ask me, "So how do you know Alexus?"

"I know lots of people all over." I knew that wasn't the answer Milo was looking for, but my business was my business, and who I knew and how I knew them was none of anyone else's business. That was a particular characteristic of mine going back to my childhood. In fact, I was always so secretive about my affairs that even my older brother had deemed me cagey. Telling people that I was the sort of person who would never give any real answers to anything so as to give anyone insight into whatever it was that I was doing. That was probably one thing that had served me well: I always minded my own business and kept my mouth shut on anything that didn't concern me.

Maybe that was why the gangster types always seemed to warm up to me; they could tell I was the sort of person to keep my mouth shut. Since gangsters are people too and have families, they don't like their business out there for everyone else to know. The real gangsters, not the street thugs, wannabe gangsters who just want to be noticed and talked about. The real gangsters liked their anonymity. To move in silence whenever they could. Most of the ones I knew had jobs, usually ones where they owned their own business or worked for a relative. Most of them were normal people and didn't carry themselves in a way that said gangster. They were active in their community, went to church, and loved holidays and family get-togethers.

Like the Uces, only a handful liked to party at the clubs. Usually, the younger ones and those who were habitual bachelors would hit the nightlife scene for fun. Let's face it: they always had a handle on the nightlife scene from a financial perspective but not as an acceptable recreation. I think it is mostly because of the conflict with family and community values that nightlife activities can impose. The majority of my interactions with the Russian/Ukrainian gangsters were in private settings, and this is how I knew Alexus. I met him at a Christmas party hosted by a mutual friend. We hit it off from jump like two peas in a pod. He was a cool cat, dressed slickly but not overdoing it.

He said to me, "Tone, if only we had met when we were younger, the trouble we could've gotten into together." We both laughed in agreement. This was how I met a lot of them, by breaking bread with them. At that time, I wasn't about the life they respected, and yet I was still able to form friendships with them.

Alexus was a "Vor," which, for the Russian mafia, meant a "made" man like in the Italian mafia. He was a frontman for one of the dealerships and also owned a limo service and construction company. He had a beautiful house on American Lake just off Gravelly Lake Drive. This same house would later become a thorn of his own making for Alexus. We would spend summers barbecuing, taking out the wave runners and pontoon boats. No criminal activities, just hanging out with friends and enjoying life the same way everyone else did. So, when I said I knew a guy who knew a guy I could talk to, the guy I knew was Alexus, and he knew a guy that I needed to go see.

He had me meet him at a restaurant called The Cliff House, where he introduced me to Pavel. We sat down and enjoyed a meal and some drinks. After dinner, we stepped outside onto the balcony to get some cigars and dessert. Pavel then said to me, "I understand you have a problem of sorts. Maybe I can be of assistance." I explained to him the situation about how the Russian kid and Preschool had a misunderstanding due to their language barriers and copious amounts of alcohol consumed, mostly by the Russian kid. Words were exchanged between them, and insults led to fists being thrown. I also let him know that Preschool and I would like to have a sit down with the powers to be in order to discuss what happened and make peace.

Pavel said he would invite us to a bathhouse they have in Seattle. He requested no extra men be brought and for us to leave the guns at home. I told him I didn't know if that would go over with Preschool, but I'd ask. When I told him this, Pavel just laughed, "It's a bathhouse; everyone will be naked except for their baby-making pistols if that's any consolation, but you can't miss this meeting. We expect you guys to come."

I relayed the message to Preschool that we had to meet with the Russians at the bathhouse in Seattle to discuss what happened with their messenger. We waited for the phone call that would tell us when the meeting would take place.

I got a phone call from Pavel telling me where and when for Preschool and me to meet with him for the sit-down. The meeting was set with another "Vor" named Algimantas, who was higher up on the food chain, like an equivalent of an underboss in the Italian mafia. He was Lithuanian, and his name in Lithuania meant "Wealth." He definitely lived up to his name as one of the top earners on the West Coast. Everyone called him "Mantis" because he was known for his savagery. The praying mantis is one of nature's most perfect predators. A ruthless hunter able to capture and kill prey much larger than themselves. He didn't party or make extravagant gestures. He was a family man, went to church, and helped with his community. Don't be fooled, though; Algimantas was a legit bonafide gangster of the likes of Al Capone. Guys like him should wear signs saying, "Don't fuck with me."

He was also an ex-Russian special forces soldier who served in the elite Spetsnaz during at least two Russian conflicts. One of them was in Afghanistan. He was like me, except a Ranger for the Russians. The Spetsnaz were a tough group, and I had nothing but respect for them. He grew up during the Cold War and was a product of the old Soviet Union. This was a man who had sat in the same room as Putin. Mantis was a master chess player in both the game and in real life.

Most people think chess is just a game. They are wrong. It's a strategy development tool. It originated around six hundred A.D. out of the Indian game Chaturanga. The game was taught to kings, generals, and their heirs, and it was not played by common folk. Today, only a small portion of people know how to play chess, even though billions of people have heard of it. There are only a few grandmasters in the world at any given time. Among those who play the game, continuing to sharpen their strategic mind, are academics, businessmen, military leaders, politicians, and, ironically, nerds and criminals. Preschool was known in prison for having one of the strongest chess games that beat out the best of the best. He has frequented games that are played for a hundred dollars a pop and made a good living on chess inside.

There are two versions of chess. "Speed chess," played primarily by criminals, and "Thinking man's chess," played by everyone else. "Thinking man's chess" is how most people perceive the game. Two opponents faced off, patiently thinking through each move as they assessed fifteen to twenty moves ahead with almost no concern on time. Time is a luxury most people never have and never will have, which is why "Speed chess" is favored by the criminal mind because there's no time in the streets. Learning to calculate the risk posed by threats and answer accordingly with a coherent strategy within seconds is an ability no street king should be without. Both versions have their benefits, which is why I prescribed playing them, both first learning from my grandfather.

Mantis served time in a Russian prison for some apparent war crimes and thus began his life of crime. In prison is where he received stars on his knees, which means, "I won't kneel before the authorities," solidifying his disgust for the Russian government. There was something to tattoos other than just trying to look cool or rebellious. There was a whole spoken language within the tattoos, which varied from culture to culture. If you know what to look for, oftentimes, a whole conversation is had with hardly a word spoken. Of the three reasons the Russians loved meeting at bathhouses, the display of tattoos had to be the most significant. Sure, they wanted to make sure no one was wearing a wire or armed, but there was something about telling every motherfucker in the room just who you were and what you were all about. I sure was glad Preschool had brought his best tattoos to the party. Even though Preschool and Mantis spoke different languages, they spoke the same code. The thing about tattoos was originally, you had to actually do something to earn the right to wear one. This was usually through some kind of feat that involved pain, suffering, or heroic or infamous deeds. Most people currently don't do a thing to earn the right to wear a tattoo. Each of us in that sauna had earned the right to wear our own ink.

When we got to the bathhouse, Pavel was there to greet us and bring us inside. We proceeded to change out of our clothes into bathrobes.

Afterward, we followed him to where we would meet Mantis to sit and discuss our future endeavors with the Russian mafia. As we were walking to go and meet Mantis, I remember thinking to myself, *Damn it, Preschool. I said nothing criminal, only the legit and gray areas,* but there we were with the Russian mafia, the fucking Russian mafia, and not for no Christmas fucking dinner. Man, I loved that dude. Not many people will ever earn my level of loyalty at this level.

Hanging up our robes, both parties sat down across from each other. Preschool and I are on one side, and Pavel and Mantis are on the other side. There's some small talk, but mostly eyeing up each other, trying to read the writing on each one's skin. There's not much to read on my skin aside from a seventy-fifth Ranger scroll, some skulls, and my PHOG tatt. Mantis spent a much longer time looking over Preschool's ink work. Both Pavel's and mine's artwork were equally unimpressive compared to the two giants in the room. However, mutual respect was gained by each. Mantis addressed all of us concerning a small problem he was having. He explained how they owned various real estate interests around the Tacoma area and how a few of their mini-mansions were being vandalized and occupied by squatters.

In a split second, my mind saw how to fix their problem and multiple ways to make money by fixing that one problem. "Speed chess" was paying off. I spoke up and said that we could help with that by offering our security services. We could be used to help remove the undesirables from the properties and keep them away for the foreseeable future. I also proposed that he give us any of the cleanup or restoration work. Then, for the best part, I convinced him to allow the two of us to host exclusive parties at the various unused locations, splitting profits. Their portion of the profits would actually cover the costs of all the security and related clean-up work we would do for them. Mantis smiled and said, "Good Ranger, ya very good."

As we were sitting there, an older man in his early fifties entered and was greeted warmly by both Mantis and Pavel. They introduced him as

Mr. Sergie. Apparently, he was a big deal. Just after that, Pavel told me that he needed to discuss something in private with me and asked that we be excused. With permission granted, we slid down to the bottom corner of the sauna just out of earshot. As Pavel began to speak to me, I could see Mr. Sergie, Mantis, and Preschool begin to have a similar conversation about possibly the same thing or something completely different. Preschool and I would never know as both he and I knew and abided by the "If it ain't said to you, it ain't meant for you" code. Out of mutual respect, we wouldn't even ask each other about things that didn't concern us.

Pavel started running by me with these hypothetical questions: if someone was going to smuggle drugs and stuff onto and off of Fort Lewis, how would they do it? He was laughing and jokingly bringing his questions across, but I knew he was serious. For some reason, I thought, "fuck it, why not," and told him how I would do it if I was him. It was my opinion that there was little to no monitoring of American Lake because it was part of four jurisdictions: the City of Lakewood, Pierce County Sheriff's Department, Washington State, and Fort Lewis. At the time, none of them coordinated with anything very well. There were private citizens owning homes, beginning within the five hundred thousand dollars for the smaller ones and moving to multi-million-dollar ones. None of them had criminal drug smuggling as a chief concern. The opportunities were almost as endless as the imagination. Yo, what the fuck was wrong with me?

Preschool:

"So Valdim tells me you are a good guy," Sergie said. "It's why I don't retaliate for what you did to his nephew. Laddy is one of my most trusted brothers. I've known him since we were children. So, I want you to know I don't forget what you did easily. His nephew is a temperamental man, so I can understand how things got hostile during his visit. I'm going to propose something to you that maybe can bring us some peace instead of trouble. Suppose you can do this for me. I'll try not to think of the insult and maybe forget it altogether, huh? Deal?"

"Deal."

Laddy is Valdim Valsilchenko. A Ukrainian ex-con I knew from Walla Walla. You would never think this guy belonged to the Russian mob, but he was known out on the streets as a Russian mobster. I mean, this guy used to play soccer with the border brother Mexicans upstate. Not that that's what disqualifies him from being a mobster, but I could never picture it. He ran with the white boys. He was always in the library with me, trying to perfect his English and talking to this Jewish banker. We became fast friends after frequenting the library so much together that he opened up to conversations about stocks and bonds. It seemed that he was well-versed in stock trades and all. He studied for his SIE and Series 7 to become a stockbroker in the real world. He got jammed up before he could get his brokerage license. It didn't stop him from appearing to know everything there was about the markets, though. He was smart. He was sharp. He told me about the pump-and-dump schemes that the Russians made millions off. He taught me stock market stuff that you don't get in a SIE or Series 7 book. Before he left prison, he came to see me and gave me his number. He said, "If you ever want to get into day trading. I'll teach you how to make money quickly. Not like those bullshit drugs you USOS are into." I never took him up on that, but I always kept that number. I'm glad I did.

"Okay, good. You know we survive in this business because of our mutual agreements and cooperation with each other. You know, if the feds take us down, they will take you down the same way. And yet they do far worse and grave criminal trespasses than we do. Anyhow, you have one chance to get this precious piece back to me. I'm saying this 'one' chance not only because failure should not be an option but because I want to remind you that we have a slim chance of getting the guy who has it. He is in the middle of an immigration battle and may get deported. So, you see, the matter is urgent and requires absolute professionalism. Another thing, the feds are trying to get this guy to give up all his friends in the U.S. for a stay in the U.S. How crazy this country you live in. You will have to get this from the guy to whom I give you the information before something happens to him, so I'd suggest you do it as soon as possible. Understood?"

"Yes, sir. I'll have it done immediately."

"Okay, good. I'm counting on you to make this happen. Then maybe we will talk about more things down the road, ah … Mr.?"

"Preschool."

"Preschool?" he says with a mischievous smile. "You mean, ah, like an elementary preschool?"

"Yeah, I know. Long story."

"Well, humor me. I have time."

I tell him the story. "So, when I was in prison, they had an older USO they called Old School. He was an elder who came from the islands and didn't speak good English. He was what they called a FOB (fresh off the boat). Since in prison people called you by your last name, he'd attempt to call me all the time and say Preschool, which everyone would then mock and call me by. I hate that name, but it stuck with me. Only friends from prison call me that. People on the streets call me Charlie."

"I like Preschool better. I'll call you Preschool. Okay?" Mr. Sergie says.

"Okay, Mr. Sergie."

Mr. Sergie was a leader of one of the strongest Bratva groups, or Russian organized crime syndicates established in the U.S. He was on the FBI's top ten list of people to harass and is sought out for his brains in building a multi-billion-dollar operation which is sourced as from fishing. But it's more like poaching and arms dealing. He was only rumored to be involved in human trafficking and cars, but we'll get to that a little later. This guy is the guy. If anyone is to blame for the car rackets in Tacoma and all around Washington State for reaching the heights it has, it's this friggin' guy. The man behind the plans.

The Russians running a real estate management company that was under fire by break-ins and vandals fell into things perfectly. They were looking for a security company they could trust to handle the situation cheaply. Ironically, the Russians don't trust anyone, but they gave us Uces a chance to prove our security business worthy. But we weren't cheap. Not by a long shot. We did manage to work it out to where everyone was happy. We even decided to turn these mini-mansions they owned into house party locations. The house party business was a great success until the local neighborhood gangs started getting crazy. Tone has somewhat mastered the house party business because he turned his mini-mansion into a successful hangout after the clubs closed. Tone was charging people to come over and hang out and party till the sun came up. It was lit. He had more half-naked women walking around than the strip clubs. Heck, he had tricks showing up in full force to spend money on these women. The same women we used to promote our clubs were now promoting Tone's house, half-naked. Tone's house was known as the after-hours.

I leave the meeting with the Russian and call one of the only people I know who can help me pull this off. A guy that had my back like a parachute strap. It didn't matter how insane of a plan I had, I knew if there was anyone I could count on, it was the leader for my one time rival gang, who now turned bestie. A rival turned loyalist. Whiskers.

"Uce. We have to do something that puts us in the line of fire. Right now, you're the only guy I can trust. Let me know?"

Whiskers responds, "Nigga. I'm with you, Uce. You ain't even gotta ask."

"Good. I know I can count on you."

"What's the plan?"

"We gotta hit this lick. There's a particular piece of jewelry we're after. Gather up some of your men that you can trust. I want guys that know what they are doing. This has to be executed perfectly."

"I trust all my guys, Uce. Otherwise, they wouldn't be around me if I didn't. Everyone I got is willing to take bullets in a hail storm for me. Just make sure the plans are solid."

"Oh, don't trip. Don't I always come through?" I laughed.

The truth is the plans I've come up with haven't always been solid. It's my fault. I haven't been able to concentrate lately. I acted rashly on a lot of plans that needed to be improvised, and still, it worked out in our favor. Luckily. But I have to take this one seriously. This is not something we can try to wing at the last minute and hope to pull off successfully on the fly. I was going to have to take my time and do my homework on this one. And if anyone was good at safety-proofing my hatched plans, it was Whiskers. We've spent many nights in cars surveillancing a place, waiting on someone we were targeting, or just doing recon. We needed to catch up anyway. What better way than spending a night in the car doing just that?

Whiskers had mentioned that I should get Cowboy on the mark. Cowboy had a rare ability to track and find people that didn't want to be found. He found and tracked the mayor's daughters, who were declared missing persons years ago. This is how the mayor ended up falling into the debt of the USOS. Cowboy was my uce that got into a car crash and woke up with a southern drawl. He spoke like he was raised on Yellowstone Mountain. Even when he spoke Samoan, it came out with a Western cowboy dialect. Hence, the name Cowboy was given to him. Not only did he wake up with a southern drawl. He woke up with a high I.Q. for weapons and tactical applications. Like he was a Texas Ranger in another life or something. This was also stirring a commotion within the ranks because Uces were starting to fear that he was a lawman in the past and might revert to being one someday soon. I was never afraid of

Cowboy turning on us. One thing that car accident never changed was his unwavering loyalty and his appetite for the kind of work we did.

The Russians are just referred to as the Russians, but they are not all Russians, which is sort of racially prejudiced. The one that me and Tone teamed up with is a Ukrainian who is big on diplomacy but not keen on working with foreigners. He is only inclined to deal with us because one of his top men is a close friend of mine from inside prison. The close friend, Vladim, or "Laddy," vouched for me as a stand-up guy who could be used to further the Russian mob's mainstay presence in other parts of Washington instead of just Bellevue, making me a temporary asset.

History of the main Russian Sergei is that he is known as the Seafood King, and he was a major player in the fish exports to the U.S. He was arrested in Russia and imprisoned by Russian officials hoping to extort him out of his hundreds of millions of dollars, to which Obama and Madam Secretary Clinton went out on a limb to have him released and extradited back to the United States. His dossier shows that he is a power player in the automotive business and is assumed to be responsible for the high car thefts throughout the United States and that he is involved in everything from stock pump and dumps to murders and extortions.

He requests that the USOS do security at a club in Seattle called the Contrast Lounge. He is also interested in having me and the USOS take down scores and high-stakes jobs if they successfully pull off the jewelry heist he has set up for a rare medallion. He requests professionals for this line of work, to which I promise to deliver nothing but my best and reassure him that I'll have my best men and have them on the first job already.

After meeting with the Russians and after intense talks, the Russians also hired the USOS to secure their property management business. They tell me they own a few mini-mansions in the Tacoma area that have been vandalized and occupied by squatters. Tone came up with the idea to start mansion parties at these places, which would bring them more revenue.

Of course, all this is contingent on the USOS retrieving the sentimental medallion to the head of the Russian mafia first.

I asked, "I don't mean no disrespect, but wouldn't it be easier to just buy the jewelry back?" *With all the money the Russians have.* I was told that the owner of the jewelry store was fond of this piece of jewelry and wouldn't let it go because it was a rare national treasure piece.

Lakewood, Washington:

At 5:15 p.m. of August 2006, four men wearing body armor stormed into the Bank of America branch in South Tacoma Way with pistols and assault rifles blazing. The four brainless turds who were waving their pistols and rifles around were guys we knew. They had talked about the trench coat bandits a lot prior to that week of the robbery. The trench coat bandits, who were also some brainless turds, robbed the bank before and made off with $3.5 million in cash. They didn't get to spend this money because one of the bandits got pulled over with two million in his car in cash. Yeah, his partner got busted for trying to buy a $400k dollar property in the same week. Just brainless shit. The four turds, along with two Canadians, came up with the plan to rob the bank. I mean, if two guys can do it, surely four guys with two foreign aid cheerleaders can pull this off as well, right? That is the worst criminal logic ever. The four who robbed the bank were not as lucky as the trench coat bandits. They didn't get that much and didn't make it more than a few days before they were all picked up. An innocent bystander outside the bank had watched them go into the bank with guns drawn and come out with duffel bags. Assuming it's a robbery, he took down the license plates of the car, which the feds found linked to someone on Ft. Lewis base. After getting the military to forgo the search warrant rights, they searched the residence of the soldier and found bank money still in the bank bands along with the car, masks, and all. It turned out the Canadian who was cheering them on was also the one who tipped off the feds, wanting to get the five grand in reward money. Ain't that about a bitch. Their cut was ten grand each for their participation. The Ft. Lewis soldiers didn't know that all along. The Canadians didn't have faith that they would share the stolen loot and decided to make some on their own by turning the four in. *shakes my head*

Even worse, the feds managed to flip one of the four brainless turds and discover he worked for Reyes as a bouncer for one of the clubs he says Preschool runs. The feds say, "Are you sure you work for Reyes because we were under the impression that Preschool owns the security company," and that was all she wrote. They learned that Reyes was also an MP for many years and had recruited a lot of ex-combat and active-duty veterans to his security team. The other half of his security company is made up of ex-felons recruited by Preschool. This was all the excuse the feds needed for forming a federal joint task force designed to take down the USOS in Operation Pineapple Express. Operation Pineapple Express, headed up by Homeland Security Officer George Tauluga, ATF agent Joe Matagi, and United States Attorney Carmelita "Carm" Sanchez, was in full swing thanks to a brainless turd.

cHapter Twenty
THe Mexicans

Reyes:

Coming from a multi-racial background, I found myself always walking a fine line between race, cultural, and social diversity and a system of hierarchies. It stemmed from my background and the diversity of my heritage. My Puerto Rican ancestry was one of acceptance and having genuine pride in who we were as a people. For the most part, we Puerto Ricans get along with everyone so long as we know our place, and that place changes often. This is something I learned early on and continued to learn throughout life. Embracing one's culture and having a genuine respect for them as a people has been an astronomical part of developing and maintaining my relationships with others. This is especially true when dealing with Latinos or Native Americans, as I like to think of them all. That is because I see no major difference, as we are all one and the same. The minor differences do not take away from our sharing of one main culture, which has many subcultures.

It seems as if almost everything in life has a hierarchy of sorts, and it is no different in the world of Latinos. They share many commonalities, from language, culture, and history to the fact that they all speak Spanish and eat rice and beans. The Americas, North, South, and Central, are home to the original peoples, the indigenous Native Americans. All of them were colonized by the Europeans, who beat everyone else to colonize the world. So, you don't have to love your friendly neighborhood colonizer, but let's give credit where credit is due. If they had shared a smaller continent, maybe the Native Americans would've been the ones colonizing the world.

Europe, the second smallest continent, is home to fifty countries. All of them started out as tribes before becoming their own independent countries after thousands of years and countless wars. By contrast, North America is made up of four countries: the United States of America, Canada, Mexico, and Greenland. Then there are seven countries in Central America and twelve in South America. There are also over twenty countries spread throughout the Caribbean. All of these were occupied by, well, you guessed it, Native Americans. What do you call people from Europe? Europeans. What do you call people from Africa? Africans. So why is it so hard for anyone to wrap their brain around calling people from any of the Americas American? More specifically, Native Americans have ancestral roots in the Americas.

The confusion comes from being colonized by Europeans, who coincidentally, also colonized themselves. Yes, Europeans colonized Europeans, beginning with the Greeks and Romans. However, there was that one fellow, Genghis Khan, from Asia who spread plenty of his seed and culture into Europe. As well as the Moors and Egyptians from North Africa. In addition to Persians from the Middle East. For the most part, though, Europe was mostly divided up and conquered by Europeans.

What we have here in the Americas was the colonization of Native Americans by a handful of European countries. Most prominently being the Spanish, French, British, Dutch, and Portuguese. This is where the point of contention among the Latinos comes from: their primary European colonizer and which American continent they preside from. For instance, anyone in North America has an opinion they are superior to the rest of the Americas. This is why Mexicans have always seen themselves as higher up on the hierarchy and are not willing to refer to themselves as Latinos. Mexico is the only Spanish country that resides in North America proper. All the others are in Central America, South

America, or on an island. This alone had placed the Mexicans at the top of the Latin hierarchy until World War II.

What happened during the war to change this, you might ask? Well, the Nazis happened. The Germans and Nazis fleeing Europe at the end of the war fled primarily to Venezuela, Chile, Argentina, Brazil, and Colombia. Although they make up only a small portion of those populations, it didn't take long for their rich European bloodline to put them at the top of the hierarchy. Mexico opposed the Nazis and actually declared war on the Axis after the Nazis torpedoed and sank two of Mexico's oil tankers. Before that, Mexico was neutral, as the Germans had economic and business interests in Mexico. Of particular interest was Mexico's oil reserves. This could possibly be another point of contention concerning why Mexico refuses to be considered Latin so as not to be affiliated with the traitors and Nazi lovers of South America.

Once, I was joking around with a friend of mine from Colombia, telling her that her name was passed down to her by the Nazis who lived in Colombia, and she said to me that Nazis never lived in Colombia. I had to explain to her that Nazis had fled to South America after World War II, and she didn't believe me because she had never heard of that before. A few days later, she came to me and told me that I was right after having researched it for herself. She grew up in Colombia, never knowing its true history, but only the history they wanted them to learn as part of the indoctrination of the colonial powers that are still in place to this day.

It doesn't matter what the specific reasons are for how the Latino hierarchy came to be; after almost six hundred years in the making, it just is what it is. Mexico has positioned itself outside of this Latino culture, claiming to have its own unique one, separate from the rest of Latin America. As for the Latinos, Colombia is generally considered to be at the top, followed by Argentina, Venezuela, and Chile. At the bottom are Panama and the island nations, as they are considered to be niggers as a result of the slave trade and all the interbreeding that took place.

Urbanized Panamanians, Puerto Ricans, Cubans, and Dominicans in the United States will typically associate themselves with Black Americans and are considered black enough to use the word "nigga" without rebuke or consequence.

Of course, in any of the countries, the darker your skin and the more indigenous you are, the lower you are considered and treated as such. When you look at any of the countries in the Americas and most of the world, especially where they were colonized by the Europeans, the lighter the skin is, the higher up a person is in status. I guess white makes right. All of this stems from the colonial class structure consisting of Peninsular (Spaniards born in Spain), Creoles (born in New Spain to Spanish parents), Mestizos (born of Spanish and Native American Indian parents), Mulattoes (born to Spanish and African parents), Africans (free or enslaved) and Native American Indians. Picture a pyramid; at the bottom or the base, it is the largest representation of the structure, and at the top, it is the smallest, with everything else in between scaling according to its location in the pyramid. So, from the top down are Peninsular, Creoles, Mestizos, Mulattoes, Africans and Native American Indians. The lasting effects of that system are still seen and felt in every part of the Americas.

We Puerto Ricans have a false superiority over the Mexicans and the rest of the Latinos because we belong to the United States and are U.S. citizens by birth. It's kind of like when arguing what is the best football franchise. Bears fans just say eighty-five Bears, and anyone who knows football has no counterargument to that. Even though the Bears as a franchise are one of the most losing teams in the history of the sport, the eighty-five Bears were the most dominant team to ever take the field. So, it's the same way that even though we are an island of mostly "niggas" we are U.S. sovereignty which trumps any other argument. In other words, "My dad will beat up your dad." Coincidently, the only people who notice or care about this Latin hierarchy happen to be Latin, have to deal with

Latinos, or are just curious white people whose colonial ancestors created this nonsense in the first place. Like I said, most people don't know any of this and still refer to all Spanish-speaking people as Mexicans who speak Mexican. Can't really blame them as we basically call all white people white and all black people black, never mind where they come from or their heritages.

We Puerto Ricans come from a long line of savage and fierce warriors known as the Tainos. Frequently at war with the Caribs, their neighboring tribe. They were organized into small clans and called their island home, Boriken, which means "Land of the Valiant and Noble Lord." They thrived on their island for thousands of years before the Spaniards arrived. After the arrival of the Europeans, it was the beginning of the end for the Tainos as they were almost wiped out to extinction. A new race and culture emerged known as Puerto Ricans, a mix of all three races (Tiano, Spaniard, and African). Not just claiming one bloodline but laying claim to all three.

In the strictest sense, Boricua is a person from Puerto Rico by birth, being born on the island. While Boriqua means "of the island," not having been born there but a descendant being born elsewhere. Although, depending on who you ask and how they feel on a particular day, you might get a different answer, and the two spellings are often interchangeable. The truth is, at the end of the day, we are all Puertorriquena's.

My grandmother came from the mountains of Puerto Rico and definitely had more characteristics of having a purer Taino bloodline than my grandfather, who was born in Guaynabo, a suburb of San Juan. He was much taller and darker than my grandmother, who had traced his roots to the Canary Islands. He grew up in El Fanguito, which means "The Mudhole," and was one of the worst slums of San Juan. A letter sent to President Truman, written by William Z. Foster, stated, "These terrifying slums are primarily of American making. The worst of them, the social cancer, El Fanguito, has, with malignant vitality, been rapidly spreading its deadly poison far and wide during the past fifteen years. These vast slums are the inevitable result of the ruthless exploitation of Puerto Rico by the American sugar trust, aided by reactionary Washington politicians." It didn't matter that Mr. Foster was the National Chairman of the Communist Party, U.S.A. He spoke the truth.

My grandfather had grown up there and was a product of that slum. His escape was joining the U.S. Army and serving during World War II. Afterward, he played professional baseball for a short time before becoming a professional hustler on the streets. He lived that street life, becoming addicted to the lifestyle and all that came with it: gambling, alcoholism, drugs, and partying. He must've been good at what he did because he was able to maintain his lifestyle into his late seventies before dying of colon cancer. Unfortunately, I didn't get to see too much of him as he and my grandmother parted ways after having eight children together. She just couldn't deal with the street life, feeling it was no way for her to raise kids.

Being a people from an island, Puerto Ricans are good-natured, fun, warm, and loving souls. We are also extremely temperamental, hostile, and even devilish if we feel disrespected or violated in any way. I'm pretty sure all Puerto Ricans are bipolar schizophrenics suffering from attention-deficit/hyperactivity disorder (ADHD). This might be why we are considered to be good lovers because we are crazy as fuck, and everyone knows crazy people often have the best sex. Plus, it goes without saying that we inherited two things from our black ancestors, big butts and big dicks.

Island people have almost no sense of time. It's true; there's White people's time, which entails arriving earlier than the agreed-upon time. Then there is Asian people's time, which varies from punctual to late depending. Then, Black people's time is to arrive at least an hour after the agreed-upon time. Latin people's time is a random occurrence of almost never being anywhere on time, even after calling ahead to change the previously agreed upon time to a later time, to which they will still be, at a minimum, an hour late. The island people's time is to show up whenever and act as if they are right on time, even if it's a day or two later. Middle Eastern time is along the lines of if God wills it, they will be there.

The reason I'm taking the time to explain all of this and why it was relative to my situation is because I had dealt with it on a regular basis concerning club promotions, security, and then my business dealings with Preschool that spilled over into street politics. So now we have the Mexicans, which is what the majority of people in the United States refer to all Spanish-speaking people as. It's just not that simple as there is a Mexican and a Latino hierarchy. Depending on which organization they belong to and what particular street hustle they are pursuing could place them in a Mexican or Latino affiliation. It's similar to how people are labeled as belonging to the Russian mob even though they are of a different European descent. So, to simplify the complexities of our Mexican situation, I'm just going to refer to the main factions simply as the Mexicans, Colombians, El Salvadoreans, Cubans, and Puerto Ricans.

Mexicans refer to everything Mexican and sometimes include groups from Central America. El Salvadoreans encompass those from El Salvador and much of Central American affiliations. The Colombians were representative of most of South America. Cubans represented the greater part of the Caribbean affiliations. Puerto Ricans, under the Latin flag, were free to deal with the Blacks, Whites, Mexicans, and, of course, the Latinos. At the time, everything that was happening on much of the West Coast and Southwest fell under Mexican control and influence. The Midwest and East Coast were divided up mostly between the Mexicans and Puerto Ricans. Down South were the Cuban and Colombian areas of influence. El Salvadoreans were from the West Coast to the East Coast, plus down South. The Pacific Northwest was an open market.

Mexicans mostly dealt with Mexicans, Colombians, El Salvadoreans, and Whites. Colombians only dealt with Mexicans, Cubans, and Latinos.

Cubans dealt with Colombians, Latinos, and Blacks. El Salvadoreans mostly dealt with Mexicans, Latinos, and Whites. Puerto Ricans dealt with everyone. Of course, anyone could sit here and scrutinize the complexities, but then this would be a twelve-hundred-page book and just as clear as it is now. So why these five? Well, it has to do with three reasons: the drug trade, the drug trade, and the drug trade. Actually, it's the drug trade, control of the streets, and control of the prisons, but the drug trade was such a big part of it all. Everyone knows the Mexicans and Colombians were first in on supplying North America and most of the rest of the world with marijuana, then cocaine, and finally methamphetamines. Before that, the Mexicans also organized themselves through street gangs, biker gangs, and the Mexican mafia to control the streets and prison system in California. This quickly spread across the Southwest.

The Colombians controlled the product and money from afar, staying out of U.S. streets and the prison system. This is where the Cubans and Puerto Ricans came in, as they were already established in the U.S. in both the streets and prison systems, as well as the heroin drug trade. The El Salvadoreans in Los Angeles formed a group called MS-13 and came up through sheer willpower and violence on a scale that no one was ready for.

At the shit-hole bar, we mostly dealt with the Mexicans and Latinos who were "Rancheros," which refers to someone who works on a farm or a ranch. This shit-hole bar was basically a Spanish country western bar. This kind of bar setting attracted a lot of the Norteños and their affiliations of similar backgrounds. That was because the music that many Mexicans identify with was based on regional styles of music. As it happened, Tierra Caliente's music developed in the late twentieth century, and music Norteño developed in the late eighteen hundreds, having regional scenes in Mexico, Guatemala, El Salvador, Colombia, Chile, and the United States, which appealed greatly with Rancheros. That style of music also had strong roots in Michoacan, Mexico, which is important to understand in terms of what eventually happened. So, as for dealing with the Mexicans at that shit-hole bar, it was the Norteños, and at another bar, it was the Sureños. The Norteños are the street-level members of the Nuestra Familia, while the Sureños are affiliated with the Mexican mafia. Norteños (northerners) are prevalent in Northern California, while the Sureños (southerners) are in Southern California.

preschool:

So, to appease the situation with the Mexicans, they wanted us to move their dope. Not just through our rinky dinky club. But they wanted us to take it to the Pacific Islands. No problem. I was excited at the prospect of a new plug. One that possibly is consistent and has a direct reach back into the labs of the Michoacan mountains. Later on in the years, we would have traveled with these guys down to Mexico to visit their war-ravaged and torn state of Michoacan, Mexico. The place was a complete and utter disaster. A battleground. A war zone. The group we were working with was the El Caballero Los Templarios. The Knights Templars. This was a group that separated from the original La Familia Cartel that once controlled Michoacan single-handedly. The splinter of the cartel led to one side being of the savior types. The churchgoers with charity and goodwill in mind. This side got its name, the Knights Templars, because of it. The other side of the split and warring faction stayed true to the exploitation and pillaging of the village, which led to the creation of a group called the AutoDefensas by the village people. The village people were getting so tired of the abuse and violence brought on by La Familia that they banded together and targeted the cartel members for death. This anti-cartel group later morphed into becoming a power cartel group in itself, just like the Los Zetas did.

We would actually be recruited to join in the battle of the two split factions by our connection. We would be ordered to occupy Nueva Italia, Apatzingán, and the capital, Morelia before the tragic event occurred, which eventually split the USOS and this particular cartel. The USOS didn't believe in the wars down south. It wasn't their business. They were businessmen before they were gunmen. Not mercenaries. The Templars didn't understand that. They believed that because we were in cahoots with the drug trade, we should be providing support for them. But it doesn't work like that. We were like the United States in the Ukraine/Russia war. We could aid them but not directly take part in their battle for territory. What they didn't know was that we were being approached by other cartels to get in on the same market, and our loyalty caused us to deny exploring different options even though those other options were looking more promising in terms of supply and demand.

Chapter Twenty-One
Leadership

Reyes:

After getting everything sorted out with the Mexicans, Russians, and the streets, things seemed to finally be running smoothly and back on track. We were enjoying the prosperity of our labors, not only for ourselves, but everyone who was involved with us was eating well. I had originally told Preschool that I was cool dealing with anything legit or even in the gray, but I didn't want to get involved in any criminal activities. As time went on, even though he never directly asked me to get my hands dirty, his actions left me no choice but to start dealing more and more with street things. What else was I supposed to do? Preschool was my dude, and I had his back. That's the thing about loyalty; it always comes at a price, and I was more than willing to pay it on his behalf.

To my amazement and relief, after the club shooting, Preschool actually listened and decided to take some time off and lay low. He told me, "Hey, Uce, I'm going to be taking a little trip to lay low."

"Perfect, that will give me a chance to try and sort some things out with everything."

"Ya, we still need to get rid of a few things."

"Don't worry about it. I'll take care of everything. You just need to go lay low until some things blow over."

Before leaving on his trip, Preschool organized a quick sit down with me, the White Boy, Dog, and Whiskers. At the meeting, he told us he was going to be gone for a little while, lying low from the cops and taking care of some other obligations. To my surprise, he told them that whatever I needed, I could ask for from them and that they should also run things by me. Looking back on it, it is so laughable how naïve I was about what was going on around me. The writings were not only on the wall figuratively but were literally written on the flesh. I came to admire Preschool and his ability to recruit. Any headhunter or department responsible for recruitment is only worth its own ability to enlist others to their cause. Preschool was a master recruiter.

Preschool:

The White Boy in this story needs his own mention, which is why I'm going to tell it. So this white boy we're going to name H.A. came from prison. We met in prison and clicked. He was in for manslaughter, killing his best friend. That tells you a lot about a guy. I mean, anyone who kills his best friend should not be the likely candidate that you choose or trust for a friend. Period. Well, he came home and was in operation of a large-scale weed operation in Canada. They were receiving their pills and weed from Canada through helicopter drops. Yup. The stories are true. Anyway, one day, this guy's new bestie he met since being home decides he doesn't need this guy anymore and rips him off. He doesn't just rip H.A. off; he pretty much ends his drug career and life by sticking the bill and blame on him for why their Canadian connection is not going to get paid. The new bestie obviously didn't know about H.A.'s past with friends who betrayed him. So, he came to me. He called and asked if I could send my men out with him, that there would be a huge payout of about $200k at the stash house his old business partner was using. I sent Pistol Pete and Ray "Bonez" with him. Giving them the instruction that if it didn't check out, they should leave the white boy lying there for the stash house owners to find him.

But, surprise, things checked out. The boys called and said, "Hey, boss, it's stuck on the wall."

"What's stuck on the wall?" I asked.

They say, "The huge vault."

I send the second clean-up crew to get it and before you know it I was sitting hand counting $200k cash that night. Now, for the life of me, I could never figure out why they would name him H.A. I asked, "Is H.A. short for home alone?" I mean, he was an annoying obnoxious kid it seemed.

He laughed. "No."

No explanation given. Never asked again. That night, this kid's house got shot up. He went to the casino, and upon his return home, his dogs were barking like crazy. Stirring up the neighborhood. He had built a side door in his house that he could easily use to check on his dogs. He was raising rare breeds of mutts. So, when he walked out the sliding door, his wife followed suit. Immediately following that, a bunch of machine guns fired. His house got shot up by the bestie's new bestie, apparently. Whoever shot the house up wasn't just some flunkies. They were trained. H.A. and his wife escaped death, luckily. The funniest thing about this is that the next day, when we all met up, I ordered all the boys to be strapped. I wanted everyone on their toes and ready. I flew all the girls out to Mexico and Hawaii for vacation while we dealt with the situation. My boy Whiskers, my trusted right hand, was handing out pistols. He handed an uce a .40 cal, another one a .40 cal., and another one a .40 cal. All the way down till it came to the White Boy. Whiskers then handed him a .25 caliber pistol.

The White Boy kept bugging me that day for a private conversation. He kept saying we needed to talk. I was addressing my men. So, I was irritated at H.A., and I finally caved and told him to meet me at the side of the house to talk briefly. When we get to the side of the house, I ask, "WHAT?"

He holds up the .25 caliber and screams, "MY HOUSE GETS SHOT UP, AND HE GIVES ME A .25? Really? A .25!"

Bursting with tears and laughing, I'm like, "Look, I know it's probably an honest mistake. I'll find out what's going on."

The White Boy was screaming the racist card and swearing everything about USOSs being shitty human beings. I could only laugh and try to deny his accusations. Ughh. Crazy shit. But I couldn't help laughing even more.

The first thing I figured out about the shooters was that they were not some random young punk gangbangers. My suspicions were right. Something that Tone picked up and showed us. He said, *look at the way they sprayed the house … they were only shooting the floor lines. So, it's sort of like they had the first guy on this side who shot off the loud rounds to scare them into dropping to the floor. Then they sprayed the floor line, hoping to hit them all in the head. Good thing they were outside checking on the dogs. These dogs saved his life.*

I concur. But now I'm pissed. The Whiteboy at first thought that it was me behind the shooting. I had to reassure him that if it was me, I would have had him shot and left at the stash house the minute we discovered the loot. I kept a huge portion of the money because that's what people don't understand. My life ain't worth two hundred thousand dollars. I'm making tons more. Why the fuck would I trouble myself with this little ass money with a huge cost if I don't have to? Not all money is good money. There's funny money. Blood money. Drug money. Your money. My money. The list is endless. The value of each of these is different, but at the end of the day, it should end up all in the same place in the street. The USOS bank. It takes money to make money, which is just one part of the truth about money. It also takes money to move money, which, for some reason, no one seems to understand.

Reyes:

Whether or not it was Preschool's intention, he passed the reins over to me at that meeting. Not just the stuff dealing with the security and club business, but everything. He said that if any of the guys had an issue that needed to be handled, then they could run it by me. This could have been interpreted in more than one way, but everyone took it the same way as I did. I mean, when I heard him say it, I actually got nervous and was thinking, what the fuck? Now, I'm getting even deeper into crossing the line from out of the gray areas into the straight-up illegal ones. The three of them were lieutenants or captains under Preschool, and here I am, an associate or something like that being placed over them. I had no idea of how any of the inner workings of their family went as I had just been along for the ride for the legitimate business dealings.

Whiskers was Preschool's right-hand man and seemed to me to be more of a consigliere, while Dog was like an enforcer, and White Boy was in charge of running money operations. At that point in time, I honestly had no clue as to exactly what was what, and I only had an inclination of what I thought everything was. Preschool always spoke highly of those three to me, and I had grown fond of them, taking a particular liking to Dog. That was in part because early on, Preschool had put Dog with me on the security stuff, and since he was about ten years younger than me, I took him in under my wing, showing him everything on how to run the security stuff. Eventually, later on, Dog would become a member of legitimate business ventures, and I would serve as my right-hand man. Whiskers and White Boy were always doing street stuff, which I avoided, like the fat girls at the clubs trying to get my number. Still, I liked them both having love for them.

So, how Preschool had put it out there, and the fact that all three of them didn't seem to have any issues going along with it, made me wonder just how deep I was getting into this family. Of course, Preschool was the boss, and everyone followed his orders. So, just like none of the three of them questioned what was put out, neither did I. We all just went along with what we perceived to be the new orders and chain of command in the absence of the boss. I remember the last thing Preschool said to me,

"Okay, Uce, you got this. It's all on you now until I get back." Not long after that, he was gone and stayed away for a few weeks.

There, I was making the decisions for more than just the promotions and security business. I would get phone calls from the three of them asking me about one thing or another and how they should handle it. Or they would come to see me and talk face-to-face. Most of which had nothing to do with the business I was trying to build. I treated this leadership position the same way I had treated all my leadership positions in the military. I always took care of my men and had a genuine interest in their development and success, treating them as friends and family rather than subordinates. I think this is what resonated with the three of them, as they could tell I wasn't trying to be anyone or anything. I was just there on a temporary basis to help everything run smoothly.

PreSCHOOL:

Every time I land in Hawaii, the feds have something to say to me. I always complain, "Why don't you fakas have a flower lei and hula dancer waiting for me when I show up? That's no way to greet a guest." I told the federal agents Kamaka and Donahue that I'd be at the Halekulani Hotel, where I'd book a suite for a few weeks of partying. That they were invited to come watch me bang chicks and drool from the hallway. Haha. I know they were envious of the lifestyles we lived. They watched us run through the prettiest girls on the island while they went home to their fat Lani moo's cow of a wife at night. They hated me, and like I said, I have enough respect for some of them. But these young rookies harassing me like this, I give them hell. I tell them about themselves, and the truth is, they can't stand it.

I only got to enjoy my short-lived vacation from the boys for three weeks, wishing it was longer. The vacation motivated me to shoot for retirement next year. This life wears on you. By the time a lot of the big USOS went to prison, they were only alive long enough through the stresses of trial and ended up dead in a matter of years. It's like they just went to prison to make the concrete grave their final resting place.

When I returned home, the energy felt funny. It felt different. Like the boys were always talking about Tone this, Tone that. I said, "Shit, you report to Tone now?"

To which the boys responded, "Nah, Uce. But you told us he's in control when you're away. No?" The way they were on his nuts, though, I couldn't tell.

I got a phone call from Dog. "Dog. What up?"

"I just want you to know that the Ft. Lewis cats got jammed up."

"Yeah. I saw the news. How did the other fiestas go?"

"They were successful. The South Tacoma one really did well. We need to talk more in person. See you tonight."

"Okay, my Uce. I love you. Thank you."

"It wasn't really me. It was Tone that made things work."

"What the fuck do you mean?"

"Just like I said. Tone saw everything through. We'll talk."

There it was again. Tone. I didn't know what to make of it other than I know now that none of these guys are reliable enough to handle things adequately on their own when I'm gone. Relying on Tone is like calling a plumber with no football experience to coach the little league football team on the fly.

Reyes:

The things that needed to be handled I handled. I was not a street guy, but I knew enough about running operations to micromanage things on the streets. Besides, I knew some of the top street operators if I needed advice while Preschool was gone. My Russian contact actually said he'd take everything and cash us out for it. At that point, asking the guys what Preschool wanted to be done with the loot after the jobs was like asking a dog what its master feeds them. They don't know anything other than his commands to "sick 'em" or "sit." They were just loyal dogs that Preschool kept on a short leash to maintain his reputation for viciousness on the streets. I had to get that fence and make sure that they were giving us the prices I knew Preschool would be happy with. Speaking to some of the boys, though, made things seem off. I should have been suspicious of everything and questioned everything when it came to Preschool. Judging by the way things had been going lately, shit, I would never think to second guess my uce, but he had been fucking up. A lot.

Preschool:

"What part of lay low don't you get?" Tone asked.

"What are you talking about?" I brushed it off, justifying setting things up and having the jobs done by saying, "I have to keep my crew sharp."

"Sharp? You got the fucking businesses hot with all these stupid moves. I thought you were sharper than this. Sharp?"

"Tone, what the fuck do you know about the streets? What the fuck do you know about the other side of the business? I'm the only reason you stay ignorant and sheltered from the truth."

"Oh yeah? Well, I had to tie up loose ends and make sure that shit went smoothly, in case you haven't been told. I had to intervene to stash the guns and the loot from the jewelry store robberies. Yeah. Because your boy, you had plans on stashing the shit with? Well, just coincidentally, I got a tip from one of my law enforcement friends that they were on to him and looking to raid his house. You were busy getting pussy and massages on the beach while I was fixing things. You left all half-assed. How do you think these guys are going to respect you? You're a fall-down black-out drunk. You start all this stupid drama with the Russians. The Mexicans. Who the fuck knows who else because we got people shooting our club, and we don't even know who?"

"You done?" I asked.

"Yeah. I'm just worried about you, brother. I love you, and you are spiraling. I need you to get your head back on. Let's get this car gassed up and rolling at top speed, my dude. And again. Please keep me out of the illegal parts of the business. I don't want anything to do with it. I was told I would be just handling the club and everything legit. Up and up is what you guys said to me at the meeting to set things up".

"I know, Tone. I love you too, bro. I'ma get this thing beat. I got a lot on my plate. I have anxiety kicking my ass. It's almost like I have to stay drunk to avoid the pain and bullshit I have to deal with and battle daily. I'll keep you on the up and up. Foreal foreal"

"We're all going through battles, brother. One day at a time, Uce. That's all we can handle."

"Yeah, I know, bro. Thanks, Tone. Truly. I appreciate you stepping up."

"Hey, what's going on?" Whiskers asked. "I hate to break up your lover's quarrel, but there's a call from Vegas. It's Mando (as in mandatory)."

"What they say?" I asked.

"They want you and Tone to fly down there on asap. They need a sit down with you two. It sounded serious."

"FUCK. Fuck they want me for? I'm not part of this crazy shit. I'm just the club owner. This shit is ridiculous." Tone snapped. "I'll ride with you on this, brother, but give me a reason to get excited for the home team again. It's like you're Pete Carol of the Seahawks calling these bullshit calls and praying like heck to relive the Superbowl days of the past."

Reyes:

When Preschool got back to town, he was mad about some bullshit. I swear it was mostly in his head. This led to me and him getting into a heated exchange, and just as we were patching things up, one of Preschool's phones started ringing. He looked over to Whiskers and motioned him to answer it. Whiskers answered and informed us that they wanted to see both Preschool and me in Vegas for a meeting. What the fuck? Like, I knew who the fuck they were anyways, as it was the first time

I heard this shit. Apparently, some uce in Vegas that Preschool had to answer up to. Not me. As far as I was concerned, I wasn't involved in their organization, and besides, I wasn't the one running around starting fights with everyone. The thing was, my name kept coming up in conversations, "Tone this," "Tone that," "Did you hear what Tone did?" So now, as far as the guys in Vegas were concerned, I was involved in their thing by name, and they wanted to meet me.

I didn't survive the desert just to get popped in Vegas for something I wasn't even officially a part of. In Iraq, I survived over thirty ops of being shot at while hunting down bad guys, plus getting blown up. I know it is a slight exaggeration, but what would you call it? Anyway, I got into business with Preschool, trusting that it'd be prosperous—not poisonous. Everything that he seemed to touch turned to shit. But fuck, I loved my uce, and if I had to go with him to see Mando in Vegas, then that was just what I would have to do. I remember thinking that if I died in Vegas, I was going to be pissed.

Decidedly, we agreed we had to take care of some things before the Vegas trip, mainly getting our house in order, starting with getting all the boys in line and wired tight. Then, we would rein in the club and security business before tightening up the business for the Russians and the Mexicans. Since Preschool's vacation to Hawaii, I had been learning more about his side of the business. Plus, we still had some loose ends to tie up on a legal and financial basis. Everyone was uneasy about the whole club shooting business because it affected them and their business interests with us, too. Legally or illegally, it was harder to make money whenever law enforcement, or anyone else for that matter, was involved and crawling up your ass with a microscope.

When I talked to CW5 about the mandatory Vegas trip, he told me stories of how he, too, grew up in the Midwest. His stepfather was a chief of police, and he learned a lot about life from him. Unfortunately, he also learned about the nasty side of law enforcement, seeing firsthand the corruption and biased treatment of certain citizens. He said law enforcement in itself wasn't a bad thing; shit, we needed police to help keep society functioning. The problem was always the bad actors and politics surrounding it. He even tried his hand at it and was a police officer for a short time before deciding to join the Army and pursue a military career instead. His stepfather taught him how shit was always going to happen, a lot of it out of his control, but to always find a way not to let the shit stick to him. Then CW5 told me what his stepfather had said to him: "No matter what, kid, in the end, always come out smelling like a rose."

CHAPTER TWENTY-TWO
ON THE MOUNTAIN (DAY 1)

REYES:

At times, it seems that all relationships and friendships go through a time of strain and tension. However, only the strongest and closest ones come through intact and better. Part of the problem was that we had become too comfortable and complacent with the life of riches and women. To rectify this, we agreed to begin putting things into perspective, starting with the security teams. So, while in the midst of this looming chaotic mess taking place within our friendship, Preschool and I decided to get our security teams trained up. A training exercise was set, and the call went out to the boys to gather for a mandatory five-day, four-night excursion up into the mountains. The boys had no idea what was in store for them, but like good soldiers, they obeyed, embarking into the unknown.

I led the training exercise. My plan was to keep it simple and as effective as I could, largely due to the limited time constraints but also because most of the boys had limited to no training at all. They were raw, loyal, obedient, savage, and eager to a point. Since I was usually up at four-thirty a.m. regardless of the circumstances, the boys were just going to love getting up early to do physical training (PT) followed by a day filled with military-style training exercises.

Some of the USOS complained that they felt they were no longer in prison and shouldn't be subject to mandatory military training exercises. The complaints even began pouring in about me and the team members who were veterans of the armed forces and how the USOS weren't in the military, so they didn't need to keep up with appearances and standards like me and the "military" employees. At the end of the first day of training, Preschool gathered all the USOS together to speak with them. He assured them that it is a much-needed training and a program designed to build camaraderie and loyalty for everyone.

Preschool and the USOS continued talking mostly in Samoan, and for the most part, whatever they were talking about seemed to put the USOS's minds at rest. As I sat there by the fire, my mind began to wander, thinking back to the beginning of my military life. I was a young nineteen-year-old kid, really just happy to be escaping from a potentially troublesome life path created by the mistakes I had made for myself. The hole I had been digging at that time seemed to have two probable outcomes: prison or an early grave. I remember thinking that if I'm going to die young, then I'm going to die with honor and do something glorious. That meant going back to high school and getting my diploma, which was an attainable goal that became a priority of mine. That meant moving back in with my parents as I prepared myself by attending the adult education courses offered in order to get my high school diploma. Only then would I be eligible to enlist in the Army?

When the day came for me to leave for basic training one of my Army recruiters came to pick me up. I hugged and kissed my parents' goodbye along with my little brother who was twelve or thirteen at the time. The night before I came home drunk and I said goodbye to my dog Caesar, sadly the last time I saw him. He was a good dog and a good friend to a troubled kid. I picked up my bags and loaded them into the truck and off we went.

The first stop for me was the Kalamazoo bus station, followed by a bus ride to Lansing. There, I stayed in a hotel, thinking I'd meet a bunch of other recruits and have one final night of partying, but I was exhausted from my previous night of partying, so I fell out early. In the morning, after breakfast, the other recruits and I were shuttled to the airport. I sat next to this kid from Benton Harbor named Anderson. He acted like a refugee fleeing a war-torn country, thankful for his freedom and new opportunity in life. I could relate, but I knew whatever hardships he was escaping were most likely due to the environment he grew up in and not the ones he created. On the plane, his seat was again next to mine, and we continued to share stories, becoming acquainted with one another. We were both excited about being on the plane as it was the first time either one of us had flown.

We landed in Columbus, Georgia, and boarded a bus full of recruits headed to Fort Benning, home of the Infantry. When we arrived, we were introduced to what is known as reception. This was simply a holding area for all the new recruits to in-process into the Army, which took about a week. While at reception, we went through paperwork and got all of our shots, haircuts, uniforms, and equipment. We also got some briefings on what to expect during basic training, some information about Fort Benning, and a safety briefing. During that week, we also became acquainted with the basics of drill and ceremony, along with military lingo. For you civilians, drill and ceremony means how to line up and march in military formations.

After about a week, the drill sergeants came to pick us up. It was definitely a shocking experience for all. We had convinced ourselves that we were already in basic training. After all, it wasn't so bad. The sergeants who had been marching us all around and taking care of us seemed to be pretty cool and laid back. They hardly raised their voices and didn't make us do any push-ups or any of the things you see in the movies. But we were in for a rude awakening. The night before we would meet our drill sergeants, we had to have all our uniforms, gear, and any of the civilian stuff we brought with us packed into the two Army duffel bags we were issued.

In the morning, we all piled out of the barracks, stacking our duffel bags in a pile before lining up in formation. We waited with anticipation.

The sergeants who had been caring for us began to snicker and laugh, saying, "Here they come." No sooner than said, it began. The shouting could be heard as they came up the driveway. Appearing before us were these intimidating soldiers who were there with a purpose and clearly meant business in every word they uttered and movement they made. Those hardened men in their brown round hats were barking orders at anything alive. Shit, they even barked at the trees and the bricks and the birds in the sky. Half the things they were saying made no sense. Ironically, we understood every bark. The glaring eyes and raspy voices speaking a foreign language echoed throughout the quad. The drill sergeants swarmed around like angry hornets, inflicting their wrath on all of us, going from one soldier to the next and then back again in no specific order. They were continuously giving conflicting commands. One drill sergeant would yell at a recruit to look at him, while another drill sergeant would yell at the same recruit to look at him. Then, both drill sergeants would scream and yell at the recruit for not looking at them before yelling at the recruit for eyeballing them.

The drill sergeants had everyone take out their ID cards and hand them over. They then went about trading ID cards with one another, divvying them up as if they were baseball cards. Determining which drill sergeants would get which recruits to fill their platoons. Once they sorted out which recruits went to their platoons, the drill sergeants formed us up and began marching us out of the quad, one platoon at a time. It wasn't long before hearing the command "double time," which simply meant to run at whatever pace the drill sergeants wanted. After about a mile or so, we came to a large field. The drill sergeants ushered us in by arranging our platoon into a large rectangular shape. Later, it became known as the PT (physical training) formation.

The drill sergeants led us in endless calisthenics, beginning with jumping jacks. Then push-ups, flutter kicks, burpees, mountain climbers, ski-jumpers, sit-ups, air squats, running in place, up, down, roll left, roll right, repeatedly. The pace and intensity were grueling and went on for maybe forty minutes or so. Initially, most recruits were able to tolerate the physical exertion. Only the weakest collapsed, quitting within the first ten minutes. Those recruits were quickly dealt with and made examples of by the drill sergeants of what *not* to do or not to do if they wanted to make it through basic training. After all, that was only day one of week one out of eighteen weeks. Some recruits began to vomit, and most would later admit to having thrown up in their own mouth and swallowing it back down for fear of appearing weak and drawing the wrath of the brown rounds. If a recruit couldn't handle that smoke session, how were they going to handle the rest of their training? As the smoke session continued, as it would become known to be called, more and more recruits fell out. A smoke session was used any time the drill sergeants wanted to discipline or condition us. This would be used by the drill sergeants a lot, as they spent the next eighteen weeks fixing our weak minds and bodies, teaching us that pain was only weakness, leaving our bodies and minds. Finally, when the drill sergeants determined we had had enough, they assembled us back up into a tight formation and began to march us toward our new home. That initial smoke session was designed to break us, showing us who was in charge, and it certainly did just that.

It was only about ten in the morning when we arrived at the barracks, which would be our home for the duration of our time on Fort Benning. All our duffel bags were in a giant pile, and the drill sergeants gave us only a few minutes to retrieve our two bags. It was a chaotic mess, but somehow, we accomplished that first task within an acceptable time that was to their liking. Securing our bags, we moved inside to our new accommodations. My new home was a fourteen-man room located on the second floor. There were six bunk beds and two single beds, each with a coinciding wall locker. I claimed one of the bottom bunks farthest from the door and closest to the windows. After locking our bags in our wall lockers, we quickly returned outside and back into our platoon formation. We spent the remainder of our morning learning how to march. That mostly involved being yelled at and doing push-ups; lots and lots of push-ups. I grew up in the Army.

"Hey Uce, what you thinking about over there? You've been deep in thought for a while. Everything okay?" Preschool had finished speaking to the USOSs and was now sitting over by the fire across from me.

"Ya, bro, I'm all good." I couldn't help but wonder how long I had been lost in my own thoughts remembering the past. It's amazing how the mind works. What had only been a few minutes in the present allowed me to relive hours and days in the past. Everything was so vivid and clear, down to the smallest details. Not only visually, but sounds, smells, and emotions. I tell Preschool that I'm just going through tomorrow's training in my head, making sure I have everything straight for what I want to do. We chit-chatted for a little while before turning in for the night.

PreSCHOOL:

The funny thing about this shit is that the boys are like children. They try to play us both as to who's the favorite parent that gives in to their desires. They were out of shape. Out of focus. And so was I. I didn't care, though. In prison, one of the things that kept us tight was that we laughed together and suffered together. We endured everything that was thrown our way together. We were literally as thick as thieves. And the solidarity and camaraderie was what made others respect us. They know that amongst all the cars in the prison system, the USOS car was by far the most loved and respected. Even our enemies loved us.

The boys complained that Tone had them doing perimeter checks on the cars and campsite. Full on walkie-talkies, and all like a military compound. I died laughing because ain't no one crazy enough to steal our cars. And if they did, they'd probably not make it that far with it. Everyone knew who the cars belonged to. Heck, even the cops knew our cars. It's still funny, though, hearing these guys complain about having to check on our own cars. People probably thought we came out in style when, really, these were our daily drivers. We all had lowriders. We all drove Caddies. Old schools on switches and pumps. It's probably why the forest rangers pounced on us, hating. They probably ain't ever seen a lowrider in these parts of town and thought that we were outsiders looking to cause trouble. We were really just there to train and get in shape for the missions we had ahead of us. I never told the boys that's what I had in mind. Your right hand should never tell your left hand what it's doing. If they are riders like they claim, they should just *be* ready so they don't have to *get* ready. Same as inside.

CHAPTER TWENTY-THREE
BASIC TRAINING (DAY 2)

REYES:

I woke up to the sound of the alarm on my wristwatch. It was something I had become well acquainted with, going back to my first days of basic training and continuing all the way through my entire time in the Army. That morning, my alarm was set to zero four thirty hours, which is four-thirty a.m. for civilians. That gave me about an hour to take care of my stuff and get squared away before having to wake up the boys at zero-five thirty. They were really hating me for all these early morning wakeups. Most of them weren't used to going to bed before midnight, so they were sucking wind. I got dressed, cleaned up my area, rolled up my sleeping bag, shaved, checked my gear, and reviewed the plan for the day, which only took me about thirty minutes. The rest of the time, I reflected before my next alarm beeped.

Those early morning wake-ups at Benning took some time getting used to, but the drill sergeants would run you all day, and by the time you were allowed to bed down at night, you'd be so exhausted that falling asleep was hardly a problem for most. You learned how to adapt to getting about four hours of sleep a night. If you were lucky, you might get some nights where you got up to six hours of sleep. The hardest part of adapting to that sleep schedule was the interrupted sleep. You see, someone always had fire-watch or was a runner for the drill sergeant who was tasked with watching over the barracks at night. Those duties were an hour in duration before the next recruit was woken up to pull their hour shift. If you were smart, you would spend that time polishing your boots or studying your field manual, but whatever you did, you better not get caught sleeping or forget to wake up your relief, making sure he was fully awake before you crawled back into your rack. The punishment for any violation was severe. Not only did the recruit get punished, but drill sergeants also believed in mass punishment for any offenses committed by any one recruit. The poor recruit who was a habitual fuck up or who had a royal fuck up was then the target of the whole platoon.

One recruit made such a fuck up. At the time, the infantry was an all-male occupation, and there were no female recruits mixed in with us. All our drill sergeants were male, and most of the supporting cadre were male as well. However, there was a female armorer assigned to our arms room. She was pretty. One day, while we were in formation marching by the company area, she walked by. Private Whittleman, this taller, goofy, red-headed kid from Mississippi, decided to catcall her. That did not go over well with Drill Sergeant Savoy, who was leading the formation. Drill Sergeant Savoy was a large black man with a menacing grin and piercing eyes. It was an immediate response, almost as if Whittleman and Savoy had planned and rehearsed it. Whittleman was in mid-cat call when Savoy whipped around and shouted, "Who the fuck just said that? Which one of you dirty, disgusting, brain dead, ignorant, piece of shit, privates woke up this morning and decided to interrupt my almost seemingly peaceful day with an unintelligible, no pussy getting, never going to see daylight the same after I put my boot so far up your ass your eyes are going to pop out, had the nerve to disrespect my formation along with that female soldier?"

We marched on for some distance in complete silence. Drill Sergeant Savoy was taking us to the hill. It was a favorite destination of the drill sergeants because it was at the edge of the company area. Past the last set of buildings, at the far end of the parking lot and away from everything and everyone. As the drill sergeants were fond of saying, "Out of sight, out of mind." The hill was only about thirty yards from top to bottom, but we would spend a few hours learning not to disrespect Drill Sergeant Savoy's formation or make cat calls while in formation, but more importantly, not to disrupt Drill Sergeant Savoy's almost seemingly peaceful day. Later, Whittleman learned the true consequences of his error in judgment as the platoon decided to issue a blanket party that night.

Sand Hill was another favorite disciplinary or motivational landmark the drill sergeants liked to use. Thankfully for our platoon, our barracks were the farthest away, and our trips there were less frequent. Believe it or not, the drill sergeants had a daily schedule to keep, and any time they took away from that schedule to punish or motivate us had to be made up. Brown rounds liked to manage their time wisely and to keep things simple. That's why our little hidden hill was so popular among the drill sergeants in my company. I was thankful for that because Sand Hill was a very large and miserable hill to run up.

Part of a recruit uniform was a pocketbook and a black pen, which had to be kept on you at all times while in BDUs (Battle Dress Uniform, the camouflage fatigues). You better not have a red pen. On one particular day, I unwittingly got a drill sergeant's attention because I was missing my pen. He smoked me for about ten minutes and then told me to go see the drill sergeant so and so and ask him for a red pen. When I reported to drill sergeant so and so, he smiled and began looking through his desk for a red pen. When he couldn't find one, he began to smoke me. Then he would send me to go see another drill sergeant and ask if they had a red pen. This continued on and on as I went about in search of a red pen. I spent the remainder of that day reporting to countless drill sergeants, getting smoked anywhere from ten minutes to maybe an hour, depending on the drill sergeant. Once I returned to my drill sergeant without a red pen, he smoked me some more. You learned a lot about yourself every time you got smoked, so the lesson that day was all about me learning about myself. Something you spend a lot of time doing during training.

There were fun times at Benning, such as going through OSUT, which stands for One Station Unit Training. This is a different initial entry program than most soldiers get and was reserved mostly for those going into a combat arms MOS. Most recruits spent eight weeks at basic training with their drill sergeants and were treated like shit because they were recruits and had to be broken of all their civilian habits. Drilled into becoming a soldier after eight weeks, they would then go to their different schools for advanced individual training (AIT) based on whatever military occupation they signed up for. While at AIT, they were treated like soldiers because they had already graduated from basic training and earned the right to be called a soldier. Most AIT schools don't have drill sergeants. Instead, they have NCO cadres who are there just to teach the necessary occupational skills. We kept the same drill sergeants for eighteen weeks and were treated like shit because, until the day we graduated, we were recruits, not soldiers.

After completing OSUT, my next stop was Airborne school. For three weeks, we did two things: learned how to land on the ground and PT with endless running. We ran for everything, and if we weren't learning something to do with landing on the ground or parachutes, we were running. All that running did help prepare me for the next step in my military career, RIP (Ranger Indoctrination Program). From all the endless marching, carrying of rucks, and running during OSUT plus the PT and running at Airborne school, my legs became like sculpted iron. I sure needed it with what was lying before me.

preschool:

In prisons, it's pretty much like the military, only less severe by twenty clicks down. I mean, we run mandatory workouts and do burpees and the routines. We also punish the masses by making everyone start all over when one guy fucks things up. But it's less severe. The training is to build solidarity and bond with your brothers. The point of the bust down is to build you up. In prison, all the Asian Pacific Islanders, Natives, and red-dot Indians run together. It's some of the funniest conversations we had after workouts that gets me. I remember one of Whiskers' guys on the inside talking about what they call his junk after having worked out. He said, girls call my thing anaconda. Another guy said they call mine Mac-11 because they get the full 11. Another guy said something else. Well, later that day, during shower time, Mac-11 was heard laughing hysterically from the showers. When asked what all the noise was about, he said, this guy said girls call his junk anaconda, but that shit looks more like a garden snake. On this occasion, one of Whiskers' guys was talking about a robbery where a guy used a floatation device to get away down the river. He had hired a bunch of people to show up there for a job interview, but it was really a robbery of an armored car early in the morning. He distracted the drivers with all the guys who showed up for the job and ended up robbing them and floating away.

Dog asked, "What's a floatation device?"

Whiskers said, "You know. The thing you make love to every night."

Who doesn't know what the fuck a floatation device is? Okay. I'm not going to lie. I was wondering the same thing, but I am glad I didn't say it out loud. I didn't want to seem clueless.

Chapter Twenty-Four
Trouble on the Mountain (Day 3)

Reyes:

At graduation from Airborne school, the Ranger cadre came to pick up the Ranger candidates. Those of us who had successfully completed Airborne were separated into two groups: Ranger candidates and everyone else. This was also the first time I met Prescott. When the Ranger cadre showed up, everyone instantly showed a level of respect, awe, and fear. Even the toughest of the Airborne cadre gave way to them. Those Ranger cadre knew they had the juice and just did not give a fuck. Ranger cadre often fill their ranks with Rangers who are taking a break from the extremely high demands of serving in a line unit. These Rangers are seasoned warriors with years of experience and expertise under their belts. What is meant by taking a break usually means taking time off from line stuff to focus on individual stuff, like preparing to try out for a tier-one unit like CAG (Delta Force) or the Ranger Reconnaissance Company (RRC). If they weren't preparing for a tier one unit selection process, then many of them had recently been promoted and were waiting for a new assignment as a squad leader, platoon sergeant, or first sergeant.

To understand this better, you must understand that the Rangers have an extremely high standard of training. TRADOC stands for Training and Doctrine Command and recruits, trains, educates, develops, and builds the Army, establishing standards and driving improvements to lead necessary changes to improve the Army's capability to accomplish its missions. TRADOC levies the requirements, and the units Army-wide fill the requirements. This means the TRADOC pulls officers and NCOs Army-wide to serve mostly as instructors and evaluators, drill sergeants, and Army recruiters. Even the Airborne cadre is part of TRADOC. RIP is different because it is only led by Rangers, so only the best teaches the best, and only the best evaluates the best. That is the Ranger way. Most of the stuff I was taught during OSUT was scoffed at by the Ranger cadre, who then taught me the proper way to continue on through Ranger bat.

There was Prescott, a giant Samoan Hercules, "scrolled and tabbed," and at that time, a staff sergeant (SSG). I was in awe of him, as was everyone else watching as he put the Airborne cadre in their place, which, evidently, were below Rangers. Even those Airborne cadres who clearly outranked him, to which he would point to the beret on his head and say, "This black beret outranks anything on your collars, or you have ever done in the Army." At that time, Rangers wore black berets, which were later changed to tan berets, as the big Army adopted black berets as part of their uniform instead of patrol caps. That was the first time I met my nemesis, who later became my mentor, leader, friend, and family.

SSG Prescott came over to the group of Ranger candidates and said, "So you want to be a Ranger? You should quit now because most of you won't make it through assessment anyways." As he said this, I swear he was looking dead at me. He proceeded to say, "If anyone wants to quit now, I'll get you orders to any unit, anywhere in the world. How about Italy? Does anyone want to go to Italy? It's a wonderful assignment, and the Italian women are beautiful, and they love Americans."

To my amazement, there were actually a handful of candidates who raised their hands for those orders in Italy. I couldn't blame them or find fault in their decision; after all, I was tempted to raise my hand as well. Italy was home to the one hundred seventy-third Airborne Brigade, aka "Sky Soldiers." Italy would surely be a great duty station, and having access to all parts of Europe, North Africa, and the Middle East during leave and time off sounded amazing. Those first few candidates who raised their hands received orders wherever they wanted to go. Then, SSG Prescott gave the same speech again and offered up the same opportunity to go anywhere and to any unit. Unfortunately for the second group of candidates who raised their hands, the only orders they would receive were to be stuck in limbo, labeled as quitters serving the needs of the Ranger cadre, basically doing every bitch detail, being treated like they were still in basic training. The only positive I could see for them was that they would be in excellent shape and acquire some skill and degree of competency before getting the orders for their permanent duty stations. The other positive was that they would often be the OPFOR (Opposition force) for any training exercises we conducted. Being stuck in that limbo might only be for a few months or as long as a couple of years.

At RIP, I began to learn the difference between "scroll bearers" and "tab wearers." For starters, the tab is a school, and the scroll, a way of life. We began to learn this as we walked around a specific and large sign that was arched and in the shape of a Ranger scroll. We had to walk around it because we hadn't yet earned the right to walk under it. As luck would have it, SSG Prescott was one of my instructors/evaluators from hell. I remember thinking at the time. I would later come to appreciate how hard he was on us and the level of expertise he possessed. Learning what it would actually take to become a Ranger was much different than what I had imagined. It wasn't so much being a physical freak of nature as one would expect. Those exceptional athletes and fitness studs seemed to be the first ones quitting as they were not used to being trashed, talked about, and treated as nothing special. The main ingredients for the successful completion of RIP were never quitting and having integrity. Rangers didn't tolerate lying or cheating the standards.

There was one candidate who couldn't complete the rope climb obstacle set forth on a particular day. Each Ranger candidate had to climb to the top of a twenty-foot rope eight times before moving on to the next obstacle. One candidate made one successful climb to the top and, after about forty minutes of continuous effort, was unable to climb to the top again. When the cadre finally stopped him and asked how many times he had successfully made it to the top, the candidate answered honestly, saying only once. The cadre told him to move on to the next obstacle. He ended up making it through selection and serving in a Ranger bat.

Another candidate, a former college athlete and a PT stud, successfully climbed the rope to the top seven times. He made a few more attempts to climb to the top and then moved on to the next obstacle. When the cadre asked him how many times he made it to the top, he replied eight. They let that PT stud continue through the rest of RIP, and he excelled at all the physical challenges, but on the day of graduation, they pulled him aside and told him he was a failure and would not be passing selection based on that lie he told on the rope climb.

The cadre watch candidates very closely and know that everyone has a breaking point and wants to see how a candidate will handle the failures. It doesn't matter how strong you are or how much endurance you think you have; the Ranger cadre is very adept at breaking you to the point of complete muscle failure and exhaustion. Yet they will require the same standard to be met just as if you were fresh and ready to go. No matter what the circumstance, how exhausted or fatigued, candidates always had to do one more for the "Ranger" in the sky.

It's a funny thing what you remember about a traumatic life experience and the things you forget. RIP was kind of like that; in a way, it was a traumatic life experience, and more importantly, it was a time for further self-awareness and growth. You really had to dig deep during the three-week selection process. The assessment was grueling, with endless PT, limited sleep, training, practical exercises, and cadre smoke sessions. The Ranger cadre was quite skilled at creating new ways to smoke a candidate. My personal favorite was a play on two words, koala and qualify, which was referred to as having to koalify a tree. The Ranger cadre would look at a candidate, point to a tree, and simply say, "Koalify that tree." A candidate would approach the designated tree and do a partial cartwheel into a handstand, planting the toes of his boot against the tree. He would then wrap his legs around the tree, carefully lift his hands off the ground, one at a time, and then hug the tree, hanging upside down until the cadre told him to stop. Sometimes, we did this as a group of candidates for corrective training, and you didn't want to be one of the first candidates to fall off your tree.

Now the hardest thing about RIP was all the damn chafing, and I think anyone who has gone through it will agree. The insides of your legs, your armpits, around your neck, the back side of your knees, everywhere was eligible to be chafed. The groin, dick, balls, and inner thighs were the absolute worst, though. It was a level of discomfort and agony I don't even have the words to explain. Skin was rubbed raw, cracked, bleeding, and tender to the touch. There wasn't much anyone could do about it except quit or suck it up and drive on. The abuse on the feet was a close second, with chafing and blisters all over them, from the ankles to the top, bottom, and sides of the feet, including the toes. The tears of pain from that experience were very real, and there was no shame in it. There was only shame in quitting.

One of the course requirements to pass selection was to pass a fitness assessment test. I was in generally good shape and felt confident that I would not have any trouble passing. What happened during the push-up phase of my test was that my evaluator was none other than Staff Sergeant Prescott, and he was known for his strict adherence to any and all Army standards. To do a correct Army pushup, you had to go all the way down to not more than a fist-sized space between your chest and the ground, then all the way up to locking out your arms before going back down. The evaluator would count out loud each correct push-up performed. What you wanted to hear was "one," "two," "three," etc. What you did not want to hear was "one," "two," "two," two," and then "all the way down. Lockout those arms," followed by "two," and the worst thing you could hear was, "Your test is being terminated." When I did my push-up test, SSG Prescott failed me.

I was so fucking angry at him and hated his guts for failing me. How dare he fail me? I remember thinking at the time that my push-ups were good, and he was just being too damned critical. Who did the robotic Samoan think he was? So, I and a few other candidates who had failed were pulled aside and asked if we wanted to recycle with the next group of RIP candidates starting next week or if we wanted to be assigned to a regular infantry company. The cadre said we had a day to think about it, but they would need an answer from us by the end of the next day. To be in the Ranger battalion, all volunteers and candidates could quit at any time they chose, and I saw many candidates quit. I thought to myself that I wasn't a quitter, but damn another three weeks? How bad did I really want to be a Ranger? After thinking about it for the night and a good portion of the next day, I decided I was all in, and nothing short of death was going to prevent me from becoming a Ranger. Fuck Prescott. I was going to show him just how tough I was and what a mistake he had made failing me. My anger toward him was my fuel for the next three weeks.

After spending three long weeks in hell, twice, for a total of six weeks, I was finally assigned to the First Ranger Battalion at Hunter Army Airfield, Savannah, Georgia. During the completion ceremony at the end, all those who passed selection and received orders were given their black beret. My scroll and black beret were given to me by SSG Prescott. He stood there emotionless and robotic as he handed me my beret, shook my hand, and said, "Good job, Ranger." As I began to walk away, I saw a quick nod and wink from Sergeant Prescott. He smiled as quickly as he had winked, and then he was back to being a stone-cold, emotionless robot again. I never saw him smile during the whole time I was in those six weeks of hell; at least at the time, it was the closest to hell I had been. I was no longer angry with him.

The rumor was that when you got to your new unit, there was endless hazing, smoke sessions, and the like. The bottom line was that we newly assigned Rangers were going to be getting our asses kicked once we arrived at our battalions. Man, I was nervous about it. I didn't really feel like going through some hazing shit; after all, I had just spent six long fucking grueling weeks earning my right to wear the scroll and proudly walk under the one outside the barracks. For all those weeks of being told I wasn't worthy or fit enough to walk under the sign of the Ranger scroll and then finally being able to walk under it probably meant more to me than those who did in only three weeks.

First Ranger Battalion at Hunter Army Airfield in Savannah, Georgia, was going to be my new home for the foreseeable future. Since everyone had a "scroll" on their sleeve, those with "tabs" were placed in leadership positions and could make the non "tabbed" Rangers do push-ups and basically anything within reason. That's anything within what's reasonable to a Ranger, but if someone crossed the line, then a non "tabbed" Ranger could call them out and engage them in a fistfight. This only occurred once for me during my time as a Ranger.

All the new Rangers went through a sort of hazing process for the first week or so as part of our introduction to life as a Ranger. This also gave all the leadership a chance to get to know us and vice versa. During that first week, it felt like draft season because all the platoon sergeants, squad leaders, and section leaders were evaluating us to determine which new Ranger would go where within the organization. Everything was an evaluation, either formally or informally. Anything from actual dick-measuring contests to formal interviews.

I'm sure you could use your imagination of just how a dick-measuring contest goes, but just in case, I'll give you a quick overview. It wasn't as bad as it sounds, as most of us had already shit, showered, and shaved next to a group of naked men since basic training, which was the epitome of no privacy and no personal space. So, it's not like we hadn't seen a bunch of dicks before. It was more about letting you know who was in charge and just where you were on the totem pole. This was especially done for those who had too much pride or an over-inflated ego.

They lined us all up and said, "All right, Rangers, whip out your dicks." Of course, no one moved, but instead, we all looked dumb-founded, thinking it was a trap of sorts. The Ranger NCOs repeated their orders and added to it, "So you think you're something real special now, do you? All of you are bona fide tough guys now? So, whip out your dicks and prove it. Let's see those big dicks on you bunch of tough guys. Unless you're afraid to show your little dick. Part of being a Ranger is getting over your biggest fears, and if a dick-measuring contest is your biggest fear, then now's the time to get over it. Or you can just quit now, tough guy." And just like that, one by one, we all had our dicks out. No one had the biggest dick because Sergeant Zacharia Olson, aka "The Anaconda," was hung like a horse, and he decided to enter this dick-measuring contest. And that thing between his legs was what every porn producer dreamed of. It seemed as if all the pride and ego among us vanished into thin air.

The formal interview process entailed being called into a room with all the leadership sitting behind a long conference table. It was run similarly to a promotion board. As I entered in my dress greens, I had to walk to the center of the room, come to the position of attention, and salute the command sergeant major who sat at the center of the large conference table. As I stood there at attention, all eyes were on me, looking me up and down, sizing me up, and analyzing me. They all took turns asking me questions. Most of the questions were based on the Army and about technical knowledge. Then, there were scenario types of questions and random off-the-wall questions. However, it was the personal questions that seemed the most difficult to answer, and I do mean personal.

The one personal question that was the most difficult one for me to answer was when I was asked why I joined the military and why I wanted to be an Army Ranger. When I first answered the question, I said, "To serve my country, to be all I can, and to serve in the best damn unit in the military, Rangers lead the way!" I felt good about my answer thinking I was some hard-core, high-speed, low-drag motherfucking warrior. The blank, non-responsive, disinterested stares told me all I needed to know at the time and that not one of them was impressed by my answer; instead, they seemed annoyed with it. SSG Prescott, who had recently been assigned there as well, took pity on me. He said my name and simply asked, "Is there anything else you'd like to add, Ranger?"

As my eyes searched the curious faces in the room, he was the one I focused on as I answered his question, "Yes, Staff Sergeant."

He said, "Well," then paused, nodded, and looked around the room. "Maybe you should tell us." Then he gave me a quick smile and a wink, the same one as he had at the graduation ceremony.

Taking a deep breath, I said, "Yes, Staff Sergeant. Before joining the Army, I was a fuck up. I dropped out of school at the end of my junior year of high school. I was partying, drinking, and doing things I had no business doing. Mostly for the thrill of it and to be the cool kid. While most of my classmates were graduating from high school and making plans for their futures, I was not. Instead, I was getting more and more out of control." As I was speaking, it felt as if the weights of guilt and shame were being lifted from my chest with each and every word, and I could feel myself becoming more relaxed. Even my voice was beginning to crack some. "I saw some of my friends going to jail, and some of them ended up going to prison. I was on a path that was going to end with me getting locked up or killed, and I didn't want to end up that way. I had to look deep within myself, remembering that as a kid, I always wanted to join the military and be a soldier. I decided to go back to school and get my diploma so I could join the Army because I wasn't interested in college. I guess I just wanted to redeem myself. If I was going to end up dead, then it was going to be while doing something honorable, making my parents proud. Deep down inside me, I can feel the calling and desire to be a part of something extraordinary, and Command Sergeant Major, respectfully, I don't want to be anything else because I already am a Ranger." This was an honest, heartfelt answer, which is what they were looking for all along.

SSG Prescott picked me to be in his squad. Thankfully, he didn't believe in all that unnecessary hazing. His philosophy was simple: we were all a tribe of elite warriors, and as a warrior, it was your duty to look after the tribe by being the best warrior you were meant to be. No one had to walk around behind Achilles to get him to be a good soldier because Achilles was more than just a good soldier; he was the best; he was a deity. So, since we were all already elite warriors of an elite tribe, by default, we were already great and just had to carry ourselves accordingly on a daily basis. It was straightforward and to the point—just do your best every day, do the right thing, and actively be an informal leader. Formal leaders lead because they hold rank or a position of authority. Informal leaders lead by example and by doing what they know needs to be done without being told.

SSG Prescott also had a very instructive way of managing the hardest-headed soldiers. He was simply just more hardheaded, and you dare not get into a physical altercation with him.

Later, he told me that he had to fail me because, at the time, I wasn't ready yet. The only way I would make it as a Ranger was if I was mentally tougher than my peers because I wasn't yet physically as strong and capable as most of the others. He said that over time, I would grow in strength and other physical aspects but needed to be mentally tough to withstand the punishment I would go through until I developed more. Going through a second time would make me mentally tougher and physically tougher, but the choice was mine to make, and I had to be certain I wanted it more than I didn't.

It was at the Ranger bat that I learned more about the differences between being a "scroll bearer" and "tab wearer." Although wearing the scroll on our shoulder made us proud as could be, without the Ranger tab, we were known as a "tables bitch." To get your scroll, you had to pass RIP and serve in the active Ranger regiment. To earn your tab, you had to complete Ranger School. To serve in any leadership position in a Ranger battalion, you had to have both your scroll and your tab. Until then, you were doing all the minor labor tasks in garrison, like mowing the grass, cleaning the latrines, buffing the floors, etc., and in the field, you did all the grunt work.

Yep, the boys there on the mountain had no idea just how easy they had it compared to how hard and miserable it really could be. All in all, day two of training with the boys went well. There was only one small hiccup that could've turned catastrophic, but luckily it didn't. All the tricked-out lowrider cars had caught the attention of a park ranger. His curiosity to look in on who were the individuals driving the cars caused alarm bells to go off in his head. I'm not saying I even blame him for being alarmed. Basically, our group was made up of some intimidating-looking people. The boys were mostly Samoan and Pacific Islanders. They were all from the street, a bunch of thugs, and I loved them, but they were still thugs. So, I could totally empathize with the park ranger's assessment of the situation.

The other half of our group was made up of veterans and active military servicemen mixed in with a couple of prior law enforcement officers. Even though they were an intimidating group, the hand-to-hand combat training and the loud shouting of motivation and accomplishments must've looked and sounded as if there was some serious brawling taking place in the middle of the woods of the park. No wonder the park Ranger was concerned and had called in backup to approach the group of ruffians.

The park Ranger used the excuse of wanting us to move the cars so that he could get a closer look and make contact with our group. This did not go over well with anyone. Some were more agitated than others by this clear case of profiling, especially when everyone was on the up and up for once. The boys took particular offense to this, seeing as they had a newfound sense of accomplishment and comradery. There was Preschool taking center stage and leading the charge of aggression toward the violation of being profiled.

Thankfully, the commotion didn't last long because the park Ranger in charge recognized me from a situation that had occurred in Iraq. He had also served in the Army as a Ranger. I remember him being in the headquarters company and working closely with Prescott, who was a master sergeant at that time. During one of the times, my platoon was tasked with QRF duty. We received a radio call that some of our Rangers were in trouble. A sniper team was cut off from its main element and trapped with no safe route for extraction. Both the sniper team and their main element were in hot shit against overwhelming enemy forces.

From the time of the radio call to my platoon, hitting the ground and engaging the enemy only took about fifty minutes. It took about three minutes to load up on the birds, about nine minutes to fly the thirty miles, less than a minute to fast rope in, and three and a half minutes to run the half mile to hurry up and wait to engage with the enemy. The thirty or so minutes it took for us to safely link up with the unit under fire was actually pretty quick when you consider how dangerous it is to link up with friendlies while they are engaged with an overwhelming force of enemy combatants. Everything has to be coordinated extra carefully, and movement slowed to prevent any kind of friendly fire incident. It's not like the movies because something like this can take hours and even days to accomplish, not just a few minutes. My squad was tasked with securing the sniper team the park Ranger was on. A minute or two later, the sniper team would've been KIA (killed in action).

It was when the park Ranger was having a discussion with Preschool and trying to de-escalate the hornets' nest he had just stepped in when he noticed me. He immediately called out my name and asked if that was me.

After exchanging a few words with him, he spoke about the time I saved his life, immediately triggering my memory of him and the day we rescued him. We shook hands, sharing some war stories. After this, I explained what we were doing and that Preschool was a relative of MSG Prescott. He jokingly told me the mountain was mine for as long as I needed it. He instructed his men to let us continue on with our excursion without any further interference.

Preschool:

The forest rangers pulled up on us and complained at first. I know the sight of a convoy of lowriders coming up to the mountain couldn't be good. In a matter of minutes, arriving at our campsite, we had forest rangers pulling in from every angle of the mountain. They were sweating us until the main one saw Tone. He knew Tone from the military and went and called off his buddies. Hugging Tone and bragging to his friends that Tone was the one he talked about back at the station. The guy who saved his ass from insurgents swarming their camp like bees. Tone stood there, kind of embarrassed as if he didn't know how to accept the compliment. Anyway, that was cool. The forest rangers pretty much gave us the run-of-the-mill afterward. Leaving us to do whatever we wanted, and that's exactly what we did in those mountains. Whatever we wanted. We built a base with dams for holding our liquor and drinks. We built a military-style bunker. It was perfect for a training ground.

CHAPTER TWENTY-FIVE
NOT THE SAME AS DAHLONEGA (DAY 4)

REYES:

As we kicked off day four of our training excursion, I couldn't keep my mind from wandering back to my time in Ranger school. As I was watching the boys accomplish team-building training exercises, this one cadence just kept playing over and over in my head.

"I hear the choppers hovering. They're hovering overhead. They've come to get the wounded. They've come to get the dead."

"Airboooooooooooooorne … Rangeeeeeeeeeeerrrs lead the way. Shoot, shoot, shoot to kill."

"My buddy's in a foxhole, a bullet in his head. The medic says he's wounded, but I know that he's dead."

"Airborne Rangers lead the way. Shoot, shoot, shoot to kill."

"I'm sitting in my foxhole, sharpening my knife. Out jumps the enemy. I had to take his life."

"Airboooooooooooooorne … Rangeeeeeeeeeeerrrs lead the way. Shoot, shoot, shoot to kill."

What is Ranger school, one might ask? Simply put, it is the Army's premier small-unit leadership course. "Can you lead people when they are tired and hungry?" When attending the sixty-one-day course, you are sleep-deprived and starved while training, on average nineteen and a half hours daily. Go ahead and try leading people under those conditions while you, too, are also subjected to the same shit daily. I know people who have a bad night's sleep or miss a meal, and they are irritable and bitchy. It's a lot like those candy bar commercials featuring stars like Betty White, Danny DeVito, Danny Trejo, and even a Gremlin. The person is hungry and nasty until they eat the candy bar because "You're not the same when you're hungry." The only difference is there isn't a candy bar made that can instantaneously fix a person at Ranger school.

Even though it is an Army school, all branches of the military can and do attend. For instance, when I went through, there were a couple of marines from Force Recon. Also, I think it's fair to mention that over the years, Ranger School has made some changes to the course mainly for safety reasons. Regardless, it is still a bear. During the time I went through, it was broken down into three phases: Darby phase, Mountain phase, and Swamp phase. Each phase was broken down into its own training emphasis, building off the last phase, which utilizes the Army's training methodology of crawl, walk, and run. This means before you can run, you must first learn to walk, and before you walk, you must first learn to crawl. Darby is the crawl phase, Mountain is the walk phase, and Swamp is the run phase.

A few things about Ranger School stand out in my mind. First, there was BOB or the big orange ball – i.e., the sun. We hated to watch Bob go down and couldn't wait for him to come up because it got warmer when he came up, and it was just one day closer to the end. Then there was shit-talking the Rain God. At a halfhearted attempt at manliness, we would say the Rain God is a pussy, daring it to rain, which made everything suck ten times worse. The single (and first) drop of water that rolled down your butt crack, the feeling sucked because more was surely going to follow.

I'd be a bit remiss if I didn't mention the word "Hooah." This word basically means anything and everything except no. I thought we used it a lot in basic training, airborne school, RIP, and the Regiment, but nothing compares to the usage of that word during Ranger school. Hooah SARNT equated to *yes, Sergeant*, and said to the point of exhaustion.

Which phase is the hardest is subjective, but this much is certain: the Swamp phase is the most miserable one. Everyone in Ranger school eventually breaks, and if they recover, they continue on, and if not, they quit or are dropped. Why does the Swamp phase suck the most? Imagine continuously being in water anywhere from ankle-deep to thigh-high, and you must occupy it, occasionally fully submerged. It gets cold in summer, and in the winter, it's a whole new level of suck. Anyone completing Ranger school during winter could earn white thread on their Ranger Tab, symbolizing they were a Winter Ranger. When crossing a river or a stream, eventually, the frigid water reaches high enough to touch your balls, creating a whole new level of thinking and misery.

The fucking Damn-it stumps were agony. They really sucked. They were Cypress tree stumps just below the surface of the water, and you couldn't see them at night. So, you would run into them and fall over. No fun. Game over, dude.

Not to mention, by the time you get to Swamp phase, you are completely sleep-deprived and nutrient-deficient. It's not uncommon for Rangers to start hallucinating and falling asleep while standing or marching. You'll have a five-minute conversation with some of the coolest, most spectacular Rangers you will ever meet just to find out you were engaged in a conversation with a tree, a fucking tree. Sometimes you even catch Rangers trying to get food out of the vending machines in the middle of the swamp, yes, more fucking trees.

So, for those who hadn't broken down before then, at night in the darkness, alone in the cold water, shivering was the last straw. You could hear the misery and agony in the air as, one by one, individuals began to break. From the common response of sniffling, whimpering, and self-pity exclamations to full-on screaming and crying. The most common phrases were, "Fuck this shit," "I'm leaving," and "I can't take it anymore," venting and empty threats, as most who made it that far weren't quitting. The Ranger instructors (RI) weren't sympathetic and would shout out things like, "Shut up, you nig Ranger-baby," "Ranger-does your pussy hurt?" and "You can quit anytime you like, and there's a hot shower, hot meal, and warm bed waiting for you."

I won't lie. I had a big pity party during this portion of Swamp phase, whimpering about and uttering some of those same phrases. I remember I was just miserable sitting on the only piece of dry ground I could find, looking down into the darkness and feeling sorry for myself. Only to be interrupted by the outbursts of others who were going through the same experience. Ultimately, I think that's what got me through those horrible, miserable days during the Swamp phase. The fact that I wasn't going through it alone and I wasn't the only one suffering had helped me realize that I wasn't weak or deficient, but only human. The military always emphasized teamwork and being part of a team. Knowing you're not alone in something can make a world of difference, especially in adversity. My fellow classmates, my team, and I were going to get through it together, and we did.

During any phase, you stand a chance of being recycled.

CHAPTER TWENTY-SIX
I AIN'T NO BABYSITTER (DAY 5)

REYES:

The boys started training hard the next morning and seemed to be coming together. That was until they noticed Preschool was a no-show, and they began to complain. "Where's Preschool?" "How come he's not here?" "Why doesn't he have to do any of this stuff?"

I couldn't fucking take it anymore, and all diplomacy went out the window. Going into full-on sergeant mode, I answered them harshly and in a manner they were not accustomed to seeing from me. I started out with an agreeable demeanor, saying, "Ya, where is he? Maybe he's not here because he has a dental appointment or something?" To which some of the boys could pick up on my sarcasm and started to smile, snicker, and laugh a little. Then I caught them all off guard saying, "Or maybe he's not here because he doesn't answer to any of you fuckers. Your asses belong to him and answer *up* to him, not the other way around, and since he's not here right now, your asses belong to me, and you fuckers answer *up* to me."

There was a group pause as they all looked bewildered and frozen in their thoughts until I could hear one of the boys say, "What the fuck, Uce?" It was June who had said it. He was another of the Uces I was fond of, and early on, like Dog, he accompanied and shadowed me on the security contracts. Sometimes, it would be just him and me riding together, going from spot to spot, checking on the boys working at all our spots. Preschool always spoke highly of him as well, and the both of them went way back. June was a solid dude and was always down for whatever needed to be done. He was loyal, which might have been the reason his comment got under my skin the way that it did. I also knew that if he fell in line, then everyone else would, too. I also knew there was a line not to cross, but I was going to walk right up to that line and stand on it. This is something I often did in the Army, and well, let's face it, I did it often in life as well. Knowing just how far to push something without actually crossing the line was one of the keys to diplomacy. Being willing, able, and ready to back up your play is another key.

Anyway, that was it. That was all I could stand listening to. They were about to see a full-on snapping and come to realize just how fucking crazy I was. "What fucker? What the fuck did you just say to me? Did you just say *what the fuck Uce*? Like you didn't understand what I just said to your motherfucking ass a minute ago, which belongs to me, and you answer to me. Not the other way around." Now picture this: I'm the smallest one out there at only five foot eight and a hundred ninety-five pounds. I'm standing in the middle of all these giant men and directly addressing one of the bigger Samoans named June, who is also most likely the toughest man out there with us. As a semblance of diplomacy returned to me, I looked him dead in his eyes and said, "Now, we are all going to do what Preschool wants us to do, and that is to train without all the bitching and complaining." Looking around at the rest of the group, I continued, "And if any of you have an issue with it, we can head to the wood line and settle our differences, and I guaran-fucking-tee that it'll be like a Pitbull fighting a mastiff, and we are both coming back from the wood line all bloodied and scarred up."

As Juney and the rest of them were thinking about this and I was seriously considering going to the wood line, I interrupted their thoughts, saying, "Now, if there aren't any more interruptions or complaints, it's time to train. Today we are going to see who bitches out first, and no one wants to be a little bitch, so everyone get down on the ground, and let's start knocking out these push-ups." And that was that. I smoked the piss out of them for the next ninety minutes. Even had a few of them puking, but the thing they all respected was that I did every exercise and every repetition with them.

After we finished our smoke session, it was time to get cleaned up, which would be the last part of our training session and team bonding. A plunge into the mountain lake we had been camping next to. Mowich Lake in Mount Rainier National Park was ice cold. After that workout, it was actually a welcomed endeavor and might not have been the case any other way. Not one complaint from the boys, but rather a form of glee and excitement to be the first one to jump in. While we were all in the water, I told them ancient warrior stories I had heard from Tavita LemaokaOAli'i Prescott, who I mentioned by name as my source. All of us in the lake shivering and bonding as warriors. If there was any animosity among us, it seemed to just disappear and be replaced with respect and understanding. Where the fuck was Preschool? He was supposed to be telling all these warrior stories. After all, he's the one with the gift of storytelling.

Later that evening, there was still no Preschool, and to be honest, I was getting a little concerned, wondering if he might be in some kind of trouble. There were no girls, alcohol, or festive celebrations either. Good thing the boys didn't know about the surprise Preschool, and I had planned for them that last night on the mountain. Instead, it was an early night, and most of the boys, being exhausted from the training excursion, ended up falling out early. It ended up just me, Dog, H.A., Whiskers, and June staying up and sitting around our campfire. Whiskers did most of the talking, cracking jokes, telling funny stories, and busting balls. At one point, June put his hand on my shoulder and said, "No hard feelings. I understand everything you did. You had to do it, much respect and love, Uce." It was a relief to me that not only did I not have to fight Juney, who would've fucked me up, but everyone seemed to have taken away from training all the positive lessons. They were in good spirits, and most importantly for me, mutual respect had been earned. Everything was everything.

PRESCHOOL:

Who would've thought me driving back into town to call the girls and tell them the last day of training was supposed to be a day of partying and camping with them would be a disastrous day? I mean, I drive to town. I bang my beautiful ebony queen. My Nubian goddess. Spending all this time in the woods without pussy does weird shit to my head. I start thinking about how it was back in prison. I hate that shit. My girl already knew the plan was to come up at the exact time and date to meet, so she got a room. Seems as I was driving back from town, one of these forest Ranger pricks followed behind me in an O.J. Simpson Bronco. I don't know what the fuck they drive. He starts pushing up on me. I started to brake check him. I'm driving in the middle of the road, swerving because I can't tell where the hell the campsite is. It all looks the same to me. They have no reception on their phones, so it's not like I can call the boys and tell them I'm lost in the middle of the woods looking for the campsite. So, as I'm driving with this guy behind me doing weird shit, he finally blurps his lights and horns. Fuck.

I ask him when he comes to the window, "Shouldn't you be harassing Yogi stealing picnic baskets?"

He loses it. Draws down and everything. I'm dying laughing because I'm drunk as fuck. Something that I promised Tone I wouldn't be doing until the end of training. I asked the guy if he knew Tone. Just my luck. He says no. He takes me back to the station to breathalyze me and release me. I'm like, you lousy cocksucker. You brought me here to let me go? And my car was towed, so I won't be able to get it soon. It was three in the morning. I had no phone or anything because it was all in the damn car when this prick drew down on me and started trippin'. Story of my life. I had to walk down the street and find a guy with a phone and tell him that if he lent me his phone, I'd pay him one hundred dollars when my girl picked me up. He was so obliging. Hell, he gave me a beer as well. Haha, I thought, fuck. Tone is not going to be happy. But fuck it. And as luck would have it, the punk ass forest Ranger pulls up on me and this stranger having a beer not far from the police station and high beams me with his spotlight on his Bronco.

I said, "What the fuck? You forget to tell me something?"

The forest ranger just smiled. "Well, you're drinking in public, and that's a violation of state law."

"State law? What the fuck are you talking about?" And before I knew it, this punk ass Yogi bear underwear sniffing ass Ranger drew down on me again. This time, he didn't have to load me in the car and marvel at how huge I was because I couldn't fit like the average person he booked. Nah, he walked me right back into the station. Haha.

Tone really ain't going to like this. But that's who I knew I had to call because he had the satellite phone for emergencies, and this was one of them emergencies.

Reyes:

I've served under many different leaders, not just in the military but in all walks of my life. For example, teachers, coaches, employers, mentors, and parents all fulfill leadership roles throughout one's life. The military is just really big on leadership, prescribing to a doctrine of formal and informal leaders. A formal leader is someone given official authority by rank or position to order others to accomplish a task or mission. On the other hand, informal leaders have no authority but know what needs to be done and persuade, influence, and motivate others to accomplish the task or mission. The Army has even dedicated a ninety-six-page field manual (FM 22-100) on the subject, titled Military Leadership. The lesson I learned early in life is that there are good leaders and bad ones. Both are able to teach you invaluable leadership lessons as well as life lessons. I would always try to emulate a good leader because I would learn from them what to do and how to be. Bad leaders always taught me what not to do and how not to be.

Honestly, in the military, I had so many more good leaders than bad ones. There are two who have always stuck out to me, and the lessons I have learned from them have served me well throughout my life. Both of them were lieutenants, which, to me, is one of the hardest ranks to hold. That's because most lieutenants aren't much older than any of the lower enlisted they are in charge of. Plus, they are in charge of their team leaders, who are roughly the same age as them, and their platoon sergeant and their squad leaders are older, and almost all have more experience than them. I'll just refer to these two as Lt. Z and Lt. C. I'm sure they would remember things just a little bit differently but would most definitely recognize themselves being referred to.

Lt. Z was the third of many platoon leaders under whom I had the honor of serving. His style of leadership was something I aspired to. For instance, we were on a training mission in the desert, and by chance, I found him in one of the connexes, suffering from heat exhaustion. He chose to suffer silently and in private rather than to show any signs of weakness in front of the men he was in charge of leading. Leaders often suffer in silence and secret. It remained our secret.

A hat or a cover, as it is referred to in the Army, must be worn at all times while in uniform and outdoors while in garrison. It gets hot in Georgia and extremely humid during the summers. Now, soldiers will take off their covers any chance they get because of all the sweating. It would get uncomfortable and annoying to wear. It just so happened that lieutenants will also remove theirs for the same reasons. On this particular day, we were all outside and had removed our covers while doing some training stuff, including Lt. Z. At some point during the training, Lt. Z had gone off somewhere else. When he came back, he was wearing his cover and barked at all of us to put our covers on. It happened that I was the senior lowest enlisted because all the sergeants were off at some mandatory briefing they had to attend with the first sergeant. So, I retorted back, "Sir, you were just walking around here without your cover on and didn't say anything before. Why are you being such a dick about it now?"

By rights, he could have brought me up on charges of insubordination, but he didn't. He wasn't even an asshole about it. Instead, he calmly said, "Maybe because I just got my ass chewed out by the commander, who got his ass chewed out by the major because none of us were wearing our cover and were out of uniform. You didn't see that, did you? So instead of arguing with the commander, I put on my cover, took my ass chewing, and am now advising the rest of you to do the same. And just because I fucked up and was corrected, does it mean I shouldn't correct others for the same thing?" Well, when he put it that way, I felt like the asshole.

Once, I made a bet with Lt. Z on one of our training ranges that my team would score higher than his. The wager was if I lost, I would have to clean his yard. If he lost, he would have to come clean my barracks room. Well, shit, his team scored higher. He said I didn't have to clean his yard, but I was a man of my word, and I damn sure wouldn't have let him off if my team had won. So, I got to his house, and it so happened that he had two big-ass Great Danes and had let the dogs shit in his yard build up over a week or so before I finally made it over to his place. It was fucking disgusting. He just laughed and laughed about it. Even to this day, if we talk, it's one of the conversations we have, and he still laughs about it. The lesson learned is that as a leader, never ask your subordinates to do anything you wouldn't do yourself or haven't done. Also, your word is who you are.

Another time, he took our platoon on a trip to Fort McAllister and got this excursion approved because he was able to justify it as relevant training and team building, which the commander signed off on. Lt. Z was always coming up with out-of-the-box ideas and was never afraid of trying out new things. He instilled in me training to standard, never to time. That meant if you finished training to the standard early, then you were finished and could go, but it also meant that if it took you all night to complete the training to standard, then that's just what it was.

For this trip, our transportation was a bus, and during the bus ride, everyone was in good spirits, getting a chance to get away from the monotony of our daily routines. As lower enlisted often do, we turned the bus ride into a game of sorts. Just fucking with one another, really, to pass the time. Someone would say something insignificant, and the rest of us would chime in, saying, "Ooooh wow, no way," and someone else would say something equally unimportant. Again, we would all chime in one at a time, saying, "Oooh," as if something important or amazing was said. It was just pure juvenile and silliness, but it made us all laugh. Well, Lt. Z, not knowing of the nonsensical game we were playing, wanted to get in and impress us. He started saying some actual important things, and we all were like, "Ooooh, wow, no way," egging him on to keep saying his impressive things. He really believed we were being genuine until he realized we were all being a bunch of assholes, and he was the butt of our joke. His face got red, and he said, "You fucking assholes got me good." He turned around and did his best to ignore us and nurse his wounded ego. Here's the point: he didn't use his rank and try to lord over us like some, well, actually, a lot of officers would have done. Instead, he took it like a champ, earning our respect, admiration, and love. To the last man in the platoon, we would've each died for him.

My experiences with Lt. C were different because he was never in my chain of command, even though we conducted numerous training missions together. It was just his leadership style and the way he talked to people. He was always genuinely interested in the other person he was engaged with. It never felt like you were talking with a superior, but more like a mentor. I never saw him use his rank to get his way or to accomplish a mission. It was always "we" needed to do this together. I'll sum up his leadership style like this. He did everything the privates did even though he didn't have to, but because he didn't see himself as better than the men he led. Instead, he always referred to them as the "boys," and when he rose to a rank and level where he could no longer be with the "boys," it was time for him to retire. Even though he was a formal leader, everything about him gave way to his true nature as an informal leader, just one of the "boys." Make no mistake about it: he was no slacker. In fact, he was one squared-away soldier and served in some of the highest capacities at elite levels. Even to this day, he is still a mentor and friend.

Thankfully for leaders like Lt. Z, Lt. C, MSG Prescott, and others, I was more than ready for Ranger school and leadership positions during my time in the Army. This is why I recognized that Preschool was a leader even if he didn't want to be one. His not wanting to step up and really be the leader he was capable of being was something I began to ascertain. I mean, it made sense. Some of the best leaders I ever had known in my life and read about never wanted to be in charge. This was clearly the case with Preschool. He didn't seem to really want to be over anyone giving out orders. It didn't matter that the guy was a natural; in his own way, he was running from it. He was half-assing it and avoiding the changes he would have to make if he was going to rise up and take this thing to the top. He probably thought no one was on to him, or maybe he didn't even realize himself. I had to get him to see that he needed to step up to the plate and take charge. It's a real phenomenon that takes the place of not wanting to be in charge of your peers (your buddies), and I've witnessed it plenty of times in the Army. Especially when someone gets promoted from specialist to sergeant. The Army fix was usually to reassign the newly promoted sergeant to another platoon or even another company so he could make the adjustments to his new leadership position without all the peer pressure from his buddies, whom he now outranked. Getting him to see it was going to be a different story, requiring a degree of persuasion and guidance on my part. After all, we, I, needed his leadership.

PreSCHOOL:

So, just my luck, when I called my girl, she wasn't answering. To make matters worse, I got picked up in Buckley and escorted back into the local police station for public intoxication. There I was in this small police station, and they allowed me to make one phone call. Since my girl wasn't picking up and I couldn't risk anyone answering my one phone call, which these yahoos were serious about when they said only one call, I had to make the one call I didn't want to make. I had to call Tone on his satellite phone, which he explicitly said was only supposed to be used in emergencies.

All I could do on the satellite phone was apologize. I know I fucked up. I know the boys are all losing respect and thinking that I'm problematic. Hell, when I returned from my vacation, the boys were cozying up to Tone and following his command. I'm not going to lie. That shit bothered me a little. But it's good to know that Tone always had my back and kept things in order when I couldn't. This stressful business kills a lot of guys younger than me. Literally, I mean, you make a miss move, and it's your life. That's the thing about the game. It's called a game. But it's real life. In any game, if you make a mistake, you can restart or respawn, and all is well. In this game, you make a wrong move, and you could end up dead. I found more and more that I could trust Tone rather than my own USOS. That's sad. I didn't want anyone to know I was thinking that because it seemed disloyal to the movement.

There's a creed in the bylaw of the USOS. That a USO can never side with someone outside the organization or talk against the movement like I mentioned before. If you are within earshot, you are just as guilty. They hung one of the boys in prison just for hearing another one vent. And stabbed the guy venting and cut out his eyelids so he could never sleep. They were serious about that part of the bylaw. There is also a code that says no one USO can sleep with another one's wife. Any organization, from Italians to Chinese and even Russians, enforces that rule with murder. Nah, not us. We worried more about gossip breaking us up rather than a girl coming in between us.

Tone came down to the station. I could see the look in his eyes. Just knowing that I was disappointing him hurt my heart. Growth is when you start taking accountability and responsibility for your actions before someone even has to tell you. The thing is, I couldn't help myself. I was stressed with all the craziness this life entailed. He reminded me that there was still Vegas we needed to go visit. And here I was, getting myself into some shit. What if I couldn't get out of jail for some reason? I'm on parole. What if, by happenstance, I got caught up? How would the boys function knowing that I was truly the glue? He told me that he ordered everyone to fall in, and surprisingly, everyone did. Everyone started feeling like Tone should be the one guiding us in our journey since he was always making up for where I was lacking. When Tone told me who was behind the bickering, I already knew. I know June was a rider. Never question me. If there was a loyal USO, it was June. He was always looking for ways to help put out the fires I was causing around town instead of wanting to wet me and be over it like the others were secretly doing. Sending kites to prison to complain. June's little brother, though, was behind the disgruntled remarks that were causing others to think negatively. That was an issue I would have to address.

After half an hour of arguing with Tone, he spat, "Why didn't you call your famous lawyer to get you out of the jam?"

"Shit, to be honest. I think he's sick of me, too. He's currently dealing with the situation of the insurance money being exposed as a fraudulent ordeal. He's trying to lay low, too."

"Look, Uce, you know I got your back. But you're fucking everything up that we built. You are bringing down the house. For what? What the fuck are you going through? Why can't you tell me? Maybe I can help?" Tone continued. "Why are you only telling me now about the lawyers being investigated for this fraud claim? You always used to tell me shit.

Now, you only tell me when it's exposed? If there's no trust, there's no us. Remember? We all we got?" Tone sounded half defeated.

"I said I'm sorry, Uce. What more can I say? The show must go on. Let's get back to the boys and party it up. I swear, when we get back from Vegas, I'm going to change shit up. I'm going to start getting back on my focus like when I was inside."

"That's if we come back from Vegas, Uce. Come on, you know the boys don't do good without a babysitter. Let's go."

CHAPTER TWENTY-SEVEN
Prescott

REYES:

Tavita LemaokaOAli'i Prescott was born on the small island of Samoa, where he spent the first eight years of his life before moving to Hawaii. His father, who was a Navy SEAL, wanted his son to have the full experience of a traditional Samoan culture, which he left to his grandmother and grandfather to teach Tavita the old ways and customs. His father would visit him as often as he could whenever the Navy would allow it. When his father was finally getting ready to retire in Hawaii, Tavita was filled with excitement and pride at the prospect of finally being reunited with his father and all his siblings. Tavita was the oldest of five brothers, three sisters, two half-brothers, and four half-sisters, most of whom lived in Hawaii.

Once in Hawaii, it would be time for Tavita to learn how to become a man. His father was strict but fair and demanded nothing but excellence from his children, never tolerating excuses from any of them. Tavita was small for a Samoan and considered a runt. While in Hawaii, this made things harder for him. Being small for his age, the other boys thought it was a good idea to pick on him and try to intimidate him into doing things against his will. After all, he was in a new neighborhood and a new school, having left all his childhood friends familiar to him in Samoa.

When Tavita's father learned of him being picked on and bullied at school, he took Tavita aside to tell him the world was always going to be full of bullies, so he might as well get used to it now and learn how to deal with it. He told him he could run or stand, and running for a Samoan wasn't a valid option. He told him that if he ran, then he would always be running from those same boys every day for the rest of his time in school. He told him that it didn't matter how big the Samoan was, but what mattered was how big the Samoan's heart was and how big the Samoan's fight was. He told him there were no excuses because Samoans were warriors, all of them from the smallest to the biggest. His father also told him that sometimes, you'll have family by your side to fight with you, and sometimes not, but regardless, you always stand with your family. However, his life experience taught him that most of the time, fights take place when you're alone, especially the biggest and most important fights.

He said, "Son, you must learn to be strong, and learning to be strong starts now. To be strong, you must never be ashamed of yourself or who you are, and you must never back down from a bully."

Not long after, Tavita found himself in conflict when the bullies came around. He really didn't want to let his father down, but he didn't want to get beat up, either. After a brief moment of hesitation, he was surprised he was able to find the inner strength and courage to stand and face his antagonists. He heard his father's voice, seeing the words he had spoken to him. As he turned to face the bullies, he felt the essence of his father standing there along with his family and his ancestors. The whole clan was with him in spirit, and it was his father's spirit that brought the most strength and courage. He found himself comforted by the spirits of his ancestors and would not bring shame to himself or them that day. Tavita would later say it was the best ass-kicking he had ever received in his life, his proudest moment. There were many more fights ahead of him and more bullies to overcome, but that day, he gained their respect. More important to him was that he had gained the respect of his father and his ancestors. Later in life, he realized the most important thing he had gained that day was his own self-worth and self-respect.

Tavita spent most of his childhood and teenage years as a runt, having to fight many battles against would-be bullies and those who thought they could easily impose their will upon him. They were all proven wrong, and even if he got his ass kicked, he smiled and laughed about it because he knew he had still won. At sixteen, he hit a growth spurt. There was one problem, though: although he grew in height, he remained unimpressive in muscular development. When he finished stretching out at eighteen, he was tall but lanky. At six foot five inches, he barely weighed one hundred and fifty pounds. Despite this, he became known as one of the toughest, most stubborn uces around. He was never a troublemaker and didn't start shit with anyone, but he would surely finish it, sometimes through sheer willpower alone. Overall, he was a good student, spending most of his time exploring the islands, playing football, and training in Muay Thai kickboxing.

He was not a fan of swimming in the ocean but wanted to follow in his father's footsteps while in Special Forces. He looked at the military branches to see what other Special Forces options were available to him other than the SEALs, which he would've joined, but to his relief, he was drawn to the Rangers. Everything about the Rangers' history and their creed resonated with him. He was a bit apprehensive to tell his father because he worried he'd be disappointed in him. To Tavita's surprise, his father's eyes filled with tears of pride and joy upon hearing his son wanted to be an Airborne Ranger. His father simply said, "Rangers lead the way," and hugged his son, then shook his hand. Sadly, not knowing that would be the last time they saw each other. His father deployed on a SEAL mission and ended up dying.

When Tavita left for basic training, he weighed one hundred and fifty-four pounds. He found basic training to be a breeze, seeing how he was a natural athlete and had spent a great deal of his time growing up engaged in physical activities and training in his two passion sports. When he finally made it to the Ranger battalion, it felt like home to him. He knew it was where he belonged, not so much because of the physical aspects but more because of the mental toughness it required to become a part of the unit. He was also required to excel in the Rangers. All those years as a runt and learning to withstand and win by force of will alone was the winning ingredient, and you either had it, or you didn't. You can almost always bring someone along physically and condition them into a better athlete or soldier, but will and determination are much harder to instill into someone, especially when they are older, and the older they are, the harder it is to do. So, they either have it or they don't, and Prescott had it in abundance.

It wasn't until about four years into his military career, around the age of twenty-two, that he started to gain weight and put on muscle. Once he started gaining, he just kept stacking on the muscles. It was a slow progression at first, creeping up to one hundred and eighty pounds, but within a year after that, he put on another forty pounds of muscle, reaching two hundred and twenty pounds by age twenty-four, and when our paths would cross, he would be a mountain of a man weighing two hundred and eighty pounds of solid muscle.

PRESCHOOL:

Paulie grew up in the same house as his brother Tavita. But it's weird they were totally the opposite. They were twins but had different views on life. They had different hopes and dreams. While Paulie started at an early age boosting cars and getting into crime, Tavita was always doing right. It was almost inevitable that he ended up in the military, following in his father's footsteps. Hell, most of his family thought he'd end up the cop that put most of his family members away, they'd joke. He just wasn't the kind of guy to play on the other side of the fence, which set a perimeter around his neighborhood. He was a straight shooter. By the book. Which is probably what spurned the envy and hatred of Paulie for him. Paulie was a sociopathic maniac by the time he could walk. He hated authority.

It was always fascinating to see two people come from the same family households go in two different directions. Tavita was always trying to live up to his old man. Paulie? He didn't care. At a young age, he thought it was stupid that his dad lost his life defending a country that didn't give a rat's ass about him. He would often complain the same thing to his brother Tavita. His brother would say, "Well, little Uce, I'd prefer to be in the military than prison. It's no way to live."

When Paulie was young, his dad used to chastise him. Get on him with that old stern military gibberish. Paulie knew early in life that he would never measure up to his dad and started to rebel. Even his mom, who was with his dad for over thirty-five years, was never good enough for him. The dad would verbally degrade, belittle, and put her down every chance he had about everything she did. Yet everything she did was for Paulie's dad. She pretty much gave her heart and soul to the dad. Even died for it and got the ass end of the stick.

Paulie said, "This motherfucka complained about all he did for his country and the government shitting on him in thanks. Yet, he shitted on my mom all these years and never once gave my mom a thank you card for any holiday. All these years, having his back. Putting food on his table. Ironed clothes on his back. Taking care of his kids while he was out serving a country that didn't give a fuck." I guess that's why Paulie formulated his own street gang and fulfilled the longing for a family with homies instead.

He built this gang that no one ever thought would spread in membership like wildfire. They had kids from every town on the island, reppin' his gang and wanting to band with Paulie. He had different types of kids, including Blacks, Mexicans, Filipinos, Hawaiians, and all. He was only sixteen when he started this gang, which became pretty much the organized crime syndicate it was ten years later with politicians and police in his pockets. A gang that ruled inside and outside of prisons in Hawaii, Washington, Oregon, Utah, and California. He ruled his gang with an iron fist, and everyone was amazed to see his growth propel to the heights it had. He started from one illegal game room to owning and running fourteen of them on the island. Each one pulled in an average of twenty to thirty thousand dollars a month. He was doing really well as a young thug entrepreneur from the slums. Before he was caught up on his last crime, which he still screams at the top of his lungs for anyone listening that it was a setup, he was starting to dominate the movie industry on the island.

Some believe that had something to do with his great fall from glory.

CHAPTER TWENTY-EIGHT
SANCHEZ

FEDS:

Carm Sanchez is a divorcee twice over, a no-life type of U.S. attorney. She's struggling to keep the kids together and a roof over their heads, hoping for a big break in the case that will get her promoted. She's sexy as hell, in a GILF type of way. She was a late bloomer. Hell, her grandchildren looked like they could be her kids.

Sanchez is teamed up with Taualuga, the Homeland Security agent who's grown up having bad experiences with Samoan gangs bullying him and his family his entire life. Taualuga is a good dad type of character. He always tries to be there for his children to tuck them in at night. He's had a hard-on for taking down bad guys for as long as he can remember. Heck, he even pulled in the cartel leader, who he heard Preschool had roughed up in hopes of turning him. They had an informant working in the cartel's American circle, and hearing that, Sanchez and Taualuga thought they had their in.

Preschool would laugh because of the balls on these two. You go and collar a cartel boss, hoping he flips on a guy who assaulted him? Really? Forget all the drugs he brings to the U.S. and all the families destroyed by his poison. Forget all the people left destitute because their husbands were stripped away from their families for working for the cartel boss. But you want to take Preschool away for a stupid assault? Haha. The fucking feds. The crazy thing is the cartel leader didn't know how to say that he got pulled in for that. He kept it quiet. That was his undoing because this stupid questioning that these pigs pulled him in for would cost him his life. Sanchez is a straight shooter most of the time. But when it came to this, she didn't object. She hates the USOS but hates the leader of the cartel even more. Her cousin was shot and hanged in Mexico City because of the American leader of the cartel who was assaulted. She couldn't care less what they did to each other.

Reyes:

Let's just say CW5 didn't have any heartache about the cartel leader being killed. The only grievance he might have had was that the cartel leader wasn't dispatched by one of the U.S. Army's special mission units. CW5 wasn't in the business of looking for bad guys to arrest. Ultimately, the intelligence he gathered led to kill packets being produced and enemies of the United States being terminated by any means necessary, and the USOS were a means to an end as far as he was concerned. He was a true believer in an ancient proverb popularized by the Romans. Instead of saying it in the modern rendition, CW5 liked to say, "Amicus meus, inimicus inimici mei." Which translates to "My friend, the enemy of my enemy." The common way it is said today is, "The enemy of my enemy is my friend."

Maybe you are wondering what a kill packet is. A textbook answer is, "They are an executive summary of intelligence information and analysis to better understand the background, history, or involvement of a target within an operational context having the highest level of clearance from the appropriate agency and person having the authority determined for issuing the termination of the target." In other words, lots and lots of intelligence (information) is collected on a specific individual, allowing for a plan of action to be created with the highest probability of a successful outcome and completion of the mission. I mean, they literally find out information about everything they need to know and then some. CW5 used nine R's for building his packets and each category would have subcategories. Residences, Relatives, Relationships, Routines, Recreations, Resources, Rackets, Recruitment, and Repercussions. Once all nine Rs were satisfied, he had all the information on someone he needed, and he could plan and justify their termination.

Since CW5 didn't particularly like hitting targets on U.S. soil because of all the complexities and red tape, there was a high probability that he, having already created a kill packet on the cartel leader, had passed along information to me. That information somehow made its way to the cartel leaders' enemies, who he had considered to be his friends. Once CW5 found out about the U.S. attorney's office's investigation into Preschool and the USOS, he began to monitor Carm Sanchez and her investigation. He saw her mistake of bringing in the cartel boss as an opportunity that he could exploit for his own benefit, which was twofold for him. Eliminating a person, he determined, was an enemy foreign national (Mexican bad guy) who was helping to aid, support, and finance terrorism. Most likely, the cartel leader did so unknowingly but still doing so, and America was conducting a global war on terrorism, so that was that. Second, he was gaining favor with a more viable source (the USOS) for human intelligence gathering and keeping them in play.

Using them to execute his kill package was just an added benefit, and CW5 did not have a single issue with taking advantage of opportunities like this one. In fact, he would tell me that if you stayed in the game long enough, the opportunities just came to you, but you had to be forward-thinking and quick enough to capitalize on them. There was that speed chess again. He was also big on plausible deniability, constantly having elaborate schemes in play to create confusion for anyone who might want to investigate him for any reason. I was beginning to realize that I was part of at least one of those elaborate schemes. And I was quickly learning this chess game. He would say things to me like, "Remember, as long as your hands are clean, my hands are clean, but even if your hands are dirty, my hands are still clean."

CHAPTER TWENTY-NINE
La Vida Loca

Reyes:

On the other side of Tacoma was this nice, upbeat Mexican nightclub called "El Tropico," owned by a married couple. The husband, John, an accountant, was in his sixties and enjoyed having his trophy wife but knew she was too much for him to ultimately keep satisfied in more ways than one. Before I met them, for many years, he fought his best to keep her satisfied and to stay married. In fact, he had financed the club for her a few years back as a last-ditch effort to win her over for good. Ultimately, he saw the writing on the wall and conceded to a marriage in name only and for financial reasons. Roseanna, the wife who went by Rose for short, was more than half his age and came from Mexico, where they had met in Puerto Vallarta. As it turned out, Rose had a thing for bad boys and an allure for adventure and excitement. It was in her nature, having grown up on the streets and getting involved with gangsters and drug dealers at an early age.

Originally, she saw John as her escape and as a means to a better, safer life for herself and her future family. She didn't want her kids growing up the way she did, along with her brothers and sisters. When they met, she was just turning twenty, and seeing her ticket out with John, she punched it. She didn't have anything negative to say about John; in fact, she adored him and loved him deeply. She was actually grateful for him and all that he did for her. The problem in their marriage came from her not being able to have kids, which was, in her words, "the only reason I left the life behind, for my children's sakes, not mine." She thought, *What is the point of a boring life if you don't have babies to raise?* You see, Rose had a thing for bad boys, and John clearly was not one in any sense of the imagination. She also had an undying thirst for thrills.

I met John and Rose when they reached out to us about doing security for their club. She was smoking hot with a body that could kill. Man, I was lost in her eyes the moment we locked eyes. Not knowing the situation at the time between her and John, I tried my best to act casual and keep things on a professional level. Then, after the initial introductions, and to my surprise, John excused himself, saying he had other business to attend to and that I would be dealing with Rose as she was the general manager of the club. As we talked about the club and security, Rose walked me over to the bar. Going behind it, she asked me what I liked to drink.

"Whiskey, neat, Crown Royal Reserve if you have it," I answered.

Looking around, she said, "How about Johnnie Walker Blue Label?"

"That'll do."

"So, tell me something, Mr. Security, do you think you can keep me safe?" She handed me my glass.

"Let's just say I'm the perfect bodyguard to handle someone's body if that someone needs their body taken care of."

"Is that so?"

"Absolutely."

There was definitely chemistry between us, and trying to keep this on a professional level wasn't going to be an easy task for me to accomplish. Then, as she poured me another glass and handed it to me, our hands touched. Locking eyes again and letting the moment linger longer before she pulled her hand away, I could feel the sexual energy. I slammed the drink, telling her I had to be somewhere and that she had my number. If she decided to use our services, or needed anything else, she could contact me day or night. My parting words were, "We are the best in the business and well worth our prices."

A few days later, she called and wanted to contract with us for security. We discussed the final price, and she agreed. It was Wednesday, and I had a security team in place the next day. Over the course of the next two months, I limited my face-to-face interactions with her, doing my best not to disrupt business. However, she kept calling me to discuss things at the club, asking irrelevant questions but wanting my thoughts. I'd give her answers to her questions, but we both knew the reason she was calling. During those phone calls, I found out that she and her husband were separated, remaining friends. He lived in a condo in downtown Seattle close to his office, while she lived in their house in Northeast Tacoma. I also learned he had a girlfriend, and their marriage was only a financial arrangement. Seeing the green light, I decided I was going to make an appearance at her club for a face-to-face.

I went to her club on a Saturday night under the guise of checking on the security we had in place there. When she saw me, she was pleasantly surprised and made her way over to me while I was talking to the boys. She put her hand on my shoulder as she leaned in to say hi. I gave her a quick hug, leaving my hand on the small part of her back, and I whispered in her ear that maybe we should go somewhere quieter to discuss further business. She said she had to take care of something first, but then we could meet in her office, and I should have a drink at the bar while I waited.

When we got to her office, she held the door open so I could enter. The tension between us was thick and needed to be cut. As she closed the door and turned around, I just grabbed her, pulled her body into mine, and kissed her before she could protest or say anything. She kissed me back, but she hadn't planned on doing either. I grabbed her ass and picked her up while we continued to explore each other's mouths as I carried her over to her desk. So right there in her office, I fucked her like I don't think she had ever been fucked before. She seemed to me to be sexually inexperienced, so I completely ravaged her that night fucking her in every inch of that office, turning her out.

I would later learn she had only been with two other men, her husband John and her high school sweetheart, who was murdered. She was a shrewd businesswoman and had learned a lot under the guidance of her husband. We ended up having a great relationship as she taught me things of a financial nature, and I taught her things in the bedroom. The best part was she didn't seem to mind being one of my side chicks.

One of the things I learned from CW5 was that even though you need to have a presence out front in any organization or operation, it doesn't always have to be you. He would tell me it was more important to be the one in charge behind the scenes than the one out front leading. This line of reasoning stems from the question, "Who has more power, the king or the kingmaker?" The modern term "kingmaker" stems from Richard Neville, the sixteenth Earl of Warwick deemed "Warwick the Kingmaker." This came about from his activities in England during, coincidently, the Wars of the Roses, which were a series of civil wars fought for control of the English throne. During that time period, Richard, being only an Earl, proved to be the one with real power as he deposed two kings from off the throne.

I was trying to pass this knowledge along to Preschool, giving him a glimpse of how I was moving. Behind the scenes, I was moving pieces that no one else had seen or knew about. Many of those pieces didn't even know about each other. I told him to just let "El Tropico" do its own thing and for us to only deal with them on a legitimate basis. If they were involved in any illegal activities and got caught, then we weren't going to be tied to any of it, which would send the feds chasing their own tails regarding us. El Tropico would be one of our scapegoats. After all, we would still reap all the benefits from an intelligence gathering standpoint, plus have legitimate money coming in and put some of the boys into earning money legally. Plus, all the hot Latina pussy generated out of that club—why ruin it?

I did everything I could to make it look like we were involved with illegal activities out of that club. I was even leaving my gym bags at Rose's house, pretending that I kept forgetting them and then having her bring them to her club for me to pick up. I'd leave other stuff with her at her house, too, only for her to bring them to the club for me to pick up as well. She was even doing my laundry at her place, dropping it off and picking up anything that needed dry cleaning. Plus, she used to love going grocery shopping for me and making sure I was eating well. Sometimes, I would actually feel bad that she was just another pawn in the big scheme of things.

Preschool:

The feds went over to Hope and tried flipping her. Little do they know, Hope is sharper than an army knife in a combat situation. She would never fold knowing as much law as she does. Knowing all the ins and outs of the way the feds operated, she despised law enforcement. They brought up her marriage and used this information as a scare tactic. That she "wouldn't want her husband to find out that she was sleeping with me." She laughed out loud. She started dialing her husband's number. "Why don't we call him and ask him how he feels about it?" The thing is, her husband already knew. He didn't care. Heck, I go by the house and visit while he's there. Sometimes, he'd watch just to take joy in the pleasure that his wife shows when she's with me. The fact that these feds were still employing these blackmail ploys on people in hopes of flipping them is shady as heck. They are a bunch of jokes. In the old days, the feds, with respect, would use the direct approach. They didn't have angles or tricks. They weren't snakes doing tricks while their director blew the pipe that made them come out of a hole in a mesmerized trans. Today, they come out of every hole known to man, and they are slicker than ever. Being upfront is the best approach to people. People hate being lied to. Hate feeling pressured to do something. Being extorted. Feeling used. They hate feeling like they have no choice in the matter. That is where the feds will always fall short. When they started investigating her, they found that I was frequently visiting her and that I had boxes and boxes to bring to her. The thing is, it could be legal work. Legal mail is strictly confidential and sensitive material. I've known the lawyers to carry out boxes and boxes just to find a loophole in Juney's case. That was a tricky, sticky situation.

They even followed Tone and found he was visiting the owner of El Tropico (a huge Hispanic night club in Tacoma) and banging her brains out. They would often see him carry a gym bag and come out with it on his visits. They assumed it was cash. Haha. A fucking gym bag is just a gym bag, you Sigmund Freud muthafuckas. And a legal box is … well, more than a legal box. It's a secured box of legal briefs that, if opened without permission, can have one of these rookies sitting colder than winter in an ice storm on top of Montana's Missoula Mountain. Yeah, they have friggin' feds up there freezing their nuts off.

chapter thirty
The Lawyer

Reyes:

A few months before the meeting with the Russians, I started dating Maria. She was a well-known Puerto Rican beauty who everybody on the Latin scene knew, and she had a good reputation, meaning she was a bit of a prude. She worked in downtown Seattle as a nurse at Harbor View Hospital. The thing is, about a month before I met her, I had met Tiffany, who I absolutely fell head over heels for but knew she wasn't girlfriend material. Tiffany was fun to hang out with and was also my way of getting intel on the Native Americans. Maria, on the other hand, was definitely girlfriend material and came without any foreseeable drama.

Seeing just how much Maria was into me and knowing at the time I wasn't going to be able to give her what she was looking for, I even tried to break up with her early in the relationship. We had been dating for maybe three months, and we were sitting in my car outside her apartment when I told her it wasn't going to work out. I told her that it would be better if we just ended it there and now. She teared up and got out of the car. A day or so later, I got a phone call from her best friend pleading Maria's case and telling me why I should be with her. It all sounded good. She was genuinely a good woman, and I thought maybe that was really what I wanted and needed. I was actually confused and apprehensive, but still, I ended up calling Maria and spent the night at her place later that day.

Preschool had his lawyers to keep the cops at bay, and I had my girls to shield me from any kind of investigation. My main girl, Maria, was spotless, and I kept her away from everything. Even though she had her suspicions and knew I was tied up in some shady things, she never asked. Now, my two main side chicks, Tiffany and Rose, both had their issues. However, none of their issues could be tied to me because I simply wasn't involved in anything shady. They did. So, even if the cops wanted to use them to get to me, they would just show me their hand without me showing them mine. In the event either one of them got busted for anything, it would alert me to the players involved. And good luck trying to keep track of all the other flings that I had and how any of them fit into anything I was doing.

I loved my girls, they were the best, and maybe I should've been a pimp or porn producer instead of a club promoter and security contractor. The best part was that none of them actually knew anything other than some hearsay or rumors they heard. I would even feed them misinformation so that in the event they were ever questioned, the cops would be stuck between chasing their own tails and chasing phantoms. Any prosecutor or judge would quickly become disgusted by all the bullshit and dead ends any cop who had a hard-on for me would bring before them. Dissension in the ranks is better than any legal team and a whole lot cheaper.

Between all my relationships, my different houses and apartments, and the mini-mansion, it was hard enough for me to keep track of where I lived, let alone anyone trying to follow me and get any kind of read on me. The only two consistent locations that could be tied to me were my office over by the casino and our club. Those were really the only two locations where I could see the cop's getting approval for a search warrant. I felt pretty insulated from any of the street stuff even though I seemed to be getting further and further into it. It was my hope that regardless of what would happen in the future, I would come out smelling like a rose. I could only hope Preschool was being as cautious and taking precautions not to get unnecessarily caught up, especially on some bullshit that could easily be avoided.

PreSCHOOL:

The same cop the feds called in a favor from, who notified Tone of the ongoing federal investigation, worked at Muy Bella previously. He called Tone to let me know. He knew if he ever needed anything, he could always count on me to make it happen. But we were not always cordial. The last time I saw this cop, he worked at the door. He wasn't a sergeant yet. He was working his way up and was as green as a marijuana plant with no buds. He came to work one day, and we were all in the club. I heard loud honking outside, and I sent him to check it out. He goes outside and comes back, saying that it's a truck that's parked outside, holding up traffic in the front of the parking lot.

"Well, why don't you tell that fucker to move, or you'll tow his car, I asked?"

"I did," he said. He claimed he was a cartel member and didn't give a shit. He spoke Spanish and spewed off mumble jumble, like arguing in Spanish, which was a competitive sport. I couldn't get into any more shit because I was already in the hot seat with my superiors, so I just walked away.

I yelled, "WHAT THE FUCK ARE WE PAYING YOU FOR THEN?"

So, he stormed out and tried to reason with the cartel member one more time before coming inside the bar, looking defeated. I go outside and start trying to reason and compromise with this guy. He says he's heard about me shooting at his friends, and he's not going to be easily swayed because he has a gun, too. I lost all my patience. So, I speak the universal language that everyone does. I punch through the window, and my hand crashes into his face. I start banging the cartel member's face against the steering wheel and telling him to pull his gun and put it in my mouth. I want him to use his gun. The truck pulls off and gets into a wreck in the oncoming traffic in the street in front of my club. As I walked back to the club with my hand bleeding, the people who were held up in traffic behind the truck cheered me on.

The cop charged out and yelled, "You can't do that in front of me. I'm an officer of the law."

To which I yell back, "Some kind of bullshit cop you are. You couldn't get a fucking truck to move." I threw a thousand dollars at the officer and told him, "You're FIRED! Now get the fuck out of here."

Since then, he's been meaning to get back in my good graces because he knows we treated him well. We paid him and his other off-duty friends two hundred bucks an hour with thousand dollar bonuses at times. Not to mention the bonuses for them not doing anything but hold up the wall for all the hours they work. I pay the boys fifteen bucks an hour, and they stay all day going above and beyond to make sure the place and environment for the patrons are safe and secured.

So, I had Cowboy and my nephew drive out to the wilderness in Smallville to drop off a Panamera Porsche to my long-time criminal defense lawyer, Michael Davis. As the two were trying to figure out the GPS on the car, which kept rerouting them continuously, they parked at an intersection. This part of town is one of those preserved white towns with nothing but hillbillies and loggers inhabiting the area. A huge truck with a Confederate flag pulls up behind the Porsche and is mad that they are just taking up the street. The truck driver is so angry he jumps out of his truck and goes to the driver's side window of the Porsche to give them a piece of his mind. The car windows are tinted, so he can't see the occupants. He gets to the window and starts banging on it, and the Porsche driver's side door opens. A 6'5", 360 pound, tribal tattooed beast of a man climbs out and hovers over the hillbilly.

The beast of a man is none other than "Cowboy," a member of my organization. "Son of a gun," The truck driver utters as he tries to get back into his truck. Cowboy is the USO that speaks with a southern drawl. He even listens to country music. A condition known as foreign accent syndrome from his car accident. No one knew what this condition was, but I would always mockingly jab at him, "It would've benefitted us if you came to from your coma knowing how to speak Chinese or even Russian. You could've helped us expand further into different continents. Instead, you come to speaking that hillbilly shit that none of us can understand and only reminds me of redneck guards at the prison. Ain't that something? Country accents don't do us any good because we ain't in the market of selling belt buckles." Cowboy grabs the truck driver from behind by the neck and pulls him backward. The truck driver, pulled by the gravity of force backward, feels a thrust of a kick that sends him flying forward.

My nephew's phone rings. He answers and it's the lawyer Michael Davis. He's screaming, "What the hell are you guys doing?"

My nephew answers casually, "Oh hey, Counselor, I was just about to call you. We're lost and at some cross-section."

"I know. I can see you guys outside from my kitchen window beating up someone in the middle of the street."

My nephew says, "Oh no, that's just Cowboy. I'm in the car. But the guy came pounding on the window asking for it."

The two were to deliver the car taken from a pimp who hired a couple of Samoans to jump the lawyer. The lawyer represented one of the pimp's hoes in a personal injury claim where she was hit by a city bus while working the streets. The lawyer took a third and gave the rest to the pimp named Jimmy "MacGeezy" Buffalino, aka "The Giraffe." It's a name he got because of his long, sleek neck, which he often covered with a silk turtleneck sweater. The Giraffe squandered his portion of the money and decided he was owed more when he found that he was broke. He believed that he was ripped off by the lawyer charging extra fees for initial court costs and whatever else the lawyer tacked on to the settlement being reached. The lawyer disagreed with him and sent him a financial statement that showed three hundred dollars was the total fee incurred for filing and initiating the settlement.

Jimmy hired these two meth-head goons to assault the lawyer regardless. Upon hearing that it was Samoans, I was furious and began to scour the whole of Tacoma, trying to figure out who it was. Eventually, my men brought me word that it was some out-of-towners. The two assailants lived in Seattle and were nephews of a good USO member in prison. Because of this, I promised not to kill them but to just break the same body parts that they broke on the lawyer. A pelvis, a rib, and a shoulder bone. Maybe a little bit more. We went to Seattle and found the two hired assailants and did to them as promised. The two assailants gave up Jimmy immediately. We later found Jimmy the Pimp and beat him to a pulp, to which he offered the car and money as compensation for damages. To spare him his life, he offered his services free of charge. His services weren't worth much, but the lawyer had a use for him, so Jimmy got to stick around.

cHapter THIrty-one
FLeetwood 94

Reyes:

Danny Duke would host these annual summer parties on his father's property down south past Olympia on sixty or so acres of land. It lasted for several days, and people would come for a day or stay longer, sleeping in tents or RVs. The outdoor tiki bar and the hot tub room were favorite spots to congregate. Playing cards or dominos was an activity everyone enjoyed, whether sober or drunk. Of course, there was music with a full-on DJ booth and speakers. There were also trails people could hike and a stream for fishing if that was what someone wanted to do. The party was for people of all ages, ethnicities, and walks of life. Danny Duke loved people and was always a gracious host.

At one of these parties, I witnessed quite the spectacle of my own making, giving me a keen insight into the female psyche. I had taken Monica along with two other females I had already fucked and was messing around with. I didn't feel bad about bringing them because, after all, I was upfront with Monica from the jump, telling her that I was going to date other women. She had willingly agreed and went along with it up to a certain point. When I picked up Monica, I told her we had to pick up two more of my friends who were going with us. When she found out the two friends were female, it put her in a certain mood, a state of irritation. To her credit, she was as cordial as she could bring herself to be after being blindsided, so that was most definitely on me. My bad, you live, and you learn.

For the most part, I was able to relax and enjoy myself with minimal pushback from Monica. Seeing it as a good sign and being a positive-minded man, I was hoping for the best outcome for the situation. That being said, Monica and I would've ended up having a threesome with one of the females, and the best-case scenario would've been all four of us getting it on. Unfortunately, Monica spent most of her time moping around like a hurt puppy. In hindsight, I guess she was just trying to process it and deal with things in her own way without freaking out. That's not how I was thinking about it at the time, though. I was frustrated with her and annoyed by her open display of jealousy and lack of excitement for the sexual energy being generated. I mean, both females were down, and I could've had a threesome with those two instead. I just didn't want to do that to Monica and ostracize her even further. Plus, it was an experience I wanted to share with her.

Later in the evening, accepting the fact that Monica wasn't going to have anything to do with what was hanging in front of her, I couldn't let those two beauties down. In one last attempt to entice Monica to drop the façade, I suggested that all four of us get into the hot tub. Both of my friends agreed with the idea and were excited to have some fun in the hot tub. Monica's objection was because she didn't bring a swimsuit. None of us did, so the three of us hopped in, me in my boxers and both Denise and Allison in their bras and panties. Denise was a beautiful ebony hottie with large breasts, and Allison was a sexy Latina number with a nice ass. Coming to the final conclusion that I had failed in my objective, I reached out to two of Pavel's younger cousins.

They had hit me up earlier and asked me where the party was, but I blew them off because they were still only seniors in high school. But then I figured, why not let these eager bucks into the action and text them the location? Since they were locals of the area, it didn't take them long to find their way to the party and onto the porch with the hot tub. Having kept the girls entertained long enough, I introduced them to Pavel's cousins, who quickly entered into the hot tub. As I sat down at the card table, drying off and getting dressed, I could still see the hot tub. Denise and Allison wasted no time unleashing their sexual energies. As they began to kiss and make out with the two cousins, both girls would stare at me, maybe hoping I would change my mind and take them back. As the two cousins fucked them, neither Denise nor Allison took their eyes off me as I played cards. The girls were happy, the boys were happy, and even Monica was pleased with herself. If I had known how things would've turned out between me and Monica in the end, I most definitely would've fucked those willing and eager beauties in a ménage à trois.

During that first summer, when we were getting acquainted, I took Preschool with me to one of these annual parties. I told Preschool to meet up with me at the Starbucks in DuPont, which is a unique small town that's home to mostly military members. It was a convenient place to meet as it was on the way just off of I-5 and tucked into its own little world, seemingly sheltered from everywhere else. It only shared its city limits with two government bodies, mostly Fort Lewis (bordering to the east and south) and a small area belonging to the Nisqually National Wildlife Refuge (bordering the west). The plan was to take two separate cars. That way, he could stay as long as he wanted or leave whenever he wanted, and I could do the same.

With me in my car was The Blonde and two of my housemates, Angelo and my cousin C'zar. Angelo was also in my unit and worked MPI with me. He was a young Italian kid who had just come back from downrange and was recovering from a collapsed lung that was a result of driving over an improvised explosive device (IED). A common occurrence in the Middle East. Shit, just about every soldier I knew coming back from over there had at least one instance with an IED. The NCOIC of MPI had encountered so many of those devices while deployed over there that while driving back here in the state, he would break out in a sweat. He would have intense flashbacks, especially driving under an overpass. The shit is real over there.

Even though he was a lot smaller than me, Angelo was really good at watching my back. There was this one incident at a house party we had gone to in Tacoma. I was outside talking with this one Mexican chick, and some young punk thought he was just gonna buck up and interrupt. At that point in time, I was in my early thirties, she was twenty-one, and this punk was eighteen or nineteen. Whatever possessed him to be so blatantly disrespectful, I'll never know. He didn't know me or what I was capable of. I let him say his piece because he knew her, but then I was like, "Look, little homie, we were talking, and you're kinda interrupting now."

He decided to step up to me and say, "She's talking to me now."

"Well, what's up then?"

That's when he started throwing punches, hitting me square on the jaw with the first one. The rest were wild and in the air, and I was able to duck under them and grab ahold of him. We were tussling for a few seconds as I was trying to get control of him, but before I could, Angelo grabbed him from behind, taking him to the ground. There's Angelo in full mount on top of this punk controlling him, telling him we were MPs and to chill out. It was too late, though, because I was already angered by the disrespect and seeing blood. I calmly walked over, removed my pistol, and was about to pistol whip the piss out of him. Fortunately, I only smacked him across his cheek once before another bystander interceded on his behalf. It was a tiny, little female, and she grabbed onto my pistol with both her hands, saying please don't shoot him. I wasn't going to shoot him. I was just going to teach him a lesson about respect. She had a death grip, and it took me a minute to break away from her, especially because I wasn't trying to hurt her adorable ass. Her little distraction had bought that punk enough time to scramble out from under Angelo, running for what he thought was his life, into the house holding his jaw. This was the first time I caught myself letting out my inner gangster, which had been manifesting since I had met Preschool.

After that, we decided it was time to leave the party. Rounding up everyone who rode with us took a few minutes. It was me, Angelo, C'zar,

Malik, this chick Jennifer who was driving, and, of course, the Mexican chick. As we were getting into the Chevy Tahoe, a bunch of gangbangers came up to the house demanding to be let in, and a fight started outside. Malik was telling me, "Come on, let's go," since I was the only one still standing outside the Tahoe when the fight broke out.

"Okay, let's do it," was my response as I turned and started walking toward the house. I made it only one or two steps before feeling Malik's hand on my shoulder.

"What are you doing? Get in the truck. We need to go."

It was only then that I realized what he had meant when he said *come on, let's go*. He read the situation, knowing it was all bad, and wanted us to leave, but I thought he had meant for us to go get in on the action. As I turned around, laughing at my own misunderstanding and trying to explain it to him, gunshots came from the direction of the house. The girl, Jennifer, wasn't wasting any time leaving, throwing the Tahoe in drive and stepping on the gas. I wasn't even all the way in yet, and thankfully, Malik and C'zar grabbed hold of me and pulled me in. I later heard that the situation escalated after we left. Friends of ours still there came piling out of the house with their own guns drawn, taking up tactical positions as many of them were prior military combat vets. Some of them even served in the Rangers as well. One of my friends had even taken up a position under a car with his AR-15. When the police came, they showed up in full force. Surprisingly, no arrests were made, and no one got in trouble.

I was already parked at the Starbucks waiting for Preschool while reminiscing about this particular Starbucks. I mean, how could I not? One time, while I was on duty, The Blonde and I had a rendezvous there. Since I worked in plainclothes, driving an unmarked police car and could leave base with it, I decided to meet The Blonde there for coffee one day. When she pulled up, I got out of my unmarked vehicle, a Ford Explorer, and greeted her with a hug as she got out of her car. That led to some kissing and ass-grabbing. Then, taking her by the hand, I took her to the passenger side of the Explorer. Opening the door, I sat down in the passenger seat, and she climbed up on my lap. Even though she was petite, we barely fit, and since it had a cage in the back, I couldn't let the seat fully back. Taking our pants off was a challenge, but we both managed, and she rode me until I was ready to bust. At which point she half stood up, bent over at the waist, and took my load in her mouth. I thought for sure someone was going to see us and report it, but it never happened. Damn, that was so hot.

My thoughts were interrupted when Preschool arrived with two Samoan passengers. He was driving his tricked-out, baby blue, four-door, 1975 Fleetwood, Brougham Cadillac Deville. Damn, he was riding in style, and at that moment, I fell in love with that automobile and wanted one too. I actually started obsessing over the idea of getting a Cadillac on the drive down to Danny Duke's place. Eventually, I knew I would get around to finding the right one. Then, it would need some restoration and take some time to do so. We said our quick hello and then were on our way down to the party. It only took us about an hour to get there from Starbucks.

When I introduced Danny Duke to Preschool, the look on Danny's face was priceless as it was at that point he knew I was backing up what I told him when I said I would handle the gray areas of the promotion and club stuff. The location was a perfect setting for Preschool and me to have a private conversation. Down there, it was completely isolated and away from everyone who might have ears to want to listen in on what we talked about that day.

PrescHOOL:

Man, I didn't know Tone all that well when he invited me to this party. He had me meet him at this Starbucks back then, and it was wearisome for me. But he had me follow him out into the middle of nowhere, and it was the most amazing thing. We got the chance to sit down and actually talk man to man about stuff, and up until this time, I really didn't know who he was, but the vision he had for a business for the two of us and wanting to include the benefits to help the boys was a standup thing. He wasn't as much of a square as he let on to be at first, having some knowledge of the streets, but he never really got down like that too much. He was like me in so many ways. I was like him in the sense that I had grown up in a different environment, a different family. I probably could've been a CEO or a computer engineer of some sort. Probably would've gone legit and enjoyed what I did, too.

I didn't know where we were going, but I almost never drove my "Blue Mackerel" anywhere that could get dirty. We just had it tricked and got the pumps and switches put in it. It had three pumps and eight batteries sitting in the back, and I was worried that where we'd be going would be off-roading for some reason. I never thought that having this Fleetwood would inspire a lot of the boys to get a Fleetwood and trick it out themselves. This gave birth to our affiliation with the USOS Car Club, one of the biggest car clubs in the world. I mean, why not? What better way to funnel money than through a not-for-profit that seemed to be building lowriders? We had exempt status, and this meant we could cut through a lot of the tax barriers we had. We could also build a car club to span the United States and get entered into shows and become recognized for something good instead of just everything bad. A king cannot have more vices than he has virtues. That's just facts. If you gamble, you consume drugs/alcohol, you trick with women, you splurge on shopping sprees, and you have habits galore. You are going to need something pulling in money to offset the cost of your lifestyle. A lot of people get into this because of the lifestyle. But this is for real for me. I'm trying to feed my family and friends and retire in a year. I always came into this thing with the most important thought in mind, which was that this is just a hustle. It's not a lifelong occupation. The rich stay rich by pretending to be broke, and the broke stay broke by pretending to be rich. I've watched too many people die young and burn out fast over this. I got kids to think about. I always had to think a step ahead. The way things were going, though, wasn't as easy as I had expected.

Reyes:

The week before going up the mountain to train the boys, I had dropped off my car at the tire shop and looked forward to picking it up. I had finally gotten my Cadillac Fleetwood. I'd been working on that car to enter it along with the USOS cars into a lowrider competition. It was a nineteen ninety-four model, dark blue with cream-colored leather seats. I had switches for hydraulic lifts and a complete sound system installed boasting two eighteen-inch subwoofers. The last detail was getting brand-new whitewalls (tires) installed. It should've been easy enough to do, right? Well, when I went to pick up my baby from the tire shop, my cream-colored seats were smeared with grease and were destroyed.

I went to the manager, a very large white guy, and inquired about the seats, hoping to find a viable solution. That motherfucker gave no fucks about my predicament and could've cared less about the damage done to my car. When I asked to speak to the owner, he said to me, "I am the owner, buddy."

"Well, okay then, as one business owner to another, you can understand my position, and I can understand yours."

"You ain't understanding nothing because there's nothing to understand other than you owe me thirty-two hundred dollars for the tires and installation."

"Hey, man, that's not even what the issue is. I have no problem paying for the tires based on what was already agreed upon. I do have a problem with someone ruining my leather seats, which will have to be replaced, and that isn't going to be cheap. Plus, the interior is going to have to be detailed. So why don't we find some common ground?"

"Fuck you, and if you want your car back, you need to pay up before we let you leave with it. Now, we can do this the easy way or the hard way, but one thing is certain. I'm getting my money today, or you're getting an ass whooping."

At that point, some of his guys had come out of the shop and started to encircle me. The wise option was to stand down, and being polite and agreeable, I said as nicely as I could, "Okay, I'm sorry for the misunderstanding, and I'll go get your money out of the car. My girl has it in her purse."

Not waiting for a response, I turned around and walked to the car my girl, Maria, was waiting in because she was the one who drove me there. I got in the front passenger seat, pulled out my cell phone, and placed it on my lap so it wouldn't be seen. I made a call on speaker. Preschool answered, and as I faced my girl like I was talking to her, I explained the situation to him. I explained that it was six or eight big-ass white dudes, including the owner.

Fortunately for me, and unfortunately for the guys at the shop, the USOS was just down the street having a cookout. I hung up with Preschool, got the thirty-two hundred my girl was holding, and told her to leave when she saw the boys pull up. I didn't know what was going to happen, but I knew I didn't want her anywhere around it. Moving as slowly as I could, I walked back over to the office portion of the shop and handed the owner the money. As he was counting the money and feeling all proud of himself, four black SUVs pulled up. When the boys started piling out and saying to me, "Hey, Uce, what's up?" The owner stopped counting the money, and a concerned look came across his face. That was the first concerned look about my situation that I had seen him have all day.

As I watched Preschool trying to diplomatically and peacefully resolve the situation, June wasn't having it and finally had enough of the owner's mouth. I guess June thought it was time for an attitude adjustment. The situation quickly escalated, and the score was settled in our favor. Every one of the shop workers would never look at life the same way afterward. Avoiding all the blood and carnage, I gathered my money from the owner's top shirt pocket, where he had put it before unsuccessfully trying to bark us out of his shop. Additionally, the owner, seeing the error of his ways and wanting to rectify it, made an agreement with us. First, the tires and work on my car were on the house, plus he would pay for my seats. In his recompense, he also volunteered to pay the medical bills of all his employees and give generous in-house credit to the USOS.

Then, after taking care of everything else, including the tire shop nonsense, we finally got around to meeting up with the Russians. It wasn't that they weren't important to us. At that time, they were the easiest to satisfy. The situation with them was going well, and as a token of their appreciation, they offered an opportunity for a mini-mansion that had recently become available. They had suggested that I should be the one moving into it because it had been my idea to resolve their problem and make money from it. They were going to let us lease it for a very reduced price as a bonus for all the money we had saved and earned for them. Two hundred a month plus paying all the utilities was the ask. Normally, at a place like that, the monthly rent was in the ballpark of three grand.

If something sounds too good to be true, then, normally, it was, but Preschool was caught up in the idea and was ready to jump on it at first. These Russians were slick and highly intelligent chess players. There was more to it, and my suspicions were at an all-time high. It just didn't sit right with me, especially in how they made the offer. I explained to Preschool why I thought it was a setup, telling him that they only wanted to keep tabs on us. How better to do it than by putting me in one of their mini-mansions? So, after some time discussing it, Preschool and I decided why not use it to put some of our girls in and use it for our own little parties. All in all, though, everything seemed to be going well for them.

In fact, things went so well with the mini-mansion operation that the main boss wanted us to have the USOS do the security for his birthday party so more of his family and friends could attend the celebration than having to work security for it. This, in turn, obligated me to attend the birthday party with Preschool. Attending a party of this magnitude as a guest of the boss put us in the good graces of the Russians. I was trying to lie as low as I possibly could, doing my best to blend in as a nobody. I didn't want to be known by anyone there. All eyes off me, please, was my goal. I wasn't trying to be a gangster. I was just there out of loyalty to my friend Preschool. At that point, I was barely even an associate and could've easily walked away, and looking back, maybe I should've. Our host, The Seafood King, seemed to enjoy our company. I managed to hide away in a corner, cracking some jokes with a couple of foot soldiers. This gave Preschool and the host some time to speak in private. Still, I couldn't help but think to myself about the upcoming trip to Vegas and just how much deeper that was going to draw me in even further than what I'd been trying to avoid.

PreSCHOOL:

We show up any day for our loved ones. If you know USOS, we travel in packs, too, especially in these mean streets. Tone called, and we were up the road at a barbecue at the park. As soon as I said, "Tone is in some trouble," the boys all forgot about the teriyaki chicken and hot dogs on the grill. One thing everyone loves more than a cookout is a rumble before the cookout. We wasted no time. We get there and calmly try to assess the situation. But the way the owner was talking said only one thing: RUMBLE. Now, have you ever met one of those guys who you know never got his ass kicked before in his life? He's cocky and punchy like he shits roses? Like he just lives on cloud nine and shits down on the world from above? Yeah. This guy was one of those.

So not long after we asked the question of what his problem was, he gave us the go fuck yourself speech. Before he could finish, June punched his face so hard—I mean, I had never seen a guy get punched like that before, where his head was trying to leave his neck, and his teeth were flying out in that direction, saying to his face, follow me. The other shop guys came at us with tools and monkey wrenches. Shoot, we love a good party. We didn't want it any other way. We had our dancing shoes on, so coming bare to a dance floor would've been disappointing. The rumble kicked into high gear and ended with all the tough guys looking like pretzels or puzzle pieces scattered in the tire shop. They were deformed and disfigured, with nothing but oil and blood to soil the garage.

This was nostalgic for Juney because his other case stemmed from a rumble in the Lakewood bar down the road. It was like one thing after another because he was still awaiting the details of the outcome of that case to see if he had to do prison time or not. The USOS got into it with the Lakewood Crips. Juney, as the rumble broke out, started beating a dude. Another guy came over and shot June in the arm. June, having beaten the shooter's friend to a pulp, starts chasing after the shooter. Yes, chasing. As. In. The. Shooter. Ran with the gun still in hand!

June catches him and beats him with his gun because his adrenaline is pumping way too high for logic to make sense that he could've just shot the guy. Nah, he beat him in the head. Years later, the Black community activists lobbied that the kid whom June beat with his own gun be released from prison. The shooter who ran—while running—was shooting behind him, and a bullet missed June and hit the shooter's own cousin at a distance behind June. The bullet killed him. The Blacks would reach out to our lawyers to hire them, not knowing they were our lawyers. My lawyer, having noticed June's involvement, asked me if he should take it. It's a highly publicized case that could do no harm other than bolster his career. We could have June testify he was the wrong guy. Make a case for reasonable doubt. Get the shooter out and meet him with a bullet at the door. But nah. He wasn't worth the bullet or the hassle. There would be many more cases that were publicized that would put our legal friends on the red carpet and on the tongues of Hollywood's elite.

CHAPTER THIRTY-TWO
Vegas

PRESCHOOL:

Reyes and I fly to Las Vegas to meet with the USOS for what they call a saofa'i.

"What's it called, a sua fa'i?" Reyes asked.

To which the USOS laughed and corrected him. Saofa'i. Sua fa'i is a banana pudding dish Polynesians make for their babies. Or what the ladies call a man's cock juices. A saofa'i is a sit down with the elders. A counsel around the fires they used to call it. The saofa'i marks the formal acceptance of a new matai (or chief) by his family and village. It's when a title and name are given along with the responsibility to a new chief to take his seat amongst other chiefs. Reyes nodded.

"This is huge, so don't fuck it up for me, Uce," I tell him.

"Yeah, I'll try not to fuck it up," Tone says. "Especially since I don't know what the fuck it is and what I can do to *NOT* fuck it up."

Before we headed out to Vegas, the best news came in. The Russians had contracted us to be security for their mini-mansions all over Washington, in particular the north Tacoma area. In layman's terms, we were given free mansions to live in and occupy to keep them protected. I mean, what better way to keep vandals and vagrants out of a mansion than to live in it and protect it twenty-four-seven? So that's what the plan was when me and Tone returned from Vegas. We would go see all the spots they had us protect and then choose the one we wanted to occupy. This would be a blast. However, as one thing goes well with the Russians, it seems something always goes bad with another group.

The USO who picks us up from the airport takes us straight to the Dolce & Gabbana store. He seemed to have been a regular because he knew the tailors and the manager well. He bought us suits because he felt that we weren't dressed for the occasion. I thought this guy was a joke. Really. Tone had a collection of suits that would make this guy's jaw detach from his face like in the cartoons. Ha. This fucking flunky. But I can't complain about free. We didn't dress up because we weren't thinking this was a formal meeting. Heck, we're used to being more forward than formal in most of these matters, and the only formalities were in the language. Especially when we had one of the four old men in the room. The four old men were members of the council, and they were all in prison on recent indictments that covered the west coast from California, Washington, Oregon, Utah, and Las Vegas. The recent indictments also included prison guards who were aids to the USOS movement, and it's funny because the one that was a correctional officer was on the news calling the other correctional officers that ratted on him "PIGS." Ain't that something? The four old men who were the pillars of the USOS foundation on the streets. They ran the gambling in Hawaii. The protection racket in different states. The drug shipments from Mexico to the South Pacific. They were truly the oil and grease to the movement. The wheels that kept it spinning. But back to this motherfucking driver. He gives us an I-get-it look.

He goes on to say annoyingly, "You guys thought this was a vacation. You brought your swim trunks but not a suit?"

"Nah, we didn't have time to pack. We just came from the mountain where we did intense training with the troops in Washington. Tone's got suits though".

"Oh, Washington troops. I like that. You guys sound militant. *Organized.*" He laughed. "Sounds fancy."

"Well, *we are* organizing things. We're doing most of the leg work for the USOS in the streets, no? I mean, considering everything is going to shit since the four old men got indicted? I came home to put things together."

The driver chuckled. "You really think you can put this shit together? You ought to listen to the big USO when you get to the meeting. You might learn something. If you really think you can put things together, you're doing it from the hot seat. That's all I can say."

That's not what I meant but I wasn't going to sit there and argue with this laughing hippopotamus looking USO. So, I just left things where they were, and we rode in silence.

The big USO in Las Vegas story is that he was a bouncer at McGraffe Casino Resort. He worked his way up and fell in love with a casino manager, and they later got married. This casino manager's dad just so happens to be the casino owner. The couple launched into a security business and later into a marble installation company and built a successful empire out of the two. They won contracts with a lot of the casinos in Las Vegas and were able to secure jobs for the boys coming home. Receiving contract after contract netted them huge profits for security and marble installments aside from their casino interests. This USO was a king on the streets. The big USO is Vinny "Vegas" Prescott. The baby brother of Paulie and Master Sergeant Vika Prescott.

"Who is this guy?" Vegas asked.

"He's my USO," I spit back.

"You're USO? This guy looks Black." Vegas continued to heckle.

Tone looked at me because he was about to answer proudly that he was Puerto Rican and get us all jammed up. Ha.

Vegas said, "The fuck going on in Washington? You guys run out of USOS? You brought an outsider?" Vegas gets up in Tone's face and inspects him like he's looking at an inanimate object from a foreign country. "This looks like a real nigga?"

"That's because he is. Don't you remember we're all real niggas." I shoot back.

"What are you?" he asks.

I answered, "He's one of us, a USO. He's my most trusted one, which tells you what I have to work with in Washington. You think they send me guys that have clean records and work experience in the businesses? Shit, all the guys they have sent me have set us back in our progress so far." I gestured at Reyes. "You know, Tone here was with your brother Vika on tour. He was by his side when he died on the same MEDEVAC."

Vinny's eyes perked up in interest at the mention of his beloved blood brother. He looked satisfied and turned from Tone in approval. The mention of his older brother brought sadness to him. You could see he turned away because he needed a moment. Vegas started to explain to me the protocols and codes of the streets, as if I didn't know after serving a mandatory minimum ten-year sentence in the feds, with over twenty years of prison time under my belt. Vinny liked me, but I could tell we were being formal. It was his orders. Grill him and remind him. Ha. It's the reason they sent the driver who rubbed us the wrong way. This was designed to rattle our cages. See if we were unstable. If we were sober. The old man hated hearing that I was partying and living it up. Again, it was the boys calling back and feeling like they could do the same thing I did if they were given the same aid and resources. That's the sadness of this thing. Fucktards that you feed are the same one's wanting to take food out of your mouth. They don't think that half a loaf of bread is still bread. That they have more than they've ever had without me. They always want more. The greed of these motherfuckers, I tell you. You could compare it to the appetite of guys on Wall Street.

Vinny is like me. He refers to me as his uncle. I think it's sincere. I've always called him my nephew. I could call on him for anything, but he wasn't built for this. He was just a parrot. A mouthpiece. Speaking and uttering his brother's creed and words. He could've done anything in the world. He had enough brains and wit. Money to add to the complications. Yet, he chooses this life. Fuck me. I'll never understand it. He could've been like his brother Vika instead. He was actually the founder of our car club's chapter. He thought it was really pimpish to have Cadillacs. He had a fondness for pimps. He surrounded himself with them. I don't know if it's a Vegas thing. But I was never big on pimps. See, I'm a player, not a pimp. A pimp will go broke without a hoe. A player will get rich with or without a bitch. That's something to say for a guy whose wife was really the brains for him. Without his wife, he'd be just another security guard.

He goes on, "No matter how far up north Clallam Bay is, you guys still operate under my Uce upstate. We good?"

"Yeah, we are good," I answered for both of us. "What we do for your uce though, if the fed's found out, it wouldn't land us back in Clallam Bay, more like Guantanamo Bay, just saying. But yeah, we hear you."

"You guys ever studied money markets?" Vinny asked.

Well, there are these financial terms for placing orders. There's one called (F.O.K), which stands for 'Fill-Or-Kill.' This particular order says if a broker-dealer can't fill an investor's order, then he's to kill it. We're all financial instruments in a world where cash rules everything around us. And the only difference between us and Wall Street is that if we can't fill our orders, then we might end up getting killed!

Reyes:

After the sit-down, I went back to my room to decompress and think about everything that was said, letting it all sink in. I have to admit they did take care of us, putting us up in a suite at a nice casino hotel resort. As I stood on the balcony admiring the view, I thought about how I couldn't believe that this was what Master Sergeant Prescott was talking about when he meant brotherhood. He shared with me that he enlisted in the armed services not only to make his father proud to follow in his footsteps but also to escape an "obligation" he felt to join the family business. This wasn't the family business I had pictured in my mind when he said it.

Maybe I should mention that the Prescott family came from a long line of island chiefs. So, I had figured he'd have been some kind of big wig running a village or something. How bad could the family business of running a village be? At the very least, I legitimately thought his family business entailed a construction business or maybe a fishing charter or something to do with tourism. Maybe I should've been more inquisitive, but that's all I saw the one time I went with him to visit his family in Samoa. His family all seemed to be working in those endeavors, and they looked happy doing so. There I was, wishing it was a construction company instead of a criminal enterprise.

The club we owned wasn't even in either of our names and had relied on a verbal agreement with the actual owners. So, there was nothing for anyone to take from us legally if things went south as we were only named as (me) the general manager and (Preschool) the marketing director. Even though things were going well with the Mexicans and the Russians, we were still looking at a messy situation with the shooting at the club. Since we didn't own it, I believed at the time we were in a position to easily walk away, and the actual owners and their insurance policies would be able to kick back any of the money we had invested into the club. What concerned me was the expectation Vegas Vinny was placing on us with this F.O.K. thing. Fuck!

Man, it was so much easier just being a simple club promoter, making an easy few hundred dollars a week, drinking all the free liquor I wanted, and banging hot chicks. Three hundred dollars a week was a good week's earnings and with no hassles. I didn't have to attend sit-downs with chiefs and gangsters. There was no flying into different states to basically be told to produce or die. It was simple, safe, and carefree. But no, I had to go and get myself mixed up in this world of chaos and thuggery. I missed the days of not having to worry about any real overheads. I found myself dealing with the reality that having too much overhead would lead to being cut down with a bullet in the back of the head. What options did I really have? I was just going to have to ride it out and hope against hope I'm wrong about everything when it comes to Preschool, my business partner, and my best friend.

As I looked out into the desert, trying to understand my situation, I couldn't help but remember the last time I was in Las Vegas, well, actually just passing through it, was with Master Sergeant Prescott (still only a staff sergeant at the time) on our way to Fort Irwin, California home to the Army's National Training Center (NTC). A thousand acres of land located in the Mojave Desert, also known as "Death Valley," utilized by the military for large-scale force-on-force training exercises. It affords soldiers the opportunity to see a brigade-sized maneuver element in full swing, engaging in combat operations. More importantly, command leadership at the brigade level and higher are able to deploy all or almost all of their assets at the same time. That is important because usually, only battalions and smaller elements are able to go into full swing during a field training exercise at their home duty stations.

OPFOR stands for opposing forces, and at NTC, it is a full-time job for the soldiers assigned there. That means they have seen tactics used by numerous units and are really good at portraying an enemy force that is competent and formidable. Beating OPFOR is tough because units are in their house, and they know all the terrain, having the advantage of knowing all the best hiding spots. For them, it's more like a regular nine-to-five work week, pretty much knowing exactly when all the engagements are going to take place. This allows them to get regular meals, showers, and as much rest as possible. It's not like they stay up all night pulling guard duty or waiting to be ambushed in the middle of the night.

Tent City is located within the containment area. That's the place where everyone gathers before going out into what we call the field. Being in the field means being in the training area, whether out in the woods, up in the mountains, down in the jungle, or desert. Within the field, there might be ranges, mock villages, or urban training facilities. In Tent City, it is just what it sounds like thousands of tents lined up and organized by individual units sharing an overhead structure to pitch their tents under. The structure is open on all sides and only designed to provide shade, keeping the intense sunshine off soldiers and equipment. While in Tent City, soldiers draw their equipment for about a week, taking up most of the time for the week. Most units do not bring their own vehicles, such as trucks and tanks, so they need this time to go through and inspect the vehicle they are assigned and address any maintenance issues before leaving the box and heading to the field. Yes, Tent City is also referred to as The Box.

The time in Tent City also allows soldiers to acclimatize to the harsh desert environment. It is also where we get all the safety briefings and information about the local wildlife. Out of all the wildlife, the desert tortoise was the only animal that could bring a whole training mission to a screeching halt as it was on the endangered species list and heavily protected by all kinds of federal and state laws. If one of those wandered into the training area, everything had to stop until the tortoise could safely be removed, or training could continue on, providing that the tortoise was safe. The dangerous animals to watch out for included scorpions, a half dozen or so venomous snakes, including the notorious western diamondback rattlesnake, mountain lions, and coyotes.

They were expressly explicit in not touching, chasing, bothering, or feeding any of the wildlife. They even warned us that while in Tent City, the coyotes were extremely bold and would circulate in and around the tents looking for food. They actually had a separate eating area for everyone to eat, as bringing food into the tent areas was a no-go. Well, apparently, one of the Rangers thought he was smarter than everyone else and decided to become friends with one of the coyotes. In the process of giving the coyote some food, I guess it wanted more than the Ranger had to offer and bit his hand. He had to get a ton of stitches and rabies shots. Funny as it was, the chain of command was not happy about the incident. Of course, everyone in Tent City heard about the incident, and I'm sure many rotations afterward heard about it. Signs started popping up everywhere, saying, "Don't feed the coyotes!"

When you are in the field, you live like you are conducting real-world missions, with the exception of being evaluated by an OC (Observation Controller) instead of real bullets. The OCs are assigned to squads all the way up to the brigade level. They give out missions like assignments for leaders and soldiers to be evaluated and graded on with a simple "GO" or "NOGO" grade. They also serve as safeties and referees on the training battlefield, trying to keep everyone safe and settle conflicts between the OPFOR and the units being evaluated.

One morning, I saw Master Sergeant Prescott praying on top of one of the mountains we were camped out on. Earlier, he had gone off on his own a good distance away from the rest of our squad and platoon "to watch the sunrise," as he had told us. There was a radio call for us to get ready to move out, so I was told to go and get him. As I walked up the mountain path to where he was, I caught a glimpse of the strongest man I knew down on his knees, silently praying as the sun was coming up over the horizon. Completely caught off guard by what I was witnessing and hesitant to interrupt him, I just stood there in silence for a moment in time. I have to admit there was a true sense of peace and magnificence in seeing that awe-inspiring silhouette of my hero against the beautiful sunrise and witnessing a humble giant connecting with his creator.

Later, after the training exercise and returning to our barracks at Hunter Army Airfield, I found myself contemplating God one night. I remember asking myself who is God and what Staff Sergeant Prescott knew about him that I didn't. I grew up Catholic, attending private Catholic schools five out of the twelve years of my formal education. Yep, Catholic school for first grade, fourth through sixth, and then eleventh grade, and if you wanted to count preschool and kindergarten that would make it seven years invested in school for a religious upbringing. Not really knowing why, I decided to turn over a new leaf in life and follow along with Master Sergeant Prescott. Whatever he was doing worked out well for him, so maybe it was exactly what I needed to be doing with my time.

I pretty much had my fill of alcohol, partying, and chasing girls, or at least I had thought. I started reading my Bible and attending church services regularly with Prescott. I prescribed to that church-going lifestyle for almost nine years. It kept me out of so much trouble I otherwise would have easily gotten myself into. Having Prescott as my squad leader for the first two years of that newfound devotion made it so much easier to bear and to deal with all the peer pressure to do otherwise. Our squad was always squared away; Prescott was squared away, and he demanded each of us to be as well, and we did. Whether churchgoer or bargoer, everyone rose to a higher level, being the absolute best they could possibly be. Prescott just had that way about him and could inspire and bring it out in others with ease.

It finally made sense to me while standing on that balcony in Vegas as to why Prescott would gravitate to the best unit in the military and walk a road in life very few are willing to or would even consider. For him, it was either walking in the light or walking in the darkness. I don't think he saw it any other way. It was what stabilized him from having to deal with family pressures and obligations, which, for him, were the ultimate forms of peer pressure. The Rangers didn't have anything like those Samoans and their family dynamics, so it was easy for Prescott not to give in to peer pressure or follow the herd but instead for him to blaze his own path in the military. As long as he was off doing his own thing in the military, it was pretty much hands off him for the rest of his family. Even the hardest of Samoan criminals don't want to suffer the wrath of their mother, grandmother, or auntie.

After all, I had similar reasons for joining the Rangers, too. I didn't want to continue down the path of falling into the wrong circles and getting myself locked up for some nonsense. My friends weren't bad, but we egged each other on to do bad things, which only escalated into doing more fucked up shit as we got older. So, in a sense, I enlisted to escape the downfall of running into the same fate Prescott felt he would've ended up in if he hadn't. It wasn't *exactly* the same, but I was pushing the envelope and following in the footsteps of friends and family who played to the streets and ended up in jail and prison.

It is funny how life is. So, there I was, back in the desert, metaphorically, physically, and spiritually. You see, it was just like I said it was when Master Sergeant Prescott was killed in action—I died that day. Maybe it was only from the result of his death or the culmination of that particular day that killed me. I guess it didn't really matter at that point because I was in it up over my head for sure. The good thing was that I wasn't alone. I was there with my friend—no, brother. A man I trusted for the last few years with having my back, living by the same code of loyalty, being loyal to a fault. I wasn't feeling sure anymore of that bond of brotherhood, though. The only question swimming through my head as I took in the cool evening breeze was, would Preschool blindly cave into his family obligations or, worse yet, his own demons?

CHapter THirty-THree
THe Gravel Pit

PreSCHOOL:

I can see Tone is going to need some time to digest the Vegas trip because the gray just got grayer for him. Welcome to my world, Uce. I knew for sure he was along for the ride even though he hadn't fully accepted his new role within the organization. For the time being, he was just going to go back to business as usual while he internally processed everything. I told him not to worry about anything, Uce. If anything goes down, I'll take the hit for it, and I don't mind going back to prison. It's like a vacation for me, and I'll have everything I need while I'm there. I got you. I know a lot of guys on the streets will tell you this when they are out making money with you but mutate like the ninja turtles master splinter the rat when they get into the interrogation room. But on the streets, all I had was my balls and my word. If my words didn't mean anything, my balls didn't mean shit. I've known killers and hard-core guys who flipped. I don't know what could ever bring them to it. But when they do, they become a nobody. A lot of them still try to hang on to the glory days of when they were someone. But the world would never accept them or respect them the same. They are less than scum. Tone speaks up, "You think I'm worried about you flipping on me? Fuck. I'm worried about getting canceled".

Getting back from Vegas, I knew I needed to tighten up my grip on the streets, especially with the new heartfelt orders dictated by Vinny. So, while we were driving back from the airport, I told Tone about the disciplinary problems I was having with the uces. I told him about how the boys are getting rambunctious and just doing things on a whim and not truly adhering to the code. Now, I don't have a problem with initiative. In fact, I appreciate anyone who can take the initiative. The issue I'm having is a bunch of nitwits taking matters into their own hands and creating more problems than they can solve.

Then Tone says to me, "Sounds like you need to take them to the hill, someplace out of sight and out of mind."

He then continues to tell me about his basic training experience of how the drill sergeants would take them to a hill far removed from everyone else and smoke the hell out of them, out of sight out of mind.

"Ya, Uce, that sounds like exactly what I need to be doing with these guys acting like flunkies. But where? Should we go back to the mountains we were at?"

"How about the gravel pits off of Waller Road? You can easily get to them the back way through the Salishan housing area."

"Perfect."

I began doing exactly that, starting off first with the young uces to give the older ones the chance to heed the warning and get in line on their own. Plus, I didn't want a full-blown rebellion taking place until the new system of discipline was instituted. I already had too much stress on my head from the inside to get things functioning like a cult, with the followers just taking leaps in blind faith.

Reyes:

When I got back from the Vegas trip, I knew Maria, Rose, and Tiffany were all going to want my attention and affection. Since I was drained mentally and emotionally from learning the harsh reality of the predicament I was in, I needed to have some fun and blow off steam, which meant I'd be seeing Tiffany first. Maria wasn't the kind of woman you blow off steam with on the account she was a bit uptight and always so serious.

With Rose, I could've definitely blown off steam with some hot sex, but it would've cost me having to deal with her unloading her burdens on me as she was then accustomed to doing. Don't get me wrong, Maria and Rose were great and fantastic women who offered a plethora of other wonderful amenities. However, in that situation, Tiffany was the only choice to be made. She was always fun, plus we always had ardent and prodigious sex together. This could easily have been attributed to the fact that she was only twenty-two at the time and I now believe to be clinically insane. As they say, the crazy ones are always the best in bed, and this statement was indeed factual. I didn't see her really crazy until many years later when my infatuation for her wore off, and I could see her through a clear and sober mind.

When our flight touched down at Seattle-Tacoma International Airport (Sea-Tac), I sent Tiffany a text to see if she was available. She was and seemed eager to see me. I picked her up at her aunt's house off Waller Road and then headed downtown Tacoma. I took her to the Matador on Pacific and Eighth for drinks and appetizers. Feeling tipsy and anxious, I wanted to go for a walk even though it was a bit chilly outside. As we were passing by The Elk Temple, which had been abandoned and boarded up at the time, I decided I wanted to take a look inside. Tiffany was scared because she was superstitious, believing in ghosts and shit. I told her not to worry about it because if a ghost kills us, I'll fuck it up when I'm also a ghost. After several attempts at trying to break through some of the boards, I decided I was making too much noise and didn't feel like having to explain myself to the police.

Moving on, we went to one of the clubs I did promotions for called CANS. It was just a few blocks away from Ninth Street. We had a few drinks there and ground on the dance floor for a little while until all my anxiety turned into a full-blown, concupiscent disposition. I took her by the hand and led her from off the dance floor to outside the main entrance. I proceeded to lead her across the street into Fireman's Park.

The park wasn't lit up and dark enough, allowing for enough privacy for my intentions. I pulled Tiffany into me and started kissing her while grabbing a handful of her ass. Turning her around and bracing her body against the park bench, I proceeded to unzip her pants, pulling them down just enough to penetrate her., Her ass cheeks were cold at first but quickly warmed from my body heat as I gyrated and thrust inside her. The intensity was magnified by the chances of getting caught—thrilling and exhilarating.

On our walk back to my car, I told Tiffany I needed to be up early in the morning for work, so it was going to be an early night for me, and I needed to take her home. After I dropped Tiffany back off at her aunt's house, I decided it was still early enough for me to go see Rose. Seeing as I had gotten out all my anxiety and was feeling revived, I was ready to deal with Rose unloading her issues on me. When I arrived at her club, I was greeted by some of my guys working the security contract. I shot the shit with them for a little while, getting all the latest intel and gossip before going inside. Rose was in her office and busy doing paperwork when I entered, locking the door behind me. She offered me a drink and quickly poured me a double shot of whisky neat. As she handed me the drink, I grabbed her arm and pulled her to me, kissing her full on the mouth. While she was still holding the drink, I turned her around and bent her over the desk. Wasting no time, I slid my hand up her thigh under her skirt, feeling her wetness. With my other hand, I quickly unzipped my pants. Then, sliding her panties over, I began ravishing her. As it turned out, she didn't have anything to dump on me that night, as everything had been going smoothly for her.

In the morning, I figured it was going to be a long twenty-four-hour shift that day, but I thought the night I had was worth being tired and miserable for a day. Besides, once the duty day ended for everyone else and they all left for the day, I went to sleep lying down on the office couch, hoping no calls would come in for me that night. Now, the office couch wasn't exactly cozy as it wasn't long enough to fully stretch out on. Plus, it was also narrow. The short length and narrow width of the couch made it almost impossible to lie down in a normal way. However, with a lot of meandering and adjustments, I could eventually get into a comfortable position. The other difficult part about sleeping in the office was that it was always cold, no matter the season. Drafty windows in the wintertime and full-blown air conditioning in the summers.

No luck for me that night because just as I was getting comfortable and finally dozing off, I heard my call sign go out over the radio about a domestic disturbance in progress. About a minute after hearing the call out on the radio, the duty cell phone rang. Dispatch's preferred method for contacting MPI was through the duty phone. This allowed them to give out confidential information and, if needed, have a longer discussion to exchange information and ask pertinent questions. Also, this kept the radio airways free and open for other matters.

As I was heading to the housing area where the domestic disturbance was happening, I could hear all the radio traffic regarding the situation. Apparently, there was a housing dispute between a husband (a soldier) and his wife (a civilian). The husband wouldn't allow her into the home, having turned off all the lights and locked all the doors and windows. Then I hear over the radio that he's dressed up in full camouflage, face painted and everything while running around with a knife. Now, keep in mind this is everything the wife is saying to the nine-one-one dispatcher who is relaying the information over the radio to all the MPs responding.

As I arrived on the scene, the patrols already had the husband at gunpoint and talked him into surrendering. Looking around the area, I quickly noticed a parked car and a huge figure with his arms crossed leaning against the car next to a woman. I recognized the man from one of the clubs I did promotions for. He was a soldier stationed at Fort Lewis and worked security for the club as a side gig. As the patrols were interviewing the husband, wife, and a few neighbors, I talked with the giant soldier.

"Hey, what's up? I know you," I said to him as he just stared at me. Not getting a response from him, I said to him again, "I know you from the club. You work security, and I do promotions for them." That time, I got a non-verbal acknowledgment. So, then I said to him, "I didn't know you were in the Army, too. What unit are you in?" He told me about his unit and how they were getting ready to deploy down range soon.

Trying to appeal to his self-preservation instincts, I said, "Look, man, I don't know what your involvement is in all of this, but I'm pretty sure your company commander and first sergeant don't need to know anything, and if you work with me right now I can help sort this out so they don't ever know because as far as I'm concerned, this is between a husband and wife. Now hang tight and stay cool while I go talk to everyone else to see what's going on. In the meantime, I want you to think about what I said to you."

I'm good friends with the patrol supervisor, which made it really easy to get a handle on the situation and dictate a favorable outcome for the big guy. While I and the patrol supervisor were discussing the situation and how we wanted to handle it, we both agreed to listen to both sides of the story before making any rash decisions. The patrols had already decided the husband was guilty of being some kind of a villain, and the wife was a poor damsel in distress. This was exactly the kind of thing my instructors at MPI school had warned us about. They said that when patrols respond to domestic calls, the majority of them automatically side with the wife or girlfriend. It was our job as investigators to be unbiased and only look at the facts and evidence.

The duty officer had also arrived on scene. Both he and the patrol supervisor out-ranked me by military pay grade, but technically, I out-ranked them by position as the duty MPI. The last thing I wanted was a pissing match because military politics can be very tricky and unforgiving. Thankfully, my skills in diplomacy were on point that night, and I won over both the duty officer and my friend, the patrol supervisor, to my way of seeing things that night. I appreciated my friend for his patience and for taking the time to help sort it out on scene, as I knew they were already having a busy night from hearing all the radio traffic to incidents they had been responding to already.

Together, the patrol supervisor and I go over to the police cruiser where the husband is being held, and we have the patrol officer take him out so we can talk with him. The husband told us that he had recently returned home from an eighteen-month deployment to find out his wife had been dating someone else. She now wanted a divorce and the kids. That night, she was trying to make him leave the house and go live somewhere else. When he refused to leave his house, she warned him, saying that her new boyfriend was a Samoan gangster involved with organized crime. He lived down toward Olympia and did security contracts for a bunch of nightclubs. When he still refused to leave, she threatened him that she would have her new boyfriend kill him since he was causing problems for her. Then she left and, a short while later, returned with the giant soldier. The husband said that's when he sent the kids over to the neighbor's house and told them to call the police. He admitted that he freaked out when he saw the big guy, who he thought was the Samoan boyfriend, which is why he grabbed a screwdriver and was outside moving around in the dark. The fatigues and the face paint he was wearing happened to be from the training he was doing earlier that day. Since he just got home from work when all the drama started, he hadn't had a chance to take a shower and change yet.

Both me and the patrol supervisor believed the husband was telling the truth, so I suggested that we go and talk to the big guy. As we were walking over to him, we walked past the wife, who was laying it on thick as the victim and over-dramatizing everything. She even tried stopping us so she could give her own version of what happened because she had seen us talking with her husband. I politely waved her off, telling her we'd be with her in a moment. I then motioned to the patrols to get her.

Talking to the big guy, I asked him about the Samoan and what his involvement was. He said he worked some security contracts for him and was asked to go with his girlfriend to help her because her husband was giving her some trouble. I had a quick pow-wow with the patrol supervisor and asked him how he wanted to handle things. He responded by asking me what I thought we should do. That's when I suggested we cut the big guy loose and escort the wife off base. He agreed.

Speaking to the big guy, I said to him, "Look, man, I appreciate you cooperating and being cool with us. Like I said before, no one needs to know you were here mixed up in any of this. You seem like a good dude, and what you need to do is stay away from these kinds of situations, especially involving husbands and wives. Moving forward, you just need to keep your nose clean and focus on your deployment and your military career. But before I cut you loose, I need a favor."

As big as he was, he was humble and took in everything I said as if he was a nephew being set straight by his uncle. I told him I needed his phone so I could call the Samoan. He was reluctant at first, but then I reassured him everything was going to be okay, and I wasn't going to throw him under the bus or anything. Unlocking his phone and bringing up the number for the Samoan, he handed over his phone. I placed the call to the Samoan, and when he answered, he was taken aback when he heard my unfamiliar voice as I said to him, "Aye uso, I'm friends with the big homie Preschool."

"Oh, wassup?"

"This is a courtesy call because there's a situation on Fort Lewis that involves you."

"Nah, I'm not aware of that."

"Don't worry, you ain't gotta say nothing, just listen to what I have to say."

"Okay. I'm listening."

"As I said, I'm friends with the USO Preschool, and this is nothing more than a courtesy call. I'm the military police investigator responding to this situation with your girlfriend, and it's not a good thing, especially since she can't keep her mouth shut. Your boy has been real cool and kept his mouth shut, but your girl can't stop running her mouth about her Samoan gangster boyfriend who lives in Olympia gonna kill her husband."

"What?"

"I'm just going to say it like this, Uce. If it was anyone else other than me responding, they would make a big deal of this for you. But that's not what I'm about, so hear me when I tell you you don't want to be getting yourself involved with the military or anything on any of our bases. They don't operate like the rest of the government and aren't under the same constraints. Once someone comes onto the base, they lose most of their rights as a citizen."

"Nah, I didn't know all that?"

"Listen, the military is going to protect its soldiers and their bases with extreme prejudice. So, this situation with your girlfriend and her husband, who is a soldier on Fort Lewis, could get out of hand for you real quick. They can also come after you. I'm going to let your boy go on his way, send your girl off base, and call it good. And we just leave it at that as long as there aren't any more incidents concerning the husband. Cool?"

"Ya, Uce."

"He's off limits."

"Okay, I gotchu, good looking. I appreciate it."

I handed the phone back to the big guy and cut him loose as the patrol supervisor was already giving instructions to the patrols to release the husband and handcuff the wife. As the patrol was placing her in the back of his patrol car, I went over and advised her of the situation. I matter-of-factly told her I didn't appreciate her trying to bring some gangster shit onto our base and that she was in way over her head. I informed her that the house belonged to the military and was issued to her husband because he was the soldier, and she had absolutely no rights to it. The only reason she was even allowed on Fort Lewis and had any privileges on the base was because of him. I explained to her that she was going to be escorted off base and no formal charges would be filed, but if she came back on base, I would personally throw the book at her. Chastising her further, I said if you don't want to be with your husband anymore, you need to do what everyone else does by filing for divorce and go see a judge.

When I spoke to the husband, I told him not to hesitate to contact me if anything happened again, regardless of how small, and I would take care of it for him. He was still worried about the Samoan gangster coming after him. I told him I already dealt with that on his behalf and there shouldn't be any issues with him going forward, but if there were, he should contact me immediately.

In the morning, when I got off duty, I called Maria while I was driving home. I told her to come to my house later that night because I needed to get home and get some sleep. She got to my house around seven, and since I had the next day off, I decided to take her somewhere nice for drinks. She was pleasantly surprised when we pulled up to Stanley and Seaforts, one of the nicer restaurants in the greater Seattle/Tacoma area. The irony of that fine dining establishment is that it's located on the east side in the hood. The protection racket for the business and its patrons doesn't come cheaply, but they can afford it at the prices they charge. When we sat outside, overlooking the city of Tacoma, she was even more excited. We shared a pleasant, romantic evening together.

I was tipsy as fuck and horny when I pulled into my garage with Maria. She was looking so damn sexy in the black dress she was wearing, showing off her long, beautiful legs. We exited the car, and I had her come over to my side, then began making out with her. Before I knew it, I had the back door open, and she placed her hands on the back seat and bent over. I buried my face in her ass that being the first time I ever ate ass. My tongue penetrated her virgin back passage as she moaned with desire. There was something intoxicating about it that night, and she was so filled with pleasure and excitement by me doing so. Maybe it was the thought of getting caught by one of my roommates or the fact that she was such a prude, and I was turning her out, or a combination, but I was being driven by a fierce, overwhelming erotic desire. By the time I fucked her, it didn't take long before I busted, and both of us, extremely satisfied, collapsed on the back seat.

Even though it would be years later before I would recognize and admit it, between the alcohol and women, I had definitely developed an unhealthy way of dealing with all of my anxiety and stress levels. I was burying things deep down, ignoring the root of my problems only to cover them up with cheap, unsterilized bandages. This only served to conceal the wounds of my soul, allowing for the infection to grow and fester inside of me.

Eventually, these bandages would have to be torn off, and the wound painfully purged.

CHapter THirty-Four
THe SHooter

PreSCHOOL:

It was one of the USOS working security who got word on who the shooter of the bar was. He found out it was a little gangbanger and apparently wasn't shooting at the pair but instead was shooting at the kid I hired as a favor to their mom. The story with this kid is that one night, I was at a party when confronted by the mother of this kid. She tells me that the kid's daddy is doing twenty years behind bars for his service to the USOS. She proceeded to tell me she sees me living my best life and not once have I offered to help her raise her pups in any way.

I responded, "Haven't you been getting envelopes?"

To which she acknowledged but still argued. Money doesn't fix everything. She then laid it on thick, telling me how I could step in and what I could do to curb her son's ambitions to pursue the same life that his dad did. She was worried about him ending up in a cell with her husband 'Pretty Boy.' Continuing to press me, she pleaded with me that the least I could do was to hire her son and set him on the right path. Reluctantly, I listened and went against all the warning bells that were going off in my head like someone had set off a fire alarm in the hall of my mind. I became overwhelmed with this feeling of generosity when I should've put that fire out by telling her to go fuck herself.

Finally, I asked, "How old is this kid?"

"Fifteen."

"Whaddaya think I'm running? A daycare? He can't work for my security or the bar. He's way too young. Hell, I can get shut down by the liquor board if they discover minors in the club. Let alone be thrown in jail for child labor law violations." I shook my head and walked off. I needed to get away from her as quickly as I could because she was killing my buzz.

Call it a guilty conscience, if you will, but an overwhelming sense got me later on after I had sobered up. I couldn't stop thinking about what the kid's mom had said to me and how she had pleaded with me for her son. She wanted a better life for him and wanted me to help. Was she crazy? I was a gangster with ambitions of being a top kingpin, so I'm the last guy she should've asked. In fact, shouldn't she have been asking someone more like Tone? Even though he was just a known associate of ours, he was more brainy. He was always aware of the situations or tried to be. He would always talk about cost-benefit analysis. Risk versus reward.

In all honesty, I thought all that was horseshit. These were things that I read in the self-help books they gave us for programming in the joint. Don't no one really reads that shit. Most of us draw in them and go to their classes because it's often run by some warped body retarded looking female. In prison, that was better than any magazine could do for you. Then it dawned on me. In a way, she was asking for someone like Tone to help her son, but she was asking through me. I understood that the life I chose to live wasn't the kind of life most people would involve themselves in. Maybe I could help him do right. I decided to put the kid on with our security.

I told him specifically he was in no way to ever set foot in the club. If he wanted to pee, he could go to the neighboring store in the strip mall or behind the club. But for no reason, no reason at all, was he ever to come into the establishment. The kid agreed, and I threw him a security shirt, telling him it's fifteen dollars an hour, four hours a night, and three nights a week to start. The kid bragged to his friends that he was working with us. By then, all the kids and their moms were down at the bar applying for work like it was a fucking family fun center job.

REYES:

A few weeks had gone by since coming back from the Vegas trip when CW5 finally called for me to meet up with him to give him a briefing. I had been anticipating his call and had begun to wonder why I hadn't heard from him. Then, out of the blue, he wanted me to meet him at one of his favorite spots. A cozy neighborhood restaurant called Hob Nob on Sixth Avenue across the street from Wright Park. They had the best breakfast menu in the area, which is one of the reasons why CW5 liked to have our meetings there. It was also a quiet little spot tucked away out of sight and out of mind from most. At the time, it was considered a hole-in-the-wall café, but in a city prone to violence, it was a safe destination for the patrons who frequented it.

The patrons who frequented this café were artsy hipster types, senior citizens, and public officials. Talk about information central. The artsy hipsters had the pulse of the city, the seniors knew everyone, and the public officials were in the know on all the goings-on behind closed doors. CW5 would sit inconspicuously for hours, first eating his breakfast, then drinking his coffee and reading the newspaper. He would also take meticulous notes on what he heard and saw. To the common onlooker, he was just jotting down random notes. Sometimes, it was a grocery list, a list of things to do, or a guest list for a party. Little did anyone know he was writing in code in plain sight. It was also helpful that CW5 had a photographic memory, and anything he read or heard, he could impressively recall with a high degree of accuracy.

He would chat it up with everyone who came in, to the point he became just an ordinary harmless patron with whom everyone was familiar. Since those who frequented the café viewed CW5 as ordinary and harmless, he posed no threat or concern to them. It was the familiar part that was key because that's when they let their guard down, opening the floodgates of information to anyone within earshot. For instance, Great Aunt Betty, meeting with her friends, would freely talk about what her nieces and nephews were up to. Or a couple of public officials would talk about different projects or problems they were facing. The artsy crowd would talk about everything and everyone, affecting their mood. Everyone was oblivious to CW5 to the point they would often forget he was there, even though they just had a five-minute conversation with him about the weather.

The first time I met him there and every time after he would introduce me as his nephew, by default making me just as ordinary, harmless and familiar. To this point we were basically invisible and could freely talk and openly discuss whatever we wanted and no would care enough to be interested in us anyway. Don't get it twisted, CW5 and I were still careful in our conversations and always aware of who was around us and within earshot.

I gave him my update of the Vegas trip and everything else since I'd last spoken with him. I told him how I had handled everything and managed to keep the peace in regard to the streets. I was feeling proud of myself and my accomplishments at keeping everything calm and cool in light of the situation.

That quickly came to an end when, with a smug look and sarcastic voice, CW5 said to me, "Are you sure about that? Word is they already took care of the shooter, gangsta style." He then began to explain what had transpired in Tacoma while we were coming back from Vegas. Honestly, I think he was trying to see if I was withholding anything from him. I wasn't, and he could see the genuinely surprised look on my face and hear it in my voice.

Trigger heard about the shooter and decided to take the initiative. In these matters, as far as I knew, no one could move on something like this unless it was okayed by Preschool himself. I knew for sure he didn't have any say in this because I was with him. I trust he would've said something, and besides, he found out when I did. His surprised look didn't seem fake at all. In fact, I had been around him long enough to know that the look he gave meant one thing. He was mad and wanted to satisfy his anger by discipline. I've watched him pistol whip his own nephew at the front of the club for trying to pimp some broken-down prostitute to the patrons of the bar in the parking lot. Hell, I think if I didn't grab the pistol in a way that jammed my hand and released the clip so it fell out, he'd have bodied his own nephew. I later asked him, "Were you really going to off him right there?"

"Look, Tone," he said. "I treat my nephew like any one of my men. He wanted to join the life, so he's part of it. Family or not." The message that sounded loudly that night to the others was, "If he's willing to do that to his own nephew, what do you think he'll do to someone who is not his family?"

Trigger heard who the shooter was and went up to the rec center to get the kid. Nobody greenlit this, but Trigger, as always, was eager to prove himself, trying to win over the affections of the higher-ups. Of all the places, he decided to wait outside the Al Davies Boys and Girls Club in the Hilltop neighborhood. That in itself was a big no-no. That was like two strikes against Trigger before he even pulled the trigger. Acting on his own without the greenlight, strike one. Going to a place where kids and families hang out to get away from the streets, strike two. Both of these actions were highly frowned upon and warranted severe consequences.

It was after the kid had finished playing basketball and, on his way home, that Trigger walked up to him, laying the kid out. To make matters worse, it was the same .44 Magnum used on a bunch of other incidents. Plus, Trigger would use the same handgun to shoot an unsuspecting father through a screen door in the same thirty-day period. Talk about leaving a trail of forensic evidence that is not hard to follow. Since most shootings are done with a 9mm, shooting with a .44 Magnum stands out.

PreSCHOOL:

It was a few weeks after getting back from Vegas that I got a phone call about a guy who owed sixty grand to the uces in Vegas, and the uces needed to collect on that bill. The guy was hiding out at his parents' house in Burien, Washington they said. Trigger overheard me conversing about this and seemed to be bugged or antsy about this conversation for some reason.

I had a meeting with all the boys to discuss it. While I was waiting for everyone to show up, Tone hit me up with some urgency, saying we needed to meet concerning the shooter. He didn't sound happy at all. In fact, the way he sounded, somehow it made me feel like I was about to hear him rant about how I'm fucking up and need to do some vacationing again.

Trigger finally said, "Look, Uce. I'll take care of it. You got too much on your plate as it is." Trigger goes on about how he is tired of everyone thinking he is just a flunky and decides he wants to change people's minds by showing everyone he can handle this shit like a professional.

The thing about it is I know Trigger has no sense of finesse or subtlety in him. He's reckless and flamboyant. I tell him to fall back and that I got someone to handle this. I just need to apply scare tactics. Nothing more. In the meantime, go shoot a tree or go to the gun range. This is not a situation to practice on.

That's how people see him, and it's because of how he handles shit, which is with repeated recklessness. Trigger and Happy are brothers who are both "trigger happy," but Trigger is the little brother who is just a little more trigger-happy. They call the young one "Trigger" and the older brother, who's serving a twenty-year bid, "Happy." Against my better judgment, I gave him my blessing to take on the solo mission to just scare the old man. My thoughts? Well, if the guy's parents tell him there were some visitors of Polynesian descent coming to their house asking about him, he'd freak out and cave in. That the next move would be to pay the debt or, worse, involve his parents.

Unbeknownst to me, Trigger had already moved on the shooter for the club.

I thought he would be the next one to be taken to the gravel pit, so why not give him the opportunity to determine his own fate as to whether or not he ends up there? Shit, I didn't know that he had already moved on this shooter thing on his own and turned the heat on the streets all the way up.

Trigger heads out. I'm still thinking of this kid whose mom pleaded with me to take off the streets. It could be a major issue.

While I was at the hangout spot, Tone walked in just as I was giving orders to my crew to track and bring in the shooter.

Cowboy responds, "You're too late. Trigger already took care of it."

"What the fuck you talking about?" I asked.

"It doesn't matter," Cowboy said. "It was done."

"What was done? When was it done?" I asked.

"While you were in Vegas."

"Uce, why the fuck am I just hearing about it now? And why didn't you say anything when Triggz is here? This whole time? And how the fuck Trigger knew about the shooter before anyone else?"

"Because you were in Vegas. Up until now, I thought you were the one who authorized it because, you know, you were in Vegas with the big guy."

"So, you're telling me Trigger took care of the shooter and is now about to go on this solo mission?"

Tone and I look at each other and think the same thing. Trigger doesn't have the brains for subtlety. So eager is he to live up to his and his brother's name that he volunteers to do the dirty work and leaves a trail of blood and bullet casings that often leads back to them.

After the Feds questioning Tone, how can anyone be comfortable? None of the uces really knew him except for me and I claim to be a good judge of character because I've been inside of prison mixing and matching with thousands of different personalities. The uces are on edge. I'm on edge. I already don't trust anyone and this is a turn of the stove to the max with the pot boiling over.

As I head for the door to find Trigger blowing up his phone to ask about the solo mission he just went on, Cowboy adds, "It's too bad about the kid. His dad isn't going to take the news well. What a shame. He was a good kid."

"What I give a fuck about the shooter. Fuck him."

"Nah, not him. I reckon you're not privy to that bit of information as well. Yeah, the little uce you hired that got the club shot up. Trigger paid him a visit, too."

My face turns pale as I look back at Cowboy with disgust before turning to walk out of the bar. Knowing that the dad of the kid, a long-time USOS member, would not be happy when he finds out and hears the news. This could spell disaster for them from the inside out. Even worse, Trigger went on a solo mission alone to White Center.

Trigger knocked on the door of the guy who owed the money. Instead of the guy, his dad came to the door. "Can I help you?"

"Yeah," Trigger said. "Can I come inside and borrow your phone?"

The guy's dad is an ex-Navy SEAL intelligence officer, so he's no dummy. He's suspicious. He asked, "What's wrong with your cell phone?" He pointed to the phone Trigger had in his hand.

Trigger, caught by surprise, could've said anything. Like, *oh, the battery's dead,* or *I don't have service.* Shit, anything. Instead, mentally challenged by the easiest questions in life to evade, he instead lifts the .44 titanium steel Smith & Wesson revolver from under his suit jacket and shoots the guy's dad through the screen door four times.

When I say worse, it gets worse. The guy's sister works for the FBI branch in Seattle, and all hell breaks loose with law enforcement swarming everywhere. If you ever see the movies where they swarm the social clubs and gangster hideouts like a hornet's nest being hit, this was the scene. They came down, kicking in doors and breaking shit. That is exactly what I was trying to avoid. A pot boiling over. These damn raids are never good for business.

Now, this guy who owes Vegas money has a bunch of information on the uces that he is willing to share with the FBI in exchange for WITSEC, but he doesn't meet the criteria for it. The feds, yes, even with his sister working for them, want things they can corroborate. His story wasn't enough to land him a paid vacation and retirement in Arizona. All the uces are out looking for this dude and even end up shooting up the mom's house and the sister's house, which then and only then, stupidly, gives the guy the criteria he needed to be put in for WITSEC.

Trigger was on the run, and the cops caught him a few days later. Trigger was going to prison, do not pass go. We had no way to communicate with him effectively, but we sent the girls and lawyers to visit him and speak to him in code. The feds were all over him like a cheap suit on a broken-down pimp. It was only a matter of time before they put the pieces together that the gun that was used to shoot the kid was a .44 Smith & Wesson. Very distinguishable from others. How? Well, for starters, not a lot of people get shot by .44 Magnums every day. It is usually a 9mm or .45 of some sort.

Reyes:

"Uce," Preschool said. "I need you to use your diplomacy to talk to the Russians. Tell them we got everything under control, but we are dealing with our own issue right now. Just turn on the news. Ugghhh. But we will handle that treasure for him. I know it's time-sensitive, Uce. Just work your magic and have them chill."

Fuck. I knew he was spinning his wheels about everyone. It was a fragile time. I knew he was trying to clean up the Trigger situation. I knew he was weary of me, too, ever since I got questioned. I was always there with him to make sure he knew who had his back through it all. Fuck. I would've taken a bullet for my guy. But still, I had to urge him to tread softly. The heat threatened to burn down the businesses and progress we had painstakingly worked so hard to gain. If anyone could smooth out situations, it was him. They called him the fireman for a reason. He was good at putting out fires. I just didn't get the logic of putting out a fire with more gasoline. But he had a method to his madness. If he slowed down from time to time, I could see him actually thinking. On those rare occasions. You could even see the light bulb go off in his head, and his eyes lit up like, "I got it." Like I said, however, it was rare in those days. I had just hoped he figured that one out soon because we were pressed for time and pushed up against a concrete wall that said, "Welcome to your new home for the next twenty years."

CHAPTER THIRTY-FIVE
A FATHER'S SON

REYES:

Everything seemed to be going in the wrong direction for me, starting with my medical status. About eight months before heading out to Vegas with Preschool, I was sitting in the doctor's office waiting for my test results. I was optimistically hopeful for the most part, although I knew my body wasn't the same. I think maybe I was just hoping it was good enough to give me the chance to follow my deepest ambition. The doctor was cool about everything. He was a straight shooter and just told it like it was. He explained to me the damage to my head, spine, and eardrums wasn't showing any signs of improvement. That meant the motion sickness and dizzy spells were going to be with me for the long haul. No more jumping out of airplanes or helicopters for me.

I wasn't going to be cleared for jump status, and there were no waivers or anyone who would sign off on me going to selection for an SMU (Special Missions Unit, aka an Operators Course). I had no idea what difficulty I would have accepting the fact that I would not become an operator as I had once hoped. Sure, there were plenty of other options to be part of the special force's community, but none of them appealed to me as I wasn't interested in any kind of permanent administration or support role. I had purposely waited until the very last possible moment before I had to re-enlist, hoping for a medical miracle to transpire. Since I was coming up on the end of my enlistment window, I had to make a decision whether or not I was going to reenlist or get out of the Army.

Reluctantly, I would have to leave the Army. That was a sad farewell for me as it seemed premature, and after all, collectively, the military and all my leaders had been a father to me for so many of my formidable years. I can say I grew up in the Army and was a proud child of my iconic father, Uncle Sam. Each leader had instilled so much of themselves in me, and I was coming to a place where I no longer had a path or purpose. I knew deep down that I was drifting from the right course in life, away from the light and into the darkness. The whole time I had been along for the ride with CW5 and Preschool, I was naïve in thinking it would end as soon as I was cleared medically. In my mind, it had been my out from the mess I had so willingly become a part of. Who was I kidding anyway?

You have to give the Army credit for how much effort they put in trying to take care of their soldiers. I was assigned to the Warrior Transition Battalion, which is a holding unit for any soldier facing medical issues upon their end of time in service. Once assigned, soldiers only have one mission, which is to take care of all their medical issues before they leave the Army. This could take weeks, months, or years, depending on the severity of the health concerns. It was a cakewalk. Show up for morning formations, do PT on your own, go to any medical appointments, and report for end-of-day formation. I mean, it wasn't like I had doctor's appointments every day all day, so I had a lot of free time to do other things. Honestly, I never had so much free time in my life.

Just after the Vegas trip, while still assigned to the WTB, one of the boys asked me if I could provide security for his Halloween party. I told him that it was no problem and that we would take care of him, so he didn't have to worry about the cost since I would be paying the boys out of my own pocket. His house was located on East Sixtieth Street at the end of a dead end. The house was a split level, and the bottom level led to the backyard. All in all, it was about twenty-five hundred square feet plus room for people to gather outside in the backyard. Since he was still renovating the downstairs, it was pretty much an open floor plan, which was perfect for the DJ to set up and for a dance floor.

I wanted to get there early enough to make sure my security team was good to go with everything. When I arrived, there were still people setting up, which was good because it gave me a chance to get a good feel for the house and how I wanted to run the security for the evening. In the midst of setting up, a fight almost broke out. One of the guys I recruited from WTB, a Samoan who was in the infantry, and a friend decided they wanted to test each other. My friend was a former Ranger and was there to help out because he was friends with the host as well. For whatever reason, these two guys decided to go at it after some words were exchanged. I had to chastise them like little kids, telling them to knock it off and that we were all on the same side for the night and were there to take care of security for the party.

I placed my two MPI co-workers at the front door checking IDs, handing out bracelets and taking money for the cover charge. I put two uces to watch downstairs. Then I had my infantry Samoan dude floating along with myself and a few of the other boys.

The party was popping, and a few hundred people came through that night. Everything was going really smoothly, and everyone was enjoying themselves until a couple of local youths tried flexing up on the party. I got a text from my dude telling me to come up front. When I got to the front door, there were three gangbangers who wanted to come in but were refusing to show their ID. These three kids, older teenagers really, lived a few blocks down and had been watching all the traffic pour in and wanted to get in on the action. I politely explained to them they could come in, but we just needed to check IDs because the party was only for twenty-one and over. I explained that we didn't want any problems with minors in case the cops came. Plus, there was still a twenty-dollar cover they would need to pay.

Well, they weren't having it and started getting belligerent. I told them I understood what they were saying and that I would go and check with the host to see if we could work something out. So, I went to find

Preschool to tell him about the situation out front. We went back out front to talk to the three gangbangers to see if we could work out an amicable solution. This time, Preschool took the lead in talking to them, and I stood at his side.

The leader barked that they don't need to show ID or pay a cover charge. He demanded we let them into the party on the basis that they were representing Acacia Blocc Compton Crips and that it was their block. Preschool did his best to be diplomatic with the three youngsters and explained to them what the deal was. He took the time to show the leader the tattoos on his forearms, showing that he was also Crip set SOS (Sons of Samoa) and that the party was a USO party. Therefore, they had no rights to it.

Meanwhile as Preschool was having a heart to heart with the leader, the other two took notice of the situation they were in. They were now fully encircled by a dozen or so of the boys, all of whom were much harder than any of the three. I could see the look in their eyes as they came to the realization of their predicament. The leader was all puffed up on his own ego and failed to see what was transpiring around him.

Still surrounded, Preschool pulled me to the side. "Uce, what do you wanna do? You want me to ghost them or what?"

"Uce, if we do that, my guy still has to live here, and it won't be good for him."

"So, what do we do then?"

"They can't come in, and they gotta go. So, let's just tell them to leave."

"All right, my Uce."

At that point Preschool again told them in no uncertain terms it was an USO party, and they couldn't come in so they needed to leave. The leader was still barking as his two friends pulled him away.

Preschool said to me, "You know, Uce, they're gonna be back."

"Ya?"

"I'm going to send Dog to get some hardware."

"Okay, Uce, whatever you think needs to happen next."

With that, he sent Dog on an errand to retrieve some of the fully automatic rifles they were holding. In less than fifteen minutes, Dog was back and posted up in the bedroom overlooking the front yard and the street. Sure enough, not long after that, the three youngsters returned with reinforcements, bringing with them one of their OGs.

The OG was respectful and asked me what was up. I explained to him the situation. He ran down his credentials, telling me he was just getting home and still fresh out of prison. I told him he was more than welcome to come in and join the party, no ID or cover charge necessary, and that we would take good care of him. He sure liked the sound of that and sent the trio and their reinforcements home. That was probably the best welcome home party he ever had, and true to my word, I made sure he was well taken care of that evening. As a matter of fact, he closed down the party and happily strolled home around six in the morning.

Right after that party, a day later, at another Halloween house party, another kid, Vic, gets shot, which would later lead to a courtroom brawl. That courtroom brawl was caught on camera and nationally televised by news outlets across the U.S. The footage is still up on YouTube, and if you type "Pierce County courtroom fight" in the search engine, it pops up.

Preschool:

The kid being hired on was the worst fucking idea. It turns out that the kid, who was working the door, went bragging to whomever and whoever would listen. Then started some drama with the Hilltop Crips' young generations at the mall. The young Crips knew that he worked at USOS's bar as the doorman and decided to pay him a visit. They shoot the bar and kick off a flurry of shit that is heavier than the little petty beef they got going. To try to rectify the situation, Trigger finds out who the kid is and toasts the kid on the Hilltop at the rec center.

They responded by shooting up one of the house parties me and Tone were operating at the mini-mansion and fatally hit a kid who wanted to work security that we hired to watch the house parties. Things go sideways, and everything hits the fan. The USOS and the Crips go to war in five prison riots back to back in Walla Walla. The kid who got shot—his dad was a big homie for the neighborhood crip gang. He was coming home after eighteen years of prison. He was looking forward to seeing his son, who he hadn't seen in over a decade. He was looking forward to changing his son's career path by showing him a different way, and while in transit in Monroe Camp after just coming from Shelton, which is the receiving unit for classification to send inmates where they are designated, he calls home and hears his son was shot down in cold blood four times by a .44 Magnum.

He heard it was the USOS and declared war on us. At this time, the law finally catches up to me and all my shenanigans, and I can't fight it off anymore. My own lawyers were saying to just go in for a few years and let the heat die down.

They said, "It's Tacoma. When you come back home, there will still be the stench of gun smoke and pee waiting for you." They accepted a plea deal instead of fighting the possession of a firearm in the first-degree charge. I surrender myself to the county and am sent up to Shelton to await my final transit location.

I run into the kid's dad and offer to meet at the big yard to take a lap. See if we can squash the beef and put things to rest. It was a long shot, but too many people were losing their freedom and lives over this stupidity. He had his prison car behind him. I had only a few Asian Pacific Islanders with me. A meeting was set and me and the kid's dad, Mad Dog, hit the yard.

"You know," Mad Dog said. "I was so excited and anxious to get to my boy. I haven't seen him in over ten years. He stopped visiting me."

"Sorry about your boy," was all I could say. He seemed broken. Like he was about to forget where he was and break down and start bawling his eyes out. But anger carried him. And he pounced back.

"Somebody got to pay for this shit."

"Look, nothing that happens inside or out is going to bring your boy back. I get it. You're mad. But he shot a few of ours, which is what triggered the whole beef. This all started with the shooting at the bar."

He looked me up and down. "How do I know you ain't the one that put the hit out on my boy? I know your rep. You're very convincing. But Conniving."

"Look, on my word as a convict. On my children. I didn't put that out. I probably would've if I found out it was him that shot at us. How would you feel if someone shot up your business? Or your home?"

"You know what. I feel you. It took me years to understand that everything has consequences. These youngsters out here are shooting shit up, stealing whips, doing dumb shit like there's no consequence. I wanted to save my son from the same streets that sent me to twenty years in the can. But fuck ..."

"Well, you getting out. If you want, maybe we can start by putting together a program that will help these kids instead of cause them to lose their life. I'm going in for two years on a pistol. But I have everything out there set up. A platform that can help you get started building your neighborhood backup. Otherwise, it's going to be a long road back to recovery for our people. We have the power to end this right here, my uce. Let me know. Sleep on it. In the meantime, I promise you that there will be no more attacks on any one of your people from mine. Tomorrow's yard, let me know?"

"Yup."

The long-time USO member, Pretty Boy, the father of the kid we hired, hears about his son being gunned down, and he loses it. Seems like Trigger got busy and hit him, too. The dad, Pretty Boy, starts spreading doubt and fear into the heart of the USOS at the very core. He brings it up to the old man, Paulie, and demands retribution. He wants Preschool and his partner Reyes's heads for this. Paulie calms him down and says he'll take care of it. Pretty Boy won't hear it and continues to rant, and rant, and rant until a month of driving the other USOS and Paulie crazy starts to take its toll.

Prison has a way of containing negativity and reciprocating it a thousand-fold. No one likes that energy or vibe, especially if you are serving a life sentence. In Paulie's case, he is serving multiples. Paulie was convicted of second-degree murder for his role in the triple homicide in South Park Seattle, WA, that involved several victims, including a dog. The dog's DNA on their clothing was what ultimately convicted them and nailed their case shut. It was the first case in United States history to be prosecuted and convicted using a dog's DNA as evidence. Initially, Paulie and his co-defendant were placed on death row, but because they were young adults, the child advocacy organizations and humanity groups who heard about it got involved and placed enough pressure on the state legislatures who pressed the prosecutor to scale back the death sentence.

chapter thirty-six
congress

Reyes:

My partner got caught up on some parole violations, and the man came for him, sending him back to prison for twelve to twenty-four months. This was not good at all. He was the glue holding everything together, and the boys responded well to his authority and leadership. Would they do the same for me? After all, I wasn't family by blood, and heck, I wasn't even a Pacific Islander. It didn't matter who was backing me or saying I was in charge because you can't make people accept you. They either do or they don't. Sure, I was good enough to call some shots and give leadership advice, but for anyone to truly bend the knee was a different thing altogether.

It was actually Dog who had brought this to my attention a year or so previously. See, he was out with the boys over on the east side of Tacoma one night and got into it with some other Pacific Islanders, mostly Samoans. While they were all fighting, Dog was pistol-whipping one of them, and his finger slipped on the trigger. The discharge, effectively ending the brawl, caught everyone by surprise, and they all scattered. Later on, everyone involved came to realize they were all related and squashed the beef, accepting one another with open arms and family love. Everyone except Dog because he wasn't a blood relative or Pacific Islander. The only reason he was untouchable at the time was because of Preschool who would never greenlight anything against Dog.

With Preschool gone, serving some time for a probation violation, and my discharge from the Army soon approaching, I was seriously thinking about going away, too. I could go back to the Midwest, down to Arizona, or maybe even travel. All of it seemed more appealing than having to deal with the carnage of what had just transpired over the past several months. No more Army. No more Russians. No more Mexicans. No more street stuff. No more CW5. No more F.O.K. A clean getaway!

To make matters worse, in light of recent events, I decided it would be a good idea to go out and blow off some steam. That led to me getting myself caught up with a DUI charge. I was surprised it took so long to get one with all the alcohol I was consuming on a regular basis. As I was coming to the conclusion in my own mind that I was out, two of the guys approached me and asked me if I would start a fight team with them. I liked the sound of that. Since I had already opened a small gym at the Tacoma Soccer Center, the transition seemed easy enough. I had opened the gym so the security team would have a place to train. So, that piece of the puzzle was already available. It could be fun, and it would be a break away from everything else. We would participate in combative sports, boxing, kickboxing, MMA, etc. I mean, how could any trouble come from owning a sports team?

Preschool:

In prison, the "reps" investigate situations that are brought up by the old man who makes the ultimate decision on the sanctions handed down. In order to strike down another USO, it takes the act of a congregating party, literally like an act of Congress. The old man gave his ruling that he didn't know who committed this act against Pretty Boy's son, and so he wasn't taking action against anyone for it at the time. The USOS don't move on account of something that doesn't involve prison politics anyway. His little brother Vinny Vegas had sent word that Preschool and his partner were with him during the incident and that Preschool had reached out to send word upstate that he had nothing to do with that. And Vinny believed him.

"Heck, it could've been the second attempt on the kid's life for all we know," Vinny had said.

But none of this would appease Pretty Boy, who was relentlessly driving a wedge between the USOS. He was starting to splinter off into his own faction and create an internal conflict that Paulie, reluctantly but swiftly, would have to deal with or risk losing control of the car.

Then Trigger got picked up. At that time, every inmate of DOC who violated parole got sent straight to Monroe Camp. The overcrowded jail situation made it convenient for Trigger to reach home base quickly. All he had to do was get to Monroe Camp, beat up on another violator, and he was on the first bus smoking back to the Bay. They could do all the intake and processing of violent inmates there. Paulie welcomed Trigger back with open arms. The way the prison is set up, Paulie is in a different wing from Pretty Boy. So, Pretty Boy has a say in the other units but ultimately reports back to Paulie.

Pretty works in the laundry, so he knows who's coming or leaving the prison. That way, they can prepare for the USOS enemies when they arrive. The USOS usually hit them right out of the bus, sending a message to the admin and their rivals that they are not allowed to walk the line there. Pretty Boy anxiously awaits Trigger with the usual care package from the USOS. He's been dying to pick Trigger's mind. He asked about his son's murder. He wanted to know if Preschool and Tone had anything to do with it. That he knows in his heart they did. His wife confirms his suspicions by relaying all the events of the streets to him. Trigger plays him like a fiddle and leads him to believe it was all Preschool. Pretty Boy couldn't wait to get the okay to send the word back to the streets to lay Preschool down. Little did he know that the old man had requested Trigger to come home. To deal with the situation he was facing. That he couldn't get anyone he trusted to handle this because Pretty Boy had built up quite a following and loyalist of soldiers siding with his ideas on revenge.

Trigger, the ever so loyal son to the old man, came as quickly as the chain bus could carry him. He waited until he and Pretty Boy were alone. When Pretty Boy's guard was down, Trigger stabbed him multiple times in the neck and the face. He commenced to strangle Pretty Boy while the guards were running in to save him. I couldn't help but think about how Tone would be strangled by the streets, metaphorically, I mean. My time here on the inside had to be a short stay, which meant I couldn't get caught up in any of the prison politics that would extend my stay in these luxurious accommodations. Since Paulie wanted me back on the streets because I was such a good earner for the cause, he would see to it that my papers were clean and in good order, even hoping for an early release date. The only thing I had to do was keep my temper in check.

"The next few years would lead to murders and more bloodshed like we were cursed by the life we chose. No matter how much damage control we throw at the system, the corruption of the human soul forces us on a downward spiral. To see how we stayed alive while being hunted, join us in book two as our story continues to unfold, and we delve deeper into "the life."

Look for part two of three, which is coming soon.